JUST ONCE

Lori Handeland

This first world edition published 2018
in Great Britain and 2019 in the USA by
SEVERN HOUSE PUBLISHERS LTD of
Eardley House, 4 Uxbridge Street, London W8 7SY.
Trade paperback edition first published
in Great Britain and the USA 2019 by
SEVERN HOUSE PUBLISHERS LTD.

British Library Cataloguing in Publication Data
A CIP catalogue record for this title is available from the British Library.

ISBN-13: 978-0-7278-8833-4 (cased)
ISBN-13: 978-1-84751-955-9 (trade paper)
ISBN-13: 978-1-4483-0164-5 (e-book)

Typeset by Palimpsest Book Production Ltd.,
Falkirk, Stirlingshire, Scotland.

JUST ONCE

Frankie

Whitefish Bay, Wisconsin. June, 2016

Francesca Sicari started up from sleep, disoriented. Her cell phone was ringing.

The TV flickered a rerun of *Two and a Half Men*, casting just enough silver-blue light across the coffee table to reveal the remnants of her take-out supper, her MacBook and her Canon camera. No sign of her iPhone.

Nothing new there. Frankie misplaced her phone a lot. Usually because she held her camera in both hands, and she was more interested in what she saw through the lens than anything that might appear on the display of a mobile device.

She followed the sound of her ringtone – 'Whooooo are you? Woo-woo, woo-woo!' – which indicated the caller was not in her contact list. She should probably let it go to voicemail, but anyone calling in the middle of the night must have a good reason. Or a bad one.

Frankie hurried into the kitchen, thrilled to see her phone plugged into the wall where it belonged, though she had no memory of doing so.

She'd come home from work, set her kung pao on the counter and become fascinated with the way the setting sun turned the cut glass vase on her farmhouse dining room table the shade of blood.

She'd spent the next hour photographing the vase with various props – a green pepper, a white tennis shoe, a yellow begonia yanked out of the garden – as the colors shifted from red, to orange, to fuchsia, gold and finally blue-gray.

Then she'd warmed up her ice-cold supper and taken it, along with the camera and her computer, into the living room. Setting everything on the restored wooden trunk that served as a coffee table, she'd uploaded the pictures she'd taken that day of the Basilica of St Josaphat on the south side of Milwaukee and started editing. Several hours later, she'd closed her burning eyes 'just for a minute'. Next thing she knew, the phone was ringing.

Woo-woo, woo-woo!

That ringtone was getting on her last nerve. She'd have to change it.

Frankie snatched up the phone. 'Hello?'

'Francesca?'

She knew that voice. Considering she'd met the woman once and talked to her on the phone never, Frankie wasn't sure why.

'Hannah?'

'Is Charley there?'

Frankie had divorced Charley Blackwell twenty-four years ago. He'd married Hannah soon afterward. Considering he'd been boffing her, that made sense. Or as much sense as anything had made back when Frankie had discovered the love of her life loved someone else.

'Why would he be here?'

'He was supposed to fly in from Africa tonight. When he didn't show, I tracked him there.'

Frankie tightened her lips over the words *how do you like it?* Not productive.

'By "there" you mean Milwaukee?'

'Yes.' Hannah's voice was clipped, but she sounded more scared than pissed. Why?

'How'd you get any info out of the airlines?'

Frankie had always had a heck of a time hunting down Charley when he didn't show. With TSA and privacy laws, she couldn't imagine it had gotten any easier.

'He was shooting for *National Geographic*. They made the reservation so they were able to pull some strings.'

Funny. They hadn't been all that willing to pull strings for Frankie.

'Maybe he got another assignment,' Frankie said.

'In Milwaukee?' Hannah didn't exactly sneer the word, but she might as well have.

'I know it isn't the Congo, but we do have worthwhile images to photograph.'

For instance, the Basilica, which was modeled after St Peter's in Rome and had one of the largest copper domes in the world. The structure was exquisite, as were many other local churches, such as the Greek Orthodox church designed by Frank Lloyd Wright. Frankie planned to go there tomorrow.

But Charley was a photojournalist. One of the few left in an era where everyone had a camera on their cell phone and speed trumped technique. That he was still employed at sixty-three was a testament to how good Charley was at his job.

In the last couple of decades since they'd called it quits he'd become even more famous. If Frankie took one of his more well-known pictures on to the street and showed it to the first person who passed by, she'd bet a hundred dollars Joe Public would recognize it.

Charley had begun his career as a combat photographer in Vietnam. He'd been drafted shortly out of high school, then re-upped for a second tour. Once the troops had been withdrawn following the Paris Accords, he'd stayed on, which meant he'd been there at the end, and the photos he'd taken of the fall of Saigon had landed him a job with Associated Press. From there he had moved to *Time* magazine, then *National Geographic*, eventually becoming a freelance photographer so he could pick and choose the best jobs from each of them.

'Charley wouldn't fly off on another assignment without letting me know,' Hannah said.

Interesting. He'd done that often enough to Frankie. She wondered how long it had taken Hannah to train the asshole out of him.

'You still seem to have lost him.'

'Be that as it may,' Hannah said, and Frankie laughed.

Hannah didn't seem the 'be that as it may' type. But what did Frankie know? As previously mentioned, she'd met her once. The circumstances had shown neither of them in their best light. How could they, considering?

Hannah had been a kid, which had only contributed to the unpleasantness. Not only because she had no idea how to handle the situation, but because her age had made the situation even more of a . . . well, situation. She hadn't been too young – as in pedophile young – but she'd been young enough to really piss Frankie off.

Charley had asked her if he'd fallen in love with a woman his own age, would that have been better? Frankie had punched him in the mouth. She still had the scar from his front tooth on her middle finger. She recalled holding that finger up, dripping blood, waving goodbye with it as Hannah fussed over his soon-to-be-capped front teeth.

Ah, good times.

'What is so goddamn funny?' Hannah asked.

'Nothing.' Frankie didn't plan to share anything more with Hannah than she already had.

The woman on the other end of the line bore little resemblance to the Hannah Frankie held in her head. Soft voiced, a bit meek, not Charley's type at all. Of course Frankie had been as wrong about Charley's type as she'd obviously been about Hannah herself. Tonight Hannah sounded anything but meek; tonight Hannah sounded a bit ball-busty.

'If he shows up there would you call me?'

'Why would he show up here?'

'Why does Charley do anything?'

Once Frankie had thought she understood Charley Blackwell better than she understood anyone, even herself. She'd been wrong. But she'd have thought, by now, that Hannah might. They'd been married longer than Frankie and Charley had.

'Are you two having problems?' Frankie asked.

'You'd like that, wouldn't you?'

Maybe twenty-four years ago – even fifteen – Frankie might have enjoyed hearing that Charley and Hannah were on the outs. She'd have called her BFF, Irene Pasternak, and chortled. But now?

'I couldn't care less.'

Hannah snorted, and irritation danced along Frankie's skin. While she didn't have any feelings about their marriage one way or another, apparently she still hated Hannah.

'If he shows up, I'll have *him* call. That work?'

If anyone had told her back then that she'd be having this conversation – *any* conversation – with Hannah Blackwell – that there'd *be* a Hannah Blackwell – Frankie wouldn't have believed it. She almost didn't believe it now.

'I'm not sure,' Hannah said. 'You might have to—'

'You know, it's almost three in the morning here. I don't have the patience for you.'

'That makes two of us.' Hannah hung up.

'Wow,' Frankie said. 'That was fun.'

She set the phone on the counter, realized she was holding her camera in the other hand, and set that down too. It wasn't the first time she'd clutched the device like a security blanket.

She headed for the stairs, intent on her bed and a few hours of real sleep, her mind still on the weird phone call. Why would Hannah think Charley would come here? Why had she seemed jittery and a little scared?

Why would you think you know what the woman feels, thinks or even sounds like when she's any kind of way?

Frankie didn't know Hannah Blackwell at all. She didn't want to.

For years Frankie had thought of the woman as the twenty-three-year-old bimbo Charley had left her for. But Hannah was no longer twenty-three or a bimbo. She was the forty-seven-year-old owner/editor of *You*, a fashion magazine in a time when magazines were tanking and being over forty in fashion meant you were on your way down the other side of the mountain. She would probably lose her company soon. Frankie should feel sorry for her. But she didn't.

The front door rattled. Frankie paused with her foot on the first step leading to the second floor, listening for a wind gust that would explain said rattling, but the late spring night was still.

The knob turned right-left, right-left.

Tick-tock. Tick-tock.

'Fancy? Open up.'

Frankie felt a chill so deep it made her dizzy. Only Charley had ever called her Fancy.

Though she'd just gotten off the phone with his wife, she still couldn't believe he was here.

Tick-tock, tick-tock.

And trying the door as if he expected it to open.

'My key doesn't work.'

'No shit.' She'd changed the locks the day after she'd seen him kissing her.

'I'm tired. I've been traveling forever.'

Frankie swirled her finger in the air – the universal sign for *whoop-de-doo.*

'I can see your shadow on the floor.'

Sure enough, she'd moved closer and the light from the TV outlined her silhouette on the reclaimed wood of the entry hall, her shadow clearly visible through the frosted glass windowpane to the side of the door.

Frankie stepped back. She didn't want to let him in. She didn't have to. This was her house and it was the middle of the night.

'I forgot to call again, didn't I?'

The hair on her arms prickled. Something was very wrong. Charley hadn't forgotten to call in twenty-four years. That's what divorce meant. He no longer had to call; she no longer had to care when he didn't.

'Come on, baby. Let me in.'

An odd sound escaped. It would have been a sob if she hadn't cried herself sick over the man long ago. It almost sounded like a laugh, but nothing was funny about this. Even though it must be a joke.

It just had to be.

'Fancy, come on.'

Charley sounded exactly as he had all those years ago whenever he'd come home late, forgotten to call, or left for some god-forsaken corner of the earth without telling her.

And none of that had ever mattered. She'd known the man she was marrying; she'd understood his passion, his conviction, his need to record how he saw the world through a camera. She'd shared that passion, but where Frankie saw light and color, contrast and composition – the way the world came together – Charley saw how the world came apart.

They said it was his gift; Frankie had always thought it more of a curse. Charley's view of life had been pretty damn dark. She'd spent a lot of her time lightening him up. Dragging him into the sun after he'd spent weeks in the rain. And if it insisted on raining, then she'd dragged him out anyway and convinced him to dance. There was nothing like dancing in the rain to make even the most jaded soul laugh.

Tick-tock.

The distant sound of Charley's laughter died. What the hell was wrong with her? Zoning off, thinking about her lying, cheating ex-husband's laughter and smiling like a fool.

'Fancy, please.'

Her smile faded as she shivered at the tone – desperation laced with terror. The last time she'd heard him speak like that . . .

Frankie opened the door.

Charley walked right inside. His duffel hit the ground. He set his camera bag next to it more gently. The twin thuds brought back the past with dizzying clarity. How many times had she stood in this hallway and heard those exact same sounds?

More than she could count – but not for a long, long time. Back when her breasts didn't need a super bra to keep them from meeting her waist and her ass didn't kiss her thighs with every step.

'I know I should have called, but I didn't want to wake you.' He shut the door, turning with a smile as his arms opened wide. His head tilted.

His hair, no longer dark, but neither was hers, remained thick and curly despite his age. His eyes shone blue against his perpetual tan, maintained by a hundred dusty, sunny countries. The only signs of his age were more lines on his face and a slight stoop to his slim shoulders. He was still tall, thin and handsome.

Jerk.

'I guess I woke you anyway. Sorry, baby.'

Frankie's mouth hung open. She snapped it shut, then crossed her arms over her chest. She'd interrupted her editing long enough to remove the bra that left marks on her shoulders and ribs to put on a very old tank top and equally old pajama bottoms. Not that this man hadn't seen it all. But he hadn't seen it the way it was now, and she didn't want him to.

Another perk of divorce.

'This isn't funny,' Frankie said.

Charley dropped his arms, clueing into the fact that she wasn't going to walk into them anytime soon. 'Why would it be funny?'

He appeared honestly confused. Charley was many things – smart, talented, expansive – but a great actor wasn't one of them. He was genuine in a way few people were. Which was probably why he was so good at his job. He could talk to anyone – from a Maasai warrior to the newly elected President of the United States – and his sincerity charmed them. Charley truly wanted to connect with his subjects – and who wasn't charmed by legitimate interest? With his incredible ability to record someone's essence through the lens of his camera, he told stories without words.

When Charley Blackwell looked at you, you felt special. When he took your picture, you became immortal. People trusted Charley. They loved him. Frankie had.

When he broke her heart, he broke it forever. Sure, she'd survived. Didn't we all? But she was never again the woman she'd been before she'd lost him.

Frankie's hands seemed empty without her camera. She felt more naked without it than without her bra. With a camera, Frankie could distance anyone just by bringing the viewfinder to her eye.

It also made a great weapon. Just ask Charley. He'd saved himself in countless dicey situations by bashing someone on the head with his Nikon. Right now, she really wanted to bash him.

'What the fuck are you doing here, Charley?'

'I live here.'

He sounded so certain that she pinched herself to see if, maybe, this was a dream. It was strange enough.

Her fingernails left half-moon marks in her arm; the pinch pinched. She didn't wake up.

'You don't live here any more.'

He laughed – the big, booming Charley laugh she'd fallen in love with. 'Did you toss my clothes on the lawn again?'

'I only did that once.' Of course the time he'd really deserved it, the time he'd admitted to boinking an editorial assistant – worse, to *loving* an editorial assistant – she'd been too devastated to do anything but curl into a ball and cry.

'Seemed like more.'

Frankie made a soft sound of amusement and his smile deepened. He grabbed her hand before she could stop him. 'Let's go to bed. I'm beat.' He started up the stairs, tugging her along.

She hung back. 'What is wrong with you?'

Because there *was* something wrong. Very.

'Nothing that twelve hours in the sack with you won't cure.'

Frankie shook her head to try and make the weird buzzing in her ears stop.

Charley took it as a 'no', which it also was. 'Still working? OK.'

He continued up the stairs, his hiking boots silent on the new plush carpet, but instead of going into what had once been their bedroom on the left, he turned into the room on the right. He immediately came out. For the first time since he'd walked through her door, uncertainty flickered across his face. 'What's going on?'

'You tell me.'

He glanced into the room again, then back. 'Where's Lisa?'

Gooseflesh broke out everywhere on Frankie's body. She tried to breathe, but the air she drew into her lungs tasted like fire, burned like it too. Maybe there was a fire, because her eyes suddenly watered as if smoke billowed all around.

Why would he ask that? How could he ask that?

Their daughter was dead.

'Did you let Lisa stay at a friend's? You knew I was coming home and that I'd want to see her.'

Frankie stood in the foyer, gaping like a kamikaze goldfish that had flipped from the bowl and on to the floor. She could not draw in enough air.

'Fancy? You OK?'

Neither of them was OK, but one of them was less OK than the other. Right now, as black dots began to dance in front of her eyes, Frankie wasn't sure which one that was.

Footsteps pounded down the stairs. Charley smacked her – hard – in the center of her back. She gasped and began to breathe again.

Charley pulled Frankie into his arms. She was so loopy she let him.

He smelled exactly the same beneath that gamey, too-long-in-a-plane smell. Since Frankie had met him he'd used a shower gel that brought to mind fresh herbs just sprouted in a sunny garden. Every time she caught a whiff of basil, Frankie thought of Charley. Right after the divorce, she'd been unable to prepare any of her mother's Italian recipes. The instant Frankie smelled those herbs she'd felt sick. It had been years before she could stomach bruschetta again, and it had once been her favorite.

Frankie stepped out of Charley's arms. It wasn't right. He wasn't right.

'I'll see Lisa tomorrow,' Charley said. 'I'm beat. You sure you're OK?'

Frankie hadn't said she was – and in fact she really wasn't – but she nodded, and he ran upstairs and disappeared into their – *her* – room. Frankie collapsed on to the couch and tried to make sense of things.

Charley seemed to have forgotten the past twenty-four years. Couldn't blame him. There had been many times during them when she'd wanted to forget too. Even odder was that he hadn't noticed her graying hair, sagging face, rounder body.

And what about the house? Frankie hadn't changed much downstairs – new carpet, but the same shade; she was pretty sure she'd painted a few walls; she'd definitely painted the kitchen cabinets to complement the new volcanic rock countertop.

But Lisa's room had more changes than simply the lack of Lisa. It was still a bedroom, but for guests. Frankie had replaced the pink throw rug with white plush, wall-to-wall. The canopy bed was now a Sleep Number, complete with a black upholstered headboard. The quilt wasn't pink either but bright red. All the stuffed animals were gone.

Frankie grabbed her computer and Googled 'stroke'. Symptoms were confusion—

'I'll say.'

Combined with trouble speaking and understanding.

Well, Charley didn't understand that he didn't live here any more but he'd certainly had no trouble talking. In Frankie's opinion, he'd had trouble shutting up.

She continued to read symptoms. Charley hadn't complained of a headache; he wasn't vomiting or having trouble seeing or walking. His face hadn't sagged. His hands and arms worked just fine. Too fine, considering the hug.

She tried 'aneurysm' next. Those often had no symptoms, but if they did they came on suddenly and consisted of a severe headache, neck pain, nausea, vomiting, sensitivity to light, loss of consciousness and seizures. Couldn't miss any of those. Charley would never have been able to walk up to her door and stroll around the house as if he still owned the place with such symptoms.

Frankie's fingers flew over the keys needed to type: 'brain tumor'.

The brain tumor hit parade was similar to the previous options. Changes in speech, hearing, vision, balance, as well as the seizures, were all present on the list but not in Charley. However, there were a few that fit his profile – namely personality changes and memory issues.

'Shit.' Frankie was going to have to call Hannah. She'd hoped she'd be able to Google her way out of it.

In an attempt to avoid the inevitable for a little while longer, Frankie dialed Irene.

'Bubala, it's four a.m.'

'Three,' Frankie corrected. Or near enough. 'You shouldn't have answered.'

'When haven't I answered? Especially in the middle of the night. You'd do the same for me.'

Frankie would. She had.

Irene and Frankie had been best friends since childhood – back when Irene had been the only Jew in school. She'd been an oddity to others, but to Frankie she'd been Irene from next door. They'd grown up together. They'd shared everything. They still did.

'Charley showed up at my house.'

Silence came over the line for so long Frankie feared Irene had fallen back asleep. Wouldn't be the first time.

'Hello?' she said.

'I'm here. I just . . .' Irene's voice trailed off.

'Yeah. That was my reaction too.'

'Why now? Did the *shiksa* throw him out?'

Irene tossed Yiddish words into her conversation whenever she could. She said she didn't want the language to die. Frankie thought she just liked how they sounded.

'I don't think so,' Frankie said. 'Though there was something off about her when she called.'

'Wait. The *shiksa* called you? Why?'

'She wanted to ask if Charley was here.'

'Why on earth would he be there?'

'Exactly. Except he is.'

'You didn't ask him why?'

'He's . . .' Now Frankie's voice trailed off. What *was* he? 'Not himself.'

Except he was himself – of twenty-four years ago.

Quickly she told Irene what had happened, leaving out the hug. She wasn't sure why.

'Bullshit,' Irene said.

'I wouldn't bullshit you at three a.m.'

'Four,' Irene corrected. 'And I wasn't talking about you. I was talking about him. *Shiksa* threw him out and he needs a place to stay. He knew you'd never let him past the front door if he wasn't . . . whatever it is he is.'

'He can afford a hotel.' Charley could afford several hotels.

'He hates hotels.'

As he lived most of his life in them, this made sense. Or maybe it didn't. Frankie had questioned on many occasions before they'd parted ways, why, if he hated hotels so much, did he continue in a job where he had to make use of so many of them? However, she didn't think Charley was capable of doing anything else. He *had* tried.

Before.

Her chest hurt; her throat went tight. Their lives would forever be divided into before and after that horrible, awful, terrible day when their daughter had died.

'Where is he now?' Irene asked, interrupting memories Frankie didn't want to have.

'Sleeping. I think.'

'Or getting naked.'

She had a vivid memory of Charley naked. Charley naked had been a beautiful thing. One of the reasons that finding out he'd been naked with Hannah had nearly ended her. How could he have taken what had been hers alone and given it to someone else?

'Why would he want me when he can have her?' Frankie asked.

'I always thought of that question the other way: why would he want her when he could have you?'

'Blond, young, brilliant editor with her own magazine and a wealthy, connected family? Who wouldn't want that?'

'Meh.'

Frankie imagined Irene's shrug.

'You're loyal. I appreciate it.'

'I'm not a moron. Youth fades. In fact, hers has. I saw her last week. She didn't appear well.'

Maybe that's what this was. Both Hannah and Charley had been ill. Nothing more than a bad flu, a nasty fever, which – for a man Charley's age – would be more dangerous than it had been for his child bride. Certainly Hannah wasn't a child any more, but she was still closer to one than Charley was.

'Why did you see her?' Frankie asked.

'Same reason I always see her. Publisher party at her mother's company.'

Irene was a literary attorney, Hannah's mom a bigwig publisher. For some reason Hannah came to the parties, even though she was a magazine editor in DC. Maybe it was the only time she saw her mother. Who knew? Who cared?

Not Frankie.

'Did you talk to her?'

'That never turns out well.'

Irene didn't pull punches. Not in her job – which was why she was one of the most sought-after attorneys in the biz – or in social situations – where she was also sought-after, though, considering her lack of a mouth filter, Frankie couldn't figure out why.

'Besides, when she sees me she runs like a little girl from a mouse.'

'More like a grown woman from a shark.'

'Whatever works,' Irene said.

'I'm going to have to call her, aren't I?'

'You could probably wait until morning. If you want to be nice.'

'Yeah, that'll happen.'

Frankie didn't want to call Hannah. One conversation a night was enough. But she wasn't going to be able to put it off either, so she might as well get it over with.

'Call me first thing and tell me how it went,' Irene said. 'Love ya.'

'You too.'

Frankie didn't know what she would have done without Irene. After. Irene had dropped everything and flown to Milwaukee. She'd stayed for weeks. Frankie couldn't remember how many. Then, when Frankie had found out about Charley and Hannah, Irene had come back and done it again.

Frankie scrolled through her recent calls. Hannah's was labeled *Private* – no number – and she didn't have it in her contacts for obvious reasons, so she headed up the steps. If Charley were awake, she'd insist he call his wife. If he were asleep, she'd use his phone and do it herself.

Pausing in the doorway, she suddenly couldn't breathe again.

Charley had left on the bathroom light, the door pulled nearly closed so the glow spread across the Berber carpet in a thin shaft, illuminating a path from bed to bathroom. It also served to illuminate the bed – new, with a frilly white comforter Frankie never would have bought when they were married.

The only man she'd ever loved lay right where he had the last time he'd slept here.

'Sweetheart,' he murmured, his voice slurred.

With sleep or with stroke/aneurysm/brain tumor? Maybe she should call 911 instead of Hannah.

'You OK?'

'Tired.' His blue eyes seemed to gleam, so bright that when he closed them the entire room dimmed. 'Come to bed.'

'You need to call your wife.'

'Fancy,' he called. 'Fancy.'

'On the phone, Charley. Call her.'

'I don't need to use the phone to call you. You're right here.' The final three words came out slowly and were followed by a soft snore.

Charley had always been able to fall asleep between one instant and the next. Probably from spending the majority of his time on the road, catching rest on trains, trucks, planes, the ground.

Frankie knew that snore. He would wake up if an IED went off, but if she tried to rouse him he'd be dead to the world.

She should be glad he wasn't actually dead to the world. In her bed.

'Goddamn it, Charley.' She went through his stained jeans – as Irene had predicted, he'd gotten naked; all his clothes were on the floor – and found his cell phone.

She pressed a thumb to the *Favorites* button, surprised to find her own name there. The man hadn't called her in two decades.

Frankie scrolled until she found Hannah and pressed again. She figured the phone would ring several times, maybe even go to voicemail. Instead, it was answered between the first and second rings.

'Where are you?'

'He's . . . uh . . . here.'

'Francesca?'

Considering Hannah had called not more than an hour ago to warn of just this possible occurrence, she seemed awfully surprised.

'Yes.'

'Did he say why he's there?'

According to Charley, he still lived here. How was Frankie going to explain that on the phone? How was she going to explain it at all, ever?

'You should probably come and get him.'

'Me? There?' Hannah said the last word as if Frankie had asked her to fly to an Ebola-ridden nation. 'Why?'

Frankie debated telling Hannah not to bother. She didn't want to see her. She specifically didn't want to see her with him. But Charley was no longer Frankie's problem. He was Hannah's.

'Because there's something wrong with Charley. He thinks we're still married. He thinks Lisa is still alive.'

'That's impossible.'

'Be that as it may,' Frankie said, and hung up.

Charley

University of Southern Illinois. Summer, 1976

Most of the students were talking – small cliques of two or three, maybe four. The drone decreased significantly when Charley Blackwell set his battered black camera bag on the gray metal table at the front of the room. There were about a dozen tables just like it dotted across the yellowing linoleum. Students sat on top of them or in the equally clunky metal chairs positioned three or four apiece.

Curious faces turned Charley's way; many became skeptical. He knew in his torn jeans and sandals, with his curly hair overgrown and shaggy, he more closely resembled a student than one of the faculty.

He was only twenty-three, but he'd been to Vietnam and back; so had many of them. The GI Bill was in full force on campuses across America. Former soldiers going to college on Uncle Sam's dime. It was the least they deserved.

Charley could have taken advantage of the bill himself. No money for college meant he'd been drafted, and while he had spent time as a grunt with a gun, he'd also had a camera. He could have come home after his first tour; instead he'd stayed and kept on shooting. The pictures he'd taken while marching through the jungle, in the midst of firefights, faces, bodies covered in blood, the tears and the laughter, then his insider's view of the final days in Saigon, had landed him here.

For the summer semester he would teach Advanced Photography, and in the fall he would begin his new job with the Associated

Press. This was the life he'd dreamed of while growing up on a farm not very far away.

'Are you Charley Blackwell?'

In the middle of searching for his notes, which must be at the bottom of his camera bag, below every camera body, lens and filter he owned, Charley glanced up and into the prettiest green eyes he'd ever seen.

'I am.' He smiled. 'And you are?'

The girl blushed, her cheeks turning apricot instead of crimson, a shade lighter than the auburn streaks in her dark brown hair. Her summer-weight short skirt and tie-dyed T-shirt were replicated all over the room, but she wore them a lot better than anyone else.

'I'm Francesca Sicari.'

'Fancy,' he said.

She lifted her eyebrows and her mouth quirked. 'People usually call me Frankie.'

He rarely did.

Charley managed not to touch her while she was his student, but it wasn't easy. That skin – dusky with a hint of peach – begged touching. Those eyes, like a wise Egyptian cat's – he found himself staring into them when he should have been teaching. Her hair, which hung to her waist as so many women's did then, was thick and straight and whenever it swayed a different shade revealed itself. He wanted to photograph that hair at dusk, at dawn and every hour in between.

She was his best student, as well as his most talented student. Frankie saw things in a way no one else did. When Charley looked at her photographs he found a world he wouldn't have without her, a world that was different from the one he saw through his lens. That's what photography was all about.

She sat in the front row of his class for six weeks and drove him mad. Whenever she was near he smelled lemons. Charley had always liked lemons, usually in his vodka and lemonade.

He later learned the streaks in her hair were from lying in the sun after combing lemon juice through the strands. Something all the girls were doing. Strangely she was the only one who smelled like lemons even after she'd washed the juice away.

They would go out with the other students – take pictures, have a beer afterward, talk about photography, the war, the election,

the death penalty, the meaning of 'Bohemian Rhapsody' –
anything, everything – then go their separate ways.

Charley dreamed of her every night.

It wasn't appropriate. He was her teacher. But he wasn't *a*
teacher. This was a short-term gig. He started counting the days
until the summer semester was over.

After that final class, the students filed out, shaking Charley's
hand, thanking him, wishing him well. Frankie sat in her chair
until everyone was gone.

Charley had been waiting for a time when there would be
only them; now that it was here he wasn't sure what to say.
They were two years apart in age, but he felt so much older.
Probably too old.

He still woke sometimes, screaming in the night. A lot of
the guys who'd come back from Vietnam did. Charley had
witnessed plenty of horrors. Recording them seemed to have
imprinted the images on his brain as well as on film. The thought
of Francesca seeing him screaming, crying, thrashing . . . he
wasn't sure he could stand it.

'I hope you enjoyed the class.'

Her lips curved. She didn't speak.

Charley opened and closed his hands, a nervous gesture he
usually soothed by picking up a camera, so he did. He trained
the lens on her.

She placed her palm over the glass. 'Maybe later.'

'Later?' he repeated stupidly.

She took his hand and led him home.

Later – after – he took pictures of her and she took pictures
of him. They were the first set of many.

For Frankie and Charley photography was how they spoke to
the world; it reflected both thoughts and feeling. Pictures were
a language they shared, one very few other people spoke. In
finding each other, they'd found someone who heard them in a
way no one else ever had. From that first day, Charley had a hard
time remembering how long he and Frankie had been together
because his life without her was dim, a time spent in shadows
best forgotten. All he wanted was to live in the world he'd
discovered with her. Who wouldn't if given the chance?

Frankie was from Milwaukee, the only child of a second-
generation German housewife and a first-generation Italian

autoworker at the American Motors plant. Frankie's desire to go to college, to become a photographer, mystified them.

'My mother wants nothing more than to clean, cook and make sure my dad's after-work coffee has just the right amount of brandy.'

'So they mystify you too.'

Frankie tilted her head so she could see into his face. 'I never thought of it like that, but yeah.'

They lay together, naked, on the pull-out couch in her studio apartment. WKTI, the local Top Forty station, played 'Sara Smile' in the background. The morning sun pushed through a gap in the curtains and flowed across Frankie's hip like golden water.

Her sheets were old, faded but soft, and they smelled like lemons too. There were books and lenses and photographs and magazines spread across every surface. Her furniture appeared to have been confiscated from basements across America – scarred end tables, an ancient television with tin foiled rabbit ears, kitchen table with teeth marks on the legs. Charley hoped they were from a dog and not a kid, but who could tell?

'It's a mysterious time for everyone in this country. Things are changing. They're going to keep changing.'

Just this summer there had been riots in South Africa; an airliner hijacked from Athens and taken to Entebbe, where the Israelis staged a raid to free the hostages; a former peanut farmer had become the Democratic presidential nominee; soldiers had died in the Korean Demilitarized Zone, in Ireland and Palestine.

'You don't think life, people, everything will settle down now that the war's over?' Her breath puffed against his chest and made him shiver.

'No,' he said. 'I don't.'

He planned to take photographs of upheaval all over the world for as long as he could. Except . . .

He peered at the woman in his arms. She had freckles on her nose. He thought he might like to stare at those freckles for the rest of his life.

Charley woke the next morning still in her bed. He didn't want to go, and that was new. Usually he left before dawn broke. Today he lingered, even though he had someplace to be.

They took a shower, drank coffee, made pancakes for breakfast, read the paper in their underwear and T-shirts. Frankie's showed the movie poster for *Jaws*, which had been released that summer. She'd seen it twice. Charley wore the concert T-shirt for David Bowie's *Diamond Dogs* Tour. He'd been in Vietnam at the time, won the thing in a card game.

Frankie didn't seem in any more hurry to see the end of him than he was to see the end of her. Eventually, he had to either go or take her with him.

'You wanna meet my parents?'

She shrugged. 'You wanna meet mine?'

Charley drove an old white VW bus. He loved that vehicle despite the rust. It was the first one he'd ever owned. However, when he pulled it to a stop at the foot of the long gravel lane that led to his family farm, his father, George, came on to the porch and spat.

'Tell me you didn't drive that hippy bus through town.'

'OK.'

He had, but why mention it? He wasn't staying.

Charley's mother and his two younger brothers – Ben was fifteen, David was seventeen – joined his father. All three men wore denim overalls, long-sleeved dark shirts and work boots, despite the heat. The males shared Charley's dark curling hair; he shared his mother's blue eyes.

Charley had never noticed before how faded everything was – the house, the barn, the cows, his family. The only real color, as far as he could see, was Fancy – green eyes, hair in every shade of brown, her swirling orange skirt, beaded moccasins and white peasant blouse. She stood out like a jeweled brooch dropped into a sea of old hay.

'This is Francesca Sicari.'

His father grunted. 'As foreign as your car.'

'I was born in Milwaukee,' Frankie said.

Charley's father just grunted again.

The visit didn't improve. Charley's mother tried, but she was as mystified by Frankie as Frankie's own parents were.

'You go to college?' Claire smoothed her chapped hands over her blue cotton dress. 'Why?'

Charley had never before noticed how prison matron his mother's clothes looked.

'I . . . uh . . .' Frankie glanced at Charley. 'Wanted to learn.'

'What?'

'Photography.'

Charley's dad cast him a quick, disgusted glance. 'Your student?'

'Not any more.'

They left right after dinner.

To her credit, Frankie only smiled when Charley's dad asked if she was a hippy.

'*I'm* a hippy, Dad,' Charley said.

'I suppose that means you aren't coming home to help.'

'I wasn't ever coming home to help.'

From the instant he'd peered through a viewfinder at the rice paddies below his helicopter, where people toiled year in and year out for very little, often caught in the crossfire of a war they hadn't wanted and didn't understand, Charley hadn't planned to do anything but frame what he saw within that square over and over again. No matter what he had to do; no matter what he had to not do.

'How'm I gonna keep the farm goin' without you?' his father demanded.

'You have Ben and Dave.'

'We could really make something of this place with one more pair of hands.'

'That's your world, not mine.'

Charley's mother gasped. His father's face turned red. Charley tensed for an argument and—

Frankie took his hand. 'Thank you for dinner. It was lovely meeting you.'

Then she led him back to the car.

He didn't meet her parents until the following spring. It didn't go much better than the meeting with his own.

Frankie still had one more year of college. Charley spent most of it on assignments for the Associated Press all over the world. He'd planned to rent a cheap apartment in a city with an international airport. Instead, he used the money he saved from not having to rent a place to fly into the small Marion, Illinois airport, or sometimes into St Louis, where he'd rent a car and drive to Carbondale. He left the VW bus with Frankie. She loved it almost as much as he did.

When Frankie graduated in May he was at the Kentucky Derby.

Charley was discouraged at the lack of hard news stories he

was sent to cover. As the new guy, he shot a lot of fluff – like the Kentucky Derby. What he wanted to do was go to Cambodia and record what the country was like since Pol Pot had become prime minister – Cambodian code for dictator – last year. But he had to pay his dues.

After the Kentucky Derby, Charley flew to Wisconsin. Frankie's parents hosted a graduation party at their two-story brick duplex in South Milwaukee, though they seemed more inclined to show off their daughter's boyfriend than their daughter's diploma. Charley spent the day talking up the Southern Illinois program and insisting that a degree in photography was really a degree.

'She'll take wedding photos?' one of Frankie's aunts asked.

'Maybe school portraits?' suggested another.

Charley gave up trying to explain photojournalism. 'Whatever she wants.'

'You don't mind her working?' asked an uncle – Paolo, he thought.

'I don't have anything to say about it.'

Across the room, Frankie caught his eye and winked.

Charley was dazzled even at a distance. They hadn't had time alone together in a month. They wouldn't have any here either since they were staying at her parents' place, in separate rooms.

'You don't plan to marry my Francesca?'

Frankie's father – Pietro at birth, Peter in America – had joined him. He was short and wiry, with leathery skin and dark, sharp eyes. Charley towered over him by nearly a foot. The guy still scared him. He was so fierce when it came to his only child.

'I . . . uh . . . well . . .' He hadn't thought of marriage. He'd been too busy thinking of . . .

Charley flushed, which probably made him appear guilty. Though of what, he couldn't say.

'She talks of nothing but you. She dates no other man. If you do not plan to make her your wife, you need to run along.'

'I travel three hundred days a year.'

'So?'

'She'd be alone all the time.'

'She'd be alone with your name, your protection—'

'Papa!' Frankie must have seen Charley's panic, because she had come to his rescue. 'I don't need his name; I have my own. And I can protect myself.'

Mr Sicari fixed Charley with a glare. 'Are you a communist?'

'Papa!' Frankie said again, but this time she was laughing. 'It isn't 1955.'

'I'm not a communist, sir.'

Mr Sicari didn't seem mollified by that, but he did stop asking Charley questions he couldn't answer. At least for the rest of the day.

Later, Frankie apologized. 'He's old fashioned. He thinks women should be married.'

'What do you think?'

They had gone for a walk along Lake Michigan, where the late May breeze still carried a hint of ice, but the water was so blue it hurt to stare at the surface beneath the sun.

'I think I'm starting a new job next week, and that's enough change for me right now.'

Frankie had taken a position as a news photographer for the *Milwaukee Journal.* Charley had written her a recommendation. Probably not exactly on the up and up, considering, except she *had* been his best student. He hadn't lied about that.

Following the graduation, Charley was sent to San Francisco where 200,000 people marched in protest of Anita Bryant's anti-gay stance, as well as the murder of Robert Hillsborough, a homosexual gardener who had been stabbed fifteen times on his way home from a club. Charley received his first Pulitzer nomination for his photos of the march.

He didn't get back to Milwaukee until autumn. The leaves were all orange and red and yellow. Charley barely noticed. He missed Frankie so much by then his stomach ached whenever he thought of her.

She met him at the airport and took him to his hotel, where they barely made it into the room before they started tearing off each other's clothes.

A half-hour later, Frankie kissed his chest and started to pick up her things.

'Where are you going?' Charley had been gearing up for round two.

'I live with my parents. They're expecting me – us really – for dinner.'

'Let's get a place of our own.'

She laughed. When he didn't, she stopped. 'You were serious?'

'I almost always am.' Charley didn't waste time with jokes or teasing. Life was serious, and in the places he worked more serious than most.

'We can't live together.'

'We have before.'

'No, you visited me at college.'

'Where you kept all my stuff and my van.'

'I still have your van.' She cocked her head and her hair flowed over one shoulder, the colors beneath the glow of the bedside lamp reminding him of the trees outside. 'I guess in some countries that's as good as married.'

'What countries?' he asked.

'Joke.' She waved her hand. 'Never mind. I can't live with you.'

'I suppose your dad would come after me with his shotgun.'

'He doesn't own a gun.'

'For this, he'd probably buy one.' Charley sat up in the hotel bed and held out his hand. She didn't take it, and he got a little scared. 'You don't want to move in with me?'

Her face softened. 'There's nothing I'd like more, but I have to live in this town and you don't.'

'I just said I'd be living with you.'

'Your idea of living with me is dropping in between assignments.' She made a 'halt' gesture. 'I understand your job. I don't want you to change. But I can't move in with you. I won't do that to my parents.'

'It isn't their life; it's ours.'

'This isn't my town; it's theirs. And it wouldn't be fair.'

At least she hadn't said it wouldn't be right. Because Charley couldn't think of anything more right than them sharing every moment they could, from now until forever. Didn't she feel the same way?

'Let's get married.'

Where had that come from? He had no idea, but as soon as he said it, he wanted to get married more than he'd ever wanted anything except, maybe, his camera.

Idiot! He definitely wanted Frankie more than a camera.

'What?' She dropped all the clothes she'd picked up back on to the floor. 'No!'

'You're telling me no?' He was not only surprised, but that

niggle of fear that had started up now deepened. What would he do if she didn't feel the same way?

'Charley.' Leaving the garments where they'd fallen, she sat on the bed. 'You've never even said that you loved me.'

He hadn't? He tried to remember an occasion when he had so that he could bring it out and prove her wrong, but his mind was blank. Had he only thought the words every time he'd seen her, touched her, woken up next to her? That couldn't be true.

He was a fool.

Charley framed her face in his palms and kissed her brow. 'I love you.' He kissed her right cheek, then her left. 'I love you.'

His mouth trailed over her eyelids. 'I love you.'

Then at last he took her lips; her hands cupped his where they still rested on her face. He lifted his head, looked into her eyes and, together, they smiled.

'Let's find an apartment,' she said.

Hannah

Washington DC, 1990

Hannah Cartwright walked along Seventeenth Street. It was her first day as an intern for *National Geographic*.

She didn't think she'd slept more than an hour, total, all of last night. She hoped she didn't fall asleep on her feet today, though the way she felt now, she didn't think she'd sleep again soon. She was so damn nervous.

From the moment her professor at NYU had suggested she apply for an internship at *National Geographic*, Hannah had been desperate to be accepted. She'd loved her journalism classes in high school; the one place she'd fit in was at her school newspaper/magazine. All she'd ever wanted was to work for *National Geographic*. Which only made her one of a hundred thousand other kids with a dream.

She'd applied for an internship in editorial – her hope to become editor-in-chief someday – but what she'd gotten was an internship in the photography department. Hannah knew nothing about photography beyond point and shoot.

Nevertheless, she'd taken the job. As her twin brother, Heath, had said: 'If you're going to be in charge of the entire shebang you're going to need to know everything. Why not start with what you know the least about?'

He had a point, but she was still scared out of her wits. What if she was fired the first day?

Hannah paused and hugged herself. Several pedestrians side-stepped, one casting her a disgusted glance, another a slightly concerned one. Was she crazy?

She felt a little crazy. Or maybe terrified was the right word. 'I bet Gloria Steinem wasn't terrified her first day on the job.'

Hannah didn't realize she'd said that out loud until more concerned, disgusted glances came her way. She straightened her spine and marched on.

Today she would begin the rest of her life. Hokey, but true. She was on her way to being the editor-in-chief of the world's most well-known magazine. Was she overreaching? Probably. But that was how people got where they wanted to go – by making goals and sticking to them, turning obstacles into opportunities.

If he could hear her thoughts, Heath would call her Pollyanna, as he so often did. Or advise her to take up a career inventing T-shirt slogans.

The twins were spending the summer with their aunt, who had just started the fashion magazine *You*. Heath would be Aunt Carol's intern. He understood so much more about fashion than Hannah ever could. He'd even dressed her that morning.

'You want to appear professional, not stodgy.' Only Heath would use a word like *stodgy*; only Heath could make it work.

While Hannah was pale, slightly round and tiny, Heath was tall, slim and golden. She swore her brother glowed. He had long fingers, long feet, even his long nose fit on his 'should have been born in the Regency era' face. Sometimes he dressed like a British lord and faked the accent. He'd never once been questioned on it.

Heath had wrinkled his long nose at Hannah's black skirt and white blouse. 'Take that off.'

'Take what off?'

'The shirt. Too *Prime of Miss Jean Brodie*. The girls, not Miss Jean.'

'I don't know what that means,' Hannah had said, but she'd taken off the shirt.

Some might find it odd – creepy even – for Hannah to do so. But she and Heath were twins. They had shared the womb, then shared a secret language. They often shared thoughts. They'd shared crushes. In fifth grade they'd both adored Tommy Savante.

'This one.' Heath pulled a deep-blue blouse from her closet.

There was a reason Heath was the fashion intern and Hannah wasn't.

'Honestly, Hannah, what would you do without me?'

'Panic,' she'd said, which was what she always said whenever he asked.

Up ahead loomed the headquarters of *National Geographic* tall and white; the windows sparkled so brightly in the morning sun Hannah was nearly blinded. She paused just to enjoy the moment. This could be the beginning of the realization of all her hopes and dreams. It *would* be. She wouldn't allow it to be anything else.

Hannah took a deep breath, then glanced at her watch. She was right on time.

'Hannah!' Julie Jones, the receptionist, greeted her as if she were both surprised and thrilled that Hannah had shown up.

Who wouldn't show up for a coveted internship at *National Geographic*?

'Let's get you settled.' Julie came out from behind her desk. A stocky woman with a cap of ebony hair and huge, pink-framed glasses, Julie was the heart of the photography department.

The rest of the day passed in a whirl of new faces and names, new experiences. Hannah sat in front of a light box in the editing room, with slide after slide after slide propped on the tiny shelves that made up row after row.

In an attempt not to miss anything, a photographer took pictures of everything. Then they culled – or she did. Out went shots that were underexposed, overexposed, those that contained a view of a thumb, a knee, the ground, the back of someone's head.

Next, doubles were shorn to singles. Unless there was some-thing different in the shot – another person, an unusual angle, two cats instead of one, better light, worse light, a filter – out it went.

But woe to the intern who got rid of a slide that was not *exactly* the same as another. Because that shot might be *the* shot.

Hannah held a magnifying loupe to her eye so she could examine the slides more closely. She thought she might go crazy if this was what she had to do every day, all summer long. Of course the photos depicted erosion in desert locales – important stuff but not exactly visually stimulating. Maybe tomorrow she'd get to examine slides of the beginning of the end of apartheid.

'Please, please, please,' she muttered.

'If you think this is bad, you should see the light room at *Sports Illustrated*.'

Hannah spun.

The man standing in the doorway wearing dirty khakis and a rumpled powder-blue Oxford shirt appeared as if he'd been on a plane since last Thanksgiving. His dark hair was a jungle of curls; his eyes were roadmaps, his skin pale beneath the tan, and his four-day beard sported several patches of gray. Considering the camera bag slung over his shoulder and his presence in this office, he must be one of the staff photographers.

'I . . . uh . . . why's that?' Hannah managed.

'Sports photographers.' He rolled his eyes, then winced. Moving eyes that bloodshot must hurt. 'They take twice the shots we do. You never know what you might miss when Jordan's driving to the hoop unless you record every millisecond of the event.'

From the number of slides in this room, Hannah thought every millisecond of the last millennium had been recorded. She took an instant to be grateful she hadn't applied for an internship at *Sports Illustrated*.

As if.

She stood, smoothing her skirt. 'I'm Hannah Cartwright.' She held out her hand, thankful she'd dried her palms on said skirt.

'Charley Blackwell.'

His palm was large and hard, as if he broke rocks for a living. Something her dad always said – though who would do that and why, she wasn't sure.

'Staff photographer?'

He patted his camera bag. 'Got it in one. You're the new intern?'

'I am.' She was unreasonably pleased that he knew who she was. Not that it was difficult to figure out. Who else would be stuck in this room all day?

He peered at the slides on her editing table. 'Sediment. Lucky you.'

'I don't mind.'

'Then you're a saint.' He opened his camera bag and removed a bunch of white plastic containers. 'You wanna work on these if you have time?'

'God, yes.' She snatched them away.

'You don't even know what they are.' He pulled out more and set them on the table.

'I don't care.'

'Well.' He stuck his big hands into his pockets and hunched his shoulders before glancing into the hall. His expression seemed woebegone. She couldn't tell if he didn't want to leave or he didn't want to stay. 'I'll see you around.'

'I'll be here.'

Charley Blackwell proved to be the most excitement she had all day.

Heath waited for Hannah at the door that night. 'How was it?'

Their aunt was still at the office and would be for hours. Starting a magazine took a lot of time. From what Hannah could tell, it took all her time.

'I edited pictures of dirt.'

'Lucky, lucky. Anything else happen?'

'Met one of the staff photographers.'

'Which one?'

'Charley Blackwell.'

Heath's eyes widened. 'He took the photos of the march in San Francisco.'

'Which march?'

'Nineteen seventy-seven. Protest against some chick who hated gays, as well as the murder of one.'

'You were eight.'

'Wrong was still wrong, even back then when they didn't think it was.'

'You remember a guy's name from a photo he took way back then?'

'He was nominated for a Pulitzer.'

The photographers at *National Geographic* were the best of the best, but apparently Charley was even better than that.

'What was he like?' Heath asked.

'He's . . .' Hannah searched for a word to describe Charley Blackwell. She meant to say *fascinating* or *interesting* or even *motivational* but she remembered his expression right before he'd left the editing room, and what came out was: 'Sad.'

Heath blinked, his ridiculously long dark lashes sweeping over his annoyingly deep blue eyes. Hannah had blue eyes, but they were much lighter, and while her eyelashes were adequate, they weren't Heath-length and they weren't black unless she used mascara. Which Heath said girls did anyway, so why was she bitching?

'Sad,' he repeated. 'As in . . .' He held up his thumb and forefinger to his forehead in an 'L', international sign of the loser.

'No. Gloomy-sad.' Hannah pulled an exaggerated frown.

'Bummer.'

'He just got back from an assignment.'

'Maybe that made him sad. Lord knows there's plenty in this world to cry about. Where was he?'

'I'm not sure. I guess I'll find out tomorrow when I open the boxes of slides he gave me to edit.'

'Cool. You'll have to tell me what you find.' Heath waggled a bottle of champagne so cheap she was surprised he'd found it in this neighborhood. 'In celebration of our first day.'

'How was yours?' Hannah kicked off her shoes.

'Fabulous!' He punctuated the exclamation by setting the champagne bottle on the butcher's block island with a thump, then turned with two full glasses and joined her on the couch. 'I was a hit.'

Hannah sipped the champagne. Horrid, just as she'd suspected.

'How could you not be? What did you do?'

'Got coffee, answered phones, sat in on meetings.'

In comparison, her day had been more to Hannah's liking. But Heath would have wilted in a small, dark room with a thousand boxes of slides. He needed light and color and people.

He sipped his own champagne, grimaced, then slammed the entire thing, setting the empty on the basswood and glass coffee table before leaning back with his hands behind his head. 'I met someone.'

'Already?' Hannah sipped more slowly. She didn't want her brother refilling her drink. One glass was doable; two of this stuff would cause a splitting headache.

'True love waits for no man.'

With Heath it was always true love. He'd had his heart broken more times than Hannah wanted to remember. Because Hannah was always the one who picked up the pieces of that heart and shoehorned them back together.

'Maybe you should wait a week or two before starting an office romance.' Or maybe not start one at all. That would be her vote.

'Beggars can't be choosers, sis.'

'You've never begged in your life.'

He lifted his eyebrow – something he'd practiced when they were fifteen until he could lift one without the other whenever he wanted.

Hannah never bothered to try. She figured the expression would make her look like she'd had a stroke, rather than arch and debonair the way it did for Heath.

'I've begged plenty – in the right situation.'

Hannah – who suspected she might be an eternal virgin – blushed. 'You know what I mean. You don't have to rush into anything.'

'The early bird gets the worm.' Now he waggled both eyebrows.

'Yuck.' Hannah punched his arm.

Heath rubbed the area, though she hadn't hit him that hard. 'Seriously, Joel's perfect for me. Tall, dark, built.' He sighed.

Well, she'd tried, but once Heath was 'in love' there was no stopping him. Thus far, he'd never been turned down. Really, what man in his right mind would turn down the young, beautiful, brilliant, amusing and clever Heath Cartwright?

'Just be careful, OK?' Hannah set her glass on the coffee table so she could take his hand.

'I'm always careful.'

'Condom careful?'

His gaze flicked away. 'Of course.'

Her fingers tightened. 'I'm not kidding. AIDS is—'

'I know what AIDS is.' He pulled away, stood, then refilled his champagne and drained it again.

She knew that he did – in theory. But Heath had yet to lose anyone to the new and terrible disease.

He would. It was inevitable. The reported number of cases in the US the previous year had reached 100,000, with 400,000 worldwide. It was an epidemic, a twentieth-century plague. And she was terrified her twin would die of it.

'Please, Heath. For me?'

Without her twin, panic would be the least of it. Their parents were . . . vague would be the best – the nicest – word. They both had careers that they loved and excelled in – their father worked on Wall Street; their mother was an executive editor at a publishing house.

The twins had never lacked for anything. They'd lived a block off Central Park. They'd gone to good schools, been raised by a perfectly lovely string of nannies. They'd taken fabulous vacations with their parents – and the nanny. More importantly they'd had each other, and that was all the two of them needed.

Really.

Sometimes Hannah wondered if their father had been more present in their lives, would Heath have—

No. Heath had always been the way he was and there was nothing wrong with that. No matter what anyone else – including their father – said.

Of course Heath thought the reason Hannah was always attracted to older boys was because of her 'daddy issues'. Hannah thought it was hardly fair of him to throw the daddy stone, considering.

'I'll be careful.' Heath bounded to his feet. 'I need to change. We're meeting for a drink, and he's already seen me in this.'

This was cream trousers, a turquoise T-shirt and a cream sport coat with the sleeves rolled up – a scrumptious cross between Kirk Cameron and Don Johnson.

'You need my help?' Hannah asked.

Heath just laughed and disappeared into his room. He left not long after.

Hannah made herself a sandwich and turned on the television. While she watched *Cheers* she paged through the stack of *National Geographic* magazines her aunt had kept. Hannah had opened them before, but she'd been reading the articles, considering the layouts. She hadn't paid much attention to the photographs. She certainly hadn't read the bylines. Now that she did, she found quite a few of them were Charley's. She thought the best ones were Charley's. Maybe she was prejudiced by Heath's words about the man, but she didn't think so.

The apartment door opened. Hannah glanced up, hoping Heath had returned early, Joel having been an incredible disappointment. Instead, her aunt dropped her Gucci bag and her keys on the antique Hepplewhite gaming table that stood just inside the door.

Carol was a stunning woman. Taller than most at five-nine, she still wore three-inch heels. She was busty and built, but she chose clothes that played that down. As she'd told Heath and Hannah, she wanted to be respected for her brain and not her boobs.

'She's respected for her bank account,' Heath had whispered when their aunt left the room.

Carol's first and second husbands had gone to the great husband hotel in the sky. Or Hell's Hotel for Hateful Husbands, if you listened to their aunt. She didn't miss them and wasn't searching for a third. She didn't need to. Both one and two had been loaded. Now she was.

'Hey.' Carol tossed her frosted blond hair out of her eyes.

Hannah couldn't recall a time she'd ever seen her aunt's hair shift enough to cover her eyes. It was usually shellacked into an immovable helmet. Must have been a really rough day.

Hannah set the magazine on the table, leaving it open to Charley's most recent published photos of Siberia. 'You hungry? I still have half a sandwich, and I'm full.'

'God, yes.' Carol kicked off her black heels, reached under her boldly printed white, yellow and black dress to yank off her pantyhose, then twisted her arm around to release her bra. 'Ah.' She plopped on the couch next to Hannah and took a huge bite out of the ham and cheese.

'Tough day?' Hannah asked.

Carol chewed a bit and swallowed. 'The usual.'

'You work too hard.'

'Is it work if you love it?'

'I don't know.' Hannah had never worked before.

Aunt Carol patted Hannah's hand. 'You will.' Her gaze flicked to the stack of *National Geographic* magazines. 'Studying?'

'Can't hurt.'

Carol leaned over to view the spread Hannah had been appraising when she came in. 'Siberia?' She gave an exaggerated shudder. 'Terrible fashion sense.'

'I don't think that's what they were going for here. Though if you wanted to do something about Siberia for *You*, I'd suggest a lot of fur.'

Carol's head tilted. 'That's not a bad idea. You sure you don't want to work for me?'

'Heath's your man. I'd be hopeless.'

'You'll learn a lot at *National Geographic*. You'll be able to work anywhere if you do well there.'

'I hope so.'

'Where do you want to work?'

'There.' Hannah shrugged. 'Who wouldn't?'

'Me.' Her aunt cast a wary glance at the photos of ice and snow. 'That kind of stuff would give me nightmares.'

'It's interesting. Gritty, exciting, real.' She left out *important* because her aunt and Heath thought fashion was important, and to a lot of people it was. Just not Hannah. Besides, she'd sound pretentious, something Heath had told her she needed to stop.

'Exactly,' Carol said. 'I get enough "real" walking home from work every night.'

Hannah peered at the photos again. When she lifted her gaze, Carol studied her as intently as Hannah had studied the glossy pages. 'What do you see?'

'Lives that are different from mine. Places I've never seen and places I have, but not in the way that he does. Dreams, disappointments, joys, heartaches. This guy is really good. I met him today. Charley Blackwell.'

'He's the best there is. Too bad he doesn't do fashion.'

Hannah tightened her lips to keep the 'Thank God' from bursting free. The idea of Charley – who'd taken such brilliant photos of so many things – circling a model wearing the latest Chanel, snapping her this way, that way and murmuring, 'Sell it to me, baby' made her kind of nauseous.

'You don't have a crush on him or anything, do you?' Carol asked.

'Me? Why would you think that?'

'The way you're staring at those pictures.'

'I have a crush on the pictures.'

'I'd just hate for you to become a cliché.'

'You lost me.'

Carol bit her lip. 'Falling for an older man. It's so . . .'

'I won't.'

'Well . . .' Aunt Carol shrugged. 'Even if you did fall for him, nothing would come of it. Charley Blackwell has a reputation.'

'He should. He's a genius.'

'I meant a reputation for faithfulness. He's in love with his wife.'

Hannah put her hand on her chest and gasped. 'Oh no!'

Carol rewarded her theatrics with a small smile. 'It is pretty amazing. In his business, in any business where you travel all the time, the loneliness gets to you. The constant opportunity is pretty hard to resist. But from what I hear, Charley has never strayed. And believe me, I'd have heard. I'd like to meet his wife. I guess she's a talented photographer herself. Though if she's that good, she wouldn't stay in Milwaukee; she'd be here or in New York. Maybe Paris or London.'

'Maybe she just likes Milwaukee.'

Carol rolled her eyes at that comment and went to bed.

Despite Carol's intentions, her aunt's words about Charley Blackwell only made Hannah more intrigued by the man. She couldn't wait to see the slides he'd brought in that day.

To that end, she was up early the next morning – just in time to meet Heath wandering in. She hadn't realized he'd not come home. She felt awful that she hadn't checked, but he was twenty-one and she was not – contrary to her behavior most of the time – his mommy. Although, she couldn't recall a single time *their* mommy had ever checked on either one of them. She'd paid someone to do that. As Mom had always said, paying top dollar was how you got the job done right.

The day was overcast, and the foggy light through the living room windows made Heath appear skeletal. For an instant she was afraid, and she didn't know why.

When Heath found her standing in the hall, dressed and ready to leave, panic flickered in his bloodshot eyes. 'What time is it?'

'Early. But you'd better get in the shower and IV some coffee before Aunt Carol sees you.'

'When have I ever not been ready to go when I needed to be?'

Hannah just sighed and headed for the door.

Heath stopped her with a hand on her arm. 'It really is love this time.'

She wanted to make a quip, but what she saw in his eyes stopped her. Instead, she kissed his forehead. 'Good for you.'

She was in the office before anyone else, so she started the Mr Coffee then opened one of Charley's containers and set the slides on the light table.

At first she thought she had the wrong box, but the ones Charley had handed her were right where she'd left them.

All the pictures were of basketball hoops. Hannah had no interest in basketball. At thirteen, she'd stopped growing, and she stood five-foot-two in shoes. Even if she'd been five-eight, she was a klutz.

But as she continued to pull out slides, then pare them down as she'd been taught, Hannah became very interested indeed. Each picture told a story – with basketball hoops.

A bare hoop mounted on weathered board – no net in sight – in the middle of Harlem. Another stood at the edge of a cornfield, beneath a stark barn light – very *Field of Dreams*. A third was fastened to a chipped avocado ceramic tile wall, the photo that of a toddler in a sudsy bath, shooting a *Nerf* basketball with pretty damn good form; the basketball blurred with speed, headed straight for the hoop. An action shot of a wheelchair game, an artsy shot of a desktop hoop made to appear large by the angle alone, the executive in the chair behind seemingly small.

The essay was brilliant.

'You're here bright and early.'

Hannah started so badly she knocked several slides off the stand. The managing editor, Ray Cantrell, stood in the doorway. A stout man with a perpetually red nose and flushed cheeks, she'd met him yesterday, but he'd barely spared her a glance. Why would he?

She was thrilled he'd seen her here, diligently doing her job.

'I wanted to get started on the slides Charley gave me.'

'Blackwell?' He came into the room, peered at the photos and scowled. 'That's not an assignment.'

'Should be,' Hannah said, then wished she'd shut up.

'Really?' Cantrell straightened. 'Why's that?'

'They're amazing.'

Seemed she couldn't shut up, even when she wished to.

'You think I should publish it?'

'I . . . well, aren't you?'

'Charley's been proposing this story for years. I didn't think it was something that fit here. I told him he could take it to other magazines.'

'But he didn't?'

'He did. No takers.'

'I can't understand that.'

Cantrell grunted, but his gaze was on the photos. 'Tell you what . . . mock up a spread.'

'Me?'

'In your spare time. You need to do what you're assigned to do first.'

'I didn't realize this wasn't it.'

'Not your fault. But from now on, the only slides you edit are the ones Julie tells you to. And these.'

'No problem.'

Hannah pulled the transparencies off the light table and replaced them in the boxes, then she went back to sediment. But while she edited dirt, she thought about basketball hoops, and she began to set up the spread in her mind.

This was her chance, and she planned to make the most of it.

Charley

Quang Nam Province, Vietnam. Spring, 1971

'Charley!'

At the shout, several soldiers grabbed their rifles and trained them on the jungle. Their eyes, already far too old for their often baby faces, narrowed. Searching, always searching.

'Whoa!' Jim Colby stepped out of the overgrowth, arms raised. No shirt in this steamy heat, his dog tags stuck to his sweaty, dark skin. Droplets of sweat beaded in his clipped Afro. 'The same baby san's here askin' for Charley that was here yesterday.'

The men put down their rifles, many cursed. *Charlie* was what they called the enemy.

'You're going to get your head blown off if you keep shouting that around here,' Charley said.

'It's your name.' Jim strolled into camp, followed by the 'baby san', what many of the guys called the village kids, be they boy or girl – sometimes it was hard to tell.

Charley was pretty sure this one was a boy, maybe six. It was also difficult to determine age since the kids were so small and skinny. He was cute – all big, dark eyes, knobby knees and elbows, huge smile with gaps in his crooked teeth. Charley had taken some great pictures of him, both with his personal Polaroid and with his military issue Leica.

'I thought we agreed to call Charley Polaroid,' the Waz said.

The Waz was Lester Wasiekowski. By the time anyone got 'Wasiekowski' out someone would be dead.

Les was from some town in Minnesota no one could pronounce any better than they could pronounce Wasiekowski. His blond hair had faded toward white; his pasty skin was perpetually the shade of a Southwestern sunset, and his pale eyes behind his big, black-rimmed glasses still appeared scared despite his having been here longer than almost any of them.

'Maybe you agreed.' Jim cast Charley a glance. 'Whaddya think about it?'

'Polaroid's fine,' Charley said.

He'd taken hundreds of Polaroid photographs of the children here then given them out. They loved watching themselves appear like magic. It was good PR.

The nickname would take some getting used to, but better than the alternative – never having time to *get* used to it because someone shouted his name and a FNG, fucking new guy – they seemed to arrive daily – panicked and shot someone, probably Charley.

Charley beckoned the boy, who joined him very slowly. Previously he'd scampered over, chattering words Charley didn't understand, leaning against his leg, wrapping his dirty fingers in Charley's belt loops.

Maybe he wasn't feeling well. How could Charley tell? The boy's skin would be as hot as Charley's own in this heat.

The kid didn't speak English and Charley's Vietnamese was limited to *Ngừng la.i,* which meant *stop; Tôi không hiê?u,* which meant *I don't understand,* and *Bên tên gì,* which meant *What is your name?*

The latter had yielded the word *Hau.*

Hau followed Charley into the tent, where the kid had been

a half-dozen times before. His dark eyes flicked around as if searching for . . . Charley had no idea.

'You hungry?' Charley hooked his fingers like a fork with one hand, dipping them into the bowl he'd fashioned with the other, before lifting them to his mouth.

Hau shook his head.

That was a first. He *must* be ill. Charley should probably get him out of here before he gave whatever he had to the rest of them.

The other guys, busy writing letters home, reading, playing cards, nodded to the boy, a few even said *xin chào* – hello in Vietnamese. There was one more word Charley knew.

Hau didn't respond.

'You OK, Hau?'

Hau stared at Charley blankly.

'Jim!' Charley shouted, and Hau skittered back a few steps.

Charley reached carefully for his Polaroid camera, hoping the familiar sight of it would calm the child.

Hau did smile his crooked smile, though it wasn't as cheery as it usually was.

Charley took the shot; the picture whirred out of the camera.

'What?' Jim ducked into the tent.

'You do anything to this kid?'

'What the hell would I do to him?'

Charley yanked the Polaroid photograph free. The ghostly, shadow-image of Hau had begun to develop already. He held it out to the child, who took it with his free hand. The other he kept in his pocket. Had he hurt that one?

'I don't know.' Charley studied Jim's face. Jim was never able to lie worth a damn. 'From the way he's acting, did you poke him with sticks?'

'What do I look like a— shit!'

Hau scooted around Charley, the steadily developing photo still clutched in his fingers. The hand that had been in his pocket now held a grenade.

He heard Jim bellowing, 'Run!'

Charley made a grab for Hau. Why, he had no idea. He should let the kid run away with the explosive device. Then Hau tossed it with a nimble flip of his dark fingers and the thing landed in the center of Charley's sleeping bag.

Bullseye.

'Get out!' Charley yelled.

Luckily the rest had been alerted by Jim's behavior and several were already gone. Others had bunched at the exit. Charley hit the pile like an NFL running back, shoving men through the opening. Then someone hit him from behind, shoving Charley out too and –

Kaboom.

Charley started up from sleep, gasping, sweating, maybe crying. His throat was raw. Had he been screaming?

Apparently, he had. Frankie seemed scared.

It took him a moment to remember where he was, *when* he was.

Nineteen seventy-seven. Not nineteen seventy-one.

Their new apartment on Brady Street in Milwaukee. Not Vietnam.

'Sorry.' He'd hoped that sleeping with Frankie would cure his nightmares. Up until now it had. He should have known they wouldn't be gone forever.

He was drenched in sweat, breathing heavily, his heart pounding so loudly he felt dizzy. He started to get out of bed; Frankie pulled him right back.

'You wanna tell me about it?' She gathered him into her arms, ignoring his protests that he was wet, and he smelled, with a nonchalant, 'You think I care?'

He lay there for a while letting her touch, her scent, her everything soothe him. She took one of his hands and kissed his fingertips, something she did when he wasn't paying attention. Like now. Now he was still hearing that damn boom.

She started humming the tune to 'Where Have all the Flowers Gone?'. Probably not the best song in this situation, but he liked how it sounded. He liked how *she* sounded. Eventually he told her. Not everything, but some of it.

For a minute silence settled over them, deep and full of questions he wasn't sure she'd ask, then she did.

'Did everyone get out?'

Charley took a breath, seeing it all again, hearing it, smelling it – that distinct odor of *kaboom* and rot. He felt the helpless panic. 'No.'

'How close were you to not getting out?'

Charley flinched at the remnant of sound that seemed to live in his head, especially in the darkest part of the night.

'I'm here,' he said, and kissed her.

'The boy?'

Charley shrugged. He had never seen Hau again, wasn't sure if the kid had gotten out or not. Hadn't wanted to ask.

'After that you re-upped?' Frankie's voice was incredulous.

'I . . . uh . . . yeah.'

'Then you stayed until the very end when you could have gone home?'

She knew the answer to both those questions. He didn't talk much about Vietnam, from what he gathered, hardly anyone who'd been there did, but he had told her that much.

'Why?' she asked.

The majority of the troops had left by 1973, though the final abandonment of Saigon hadn't happened until spring 1975. Every time he thought of the final days, he heard the *whoop-whoop* of the helicopters. There had seemed to be hundreds, but there hadn't been enough to get everyone out that needed to get out.

'Charley?' Frankie murmured.

What had she asked him? Oh, yeah. *Why?*

Why had he stayed when he could have gone home?

'By the end of my first tour I was solidly a combat photographer.' Sure he'd carried a gun; they all did, but he'd used his camera more. The pictures he'd taken, that they'd all taken, had done more to end that war than their weapons ever had. 'I couldn't stop. I had to stay. I had to see.'

'You had to make sure others saw.'

'Yeah,' he said, and kissed her again.

No one had ever understood him the way that she did.

Later, Charley woke alone. The sounds of the new apartment were unfamiliar, and he sat up in bed, trying to get oriented. He heard a distant gunshot, which was not distant enough for his taste.

While they'd chosen the area because it had been ripe with counterculture and a locus for the anti-war movement, lately the neighborhood appeared a little seedy. Frankie had high hopes that would turn around. She loved living in a place where she could walk to an Italian bakery or a locally owned market. Charley had told her not to do either one at night, and she had laughed.

'I've lived in this city most of my life. You don't have to worry.'

But he did worry. Because he saw a lot of places where the gunshots weren't distant enough.

He found Frankie curled up on their thrift-shop couch, wearing the white T-shirt he'd left on the floor, her smooth, tanned legs folded beneath her as she stared into space. Had she been crying?

'Fancy?'

Her gaze flew to his. She'd definitely been crying.

'What's wrong?' He gathered her into his arms.

'I had a dream.' Her voice was muffled against his throat, her breath warm and moist on his skin.

'I dreamed that close call you told me about was a lot closer. And . . . and . . .' Now her breath hitched. 'You were gone.'

'Gone?' he repeated stupidly.

'Dead. I never saw you again. Some asshole came to the door and handed me your cameras.'

Now she sounded mad. Charley liked it better than sad. Seeing her sad made his chest hurt. He didn't want to see her sad ever again.

'Our life . . .' She took a deep breath that hitched in the middle.

Charley wanted to punch whoever had caused that hitch, then he realized it was him.

'The life we're going to have, it never happened.'

'It hasn't happened,' he said, then wanted to bite his tongue as her eyes narrowed.

'I dream of it. Our perfect life. The pictures we'll take. The places we'll see. The people we'll meet. The time we'll spend together.'

He dreamed of that sometimes too, though when he woke up he wondered exactly how all that would happen with him on the road and her here. But they did have a lifetime, which was a long time, though he couldn't see how it could ever be enough.

'You make me believe I can do anything.' She ducked her head. 'I know it's not very Betty Friedan, but I never felt like I could be the me I wanted to be until I met you.'

'That's exactly it,' he said. 'For me too.'

She touched his face. 'I like my perfect-life dreams so much better than the one where you're dead from a grenade and some asshole turns up at the door with your cameras.'

'Baby, that happened years ago in another country.' He didn't point out that she hadn't known him then; no one would have come to her door. That would only make her cry more to think they might never have had even this much time together. He kind of wanted to cry when he thought about it, too.

'I know. But there'll be other close calls, won't there?'

He didn't mention that he'd had several since he'd met her. He wasn't stupid.

'Let's get married,' he said.

'You already asked me that, and I said yes.'

She'd actually agreed to get an apartment; she'd never agreed to marry him. Though he'd bulldozed ahead, purchased a ring, told his parents and hers that they were engaged.

'I mean now,' he said.

She lifted her head, blinked. 'It's after midnight.'

'In the morning then.'

When she laughed, his chest stopped aching. Just like that.

'I think we need a license,' she said, 'and that takes a few weeks.'

'Is there anywhere you don't need a license?'

'Doubtful.'

Neither of their families had been all that happy about their engagement. The idea of a wedding surrounded by those hangdog faces was one of the reasons they hadn't set a date.

'A place where people get married on a whim,' Frankie murmured.

'Vegas,' they said together.

They planned to leave the next morning, but before they were even out of bed Charley had a call from AP.

'Hold on,' he said into the receiver, then set his hand over the mouthpiece. 'They want me to go to Montenegro. Yugoslavia. I think. There's been a war there for so long, I'm not certain what, exactly, the area's called any more.'

'There's a lot of that going around.' Frankie's brow furrowed. 'I know photojournalists photograph the news and the news isn't often happy. You gotta do what you gotta do. Vegas will still be there when you get back. I'll be there.'

He kissed her long and well while his boss called, 'Charley? Come on, Charley!' on the other end of the phone.

Then he packed his bag and flew away.

And nearly died in a flooded field, in a place he wasn't sure he knew the name of beyond Yugoslavia.

He arrived late at McCarran Airport. Flights out of Yugoslavia were rarely on time. Sometimes flights didn't leave at all, so he counted himself lucky.

Though the assignment had been to shoot a story about peace after centuries of war, in a lot of areas there had still been war.

In the terminal he paused, uncertain. The plan had been for him to meet her plane, as his would arrive several hours earlier. Instead it was hours and hours later. She was probably at the hotel. Which one had it been?

He rubbed his head. Couldn't remember. He needed to find a phone and call . . .

'Crap.'

The only people who knew the hotel were Frankie and himself, and he couldn't call the hotel to see if she was there since he didn't know where to call. Why didn't he write things down? Maybe she'd told her mother.

'Charley!'

He turned and Frankie launched herself into his arms. He buried his face in hair that smelled of lemons, and the world came into focus.

He twirled her in a circle. People around them smiled and laughed. Frankie was laughing too, her face lit up like the Strip itself.

When he set her down, he saw she was garbed for a wedding in a dress of antique lace, her shoulders bare, flowers in her hair. He lifted the long skirt to see if she was barefoot. She wasn't.

'Do you plan on wearing combat boots to the chapel?'

'Gotta wear shoes in the airport. Fascists.' She kissed his nose. 'I asked about your plane and they said it was in the air, just late. I went into the restroom and got ready.' She did a *voilà* gesture.

'You've been sitting here in your wedding dress ever since? Why?'

'Because we're getting married.'

'You could have gone to the hotel. Rested. Gambled. Had a drink.'

'When I enter Caesars Palace, I plan to be Mrs Charles Blackwell.'

Caesars! How could he have forgotten that?

'I thought you weren't changing your name.'

Now that Frankie was making her own reputation in news photography, she didn't want to change her name and start all over again to gain recognition. She also didn't want to ride on the fame of Charley Blackwell. She didn't need to.

'I'm still not changing it legally. But I'll *be* Mrs Charles Blackwell.' She looped her arm through his. 'As soon as I get you to the chapel.'

'The license?' he asked.

'We can stop at the courthouse on the way.'

'Now?' It was dark outside.

'In Vegas, everything's open late.'

Charley paused in front of the restroom. 'I'll just clean up a little.' Except he had nothing to wear that wasn't wrinkled, damp or worse. He'd planned to arrive in plenty of time to buy new clothes. He should know better.

'Here.' Frankie held out a shopping bag. 'I had a few free hours.'

In the bag were tan slacks and a cream shirt that matched her dress.

'No shoes?'

'If I'm not wearing any, why should you?'

In the restroom he spent most of his time scrubbing his feet in the sink. He didn't even get any strange glances. It was Vegas.

There was a line at the courthouse and also at A Little White Wedding Chapel. They stood on the well-worn, too-bright carpet and passed the time by examining the photos of celebrity weddings that had taken place there.

The crease between Frankie's eyebrows that she got whenever she was thinking too hard appeared.

He took her hand. 'What's wrong?'

'Do any of these marriages last? Maybe we're cursing ourselves by coming here.'

'There's no such thing as a curse. Besides, what about Paul and Jo?' Charley pointed at the photo of Paul Newman and Joanne Woodward, then tugged on a lock of Frankie's hair until she met his eyes. 'Doesn't she seem like a Jo to you rather than a Joanne? I bet Paul's called her that – for nearly twenty-five years. That'll be us. We're built to last.'

He kissed her then, and he didn't stop until the couple behind them shuffled and coughed.

'It's our turn at the altar,' Charley said. 'Ready?'

She faced forward. 'Set.'

'Let's go.'

Frankie

Frankie abandoned sleep for the night. Her brain was far too busy.

After hanging up on Hannah, she took a shower, got dressed, made coffee. Then she stared out the kitchen window until office hours began and she could make an appointment for Charley with her doctor.

She probably should have waited for Hannah, but what if he had convulsions or a stroke or a heart attack before she got here? What if Hannah insisted on taking him back to DC and he expired on the plane?

'*Zeisele*, why is that your problem?' Irene asked when she called just after eight thirty that morning.

'Wasn't I supposed to call you?'

'You forgot.'

She had. Although 8:30 a.m. was early for Irene to conclude this, why argue?

Charley continued to sleep. Frankie had gone in to make sure he was still breathing. He was.

'He's in my bed,' she said. 'Doesn't that make him my problem?'

'Only if you let it.'

'I think this has gone past my control.'

'Because you let it.'

'Shut up, Irene,' Frankie muttered.

'You know I'm still on the phone, right?'

'Not any more.' Frankie hung up. She was getting quite good at it.

'How's Irene?'

Charley stood in the doorway – shirtless, barefoot. Still thought he owned the place.

'She's . . . uh . . . Never mind. How are you feeling?'

'Great.'

He went to the coffee pot, reached into the cabinet where she'd always kept the cups and poured himself one. After taking a sip – he closed his eyes and enjoyed that first hit of heaven the same way he always had – he turned and gifted her with the smile that had won her heart. Before he'd broken it.

They'd always been two peas in a pod, wanting the same things, loving the same things. They'd encouraged and supported each other. No one had ever believed in Frankie the way that Charley had. No one had ever looked at her, talked to her, or respected her – before him or since – in quite the same way. She hadn't realized how much she'd missed that until he'd strolled back in and started doing it again.

'You should have woken me when Lisa came home.'

Her warm bubble of nostalgia disintegrated. Guess she wouldn't have to ask him leading questions to discover if he was still cuckoo.

'I wish I'd been up to see her off to school.'

Frankie didn't bother to point out that she never would have let their daughter stay over at someone's house on a school night. And if she had, then Lisa probably wouldn't have come home before school but been dropped at the same by the equally insane mother who'd allowed a sleepover on a weekday. Charley wouldn't have known this even when he'd lived here. Frankie had dealt with their daughter's day-to-day life; Charley had dropped in once in a while and been Lisa's hero.

'What do you want to do today?' Charley asked.

I want to get you to the doctor then out of my house.

'I made an appointment for you with Dr Halverson.'

He drank his coffee, staring at her over the rim. 'That's your doctor.'

'You don't have one in town.'

He'd always seen doctors in New York or DC. As he was there more than here, it had made sense.

'I don't need a doctor.'

Frankie took a breath. 'Charley, you seem to have forgotten a few things.'

He shrugged, filled his cup again. 'Jet lag is a killer.'

'Where did you fly in from?'

'Botswana. Wildlife shoot. You know the country is one of the great safari destinations in Africa?'

'Show me your boarding pass.'

He frowned. 'Why?'

'Humor me.'

After setting his cup on the counter, he went to the front hall. On the way he paused to stare at a new photo she'd framed – a black lab puppy curled up in a bright red wicker basket sound asleep. Frankie waited for him to ask what had happened to the one that had been there in the past – their wedding picture – but he didn't. Instead he said, 'Nice,' before taking his boarding pass out of his duffel and handing it to her.

'This says DC,' Frankie pointed out.

'I certainly couldn't get a plane from Botswana to Milwaukee. Weird though. I had to book from DC to here. I didn't have a connecting flight. I'll have to talk to Sheila about that.'

Sheila had been in charge of travel arrangements at *National Geographic* back in the day. Was she still? Charley thought so.

He seemed to be functioning fine in his work universe, and why wouldn't he be? His work had always been his universe.

'What year is it?'

'Don't you know?' He laughed, taking back the boarding pass and crumpling it in his hand, but he continued to tighten his fingers around the paper until his knuckles whitened.

'Charley? The year?'

His forehead creased. 'I . . .' His free hand came up and began to massage his temple. 'I'm gonna lie down for a sec. Then we'll do whatever you want for the rest of the day, OK?'

He kissed her before she could back away – a quick peck and he was gone – up the stairs and into her room.

'This is bad,' Frankie said to the empty hallway.

Two hours later they sat in the waiting room. Apparently Dr Halverson, or her decorator, had bought into the 'blue is the color of calm' propaganda – indigo seat covers, lapis walls, cobalt carpet. For Frankie, it wasn't working.

At the house, Charley had fallen into a slumber like an exhausted two-year-old, but when she woke him he was cheery. She'd decided not to ask him again what year it was. Let Halverson do it.

She'd convinced him to visit the doctor by telling him she'd received a notice from 'their' insurance company stating that he needed to have a physical by the end of this week.

'I'd rather see my doctor,' he said.

'Let's just get it over with.'

'Sure, Fancy. Anything you want.'

He sounded so much like Her Charley it was maddening. Because he wasn't Frankie's Charley any more; he was Hannah's.

Speaking of Hannah, she wasn't getting into Milwaukee until late afternoon. Maybe by then Dr Halverson would have given Charley a pill that caused him to remember everything, and he'd be on the next plane out of Frankie's business.

As this wasn't Wonderland, Frankie doubted a pill would change much, but she was ever hopeful.

'Charley Blackwell.'

Charley, who'd been critiquing *People* magazine under his breath, glanced up as the nurse called his name, then stood along with Frankie.

'You don't need to go in,' he said.

'I'd like to, if that's OK.'

'Sure, baby.'

Every time he said that Frankie had to fight not to flinch.

The nurse, who appeared all of fifteen and didn't help the image by wearing scrubs that featured Sponge Bob, weighed Charley.

'Huh,' he said. 'Didn't realize I'd put on that much weight.'

He was twenty pounds heavier than when he'd been married to Frankie, and Frankie was at least the same. Not that he'd noticed. If she didn't hate him so much, she might like him again just for that.

The nurse ushered them into a cornflower-blue exam room, where she took Charley's blood pressure, his pulse, his temperature – the usual – then set a laptop on the counter and left.

The doctor came in almost immediately. She must have been hovering in the hall. That alone clued Frankie in that Halverson had gotten a heads-up from her receptionist about Frankie's call. Her quick glance Frankie's way confirmed it.

'So what's going on, Mr Blackwell?'

Dr Halverson was a tall, solid, no-nonsense woman, who kept her hair no-nonsense short and had let it go gray to match her eyes. She had been Frankie's doctor since right after Lisa died. Halverson had been very kind. She and Frankie were of an age, and the doctor had children as well. It probably hadn't been easy for her to see Frankie, imagine herself in the same position. Or maybe that was why she'd been so helpful, because she could imagine it, as any mother could. The trick, Frankie had found, was to stop imagining it.

'Frankie said I need a check-up for our insurance company. I've been out of the country, and I guess it's gotta be done this week.'

'How have you been feeling?'

'Good.'

'Anything abnormal going on?'

'Not really.' His brow creased again. 'More headaches than usual I guess. I probably wasn't hydrating enough in Africa. I'm not sure anyone can.'

'Africa.' She typed something into the computer. 'We'll want to draw blood. Might be a parasite.'

'That causes headaches?' Charley asked.

'Mmm.' The doctor typed some more. 'Hop on the table, please.'

She listened to Charley's heart, tapped his knees, felt his stomach, had him breathe deeply, cough and so on.

'You seem healthy, Mr Blackwell.'

'I try. Do you take care of my daughter as well?'

'Your daughter?'

'Lisa. Maybe she goes to a pediatrician. I'm embarrassed to say that Frankie takes care of all that.' He took Frankie's hand. 'Frankie's my gem and Lisa's my jewel.'

Frankie didn't think she managed not to flinch from that hit. At least no one noticed.

'You were born in what year, Mr Blackwell?'

'Nineteen fifty-three.'

'And what day is it?'

'June second.'

'The year?'

His gaze went to Frankie. 'Why does everyone keep asking me that?'

'How about an answer?' Frankie responded.

Charley released a put-upon sigh. 'Lisa was born in . . .' Charley's forehead creased. 'Nineteen eighty-four. She's five? So it's Nineteen eighty-nine.' He glanced at Frankie again. 'Right?'

Frankie's eyes flicked to Dr Halverson. Should she agree or shouldn't she?

The doctor must have sensed her dilemma, or recognized panic, because she moved on. 'OK, Mr Blackwell, I'm going to order some tests. Blood. Urine. CT scan.'

'Is that really necessary?' Charley hopped off the exam table.

'Definitely,' Frankie muttered.

'Whatever you say, Fancy.'

Halverson lifted her eyebrows at the nickname, or maybe it was the way he said it – as if he'd loved Frankie for a lifetime and loved her still.

How many hours until his wife showed up? He was killing her here.

'I'll send the medical assistant to draw blood. She'll bring you a cup for the urine. I'll see if I can get you in for that CT scan today. You aren't claustrophobic, are you?'

'No.'

Dr Halverson turned her gaze on Frankie, who shrugged. 'He wasn't on my watch.'

Charley frowned. 'What does that mean?'

Halverson fled.

'Your watch?' Charley pressed. 'I don't—'

Thankfully the medical assistant came in and started up the medical assistant banter designed to take a patient's mind off the coming needle.

Frankie took the opportunity to slip into the hall and chase Dr Halverson, who was just getting off the phone with the CT lab.

'What is wrong with him?' she asked.

'Hard to say. I've never seen selective memory loss like this before. Doesn't mean it can't happen. I'm not an expert on the brain. That area is one of medicine's last great mysteries. Weird stuff goes on in there that no one can fathom.'

Like the love of my life leaving me for a woman young enough to be my . . . much younger sister? That had certainly been unfathomable. Almost as unfathomable as his coming back now as if it had never happened.

'What am I supposed to do with him?' Frankie asked.

'Take him to the hospital and get that CT scan.' The doctor tore off an order from her pad and handed it to Frankie. 'Three o'clock.'

She shouldn't have taken it, but then she was too befuddled by everything to realize that. And later . . . Later things just got worse.

'We'll go from there,' Halverson continued.

'*We* aren't going anywhere. He's not my monkey any more.'

'Excuse me?' Dr Halverson said.

'Russian proverb. Designed to keep people sane. "Not my circus. Not my monkeys." He's not. Hasn't been since he . . . you know.'

'Yes.' Halverson glanced longingly down the hall toward the exit. Frankie understood the sentiment. 'When's the ringmaster supposed to show up?'

'On her way.'

'Will she be here by three this afternoon?'

'Probably not.'

'I guess he's your monkey until then. Good luck.' She ducked through another door and greeted her next patient.

Charley stepped out of the exam room, waggled the urine sample container with a grin and went into the bathroom. If Frankie wanted to make an escape, now was the time.

Except Charley knew where she lived. He thought *he* lived there too. What was she going to do, hide inside with the doors locked until Hannah showed up? The idea was far too appealing.

Instead, Frankie waited until Charley was done, then they started for her house.

'I've never heard of a CT scan being part of a check-up.' Charley had been staring out the window, saying 'huh' and 'hmm' and 'wow, that's new' every so often.

'Cadillac insurance. They run every test they can.' She had no idea if that were true. Did anyone have Cadillac insurance any more? Frankie didn't. But what else could she say?

'Let's have lunch!' He pointed to DelMonico's.

Frankie drove right past. She was *not* having lunch with him at 'their place'.

'Hey! I'm hungry.'

'It's eleven a.m.'

'So?'

'Not open until four, but there's another restaurant. Sobelman's. Near Marquette University.'

Sobelman's not only had the best burgers, in Frankie's opinion, but it held no memories. They'd never been there together. The place opened after he'd gone. It also had the added bonus of being small, loud and always busy. The less they talked, the better.

They sat at the bar and ordered.

'Frankie?'

One of her former colleagues at the *Journal* – now the *Journal Sentinel* since the morning *Sentinel* and the evening *Journal* had merged years ago thanks to the Internet – stood behind them.

'Everett. Hey.' Frankie's voice sounded as enthused as she felt.

She'd never much cared for Everett Geffard. He thought he was God's gift to photography. What made it especially galling was that a lot of other people did too. Frankie had never understood why. He had no originality, no vision – something a photographer shouldn't be without.

'How've you been? What are you up to?' He glanced at Charley and his eyes widened. 'Charley Blackwell?'

They'd never met, but every photographer knew Charley.

Charley stood; introductions ensued; the two men shook hands.

'What are you doing?'

'Eating,' Frankie said.

'Together?'

'Yep.'

'What—'

Frankie cast Everett such an evil glare he swallowed whatever he'd been about to say.

Charley and Frankie's break-up had been unpleasant. Following so closely after Lisa's death, it had been water-cooler fodder for a long, long time.

'We . . . uh . . . miss you at the paper, Frankie. Take care.'

He left, meeting up with some others by the door, none of whom she recognized. Frankie had been gone from the place for over twenty years. She was surprised she knew anyone who worked there these days.

'That's the guy who drove you nuts.' Charley took a swig of his soft drink. 'What did he mean about missing you at the paper?'

She didn't want to keep lying to him. Hell, she didn't want to keep talking to him, but she was having a hard time avoiding it. 'I don't work there any more.'

'Since when?'

Frankie sipped her ice tea. 'A while.'

'You were always better than that place.'

He'd been dead set against her leaving, back when she'd actually left.

'You're a photojournalist,' he'd said.

Well, actually, he'd said a lot more than that. Charley had disdained 'artsy' photographers, which was what Frankie had become.

'No, *you're* a photojournalist. I can't bear to see reality through that lens any more.' By then, she'd seen far too much reality in her life. 'You live for it.'

And since she was right, since one of the reasons she couldn't stand reality was because all Charley did was chase it, he'd let it go.

Frankie had been desperate to find beauty, and that wasn't as easy as people thought. Even harder if everything in the world suddenly appeared ugly and bleak no matter how anyone tried to spin it. So Frankie had started to create beauty, and Charley had found someone he could respect somewhere else.

Instead of turning to each other in tragedy, they'd turned away, and then fallen apart. She'd never seen it coming.

Once they'd eaten and were back at the house, Charley took a nap while Frankie did some work. Around two thirty, she received a text from Hannah.

Landed early. Should I come to your place?

Charley still dozed on the couch.

Quickly Frankie texted back: *He'll be having a test. Meet us at Columbia St Mary's on Lake Drive.*

'Charley.'

He didn't wake up.

'Charley!'

Frankie shook him. His hand encircled her wrist. He yanked her on top of him and kissed her the way he always used to. As if she were everything, as if without her there was nothing. She knew those things to be a lie, and still his mouth made her believe them all over again. It was like coming home. With his lips on hers, she forgot a lot of things, almost everything – betrayal and heartache, infidelity, aging, loneliness. But she couldn't forget death.

She'd never forget that. She'd never forget their little girl.

Frankie sat up, pulling her mouth from his with an audible smack. He reached for her again.

She stood. 'Stop.'

'Never.'

She narrowed her eyes. 'We need to get to St Mary's for that CT scan.'

'Waste of money.'

'Not your money.' Frankie grabbed her crocheted Sak purse and the car keys. 'Let's go.'

The drive from Whitefish Bay, an upscale suburb located just north of Milwaukee proper, with neighborhoods of stately older houses, many built in the twenties of Cream City brick just like hers, took fifteen minutes.

'Why's it so empty?' Charley asked as they walked across the sparkling vinyl floor toward the Imaging Department. 'This is kind of creepy.'

'No one gets to stay in the hospital for very long these days.'

Frankie could tell by Charley's expression that he wanted to photograph the creepy.

He'd broken her heart. She still kind of hated him. But he was the most talented photographer she knew, and the world should see itself through his eyes for as long as possible. Sure there'd be another talented photographer along any second, there probably already was, but there would never be another Charley Blackwell.

His vision. It had always stunned her. Nearly as much as the man himself.

They checked in, waited only a minute or two before Charley's name was called.

'Your wife is perfectly welcome to come back with you, Mr Blackwell.'

'I'm not—' Frankie snapped her lips shut over the automatic denial.

Charley pulled her to her feet.

The technician, a twenty-something blond whose nametag read *Emma*, got right down to business, asking a few questions, then urging Charley on to the table.

'You can stay in the room, Mrs Blackwell.'

Frankie had never legally changed her name from Sicari, which was quite handy since she would only have had to change it back. But she'd been called Mrs Blackwell at Lisa's school, as well as by her friends often enough, that she'd missed it when it had stopped. Now the address just made her feel like a liar.

'Maybe I should . . .' Frankie sidled toward the door.

'It's perfectly safe. You get less radiation from a CT scan these days than you get on an airplane. As long as you're not pregnant.' Emma chuckled.

'Not yet,' Charley answered cheerily. 'But we might start trying.'

Emma stopped laughing and glanced at Frankie with wide eyes.

'You *are* scanning his brain.' If she'd just get to it.

'Right.' All humor fled. 'I'll step out for a bit. Won't take long.'

Frankie hovered near the wall as the table slid into the tube. He started to sit up.

'Mr Blackwell!' The technician's voice came over the intercom. 'You have to hold still for the test.'

He lay down. The table continued to move. Nearly half his body was inside when he went rigid. His hands clenched.

Charley screamed.

The sound was so chilling, so ear-splitting, goose bumps lifted all over Frankie. She understood for the first time, and she hoped the last, what a blood-curdling shriek sounded like.

She rushed to him. She had to.

The table slid out of the tube. Charley couldn't see that because he had his eyes closed tight. Frankie tried to calm him by putting her hand on his leg and calling his name, but he thrashed wildly and kept screaming.

The technician ran in. 'They said he wasn't claustrophobic.'

'He wasn't the last I knew.'

Which, to be fair, was twenty-four years ago.

'He is now.'

The voice from the doorway made Frankie turn.

Despite what Irene had said, Hannah *had* aged well. She didn't look forty-seven, though forty-seven didn't look like it used to. What did they say? Forty was the new thirty? Did that make sixty the new fifty? If only. At least Hannah hadn't gotten thin over time. She'd always been short and a bit on the pudgy side. She still was.

'Since the World Trade Center. He was . . . there.'

Of course he was. Where else would Charley have been when the world almost ended?

'Why didn't you tell me?' Frankie demanded.

'You said tests not scan.'

She had Frankie there. Still . . .

'A heads-up would have been nice.'

'I'm not very nice,' Hannah said.

Something Frankie had begun to suspect already.

The Hannah Frankie had known had been young and meek. This Hannah was anything but. Right now, Frankie kind of wanted the youngster back.

'If he keeps screaming,' the technician said, 'I'll have to sedate him.'

Hannah grabbed one of Charley's thrashing hands, ducking the other when it swung. 'Charley. Hey!' Her fingers tightened. 'Everything's OK.'

Charley stopped screaming, but he still emitted guttural, panicked sounds that made Frankie twitchy. She remembered his nightmares, how she'd calmed him with songs and kisses.

When he was shaking and crying, he wasn't the man she thought she knew. Then again, had he *ever* been the man she thought she knew?

Soon after they'd married, she'd done some research on PTSD. They hadn't known much at the time, but there had been one theory she liked, mostly because it agreed with what she'd already been doing. The doctor believed that reliving traumatic memories while in a calm, peaceful state would eventually cause those memories to become associated with peace and calm. They faded. Charley's had.

Hannah continued to murmur and whisper, patting Charley, petting him. Watching made Frankie even twitchier. She'd never seen them as a couple beyond that one, fateful kiss. She didn't want to.

Charley yanked his hands from Hannah's. 'Who the fuck are you?'

Shocked silence fell over the room.

Frankie muttered, 'Shit.' She'd been hoping that once Charley saw Hannah he'd remember everything and skip right out of her life, same as last time. But she wasn't that lucky.

'I'm your wife.' Hannah's voice was strained.

'My wife is right there.' He pointed at Frankie. 'Does this woman belong in psychiatric?'

'Someone does,' Hannah said.

The tech's lips tightened. 'We need to get this CT scan done.'

Frankie had had enough. 'Charley, you need this test. If you can't be still and quiet, you'll have to be sedated.'

'Maybe if you hold my hand.'

She laughed, then realized he was serious. That was happening a lot lately.

She gave him her hand, saw Hannah's face, felt almost bad for her, then remembered . . . everything.

'You should probably wait outside,' Frankie said.

'You should probably let go of my husband.'

'Not your husband,' Charley snapped. 'Can someone get this nutcase out of here?'

'You should go,' the tech said.

Hannah's eyes narrowed, but she left.

The table slid into the machine. Charley tensed. Frankie tightened her fingers around his.

'Talk to me, Fancy.'

'About what?'

'Tell me what Lisa's been doing since I saw her last.'

She nearly pulled away and ran, but he held on ever tighter.

'Didn't she have a music concert?' he asked. 'I'm sorry I didn't get home in time. Tell me how it went so I don't think about this.'

Frankie closed her eyes, and for a minute she could see it all again; she could see Lisa. Taller than the others, lanky like Charley, with Frankie's green eyes and Charley's curly, dark hair. Lisa had Frankie's freckles too. Charley had loved them. He had loved her.

Considering he hadn't wanted children, Charley's adoration of his daughter had always seemed like a special gift – almost as special as the gift of Lisa herself.

Frankie never allowed these memories to surface. They hurt too much. But, right now, it wasn't so bad. In fact, it felt almost good to remember.

With him.

She described the music concert that had happened decades ago. She'd just reached the end and begun to worry about what she'd say next when the machine went off, the table slid free and Emma returned.

'Your doctor will call with the results.'

Charley hopped to the floor. Frankie didn't realize he still held her hand until he released it and brushed a thumb across her cheek. 'You're crying.'

She scrubbed her palms over her face. 'I'm fine.'

'You always were a softy.'

She had been. She wasn't any more. She had no reason to be.

In the waiting room, Hannah waited. As soon as she saw them, she marched right up.

'Hasn't someone from psych collected you yet?' Charley tried to push past her.

She shoved her phone under his nose. 'If I'm not your wife, how do you explain this photo?'

He gave an impatient grunt, but he looked at the picture. Charley always looked at pictures. Then he grabbed the phone. 'What the hell is this?'

'Our wedding photograph.'

Frankie leaned over so she could see, then wished she hadn't.

Hannah gleamed with happiness. Her dress was yards and yards of white lace, a long, long train, big skirt, ruffles around the bodice – a little Scarlett O'Hara but most dresses were back then. Charley wore a black tuxedo. He'd been nearly as stunning as Hannah. How could he have smiled for the camera so soon after all he'd done?

'It's a fake,' Charley said.

Apparently what he should consider a sci-fi phone didn't seem strange to him, only the photo did. Odd, but no more so than anything else he'd forgotten or ignored since he'd walked back into Frankie's life.

'Not a fake.' Hannah pulled her driver's license out of her purse. 'Neither is this. I'm Hannah Blackwell. Says so right there.' She tapped the name.

Charley swayed.

Frankie grabbed one elbow at the same time Hannah grabbed the other. For an instant Frankie imagined them tugging on Charley like a wishbone.

'I know we haven't been getting along, but this is pathetic. I still love you. You still love me. Let's go home.' Hannah pulled on his arm.

Charley yanked free. 'I am home.'

'You divorced her twenty-four years ago.'

Actually, Frankie had divorced him, but she decided to stay out of it.

'I wouldn't.'

'You did. After we had an affair. After Lisa—'

'Shut up,' Frankie said.

Shockingly, Hannah did.

'Fancy?' Charley's voice wavered. 'Tell her I'd never hurt you. I'd never cheat on you. I'd *never* leave you.'

'You did,' Hannah said.

Charley's eyes rolled up, and he went down so fast Frankie barely caught him before his head smacked the floor.

People came running from all directions. It was mayhem. They got Charley on a gurney and took him to the ER.

'You should probably go with him,' Frankie said.

Hannah didn't answer. Because Hannah was gone.

Three hours later Charley had a room of his own in the nearly empty hospital.

Dr Halverson bustled in. If she was surprised to see Frankie, she didn't show it.

'I have the results of your tests.' She opened her laptop and tapped the keys. 'No illness, no parasite that we can see from the blood and urine analysis.'

Charley threw back the covers. 'Great. Thanks for your time.'

'Stay,' Frankie ordered.

Dr Halverson's lips twitched once before the mask came back.

Frankie didn't like that mask. The doctor was always friendly and animated with her. That she wasn't told Frankie, even before the doctor told her, that the news wasn't good.

'The CT scan shows a mass in the brain.'

'Well, I do have a mass of brains,' Charley said.

No one laughed.

'What kind of mass?' Frankie asked.

'That's a question for the oncologist. I sent your results to Dr Lanier. He's the best at this kind of thing.'

'*What* kind of thing?' Frankie pressed.

Halverson stood. 'That's for Lanier to decide. He's ordered a PET scan while you're here as well.'

'A what?' Charley asked.

'Positron emission tomography. An imaging test to check if there's anything else in your body we need to address.'

'Anything else?' Frankie repeated. 'Like what?'

'Again, Dr Lanier will discuss this with you. Don't worry, Mr Blackwell. The machine isn't enclosed like the CT scan.'

'OK,' Charley said, but he didn't seem very sure.

When Halverson left, Frankie followed her out the door. 'Wait a second.'

'I really can't tell you any more.'

'Because we're no longer married?'

'Because I don't know. He has a mass.'

'A tumor?'

Dr Halverson nodded.

'Which must be cancerous since he's seeing an oncologist.'

'That's what Dr Lanier will determine.'

'How?'

'Any number of ways.'

'Why are you being so vague?'

'With the brain, most of what we know is vague.'

Frankie didn't like the sound of that. But she hadn't liked the sound of much since Charley had come knocking.

'I can't stay here. I can't help him or be here for him. I'm not his wife.'

'He doesn't remember his wife.'

'That doesn't mean she isn't.'

Dr Halverson didn't answer.

'You understand, right?' Frankie didn't know why she wanted the doctor to absolve her.

'I understand that in his mind none of the things that happened in the past two decades actually happened.'

'That doesn't mean they didn't.'

'To him it does.'

Charley

Mexico City. May, 1980

Charley rose before the sun, slipping out of the bed so he didn't wake Frankie. He got dressed in the bathroom, then grabbed his Nikon and snuck out. If he was lucky he'd be back before she woke, and she'd never know he'd been gone.

Stepping out of the Hotel Genève and on to the dark streets, he hurried from the tourist area toward the area tourists should never go.

If Frankie had woken, she'd have wanted to grab her own camera and come along. He would have hesitated to bring her where he was going. Not only was it not safe, but he would not be able to focus – *ha* – on his subjects if he had to worry about her. Besides, she would have insisted on photographing the sun coming up, or the mist swirling across cobblestones. Something artsy, not real. Fine for her, but stuff like that made his teeth ache.

Charley was still at AP, though he was beginning to get itchy feet. Something Frankie didn't understand since he was on the road all the time. How could he want to move on, when all he did was . . . move on?

The need was more about the feeling inside him than the places he went, a near obsessive desire to record the world – both its tragedies and triumphs. But Charley couldn't seem to articulate that inner yearning well enough for Frankie to grasp what he meant, and it didn't matter. Frankie told him to do whatever he needed to do, go wherever he had to go, she'd always support him.

Before he'd had Frankie to come home to, he'd wandered, but it had been more about running *from* something rather than *to* something. He'd had to get out of Illinois, away from his father and the farm. Now he had to find the next astonishing picture, and the next and the next – with a little Frankie time in between.

His wife still worked at the *Milwaukee Journal*, but when she wasn't, Frankie didn't want to shoot work-type pictures. Charley had tried to grasp the point of photographing a swirling sand dune or an aquamarine ocean. Sure they were pretty, but they didn't *change* anything. Only tragedy, sorrow, perhaps a little blood, a lot of sweat and a few tears could do that.

'I see enough sadness every day,' Frankie said. 'Don't you?'

He did, but recording it was something he couldn't stop – even when he was on vacation. This morning he planned to photograph the young men he'd seen in the alleys: their homes, their parents, children, grandparents. Then he'd hurry back to the hotel and take his wife to brunch.

He brought only one camera and a light meter, then filled his pockets with film. Flashing a bag of expensive equipment wasn't a smart idea where he was going.

He spent an hour walking up and down the streets where the sewage swirled into the rainwater. Little kids played in the sludge like it was the local swimming pool. He handed out coins to the people who allowed him to photograph them. An old, toothless woman making tamales just outside her doorway. An ancient man whittling himself a new walking stick. A young, very pregnant woman carrying a basket on her head, three children of varying heights following in her wake and a stray dog too.

He lost track of time – nothing new. What was new was that he needed to get back to Frankie, so he did something he shouldn't have. He took a shortcut down a side street. It was empty. It was daytime. What could happen?

He was halfway down the alley when a shuffle too close behind made Charley turn. He ducked just in time to avoid the two-by-four that had been meant for his head.

The wood glanced off his shoulder. Before he could recover his attacker swung again, catching Charley in the arm. If his camera hadn't been around his neck, he'd have dropped it as his hand went numb.

He recognized the young man as one of those who'd stood smoking and watching Charley earlier. He'd been alone. He hadn't seemed like a threat.

Foolish. The kid was thin, dark and twitchy. He was either on drugs or he wanted to be.

'*Damelo.*' The guy pointed to Charley's Nikon, then curved his fingers toward his palm in a beckoning gesture.

Charley shook his head.

The man took out a knife. '*Damelo.*'

'OK.' Holding up both hands in a gesture of surrender, Charley began to remove the camera from around his neck.

The fellow lunged, jabbing at Charley with the knife.

Charley swung. The Nikon, several pounds of solid metal on the end of a leather strip, connected with the guy's temple and he went down like a puppet off his string.

Charley never glanced back until he reached the stone entryway of the Hotel Genève.

He wiped his forehead and blood dripped off his arm. A bright shiny trail led across the ceramic tile behind him.

'*Señor*, you need the doctor.'

'*Si. Gracias.*'

He led Charley to another room, away from the guests, then made a call. In less than five minutes a man arrived with a black bag and stitched Charley's arm.

'*Policia?*' the doorman asked.

Charley shook his head. What was the point? The kid was long gone.

Besides, the less hoopla that surrounded this the better. He'd prefer that his wife never discover what had transpired, but considering the bloody state of his clothes and the stitches in his arm, that wasn't going to happen.

After thanking both the doorman and the doctor, then paying them, Charley hurried to his room. Frankie sat on the veranda drinking coffee, wearing the orange kaftan she'd bought in the marketplace the day before. She turned with a smile that froze as her eyes went wide. She dropped the cup, and it shattered on the tile.

'Stay!' he ordered, her bare feet only centimeters from the broken glass. 'I'm fine.'

'With that much blood on your shirt you cannot be fine.'

'Still have my camera.'

'And stitches.'

'You should see the other guy.' He lifted his Nikon. Not a mark on it. 'This thing is *great*.'

She touched his face. 'You're great. Every time I see you I think I can't love you more and then . . . I do.' Her voice went thick on the last two words.

'Why?' he whispered. He knew why he loved her – just her voice, her scent, the sight of her could make him sane again – but why in God's name did she love him?

'Because you're . . . you.'

He rolled his eyes. 'That's not a reason.'

'Why do people fall in love?' She brushed her fingers over his hair. 'Because I like curly hair?' She touched his lips. 'The way you say my name?' She tapped his forehead. 'The way you think?' She lifted both hands and traced his eyelids with her thumbs as she murmured, 'The way that you see.'

'The world?'

She gifted him with a small smile. 'Mostly the way that you see me.'

He put the camera aside and kissed her. One thing led to another, and they never did get brunch.

When Charley woke, the curtains were drawn; the room was dim and someone was retching in the bathroom. He opened the door.

Frankie waved him away. Her face was chalk white. 'Don't watch.'

He didn't want to, but he couldn't just leave her there.

An insidious thought hustled in. Was she pregnant?

No. Despite all the recent uproar over side effects, Frankie was on the pill. Her doctor assured her that she was young, healthy and proper monitoring would negate any possible issues.

'Must have been something I ate,' she managed between dry heaves.

'You didn't drink the water, did you?'

'Of course not.' *Gack.* 'Except . . .'

'Except what?'

'I brushed my teeth. Would that do it?'

'Maybe.'

She dry heaved again.

'Probably.'

He wet a cloth with cold water and washed her face, then got her a clean nightgown and helped her back to bed. He crawled in next to her, pulling her into his arms. 'For a minute I was afraid you were pregnant.'

Frankie stilled. 'You sound like that would be a bad thing.'

'Wouldn't it?'

'We *are* married.'

They hadn't discussed children beyond the agreement to use contraception, which to him meant none but to her meant . . . what? He'd thought they'd talked about everything, but they hadn't talked about this, and he wasn't sure why.

'You want kids?' he asked.

'Of course.' She leaned back to see his face. 'You don't?'

'I . . .' he began. All he'd ever wanted was his career and her. He'd never thought of kids, but now that he did . . . 'No.'

'No,' she repeated. 'You don't want any children, ever?'

'The world is so fucked up, Fancy.'

'And our child might fix it.'

'You believe that?'

'Yes! You want to just let the world implode?'

'I'm not sure there's any stopping it.'

'So you plan to photograph the flames and do nothing?'

'Yes?' The word came out a question because he knew it was the wrong answer, but it *was* his answer.

She sat up, pulling herself out of his arms. The movement was too sudden and her face whitened again. She lay back down, closed her eyes.

Panic fluttered. Would she leave him over this? 'Sweetheart—'

She held up a hand, kept her eyes closed. 'Give me a second.'

'I'll order room service. Some soup maybe? Toast.'

The hand she'd held up slapped over her mouth, and she pressed it there for several seconds before lowering it to rest on her stomach. 'Do *not* speak of food.'

'Sorry.'

'What about adoption?'

He'd never considered that either.

Frankie opened her eyes. She was still so pale they glowed brilliant green even in the half-light. 'Wouldn't it help the world to raise a child who has no one?'

'I suppose.'

'You don't like kids?'

'Sure.' Some of his best pictures were of kids. They were so natural, so at ease, even around a camera.

'Then why not have some?'

Some? How had they gotten from one to some?

'I'll still be gone all the time. You'll be alone.'

'I wouldn't be alone or lonely if I had a child.'

'You're lonely?' This was the first he'd heard of it.

This was the first he'd heard of a lot of things. He loved his wife more than he'd ever thought he could love anyone. He knew her as well as he knew anyone. But he was beginning to realize that he didn't know her as well as he should.

'No,' Frankie said. 'Well, yes. Sometimes.'

Charley became uneasy. Lonely wives as beautiful as Frankie weren't lonely very long.

'You could travel with me.' He did better alone, but he wouldn't do well at all if he lost her.

'I have a job. And you do better alone.'

God, he loved her so much.

'Maybe we could adopt one child,' he said.

She drew up her knees and wrapped her arms around them. 'Your mouth says one thing, your face says another.'

'What does my face say?'

'Maybe we could be saddled with a bone-marrow-sucking troll, which we have to walk over a pit of poisonous vipers, barefoot, to obtain.'

Charley touched his face. 'It says that?'

'Uh-huh.' Frankie took his hand.

Hers was still ice cold, so he took the other one too and held them between his to warm them. 'I'd do anything for you.'

'And I'd do the same for you.' She took a deep breath and something flickered in her eyes – there and then gone so fast Charley wasn't sure what it was, though he didn't like it. 'No kids. OK.'

'I didn't say—'

'You didn't have to. A child isn't something you do for someone else. You do it for the child or you don't do it at all.'

She was right, and since she was agreeing with what he wanted, he let her.

'Let's sleep a while.' He pulled her into his arms and told himself everything was all right.

When the phone rang, Frankie was so deeply asleep she didn't wake up. Charley grabbed it before the second ring.

'Charley?'

He had to stretch the cord to its limit to get into the bathroom so he could find out what was so important that his boss had called him while he was on vacation. He couldn't recall it ever happening before. He actually couldn't recall being on vacation before.

'Mt St Helens erupted in Washington,' Stanley said. 'They're saying it looks like a bomb went off.'

'Casualties?'

'Yeah. Don't know how many yet. I need you to get there and find out.'

Through the crack in the door he saw his sleeping wife, too pale, so still. 'I can't.'

'The last time we had an eruption like this was . . .' Paper rustled. 'Maybe 1912? This is the biggest story of the year.'

Considering the continuing hostage crisis in Iran and the upcoming presidential election, doubtful. But the tingle Charley always listened to started up at the base of his spine.

His gaze went to Frankie again. 'Get someone else. I'm on vacation.'

'You're never on vacation.'

'I am now. I'll be home next week.'

'Really?'

'Yes, I'll really be home next week.'

'I mean you're really not going to Washington?'

'I'm really not going to Washington,' Charley repeated, then crawled back beneath the covers.

'Did I just hear you tell Stanley to get someone else?'

Charley sighed. *Now* she woke up.

'You did.'

'You sure?'

He nodded because he didn't think he could say the words again. But Frankie had just given up children for him, the least he could do was give up one assignment for her. Although it probably shouldn't have been that assignment.

The photographer Stanley sent to Washington won a Pulitzer.

Hannah

Washington DC. September, 1990

Heath had been coughing for the past week. He blamed the cigarettes he shouldn't smoke and the slight flu he'd contracted. Luckily neither Hannah nor Carol had caught the bug. He'd had a sore throat and headache, followed by vomiting. Not pretty but it hadn't lasted long.

Hannah rapped on the bathroom door. 'I want you to see a doctor.'

He opened the door, coughed again, then kissed her forehead. 'I'm fine, worrywart. Go to work.'

Today was Hannah's last day at *National Geographic*. Tomorrow she'd start packing to return to New York. She hadn't gotten a job yet, so she'd have to live with her parents.

Carol had hired Heath full time at *You*. Hannah was so jealous she could taste it.

She'd enjoyed her internship; everyone at *National Geographic* said she'd done a great job. But when she'd asked about a position, she'd been told there wasn't an opening.

She hadn't seen Charley Blackwell again. He'd been out on assignments all summer. Charley was a star at *National Geographic*. All the plum projects went to him. He always got the best shots. He'd won a Pulitzer six or seven years ago with his photo of the bombing of the Marine barracks in Beirut.

Right place, right time Charley, they called him.

Hannah thought, in the case of a terrorist bombing, that should be *wrong place, wrong time*, but she didn't mention it.

He'd been nominated for a Pulitzer on several occasions before – the first one being the photograph from San Francisco that Heath had mentioned – and a few times since.

So when Charley Blackwell walked into the *National Geographic* offices on Hannah's last day, she wasn't the only one excited by it.

He wore trousers the color of sand, and his black shirt made his blue eyes gleam. His teeth seemed blazingly white, or maybe that was just in contrast to his tan. Add to all that a pair of scuffed boat shoes worn without socks and he appeared to have been hanging out in Hyannis Port with the Kennedys all summer when, in reality, he'd been in countries where people would kill for air conditioning or less.

He hung around, had lunch with an editor, met with the boss; he was on the way out when he stopped in the editing room.

'Hey . . .' He snapped his fingers.

'Hannah,' she supplied.

'Right. Sorry. Do you have those slides I gave you?'

She handed him a bag with the containers.

'Thanks.' He started to leave.

'I loved the essay,' she said.

She could tell he wanted to go, maybe needed to, but he came back. 'You did?'

'I thought it was . . .' She searched for the perfect word to describe what those photos had made her feel and couldn't find one. She had to settle for the lame: 'Brilliant.'

He didn't appear impressed with her critique.

She ground her teeth, centered her thoughts and tried again. 'Basketball hoops are the same everywhere – like people are the same – and then again they're not.'

'Just like people,' he said.

'Yes.'

He looked at her, really looked at her. 'I didn't think anyone would get that but me.'

'Why – uh – did you start photographing basketball hoops?'

Charley shrugged. 'I wanted to do something . . .' His gaze drifted off along with his voice.

'Happy?'

He gave a short, sharp shake of his head. His frown made Hannah feel like a fool. Of course not *happy*. Charley Blackwell didn't do happy. She'd often wondered why.

'Different,' he said, though the word sounded more like a question than an answer. 'Not artsy exactly, but . . .' His sigh was also short and sharp; he threw up his hands. 'I don't know. It seemed like a good idea at the time, but I guess not.'

Into the silence that descended, Hannah blurted, 'I put together a layout.'

Charley had been gazing down the hall toward the elevator, but his head snapped around as she pulled the mock-up from beneath the light table, then he came over to study it.

He smelled like the whole wide world in a bottle. Hannah watched his face and forced herself to breathe.

'This is perfect.' His gaze remained on her work.

'What's perfect?' Ray Cantrell stepped into the room. 'I thought you had to get home for your kid's whatsit, since you missed the last one.'

'Concert,' Charley said. 'Maybe a recital.' Charley tapped the mock-up. 'Check this out.'

Cantrell cast Hannah a narrow glance.

She held up her hands. 'All on my own time.'

He grunted. 'This is good. Really good. There's something . . .' His gaze narrowed, then widened. 'They're all the same, but then again, they're not.'

Hannah blinked. So did Charley.

Cantrell peered back and forth between the two of them. 'I'll find a place for it in one of the upcoming issues.'

He walked out, leaving them to stare silently after him.

'What just happened?' Charley asked.

'No idea.'

'I've been trying to get this essay published in a magazine – any magazine – for years.'

'Congratulations,' Hannah said. 'Now you have.'

'I think you have. Thank you.'

'I was just practicing.'

'If that was your practice, I can't wait to see your game day.'

Hannah's cheeks heated. 'If I only had a job.'

Confusion flickered. 'You work here.'

'Not after today.'

'What? Why?'

'Summer internships come to an end.'

'They should hire you.'

'Yes, they should, but there's no opening.'

'Oh.' He glanced out the door again. 'Sorry.'

'Yeah. Me too.'

Hannah gathered her things. By the time she'd finished, Charley was gone.

She arrived at the apartment later than usual. Julie and a few of the others had brought a cake for her last day. While she didn't need any cake – editing slides all summer had done nothing to slim her hips – it would have been rude not to eat some. Besides, it was great cake – chocolate fudge with cherry filling – her new favorite.

Just inside the door, she paused. The furniture was beige, the carpets white, the tables a pale brown wood and glass. Waterford crystal figurines graced the bookshelves, along with hardcover books Aunt Carol didn't have the time to read. This was a wealthy single woman's apartment, and Hannah wanted one. She would miss the place almost as much as she'd miss her job.

She heard a noise back where the bedrooms – also white and beige – lay. Too early for Carol to be home. Probably Heath.

She headed in that direction, faltering to a stop when she recognized the sound. Her brother was crying.

She hovered where she was, uncertain what to do. When Heath cried, it was serious.

His door was ajar. She pushed it open.

He was a mess. Red eyes, pink nose, there were used tissues all over his bed.

She grabbed another box from the hall closet and then wiped

his face, an exercise in futility since the tears just kept seeping out of his eyes and down his cheeks. 'What's wrong?'

'One of my friends has AIDS.'

Hannah's heart thudded so hard she thought it might come out of her chest. She fought not to let the dread invade her words. Heath was upset enough already.

'What type of friend?'

'What kind of question is that?' His voice broke.

'You know what kind of question it is, Heath.'

'I didn't sleep with him, if that's what you're asking.'

She tightened her lips over the 'Thank God'. It would only send Heath into a rant over her selfishness or a rant over God. Neither would be productive right now.

'Who is it?'

'Terry.'

She searched her memory for a mention of Terry, found none. Heath had so many friends. Unlike Hannah, who had Heath.

'I don't—'

'He works at the coffee shop in the lobby of the magazine. We went out for drinks a few times. He's a nice guy, but he had a boyfriend.'

'Had?'

'Bastard ran like a rabbit as soon as he heard the diagnosis.'

'You won't.'

'No.' He lifted his beautiful, haunted, red-rimmed eyes to hers. 'He doesn't deserve this.'

'No one does.'

Since the disease had been discovered in the early eighties, they'd come a long way. Back then half the people who contracted AIDS died within a year. The public freaked out – refusing to allow children with HIV to attend schools, forcing doctors who treated those patients out of their clinics. No one had been sure how the disease was transmitted, or how easily, and they'd over-reacted. Even now, when science had proved that hugging or kissing or breathing the same air as a 'homo' or a 'hemo' could not transfer HIV, people didn't believe it.

Hannah managed to get Heath calmed down, only to have him freak out again when he remembered she was leaving the next day.

'You can't!'

'I'll be a short train ride away.' Was less than three hours short?

'Get a job here. Any job. Work at the coffee shop with Terry. Please! I need you.'

'I don't think Mom and Dad are going to go for that.'

Heath stared at his hands. 'They were happy that I was staying here.'

'They were happy you got a job you love.'

Heath snorted.

She handed him a tissue. Snorting was not advisable after a crying jag.

'I don't think I could live with them again.' Heath blew his nose. 'Mom tries, but she still looks at me as if she's trying to figure out how she broke me. Dad doesn't look at me at all.'

'There's nothing wrong with you.'

'Tell it to the world, sister.'

'I will.' Someday she'd have a powerful job and people would listen to her, and she'd tell them all that being gay was OK.

Distraction and amusement were in order – for both of them.

'Let's order Mexican and watch *Young Frankenstein*.'

Heath's favorite movie. Hers too. They'd paid big bucks for a pirated edition, because Mel Brooks was a goddamn genius.

Several hours later – full of rice, beans and tortillas – Heath dozed and Hannah cleaned up the mess. In the kitchen, a light blinked on the message machine. She pressed the button and Ray Cantrell's voice flowed out.

'Hannah, we want you to stay on permanently. Come in at the same time tomorrow and we'll talk.'

What had changed?

'You can thank Charley Blackwell,' Cantrell continued. 'He thinks you're going to be the best editor we've ever hired. Don't make me sorry I listened to him.'

Click.

She returned to the living room and covered her brother with the soft beige throw that lay across the back of the slightly lighter beige couch. She considered waking him to share her news, but he needed the rest. He had to get over that cough.

Though now that she thought about it, Heath hadn't coughed once since she'd been home. He must be getting better.

Hannah shut off the lights and went to bed. Things were looking up for them both.

Charley

Whitefish Bay, Wisconsin. October, 1983

Frankie was in the kitchen, smooth right shoulder slipping free of her gray sweatshirt, standing on the second highest rung of the ladder as she slopped white paint over the atrocious lemon yellow.

They'd bought a fixer-upper in a near northern suburb of Milwaukee. Their Brady Street apartment just wasn't big enough any more. Where had all the stuff come from? Since Charley was there maybe two or three days a month, he didn't think it was his, except somehow, a lot of it was.

The whole place needed work – both cosmetic and structural. Work he wasn't going to be able to do, not only because he was never here but because he just wasn't handy. Never had been.

But Frankie was, thanks to her father who she'd followed around as a child while he not only fixed their duplex but whatever went wrong with the neighbors' as well. What she didn't know how to do, she'd ask for her dad's help with or hit the library and learn how to do it herself.

'It'll keep me occupied when you're gone,' she'd said.

'You need to keep occupied?'

She shrugged and didn't meet his eyes, which he took to mean *yes*. He supposed it was better that she did house renovations than the mailman.

Where had that thought come from? Frankie would never cheat on him, just as he would never cheat on her. In all the years they'd been married – six now, hard to believe, they had gone so fast – he'd never been tempted. He found that hard to believe too, as did many of his lying, cheating colleagues. Even his old Vietnam buddy the Waz – now a police chief in his hometown of 'whatever the hell it was' Minnesota – had cheated. Multiple times.

'After what we lived through, Polaroid, don't we deserve it?' he'd asked.

'Frankie doesn't deserve it,' Charley had said quietly, and hung up.

He hadn't talked to the Waz since, though he probably should. A lot of the guys he'd served with hadn't come back. Those who did come back had problems. Cheating was the least of them. He'd heard of multiple vets with cancers of all kinds. There were whispers that Agent Orange, a super weed killer sprayed on the jungle to make it less jungly, was the culprit in many of those cases. Charley wouldn't be surprised. They must have dropped millions of gallons of that crap all over Vietnam, Cambodia, Laos and the GIs.

In the bathroom mirror, speckles of white paint stood out starkly on Charley's tanned face. He'd recently returned from his third assignment for *Time* magazine, where he'd moved from AP just this year.

Benigno Aquino, a rival of Ferdinand Marcos, had been assassinated in Manila in late August. The political unrest that followed, while less violent than expected, had still kept Charley in the country longer than he'd planned and he'd arrived in Milwaukee just in time for their closing.

After signing all the paperwork, they'd celebrated at DelMonico's, sharing their favorite Chianti and an order of bruschetta. They'd fed each other off their single plate and Frankie had outlined her plans for the house with an enthusiasm Charley didn't share but could appreciate in her. He loved listening to her talk about something that excited her, loved the way her voice would deepen, her eyes would spark and her cheeks would flush. He'd taken her hand and been captivated by how much warmer her skin was than his own; her passion seemed to seep out of her body and into his.

She made him feel alive in a way that little else could but a close brush with death. An embarrassing truth that he did his best to keep to himself. He was sure his fascination with the razor edge of existence wasn't healthy, but he couldn't seem to stop himself from seeking it out and balancing right on the precipice, photographing the world all around him as it balanced there too.

The phone started ringing.

'I'll get it!' Charley did not want Frankie hustling down the ladder to answer a call.

Instead, he hurried down the stairs to snatch up the yellow receiver of the Snoopy phone perched on a TV tray in the hall.

He always felt foolish when he used the thing, but Frankie loved it. 'Charley Blackwell.'

'You gotta get to Beirut.'

Neither Charley nor his new boss, Phil Tupman, cared much for the word 'hello'.

'I thought there was a ceasefire.'

The Lebanese civil war had been raging since 1975. Now that Syria and Israel were involved, along with a supposed peacekeeping force headed by the US, things had only gotten worse.

'A Lebanese ceasefire is like any other country's war. There's been fighting in the mountains for the past month. The day the ceasefire went into effect, the *USS New Jersey* showed up in Beirut, there are a dozen Navy ships floating off the Lebanese coast and two thousand more Marines have landed.'

'Way to host a ceasefire.'

'The American way. Things have settled down, but . . .' Phil let out a short, sharp breath. 'Reagan just sent tanks and long-range artillery to the Lebanese army.'

'Shit,' Charley said.

'It's gonna hit the fan.'

'I'm on my way.' Charley hung up.

'Where to this time?' Frankie stood in the doorway of the still electric-yellow kitchen.

'I shouldn't go.'

He hadn't wanted a house, thought it was too much maintenance and responsibility, but Frankie had wanted one so badly, and promised to do everything, that he'd caved. Now he wished he hadn't.

'Go where?'

'Beirut.'

She winced.

'There's a ceasefire.'

'Yeah, I've seen how much they've ceased firing on the evening news.'

'If the place was peaceful, I wouldn't be going there.'

'I thought you said you shouldn't.' She smiled, but not with her eyes.

That smile always gave him a shiver, as if the Frankie he adored had floated off somewhere else, leaving this shell behind.

'I probably never should.'

He pulled her into his arms and kissed her forehead. She smelled like paint, or maybe he did. 'I love you.'

'I know.'

She wanted to drive him to O'Hare Airport – getting a flight to Beirut from Milwaukee . . . well, good luck with that – but he refused.

He packed his bag, kissed her until she stopped thinking, until he did, then managed to pull his lips from hers and get in the car.

'I'll call as soon as I land and find a phone,' he promised.

'Safe trip.' Frankie backed away.

She never clung; she never asked him to stay. Sure, she might try and convince him that a hot zone was too hot, but that was her limit, and he worshipped her for it.

Seventeen hours later Charley landed at Beirut International Airport. As he got off the plane in the unusually silent terminal, he glanced at his watch. Six twenty a.m. At home it was not quite two thirty p.m. He headed for the bank of telephones.

And the world did a weird sort of shimmy.

Then came the sound – waves of thunder louder than any thunder ever born.

A bomb.

Charley hurried for the exit along with everyone else; his hand reached automatically for his camera; he found the right one by touch without even glancing in the bag that hung on his shoulder.

He shot pictures until someone made him stop.

There were heavy casualties. Charley helped as much as he could; he'd become adept at performing first aid while taking photographs. He could do just about anything while taking photographs.

A suicide bomber had driven a nineteen-ton truck bomb into the lobby of the Marine Battalion Landing building and detonated it. In the end, 241 American, fifty-eight French and six civilians were dead, and over 150 injured.

But none of this was known right away. Right away all they knew was that the ceasefire was crap – no news to anyone in Beirut – and that people were willing to blow themselves up for a cause.

'Peacekeeping forces lose over three hundred lives, terrorists lose two,' Charley said when he finally called Phil sometime in the early morning hours of the following day. 'They win.'

'Like hell they win. Who blows themselves up? Who does that?'

'*Dinky dau*,' Charley murmured.

'You OK, Charley?'

'Yeah, just something we said in Vietnam. Means crazy. You bam bam.' Another way the locals had said *crazy*.

'You called Frankie, right?'

The world shimmied, and he could have sworn he heard another bomb go off. He put his hand against his chest. Nope, that pounding was just his heart, though he could swear the thing had stopped.

'Oh, God.'

'You better pray harder than that, son. She's called here three times.' Phil hung up.

As soon as Charley heard a dial tone, he placed another call. He was a dead man.

Hannah

Washington DC, 1991

Winter in DC was a lot nicer than winter in New York City. Considering the two cities were only two hundred and twenty-odd miles apart, Hannah couldn't get over the difference. They'd yet to have snow or temperatures below freezing and February was half over.

'Hannah!'

She would have known her brother had arrived at the apartment from the force of his door slam alone.

Hannah and Heath had continued to live with Carol. They'd tried to find an apartment of their own, but anything they could afford, even together, was in a neighborhood they shouldn't walk anywhere near, let alone live in. Besides, Aunt Carol was hardly ever at home and was happy for them to stay. She even refused rent money.

'Hannah!' Heath bellowed.

The apartment wasn't that large; he should have found her by now. Sometimes she worried about him.

Actually all of the time she worried about him.

He'd already dumped Joel – better than being dumped by, as Heath had informed her – flitted through Harvey and landed on Kent. She spent a lot of time shoving condoms into his wallet. She assumed he used them since whenever she cracked open his wallet to check, it was empty. She wasn't sure if she should be happy about that or more concerned.

Hannah thrust the photographs of the Gulf War, which she'd brought home to caption, into a manila envelope just as Heath barreled into her room still wearing his brand-new black leather jacket and flopped on to her bed, arms outspread as if he were falling into a swimming pool.

Drama, thy name is Heath.

His cheeks were flushed with cold or anticipation, which made his eyes shine like he was on something.

Her eyes narrowed. Was he on something?

'I'm so excited to meet him,' Heath said. 'And so nervous I couldn't sleep. I got up at five and took a walk.'

Hannah's skin prickled. At least he hadn't been out all night. Though they lived in a very nice section of DC thanks to Aunt Carol, a gay man, out in the dark, alone . . . well, anything could happen. Anything could happen to anyone, anywhere, really, which she learned the truth of every day just by glancing at the news.

'You probably shouldn't—' she began.

'Contrary to popular belief, the man on the street can't tell I'm gay just by smelling me.'

Unfortunately – no, she corrected herself, *fortunately* – Heath was Heath. He didn't hide who he was. He *was* who he was, and she was pretty sure anyone could see it. If that anyone was a homophobic, violent asshole . . .

The prickle became a shiver. She spoke quickly so Heath wouldn't notice. 'Sweetie, could you humor me and play it super safe?'

He rolled his eyes. 'Yes, ma'am. Now, back to Charley Blackwell. I'll come to your office after work and you'll introduce me, right?'

'Of course. Charley will be thrilled to meet you.'

She'd gotten to know Charley a little over the past several months. He'd been grateful for her help with his basketball essay.

It had received great feedback. Those higher up had asked for more spreads like that. They called it 'Americana', which was probably as good a name as any.

He'd told her several times how grateful he was for her help. Hannah had been equally grateful for Charley's intervention, which had gotten her a job. The next time he'd been in the office, they'd argued over who would take whom to lunch.

Hannah, who was usually painfully shy around men, wasn't around Charley and she didn't know why. Maybe it was because while he respected her talent, he had no interest in her except as his colleague.

Should she be upset about that? She wasn't. She was just glad that whenever Charley was in the office he spent some time with her.

'There's no way Charley will be as thrilled as I am,' Heath said before he hurried to work.

Later, after his meeting with the boss, Charley came searching for Hannah and found her in the sorting room.

While Hannah might no longer be the summer intern, she was still a low woman on the totem pole and she got to edit a lot of slides. Today's selection was for an upcoming feature on Eastern Europe.

Charley leaned over her shoulder; she held very still. His breath puffed past her cheek and she had to fight not to turn her head. He was so close, she just wanted to sit and enjoy him.

Despite her aunt's warnings, Hannah had a little crush and she knew it.

'You have an incredible eye, Hannah. I suspected it with the basketball essay, but I know it now.'

'Guess Ray won't fire you for convincing him to hire me.'

'It didn't take much convincing.'

Hannah didn't believe that, but further arguing would only make it seem like she wanted more kudos. She did, especially from Charley, but not enough to beg. She glanced at her watch.

'You got an appointment?'

'I . . .' She frowned at the elevator.

Heath had been bugging her to introduce him to Charley Blackwell since Hannah had met the man. Now he was late?

'My twin brother was supposed to meet me here after work.'

'You didn't tell me you had a twin.'

Hannah hadn't told Charley much about herself. Why would she? Theirs was a business relationship and it always would be.

'He wants to meet you so badly. He's a fan.'

'Of photography?'

'Of your photography.' She peered at her watch again. Over a half-hour late now. She was going to punch him in the nose.

'Give him a call. Maybe he got held up.'

Hannah used the phone on the light table to dial her brother's extension at *You*. No answer. She disconnected and dialed her aunt's.

'He isn't there yet?' Carol sounded distracted, harried. In the background people shouted and more phones rang. 'He went home to change. You know how Heath is.'

'Yeah. Thanks.' Hannah hung up, then continued to stare at the phone, biting her lip.

'Find out anything?'

'What?' For the first time ever, Hannah had forgotten Charley.

Her twin ESP was buzzing so loudly she was having a hard time hearing anything else, or thinking about anything but finding her brother. Something wasn't right.

She stood. 'I need to go.'

'I'll go with you.'

'No, I'm OK.'

He took her arm. 'You're not. Anyone can see that.'

'You have a flight, don't you?'

'I've always got a flight. And there's always another one.'

'You don't have to—'

'I want to. If your brother's just late, no harm done, we'll have a drink.'

He didn't mention what they'd do if Heath wasn't 'just late' and she kind of loved him for that. Because she was thinking of all the things that could have kept Heath away from meeting the legend and none of them were good. She remembered having a conversation with him that morning about being careful, about not walking around alone after dark.

She glanced at the window. Going on six o'clock in February. Definitely dark.

Hannah grabbed her Chanel jacket, then her coat and left without turning off the light table.

Charley was right behind her.

She stepped on to Seventeenth Street and her breath caught at the cold. For the first time that winter the temperature had dipped toward freezing and she could smell snow.

'This is going to royally fuck with the cherry blossoms,' Charley said.

Her laughter came in a startled burst, sounding so non-laughter-like she made herself stop. She had to *think*. Where could Heath be?

'Did they say where he'd gone?'

Hannah cast Charley a grateful glance. 'Home to change.'

They never got that far.

As they turned on to the block where she lived, Hannah heard shouts down the narrow opening between two of the glossy high-rise buildings. She wouldn't have given those shouts a second thought – all her thoughts were for her brother – but she caught one word in a jumble of so many others.

Faggot!

'Hannah, wait!' Charley made a grab for her arm, but she ducked between the buildings and ran.

There were three of them. Two were kicking, one was shouting, perhaps for them to stop, perhaps to urge them on. She wasn't even sure the body on the ground was her brother. At that point she didn't care.

'Get away from him!'

The kickers cast her a glance but kept on kicking.

The shouter shouted, 'Mind your own business!'

She recognized Heath's favorite Panama hat even though it had been stomped on until it was flat. Like his nose.

'He is her business, boys.'

The shouter rolled his eyes. 'Get lost, old man.' Then he kicked Heath too.

Hannah cried out and stepped forward. She wasn't sure what she planned to do. Hit them or help Heath?

The sound of a camera motor whirring, of dozens of photographs being taken in an instant, permeated the silence. Everyone froze.

Hannah hadn't realized Charley had brought a camera.

'I'd be getting lost if I were you. The authorities are going to love the mug shots I already took.' Charley replaced his finger on the motor drive.

The continued clicking seemed to confuse them. At least enough so they stopped what they were doing.

Then the only one who'd spoken so far scowled. 'Give me that, asshole.'

'Get out of the way, Hannah,' Charley murmured, and she did.

Charley swung the camera like David swung stones at Goliath.

The device smacked the advancing attacker beneath the chin with a *thunk*, and he dropped to his knees.

The other two ran.

The man shook his head; blood splattered across the toes of Hannah's pumps. He lurched to his feet.

Charley began to swing his camera on the strap, back and forth, back and forth. 'Care for round two?'

That guy ran as well.

Hannah fell on the ground next to Heath. He was coming around.

He blinked at her as if trying to make the two heads she sported merge into one. 'Hannah?'

'Of course it's Hannah, you idiot.' Then she started to bawl.

The scuffle of a shoe against the pavement made her spin, fists raised.

'You need to get help,' Charley said.

'I can't leave him.' Hannah took one of Heath's hands. His fingers felt funny – loose and spiky. Broken.

'I can't leave you here alone,' Charley said. 'I think they're gone, but—'

'He's right.' Heath patted her knee with his free, also bloodied hand.

Charley helped her to her feet. 'Go to the closest building and have the doorman call 911. Then run right back.'

Hannah didn't want to leave Heath, but she had to admit that she'd rather Charley and his camera stayed with her brother.

She hurried to the closest building, wondering if the doorman would think she was pulling a prank. However, she hadn't taken two steps inside when the man rushed to her.

'Are you all right?'

'I . . . me . . . what?'

He pointed and she looked down. Her brother's blood stained her clothes.

'Not mine. My brother. Help. Please. They . . . he . . .'

The doorman understood. Hannah wasn't sure how. He called 911 and translated her halting explanation to the operator. Then she rushed back to the alley. As she approached she heard the two men talking.

'I'm a huge fan.' Heath's voice sounded mushy and she thought she might cry. 'The pictures you took of the 1977 march in San Francisco were amazing.'

'You couldn't have been very old in 1977.'

'Old enough to know amazing.'

'I bet you were,' Charley said.

Hannah wanted to hug Charley.

'How you doing?' she asked.

'Everything hurts,' Heath said.

'You're lucky, because if something didn't hurt, I'd make it. What the hell, Heath? I told you to be careful.'

'Do you think I corralled those assholes and asked them to beat the hell out of me?'

'You shouldn't walk where there aren't a hundred' – she'd actually prefer a thousand – 'people.'

'I didn't.'

'Then why . . .?' She lifted her hands to indicate the dark alley.

'One of them stood at the entrance and asked for a light,' Charley said. 'When Heath came over to share, the other two dragged him down here.'

'Why?'

'Why do you think, Hannah?' Heath asked softly.

'Did you know them?'

'No.'

Would it be better or worse if he had?

'They said one less fudge packer in the world would be one less case of AIDS.'

Charley growled and his fingers tightened on his camera strap as if he wanted to swing it again.

In the distance, a siren wailed.

'If they were so worried about AIDS they shouldn't have made you bleed.'

'I doubt they were thinking much past kicking my ass.'

A sob nearly escaped but Hannah slapped her hands over her lips to capture it.

Heath's eyes were swollen shut by now; he couldn't see her,

but she could tell by the way his poor bruised mouth tightened that he had heard the sound and her muffling of it.

Charley touched her shoulder. 'You want to meet the EMTs?'

Instead of waiting for her answer, which would have been *no,* Charley gave her a little shove before crouching next to Heath.

'So what do you do all day, my friend, when you aren't getting your ass kicked?'

Her brother actually laughed, then grabbed his stomach. 'Ugh, what's that saying?'

'It only hurts when I laugh.' Charley's gaze met Hannah's and he jerked his head toward the approaching siren.

He was right. Heath needed his mind off this as much as it could be, and her choking back tears was not going to accomplish that.

Hannah hoofed it to the street, where people had begun to gather at the entrance and peer into the gloom.

'What happened?' someone asked.

Hannah ignored them, waving down the ambulance. A police cruiser pulled in right behind.

Two burly EMTs jumped out and grabbed a gurney. One plopped a bag on top and they took off in the direction of Heath and Charley before Hannah could say a word. She followed so closely that when they stopped she bounced off the back of the one bringing up the rear.

'Shit,' he muttered.

Hannah didn't think it was because she'd bumped into him.

'That's a lot of blood,' the other said.

'Hence our call to emergency services, gentlemen.' Charley backed away so the EMTs could do their thing.

Neither one did.

'He was unconscious before,' Charley said. 'He is again now. You should probably check the old noggin sooner rather than later.'

Still, no one moved.

'What's the problem?' Hannah demanded.

The EMT closest to her nudged Heath's hat with his toe. 'Is he gay?'

'What difference does that make?' Hannah's voice went high and shrill, not a good sound for her but her throat felt tight, as if she might choke on every sentence she had to say to these men.

'I'm not getting AIDS because of my job.'

'He doesn't have AIDS.'

'Are you sure?'

'Yes!'

Still they hesitated.

'Don't you have gloves?' Charley asked.

'Of course, but . . .' The EMT cast another uneasy glance at Heath.

'You know you can't get AIDS from blood on your clothes or your skin, right?' Hannah probably sounded like Sister Agnes teaching catechism, but right now she was having a hard time not rapping these guys with the closest thing she could find to a ruler.

How about that two-by-four next to the dumpster?

Hannah took one step toward it and Charley bent, scooped Heath into his arms and plopped him on to the gurney. 'Do your goddamn job or I'll make sure you lose it.'

To punctuate his threat, Charley took several shots of the EMTs' startled faces.

The bright flare of the camera flash brought one of the officers in their direction. Charley kept taking pictures.

'You need to stop that, sir.'

'Sorry, no can do. I'm documenting the incident at the victim's request. I'll share my photos with you. I have at least a dozen of the assailants.'

The cop, a man near to Charley's age from the gray in what was left of his hair, tilted his head. 'Well, those are gonna come in handy.'

How right he was. Not only did Charley's photographs lead to the arrest of all three dickwads – their mug shots matched almost perfectly – but they looked very nice blown up to poster-sized prints at the trial.

Their court-appointed lawyers petitioned for the posters to be disallowed as evidence. Since the grounds for the appeal were that the evidence of their clients in living color, captured in mid-assault was damaging to their case, the request was denied.

Charley accompanied them to the hospital. Hannah was never sure afterwards how she would have managed without him.

Heath was in surgery – internal bleeding – when she heard Charley on the phone. 'I'm sorry, Fancy. I know I promised I'd be there but . . .'

Charley's wife's name was Francesca. Apparently he called her Fancy.

'I couldn't just leave the kid.'

Was he talking about Heath or Hannah? Didn't really matter. If he thought one of them was a kid, by default he thought the other one was as well. They'd been born on the same day.

'As soon as things are stable, I'll be on the next plane, Fancy. I promise.'

Would a man ever say Hannah's name the way that Charley Blackwell said *Fancy*?

Charley's gaze met hers and Hannah's cheeks flamed. He knew she'd been listening, but really how could she not? He hadn't kept his voice down.

What he didn't know was what she'd been thinking and she had to make sure he never did. She was pathetic, but she didn't want to be *that* pathetic.

Charley sat next to her, then took her hand. 'He'll be OK.'

Hannah nodded, but she didn't know for sure if Heath would be and that scared her. 'You don't have to stay.'

'I'm not going to go until he's out of surgery.'

Nothing she could say would make him.

Several hours later, Hannah visited her brother in recovery. He appeared so pale, as if he had no blood left. She set her fingertips on the back of one splinted hand, hoping to feel, as she always had before, the essence of her twin, but right now there was nothing.

Hannah had given blood, asking that hers be used for her brother, not because of any fear of AIDS in the blood supply – that fear had ended in 1985, when a screening test for all donated blood became available – but because she had an irrational belief that her blood would save him.

She returned to the room that would be Heath's once he was out of recovery.

Charley was already there. 'How is he?'

'Alive.'

The idea that Heath could have died tonight hit her so hard she had to close her eyes. What would she do if she didn't have him? That empty place inside of her would expand and expand until it consumed her.

'Are your parents coming?' Charley asked.

'Tomorrow. Father had a charity dinner. Mother had a book launch party.'

Charley blinked. 'So?'

'Exactly.'

'Will you be OK until they get here?'

'I'm OK now.'

From the look he gave her, she wasn't a very good liar.

'Seriously, I'm gonna crash. They said Heath won't wake up until morning. By the time we're both coherent, they'll be here. You go on. I'm good.'

Charley seemed like he wanted to argue, but she let her eyes flutter as if she could barely keep them open. She wasn't even acting – much.

'OK.' He stood, then hovered as if he wasn't sure if he should hug her.

If he hugged her, she just might cling, so she shut her eyes. 'Bye.'

'I'll call tomorrow.'

'Mmm,' Hannah said.

Charley left, but almost immediately he came back.

'Charley, I told you . . .' Hannah opened her eyes.

A doctor stood in front of her with a patient chart. He looked a little sick himself. 'Are you Mr Cartwright's next of kin?'

'Yes.'

'I'm sorry to have to tell you this, but . . .'

For a minute she thought Heath had died and she couldn't breathe right. Then the doctor finished his sentence and Hannah didn't think she breathed right ever again.

Frankie

'If what he doesn't remember didn't happen,' Frankie said, 'then my dead daughter shouldn't be dead any more.'

How many times had she wished, hoped, prayed and dreamed *that*? More than she'd wished, hoped, prayed and dreamed that Charley would come back to her.

'Frankie.' Dr Halverson sighed. 'You can walk away, let the wife handle it.'

'Great.' Frankie started to do just that.

'But he'll be confused, hurt.'

'About time,' Frankie muttered, but even she heard how petty she sounded. She paused, turned. 'One of the perks of divorce . . . I don't have to deal with this, or with him.' She'd been finding a lot of perks in divorce lately when she never had before. 'I don't have to watch him die.'

'Who said he's going to die?'

In the past, Frankie would have made some sort of quip about the doctor having gotten her hopes up only to dash them again. Except the idea of Charley dying just wasn't as much fun to contemplate as it used to be.

Was that because he might? Or because the Charley in that room behind her wasn't the Charley she'd wished dead, but the one she'd loved so much she thought *she* might die when she lost him?

'Brain cancer isn't known for being one of the "good ones to have",' Frankie said.

Dr Halverson glanced away. 'Wait until you hear a prognosis from Dr Lanier before you start throwing dirt on his grave.'

'Who's going to tell the wife the prognosis?'

'I tried to find her but she's left the hospital.'

That was weird.

'I can give you her number.'

'I can't talk to her about his medical condition.'

'She's his wife.'

'So she says.'

'So I say too.'

The doctor spread her hands. 'On his intake forms, he lists you as his wife, not her.'

'He's got a mass in his brain.'

'Unless you have documented proof she's who she says she is and that she's his wife, my hands are tied.'

Frustration bubbled so hot and acidic in her throat, Frankie wondered if the ulcer she'd always expected was finally here. 'Which means the only way she'll know Charley's condition is for him to tell her, and he isn't going to because he thinks she's a nut.'

'You could tell her.'

Frankie rubbed between her eyes. 'I just *knew* you were going to say that.'

'Your other option is to walk away. The wife will be screaming for information. Charley will be freaked out that you're gone, that she's here.'

'That sounds more like your problem than mine.'

'We can't prevent him from leaving and when he does, won't he come home to you?'

'Not his home.'

'Tell it to Charley.'

Frankie's jaw was starting to ache from clenching her teeth. 'Fine. I'll talk to Hannah.'

'Good.' Halverson fled.

Frankie was getting very sick of seeing the ass end of Halverson. She was getting pretty sick of seeing the front end of her too.

And she'd always been so fond of the woman.

Frankie pulled out her cell and tapped in Hannah's phone number, even though she'd only seen it once on Charley's phone. She'd always had a good memory. A blessing when she wanted to recall something like a phone number. A curse when she could remember the exact way that Charley had smelled the first time he'd kissed her.

She almost hung up and fled as she'd threatened. She could pack her bag and abscond to Irene's. Although Charley knew where Irene lived too.

The phone was picked up on the other end of the line. 'Francesca?'

Frankie nearly complimented Hannah on her excellent guess, though with a 414 area code, who else could it be?

'How is he?'

Frankie suddenly realized she shouldn't be telling Hannah the news over the phone. Although why she was being considerate of the woman, she wasn't quite sure. Hannah had never done the same for her.

'You OK?' Hannah asked.

Frankie hadn't really been OK since the summer of '91.

'Where are you?'

'Hyatt.'

'Downtown?'

'Is there another one?'

Frankie managed, barely, to keep from snapping something equally sarcastic back.

'I'll be there in twenty minutes.'

'I didn't invite you.'

'I didn't ask you to.' Frankie hung up.

She glanced at the door to Charley's room. Should she tell him where she was going?

No. That would only lead to a head-splitting discussion of Hannah's identity, or lies to avoid the same. However, if she just left, he might start searching for her.

Odd, since when he was Her Charley he hadn't been all that concerned where she was or what she was doing when she wasn't in his sight. No more than she'd been concerned about what he was doing when he wasn't with her.

Of course she'd been a dumbass but—

'Shit.' Frankie strode to the door, then stood there frozen.

Charley had fallen asleep. That, combined with the lights being low and the sun having gone down, had taken a lot of the age off his face. She needed to stop thinking of him as *Her Charley*, even sarcastically, because when he looked like this she could easily start believing it.

It had taken her years to get over the man; for a long time she had thought she never would. She'd entertained crazy ideas, including drug use and a lobotomy. Actually those two had been the least crazy in an arsenal of crazy. She'd settled for alcohol and overwork. She wouldn't recommend them.

On the way out, Frankie stopped at the nurses' station and told them that if Charley woke and asked for her, to tell him she'd be back in the morning.

'You're his wife?' asked the twenty-something with the brunette braid and John Lennon glasses who sat behind the computer.

Frankie almost explained, then decided she was too tired and likely to get a lot more so since *Frankie's Day of Fun* wasn't over yet.

'Sure,' she said. 'Sure.'

She turned south on to Lake Drive to add a few minutes to her commute. Besides, the navy blue expanse of Lake Michigan, stars seeming to dance gently atop the waves, was a soothing sight, and she needed one.

Frankie left her window open; a soft breeze that smelled faintly of fish stirred her hair. She flicked the radio from the classic rock station, which was playing Duran Duran's 'The Reflex' – she didn't think that was funny – to soft rock, then turned up

'A Horse With No Name' so loud she didn't have to think. That song had always fried her brain.

The downtown streets were busy, especially around the Hyatt. Considering the high heels on the women and suits on the men, there must be an event at the Marcus Center for the Performing Arts. The last time she'd been there it had still been referred to as the plain old PAC – Performing Arts Center, and she'd been on assignment for the *Milwaukee Journal*, which still lay directly across Kilbourn Avenue from the Hyatt. Except for the sign, which now read *The Milwaukee Journal Sentinel*, the place appeared exactly the same despite the two-plus decades that had passed since she'd worked there.

Frankie dialed Hannah again. 'Room number?' she asked when Hannah answered.

'I'll come down.'

She hung up before Frankie could suggest that what they had to talk about Hannah probably didn't want to do in public. Apparently Hannah didn't want Frankie in her room and who was Frankie to argue? She'd prefer Hannah wasn't in her state.

Frankie waited for Charley's wife to step off the elevator and see her loitering in the lobby, then she went into the bar, found a table in the darkest, loneliest corner and took a seat.

Hannah joined her wearing loose jeans and a Washington Nationals sweatshirt. She'd put her hair in a ponytail and washed her face. The lack of make-up made her look older somehow, though she'd never look Frankie's age.

Well, eventually she would, but Frankie wouldn't be around to see it.

The waitress arrived before they could say a word.

'Glenfiddich,' Frankie ordered. 'Oldest you got on the rocks.'

'Same,' Hannah said.

The waitress sped toward the bar on spiky kitten heels. She must be new at the job. Every other waitress wore flats.

'You don't seem like a Scotch kind of girl,' Frankie said.

'Not a girl. What do you want, Fancy?'

Everything inside Frankie tensed. 'Don't call me that.'

'Isn't it your nickname?'

'No.'

'Francesca then.'

Few people had called Frankie by that name. Strangers. Her

mother when she was angry and then, later, Charley. One of the
most difficult things to get used to in their break-up had been
when he'd started calling her by her first name. From what she
could recall he'd never called her *Francesca* in all the years she'd
known him.

Until after.

'Frankie's fine.'

The waitress brought their drinks. Both of them took a
healthy sip.

Frankie waited for Hannah to choke, but she didn't, proving
she'd imbibed expensive Scotch before.

Hannah wasn't at all like Frankie had imagined, back when
she'd still imagined things like that. Had she changed? Most likely.
Frankie certainly had.

'Charley has brain cancer.' Frankie hadn't meant to blurt it out
like that. Then again, wasn't it best to rip off the Band-Aid?

'That's ridiculous.'

'Isn't it?'

The idea of Charley Blackwell getting sick, sicker, sickest *was*
ridiculous.

'Why did you say it then?' Hannah sipped her drink.

'Because he does.'

'Were those the doctor's exact words?'

'She said he has a mass. She made an appointment for him
with an oncologist. You do the math.'

Hannah drank more of her Scotch. 'Why are *you* telling me
this?'

Quickly Frankie explained the path that had brought her to
be sipping fifteen-dollar-a-shot Scotch in the lobby of one of the
finest hotels in town.

When Frankie finished, Hannah stared into what was left of
her drink. She didn't seem upset. Then again, Frankie had no
idea what Hannah upset was like. Maybe she was the type who
stepped up in an emergency, handled everything with the detach-
ment of the hired help then lost her shit in private.

Charley would love that. He certainly hadn't loved how Frankie
had fallen apart.

'He should see the best there is.' Hannah pulled out her phone
and started texting.

'How do you know Lanier isn't it?'

'Because if he was he wouldn't be in Milwaukee.'

Frankie drank more Scotch. It was that or throw it in Hannah's face.

'I can hear your teeth grinding.' Hannah lifted her gaze from her phone. 'Do you really believe that the best oncologist for brain cancer – if that's even what this is – would be practicing here?'

'You say that like this is Bumfuck, Wisconsin with only one ancient GP who works out of his home office. Did you know that Children's Hospital of Wisconsin is number four on the list of best children's hospitals in the country?'

The only reason Frankie did was that she'd sold some stock photos to several hospitals in town to use on their websites.

'If Charley were a child that might impress me.'

'Froedtert Hospital has been on the list of the top one hundred hospitals for four years running.'

'If it isn't the number-one hospital for oncology, then don't waste my time.' Hannah set down the phone and leaned forward. 'This is Charley we're talking about. You want to entrust that brain to just anyone?'

'I don't think Lanier is just anyone. Oncologists at Froedtert don't get their degrees off the Internet.'

'I'm not entrusting the brain that can see the world the way his does to anyone but the best,' Hannah said. 'And if you don't agree, we're gonna have problems.'

That startled a laugh from Frankie. All they had were problems.

'Who's the best?' Frankie asked.

Hannah's phone chimed an incoming text and she read it aloud. 'Dr Arnold Kettering at the Mayo Clinic. Voted number one by *America's Top Physicians*.'

'Is that a club or something?'

'*America's Top Physicians* is a series of books, updated every year. Each specialty is voted on by its peers.'

'Never heard of it.'

'Have you ever needed to find a medical specialist?'

'No.'

'I have.' For an instant her cool, competent façade faded and the shy, lost young woman Frankie remembered peeked out.

Her brother, Frankie thought.

'Hannah,' she began, but Hannah's phone chimed again and whatever Frankie might have seen was gone as fast as it had come.

Hannah peered at the screen.

'How are you going to get an appointment with a guy like that?' Frankie asked.

Hannah smiled. 'I just did.'

'How?' Frankie repeated.

'My mother publishes *America's Top Physicians*.'

'Convenient.'

'Today? Very. Charley has an appointment tomorrow afternoon. My assistant got us on a plane to Rochester in the morning, so . . .' She slammed the rest of her Scotch. 'Thanks for your help.' She left.

Frankie kept sipping her Scotch. It wasn't until she was done that she realized two things.

One, Hannah had been adamant that Charley's brain be saved because of its brilliance; she'd never mentioned saving him because she couldn't live without the man she loved. Which was damn strange in Frankie's opinion.

'Not my monkey,' Frankie murmured. Not her problem, not her business.

Not hers, and he hadn't been for a long, long time.

The second realization was that Hannah had walked out and left Frankie with the check.

She couldn't decide which realization annoyed her more.

Charley

Beirut, 1983

'I thought you were dead.'

Charley heard no tears in his wife's voice; he heard no anger either. He heard no emotion whatsoever and it scared him.

'Baby—'

'Don't.'

Still no emotion, but the word sliced through his own like shrapnel had sliced through over two hundred Marines.

'You know what they're showing on the news?'

He did. He'd been seeing it firsthand all day.

'I've been staring at the television for some sign of you. I don't know, maybe a foot? An arm?'

The words were furious now, but the voice? Still nothin'.

In the past, Frankie would get angry – she had a temper, courtesy of her Italian roots – but that anger burned out pretty fast. Flash-bang. He almost wished she'd flash-bang now. That he understood. This . . . he had no clue.

'I was on my way to call when everything . . .' He paused. What was the right thing to say now?

'Went boom?' she asked conversationally.

'Uh . . . yeah.'

'Well, I understand how that might put you off your game. Except it didn't, did it? I'm sure you've been on your game like you've never been on it before.'

'I'm sorry.'

'For doing your job? No, you aren't.'

He'd meant he was sorry he'd scared her. Except she didn't sound scared either.

'And you shouldn't be,' she continued. 'I don't want you to be.'

'What do you want, Fancy?'

The silence that came over the line made him remember the silence that had followed the explosion. His heart seemed to stop, then start with a painful jolt. There was no sound, because there was so much sound. Everything seemed so slow, and then it went so fast.

'I want you to call me so I don't . . .' Her voice broke.

Though he hated to hear her cry, he was thrilled that she'd stopped being so . . . He couldn't come up with a word for what she'd been. If he'd been with her, he'd have photographed her face with black and white film – stark and stunning. She no doubt looked both beautiful and terrible right now.

'So you don't what?' he asked softly.

At first he didn't understand what the click was. He kept waiting for her to answer his question. When she didn't, he called her name. He was glad he was in his hotel room, alone, because he would have appeared pretty foolish repeating 'Fancy? Frankie! Francesca!' for as long as he had before he figured out she'd hung up on him.

Beirut was a war zone, literally. Every day he thought about leaving; every day he became caught up in a new panorama of sight that he couldn't help but record. Charley didn't get back to Milwaukee for weeks. He called Frankie each morning, sometimes twice, tried again each night.

She didn't answer.

He was terrified he'd get to the house and it would be empty, that the air within would no longer smell like lemons. That it never would again.

When he arrived, he took a deep breath before he inserted his key into the lock. When it still worked, he let out that breath and pushed open the door.

The place was empty of human habitation, but all her things were there. The painting was done. She'd bought a few throw rugs; she'd framed some of their photographs. One of his depicted a man fishing off a dock, his silhouette black against a magenta sky. What you couldn't see was that the sky was magenta because of a raging forest fire in northern California, which had killed a dozen people and fried thousands of acres. Not one of his favorites, but a picture of starving children or a bombed wasteland was no doubt a decorating faux pas.

Her photograph *was* one of his favorites. A little blond girl wearing a hunter's orange sweater, nose-to-nose with a black kitten, back arched like a Halloween cat.

Their wedding picture also hung in the hall. That gave him more hope than the turn of his key in the lock. Best of all, he smelled lemons the instant he crossed the threshold. Frankie might be gone now, but she'd been here recently.

He ran up the stairs. The bed had been slept in. Her pillow still had an indentation from her head. He laid his right where hers had been.

Where was she?

Wait. What day was it?

He was fuzzy since he'd been on a plane since . . . he couldn't recall. Right now it felt like he'd boarded in Beirut a decade ago.

Charley glanced at his watch, a gift from Frankie that told him not only the time, but the day, date and year.

'Wednesday. She's at work, dummy.'

The last word came out slurred as he tumbled into sleep.

He awoke to twilight pushing against the windows and Frankie pushing against his shoulder. How long had she been trying to wake him? From the impatience in her 'Charley, wake up!' it had been quite a while.

'Hey.' He snatched her hand and held on when she would have pulled away. 'You're here.'

'Why are you?'

'What?' He was fuzzier now than he'd been when he'd arrived.

'What are you doing here?'

'I live here.' A thought occurred to him. He'd made sure her things were still where they belonged, but were his? Had she tossed them out? Would she toss *him* out?

'Don't I?' He sat up. 'Live here?'

'I don't know, do you?'

A conversation made up of questions and no answers really wasn't a conversation. He'd never realized that.

Charley crossed the floor and checked his closet. Kind of empty. His dresser appeared the same.

'I . . . uh . . . threw your stuff on the lawn.'

Charley had walked through the front yard and seen no clothes. Maybe the neighbors had taken what they wanted. Like a fire sale.

'Backyard.' Frankie pointed in the other direction. 'I was enjoying myself too much to share it with the world.'

The image of her tossing his stuff on to the lawn and laughing, maybe dancing too, caused that chill he'd had earlier to return. He'd really fucked up this time.

'Fancy, please.'

She wrapped her arms around herself and turned her head, staring at their bathroom door but not at him. 'Please, what?'

'Forgive me. I . . .' He wasn't sure what to say.

He wouldn't do it again? He would and she knew it.

He was sorry? He was.

She didn't care.

He'd make it up to her? How? Could he give her back the day of fear, somehow make it go away? What if he plucked it from her brain so that she didn't remember? Did that mean it had never happened at all?

Wouldn't that be great? But as far as he knew there was no such technology.

'I do forgive you.'

'You do?'

'Of course. You weren't maliciously trying to scare me to death.'

Since that seemed to be rhetorical, he remained silent.

'But I don't want to go through that again. Ever.'

She held up her hand before he could speak, though he hadn't planned to. He couldn't promise she wouldn't be scared to death again, and he shouldn't.

'I don't want to go through it, but I probably will, and there's something you should know about that.'

'About what?'

'About what happens when I'm so afraid I've lost you that I can barely breathe.'

Confusion filled him. She sounded like the condition was one she perpetually experienced, but if that were the case, this was the first he'd heard of it.

'Hold on.' He put his hand to his head, wavered a bit. When was the last time he'd eaten? 'Just let me . . .' He weaved toward the bathroom. 'Throw some water on my face. I'm not all here right now.'

Frankie snorted, a sound that very clearly said without words: *Right now? When were you ever all here?*

He tried to catch her gaze, but she now stared at the ceiling. She looked as if she might start to whistle. It was a guilty expression, but he had no idea what she might be guilty of. She'd already admitted to tossing his clothes on to the lawn. All of a sudden he didn't want to hear what she had to tell him.

Not now. Not ever.

Charley reached the bathroom, shut the door – he needed to get his head straight and he wasn't sure he could do it with her watching – then turned on the faucet. He considered stripping down and jumping into a cold shower. But while he didn't want to hear what she had to say, he also feared that if he didn't get back out there and let her say it, she might just leave and not say anything to him ever again.

He hated this, and he had no one to blame but himself. Even so, a tiny niggle of annoyance pushed right at the center of his chest.

Frankie knew who he was, what he was, how he was. Why was now any different from any of the other times he'd forgotten to call? Sure, this time the place he'd been had gone boom, but still, once she knew he was fine, why hadn't she been happy? Why couldn't she move on?

Charley finished splashing his face, reached for a towel, dropped it into the trash. His hands weren't steady. He really needed to eat something.

He retrieved the towel and froze, half bent over, staring at what lay beneath.

EPT Pregnancy Test.

'Shit.'

Not only was the box open, but when he picked it up and shook it like a maraca, nothing came out.

He peered into the depths of the receptacle. The plastic pregnancy indicator lay at the bottom. He grabbed it, as well as the instructions on how to interpret the results. He read them through several times but even he could see the test was . . .

Positive.

'Shit,' he said again.

If he'd thought he was out of it going into the bathroom, that was nothing when compared to how he felt leaving it.

Frankie still stared at the ceiling. How long had he been in there? An instant? It felt like a year.

'Is this what you wanted to tell me?' He held up the stick.

She lowered her gaze.

He waited for her to flinch, to blanch, to pale.

Instead, she sighed. 'No.'

'No?' he said louder than he'd ever said anything to her in their lives together.

She didn't seem to notice.

'It follows what I wanted to tell you. Direct result of. After effect.'

'Fancy, you're not making any sense.' And someone really needed to.

She bit her lip, took a breath, stared at her feet and he had a moment of clarity that made him dizzy again.

She couldn't meet his eyes, had been acting guilty since he'd arrived. She'd said she was pregnant as the direct result of something she needed to tell him. Something that had come about because of his idiocy in Beirut.

'It's not mine,' he said.

She picked up the decorative lamp on the dresser, yanked the cord out of the wall and threw it at his head.

He dodged. The thing glanced off his shoulder and bounced harmlessly to the shag carpet.

'Fuck you,' she said in a conversational tone that was a direct contrast to her lamp throwing.

'I . . .' he began, and then stopped. He had no idea what to say, what to do, what to think.

That he'd suggested Frankie had cheated on him should have been laughable. However, the positive pregnancy test in his hand was making him say, think and do all sorts of crazy things. It was obviously having the same effect on her.

'Did you know that whenever you're in danger I puke?'

Since he was never around her when he was in danger . . . 'No.'

'The first time was in Mexico City. You walked in with blood all over your clothes and five stitches in your arm.'

'Little asshole wanted my camera.'

'Yes!' She threw up her hands. 'You couldn't just give it to him?'

'I tried. He cut me anyway. Not my fault.'

'It's never your fault. That's not the point. The point is that it makes me physically ill to think of losing you.'

She *had* gotten sick in Mexico, he remembered, blamed it on the water. Had she been lying, or hadn't she realized until later the reason behind the hours spent worshipping the porcelain god?

He'd known she got upset when he had close calls, which was why he'd stopped telling her about them, but he hadn't known how upset.

'Why didn't you tell me?'

'What could you do about it except worry? And what if you were worrying about me when you should have been paying attention to the next asshole with a knife who wanted your camera?'

'OK. I see your point. But how does this all connect?' He waved the pregnancy stick again. He should probably put it down.

Then wash his hands.

'You remember the day you left for Beirut?'

'Vaguely.'

She cast him a nasty glance and he held up his hands in

surrender. He'd been telling the truth. Considering all that had happened since, he only vaguely remembered the last time he'd been in this house.

'You were . . . uh . . . painting,' he said.

He wished he could go back to that day and . . .

'I was,' she agreed. 'After.'

'After,' he repeated, and she gifted him with another scathing glance, then pointed at the bed.

He peered at the mussed sheets for several seconds and then . . . 'Oh!'

They'd woken for the first time in their new home and he'd said, *Let's christen the bedroom.*

So they had. Then they'd christened the bathroom, too.

It was that memory – of warm sheets, warm Frankie, lemons and light and smooth skin Frankie – that he'd thought about in the middle of those dank, dark, still smelling of ashes, smoke and death nights in Beirut. Even though he'd feared Frankie might be gone from his life forever, she would never be gone from his memories.

'You're on the pill.' He almost added *right?* but wanted to avoid more scathing glances.

Or a lamp to the head.

'Which works great,' she said. 'Unless you throw it up.'

'Throwing up one pill can do this?' He waved the stick again.

'Apparently, it only takes once.' Her voice was dry.

He studied the plastic. 'How accurate can a stick in a box be?'

'Pretty accurate, but the instructions tell you to follow up with your physician.'

'Excellent. Let's go.'

'Already went.' Her gaze met his, not scathing, not sad, but kind of hopeful. 'I'm about six weeks along.'

All the air rushed out of him and he sat on the bed so he wouldn't sit on the floor.

She seemed to be waiting for something, but it took him a few minutes to figure out what it was. 'You want me to go with you?'

He'd have to clear his schedule for a week or so, but he could. He would. For her.

'I don't have to go back for a month.' She smiled at him, and it was so close to her old smile the knot in his chest loosened just a bit.

This wouldn't be easy, but together maybe they could make everything all right.

'If you're here then,' she continued, 'I'd be glad for you to come along. If you're not . . .' She shrugged as if she were dismissing the lack of a spoon at the dinner table. 'I'll manage. You can come next time.'

'There'd better not be a next time.'

Confusion flickered in her previously happy eyes.

'And why wait a month? Shouldn't you get it done right away?'

Confusion fled. Everything stilled.

'What is it you think I'm getting done?'

'An abortion.'

She choked, coughed.

'We agreed not to bring children into this world.' After what he'd just witnessed in Beirut, he was still on board with that decision.

'We agreed not to try.'

If he'd been panicked at the thought of her being gone when he arrived, and then that she might throw him out, and later that she was pregnant by another man, he discovered he hadn't known *panicked* at all.

'I thought you believed in a woman's right to choose,' he said.

'I choose to have a baby.'

'What about what I choose?'

Her hands went to her stomach. He didn't think she knew she'd made the gesture, which made it all the more poignant and telling.

'You don't choose us?' she asked softly.

'I choose *us*.' He flicked his finger back and forth between the two of them.

'Us now includes one more.'

'It doesn't have to.'

Her face hardened into that of a woman she'd never been before, one he'd never thought to see.

A mother.

'Yes, it does.'

He tried one last time. 'Hundreds of women have died, thousands have marched so that you could have the right to an abortion.'

'They've died and they've marched so that I have the right *not* to have an abortion, too, Charley.'

Hannah

'I've heard that they have all sorts of new meds that can help someone who's HIV positive live for years.'

'Heath isn't HIV positive, Mother. He has AIDS.'

And had probably had it for a while now.

Hannah thought back to when he'd been coughing so much she'd wanted to smother him just to make him stop. That memory gave her the shivers now, both because of her annoyance at Heath for refusing to go to the doctor and for her easy acceptance of the same. But the symptoms had gone away, making her, and Heath, believe he'd only had a cold.

Even earlier that year, when he'd had a sore throat and a fever, he'd blamed a virus.

He'd been right. Blame the HIV virus.

Since the night of Heath's beating, when her whole world changed, Hannah had become very knowledgeable about HIV and AIDS. There was so much misinformation out there. Her mother seemed to have read all of it.

'Can't they give him the new meds anyway? Won't it kill whatever he's got?'

'No, whatever he's got is going to kill him.'

'Hannah! You need to be positive!'

She tried, but mostly she failed. Because facts were facts and they weren't very positive.

HIV, human immunodeficiency virus, caused the immune system of whoever was infected with it to shut down. Eventually patients contracted a disease that killed them.

In the early eighties, doctors had been stumped by previously healthy young men presenting with old men's diseases, such as rare lung infections or aggressive cancers. A few years later they identified LAV (lymphadenopathy-associated virus) as the culprit.

Fast forward four more years before AZT, an antiviral drug, was approved for those who had tested positive for HIV. AZT slowed down the damage to the immune system caused by HIV, but in the end it could not prevent AIDS.

'What are the doctors doing?' her mother demanded.

More than you are.

Hannah kept the thought to herself. Her parents were sending money. That's what they did. What they did not do was talk to Heath very often, come and help, or even visit other than the one time following the beating. Heath had still been unconscious after surgery – lucky him – because their parents had not known what to say or do besides stare and ask questions that only proved they had no idea about the life their son lived, or the life he would soon be living, which would invariably lead to death. They'd left before he'd woken, and they hadn't been back.

'They're treating his symptoms.'

'Which are?'

They had this conversation every week, which was how often Belinda called. Monday morning, nine a.m. on the dot, as soon as she reached her sunny Fifth Avenue office.

As Hannah heard the clatter of a keyboard during their conversations, she assumed her mother took notes so she could relate to their father the contents of every phone call.

Otherwise she was working.

Hannah wouldn't put it past her, nor would she put it past their father to ignore this problem as he'd ignored every other.

'The mouth lesions are almost gone,' Hannah said.

Heath had refused to go to work while he'd had them.

'I look like I have herpes!'

Actually the lesions *were* herpes, but Hannah had refrained from saying so.

Aunt Carol was being her typical angelic self. She allowed Heath to work at home if he wasn't well enough to come to the office, or even if he didn't think he was well enough to come to the office. She allowed him to work at the office if he wanted to. And when either of them thanked her she waved them off and said, 'I'll take Heath whenever and however I can get him. He's my best employee. And my favorite.'

Heath had an equal affection for both Carol and his job. He loved *You* with a near obsessive devotion. Sometimes Hannah thought he mourned not working more than he mourned not being the Heath he used to be.

'That's a relief,' their mother continued. 'He looked like a leper.'

Hannah rubbed her forehead. She was in the slide sorting room with the door closed. Her new Monday morning ritual.

'Not helping,' Hannah murmured.

'I'm doing all I can.'

The sad thing . . . her mother was telling the truth.

'His swollen lymph nodes?'

'Come and go,' Hannah answered.

Same with the night sweats. But the fatigue and the continued weight loss seemed to stick around. The more run down Heath became, the easier it would be for him to contract whatever disease was lurking around waiting to kill him.

Hannah bought every Mel Brooks movie pirated to VHS. Laughter was the best medicine, right? She bought him books and music and funny T-shirts, anything for a smile. But Heath didn't laugh much any more. Not even at Mel.

Every night on the way home from work she stopped and bought Heath's favorite meal from the restaurants he'd favored. Nothing tempted him. Neither knish nor falafel. Not a *soo-yook* or *thit xa xiu*. Not more than a bite of a burrito, a fajita or a tamale passed his lips. Soup received a sneer. Toast got her an eye roll. Crackers – plain, white, salted – were his staple.

How long could someone survive on crackers?

She couldn't count the number of times she'd woken on the floor of his room after she'd gotten him a cold cloth, a puke bowl, a tissue, then been unable to leave him alone. And though she was almost as exhausted as he was, she didn't mind. Because every minute near him was a minute she might not have the chance to steal again.

'Heath would like to see you.' He hadn't said so, would *never* say so, but Hannah knew it hurt him that their parents had stayed away.

'Of course. I'll check my schedule. Talk to you soon.' Her mother hung up.

'Well, I'd hate for the call to end any differently this week than it has every other week.' Hannah gently replaced the receiver in the cradle. Gently because what she really wanted to do was slam it hard enough to shatter, but it wasn't her phone.

'Your mother?'

Hannah let out an 'eep!' and spun.

Charley stood in the doorway. He must have just flown in from somewhere far away. His khakis were as rumpled as his hair.

'Hey,' she said.

He stepped closer and laid a hand on her shoulder. 'How is he?'

She was tempted to cover his hand with hers, but she didn't. Charley and Hannah were friends. The instant she tried to make it anything else, she would lose him. Right now, she couldn't afford to lose anything else.

'Better,' she said. 'Today's a good day.'

Heath had gone to work at *You* today. He'd been pretty excited about it. He'd missed two weeks with the leprosy lesions.

He'd bought a new hat for the occasion. Some kind of beanie-ish golf thing in red, which she hated, but he adored. Better than the endless array of baseball caps everyone seemed to be wearing nowadays.

'Should we go to dinner and celebrate tonight?' Charley asked.

'That would be great.'

Sometimes, with Charley, Heath ate more than a bite or two.

Charley and Heath had become pals. If Heath had idolized the man before he'd met him, that was nothing compared to how he felt about Charley Blackwell after the night of the beating. Whenever Charley was in town the three of them did something together. Pals forever more.

Hannah sighed.

'You OK?' Charley had been on the way out to whatever meeting he'd been in for, but he paused.

'Yes,' she said, too brightly. 'All good.'

Her throat hurt and she swallowed, which only made her cough because it was hard to swallow. That happened to her a lot lately.

A glass of water from the water cooler appeared in front of her and she accepted it gratefully, gulped it pathetically. At least it went down, though her throat still felt thick. She hoped she wasn't getting sick. What if she was the one who infected Heath with the illness that killed him?

Her brain was constantly filled with *what ifs* and they were driving her crazy.

'I'll meet you at your apartment at six,' Charley said. 'Champagne. On me.'

That made her smile, if only at the thought of Heath's joy. He loved champagne. She planned to make sure he had as much of it as he wanted for as long as he wanted it.

Hannah left work late because she'd gotten caught up in a story she was working on, something that hadn't happened in a while, and had to hurry home to get ready for dinner.

She'd called Heath earlier to inform him of their plans and ask him to indulge in his second favorite pastime, dressing her to go out, his favorite pastime being the dressing of himself. She hoped he'd gotten home early enough so that her outfit was laid out and he was already wearing his.

'Hannah!' Charley caught the door to the apartment building before it swung closed behind her. 'Perfect timing.'

'Are you early?' She could not be *that* late.

'Yeah. Sorry. Didn't have anywhere else to be so I thought I'd be here.'

He'd changed from his earlier pair of khakis into tan slacks, lost the black *Charley Blackwell World Tour* T-shirt that his wife had made every year listing all the places he'd been. Charley thought the shirt was funny; Hannah thought it was a very clever dig.

In the place of the T-shirt he wore an open-collared pale blue button down. Over his shoulder he'd slung a sport coat a shade darker than his slacks. His hair was wet and curled madly in the humidity.

He still smelled like a life she'd never have full of sun and wind, full of beauty and opportunity.

Hannah drew her key for the apartment but the door was ajar. She stood there frowning at it like an idiot.

Charley muscled in front of her and went in first.

Though the sun still shone outside, the apartment was dark behind the drawn blinds.

'Heath?' Charley called.

Something moved on the couch.

Hannah reached in and flicked on the lights.

Her brother sat poker straight. He'd been staring ahead, but now he blinked and glanced at her and Charley as if he didn't know them.

Had another friend been diagnosed? Had another acquaintance died?

Or worse. Had the doctor called?

Hannah hurried forward and set her hand on his forehead. Clammy.

He pushed her away. 'I'm fine.'

She could tell by his voice he was anything but.

On the coffee table sat several empty soda cans, an empty Snickers wrapper and an empty box of Milk Duds.

'You trying to OD on sugar?' she asked.

Though she should be happy he'd eaten something, anything, *what* he'd eaten was 'not-Heath' and it scared her. What else would he do that he'd never done?

Die.

'There are worse ways to go,' he said, and then he started laughing.

Not a good kind of laughter.

Charley inched past her so he could sit next to her brother on the couch. He put his arm around Heath. At least her brother stopped laughing.

'What happened, bud?'

One last burble of laughter escaped, which sounded almost like a sob, and Hannah realized both of her hands had curled into fists. But whom should she punch?

'Three people quit at *You* today.'

'OK,' Charley said reasonably. 'That happens, though usually not all at once.'

'It does when they quit because they don't want to use the same bathroom as the AIDS guy.'

Hannah muttered a curse.

Charley sent her a warning glance.

She backed up, out of their space, though not out of the room. She tried to uncurl her fingers but she couldn't.

'It's difficult when people are ignorant.'

'Difficult?' Heath laughed again, but this time he sounded amused. 'OK. Sure.'

'Did you explain that they can't get AIDS from a toilet seat?'

'I shouldn't have to.'

'You're right, you shouldn't. But I've discovered in my long, long life that much of it has been spent doing things I shouldn't have to.'

'They're gone. I'm not gonna waste another minute on them.'

'Good for you.' Hannah managed to uncurl her fingers. Almost.

Heath leaned forward so he could see her. 'Hey,' he said as if he hadn't known she was there.

Seeing the two of them on the couch, sitting so close, with Charley's arm around Heath as if it were the most natural thing in the world made Hannah's eyes burn. This was how it should have been between Heath and their father.

'What did Aunt Carol say when they quit?'

'Well, they didn't quit at first. At first they tried to get her to fire me.'

Obviously they didn't know Aunt Carol.

'She told them not to let the door hit them on the way out. Then she announced to the entire staff that anyone who felt the same could vacate and the next time someone asked her to choose between them and her family, she might not be so nice.'

'I love Aunt Carol.'

'Me too.' Heath laid his head on Charley's shoulder.

Hannah thought she might cry.

'Heath?' Charley whispered.

'Mmm?' Heath sounded half asleep.

Maybe they should let him rest instead of going out to celebrate. What, exactly, *were* they celebrating? She could no longer recall.

'I should record this,' Charley said.

'Record?' For an instant Hannah thought Charley meant record their conversations with a tape recorder, and she couldn't figure out why, unless it was for some legality later.

After.

Then she saw Charley absently turning the focus, this way and that, on the lens of the camera in his lap, something he often did when thinking. Again she hadn't noticed he had a camera, probably because he always, always did.

'You want to record what?' she asked.

'This. Him. All of it.'

'You want to photograph . . .' She couldn't say it.

Slowly Heath straightened. 'He wants to photograph me dying.'

'No,' Hannah said.

Was she saying no to the photographing or the dying?

Yes.

Heath stood and began to pace. 'People need to see. They need to know.'

'How it looks to die?' Hannah snapped.

'There's dying,' Heath said. 'And there's dying from AIDS. They aren't the same thing.'

'You're the same kind of dead.' Hannah couldn't believe she was having this conversation when she hadn't been able to say the word *dead* since his diagnosis.

Had she thought that by not saying it she'd prevent it from happening? She was as stupid as the people who'd just quit *You.*

'Things are going to get worse before they get better,' Heath said.

A metaphor for dying if ever there was one.

'There have been articles written and speeches given but not enough is being done to stop this,' Charley said. 'Words are easy for someone to read or hear and forget about later. But a picture – a lot of pictures – those stay with people.'

Hannah knew he was right; she still didn't like it.

'Heath, you didn't want to go to work with a mouth lesion because you didn't want anyone to see you like that and now you're going to let Charley photograph . . .' Her voice broke.

'Everything,' Heath finished. 'All of it. It's the only way.' He smiled the smile she'd been mourning for months now. 'I think this calls for champagne.'

Frankie

'*Mazel tov*, he's no longer your problem, Frankie. You should be thrilled.'

Irene had called at *Oh-God thirty* that morning. Translation *six thirty*, which she was happy to point out was seven thirty where it counted.

Sometimes Irene's *why would anyone choose not to live in Manhattan* theme was more annoying than others. *Oh-God thirty* was one of them.

'I *am* thrilled.' Frankie struggled to make coffee, her hands not working very well since she hadn't had coffee. She needed to buy a Keurig.

'Then sound thrilled, *nudnik.*' Silence came over the line, followed by, 'You need me to come out there?'

'No!' Frankie fumbled the glass carafe and nearly broke it against the side of the sink. She was not up to *in-person Irene* right now.

Frankie managed to get the coffee pot loaded and push the *brew* button. She nearly started applauding.

'I have work.' Nothing that couldn't wait, but she wasn't telling Irene that.

'What's the matter, sweetie?'

'No Yiddish? You feel OK?'

'It's not me I'm worried about. I thought you were over him a long time ago.'

'I thought I was too.'

Sounds of movement came from Irene's side of the line – swooshing sheets, thumping covers. Was she still in bed?

'You're not over him? I was just baiting you.'

Frankie retrieved her favorite cup – a golden yellow Pottery Barn special that held at least twelve ounces – and poured the half-inch of sludge from the carafe into it. 'He thinks he's My Charley.'

'What the hell does that mean?'

'He doesn't remember her; he only remembers me. Us. The way it was when . . .'

'The way it was when you had no idea he was boffing a child?'

Hannah wasn't a child any more. From what Frankie could tell, she wasn't even Hannah any more. And if Frankie said that to Irene, there'd be no stopping her friend from hopping on the next plane.

'It's just—' Frankie began, and someone rattled the front door.

She knew very well who that someone was even before Charley shouted, 'Fancy, I forgot my key.'

'Déjà vu all over again,' Frankie said.

'Is he at the door?'

'Yes.'

'Her too?'

'I don't think so.'

'Don't answer.'

Frankie had already considered that, except . . . 'He needs to be on that plane to the Mayo Clinic, not wandering around my house or the neighborhood.'

'Frankie, this is ridiculous. You need to—'

'I'll call you later.' Frankie hung up while Irene was still talking and opened the door.

Charley walked in, stopping to give her a kiss on the way. She nearly kissed him back. Maybe she should go along to Rochester and have her own head examined.

'Why are you here?' Frankie demanded.

'I live here.'

'Stop.' Frankie held up a hand. She was not doing this again. 'You're supposed to be at the hospital.'

'Crazy showed up and tried to get me to go to the airport with her. While security was sorting things out, I caught a cab.'

'Security? Why were they there?'

'There might have been some shouting. A little name calling.'

Charley had never been much of a shouter. That was Frankie's thing. But she couldn't imagine Hannah shouting either.

Charley was dressed in fresh clothes instead of the ones he'd been wearing when she'd taken him to the hospital for the CT scan. Had that been only yesterday?

'Where'd you get those?' She waved her hand to indicate the khaki Dockers and mint-green golf shirt.

'Cuckoo for Cocoa Puffs brought them. I wasn't going to shoot a gift horse. Though I was tempted.'

'Look a gift horse,' she corrected, and at his blank expression continued. 'The saying is "look a gift horse in the mouth".'

'Why would I look in a horse's mouth?'

'Never mind.'

Had he screwed up the saying because of the brain mass? Maybe it was just his age. Frankie screwed things up all the time.

Did it matter? She wasn't sure. There was a lot she wasn't sure of any more.

'Hannah is taking you to see a specialist at the Mayo Clinic.'

'Why would I fly anywhere with that nut? She's still telling people she's my wife.'

Why had she thought Charley would skip off merrily with someone he considered a stranger? Because she wanted him to.

The doorbell rang.

Charley grabbed her arm. 'Don't answer it.'

If only she'd taken that advice herself.

Bam! Bam! Bam!

'Francesca! Open the damn door.'

'It's her,' Charley whispered. 'Psycho.'

The situation would be comical if it wasn't so . . . not.

Frankie opened the door, dodging Charley's continued attempts to stop her.

Just as Charley had a few minutes ago, Hannah waltzed right in. 'We need to go now if we're going to make that plane.'

She wore a fitted jacket and bellbottom pantsuit the color of honey. Her slingback heels matched, as did her purse. Her hair – a shade lighter than the suit, three shades lighter than it had been way back when – was smoothed into a chignon that rested against the collar of the jacket.

Even if Frankie hadn't still been wearing her Tinker Bell pajama bottoms with her Walking Dead T-shirt, she'd have felt frumpy.

'I'm not going anywhere with you, Batshit. You need a check-up from the neck up.'

Hannah glanced at Frankie. 'A little help here?'

Well, the sooner she got them out of her house the sooner she could . . . do anything else but this.

'Charley, Hannah's taking you to see a specialist at the Mayo Clinic,' Frankie repeated. 'You remember Dr Halverson telling you they saw a mass in your brain?'

'I was there, Fancy. Of course I remember.'

Frankie resisted the urge to roll her own eyes at his annoyed tone. The sum total of what he didn't remember could fill a book, yet he was irritated at her for asking if he remembered something.

'You need to see a specialist.'

'If Frankie comes along, will you get on the plane?' Hannah, at last, sounded a little frazzled. Her phone buzzed, but she ignored it.

'Not,' Frankie said.

'She can't leave Lisa home alone.' Charley peered up the stairs. 'Where is she?'

Hannah's glance at Frankie was wide-eyed.

'Camp,' Frankie said. If he didn't stop asking about Lisa she just might lose it.

'Oh.' Charley's face, which had lit up on the word *Lisa*, now fell. He didn't seem to think it odd that yesterday he'd thought she was at school and now she was at camp. But, again, he'd never known their daughter's schedule beyond what Frankie had told him.

'I miss her, Fancy,' he whispered.

Frankie's chest suddenly hurt so badly she couldn't breathe. Maybe she'd have a heart attack and she wouldn't have to do this any more.

'Quit calling her that!'

'Quit breathing my air.'

'You need to—'

If they had a throw down in the middle of her foyer . . .

'Charley, Hannah is a . . .' Her mouth twisted; she could barely get the rest out. 'A friend of mine. I asked her for help. She's been telling people she's your wife to avoid issues with privacy and security.'

Charley's forehead creased.

So did Hannah's.

Frankie barreled on while they were both still confused. 'I'm not flying to Rochester.' The idea of being locked on a plane with the two of them for a few hours was more than she could take. 'But Charley still has the appointment with Dr Lanier. We can go to that.'

'But he isn't the b—' Hannah began.

'He'll do for now,' Frankie interrupted.

Charley sat on the staircase. He was pale, and he rubbed his fingertips along his temple.

'Headache?' Hannah asked.

Charley grunted.

Hannah pulled a pill bottle out of her purse, started toward him, then hesitated and handed it to Frankie. 'These should help.' She went to the door and Frankie followed. Hannah stepped on to the stoop before turning back. 'I'll meet you at Lanier's office. What time?'

'Ten. He's at Froedtert Hospital. You know where it—?'

'I have GPS; that'll get me there.' She headed for a shiny black rent-a-Cadillac as she pulled her phone out of her purse and began to answer texts.

When Frankie returned to the house, Charley no longer sat on the steps. The bathroom was empty, as was the living room and the kitchen. She hurried upstairs, flicking a gaze at the pill bottle.

Hannah Blackwell. For migraine headache. One tab at onset. May take a second after two hours.

Frankie wasn't giving them to Charley even if they did help. How long had he been having headaches that they'd masked with meds? If they'd gone right to a neurologist would this all have been solved before he showed up on her doorstep lost in the eighties?

They'd never know.

Two hours later, they were on their way to see Dr Lanier. Located on the same campus as the Children's Hospital of Wisconsin and the Medical College of Wisconsin, the place, inside and out, was a madhouse.

The oncology department had been remodeled recently. Everything appeared glossy and new. The reception desk was a light shade of faux wood, which matched the faux wood floor. The walls were a soothing gray, decorated with photographs depicting Wisconsin – fall foliage, Lake Michigan, the capitol building at dawn.

Charley studied them for a long time before he sat in one of the well-cushioned plastic chairs.

Frankie placed herself between Charley and Hannah, who'd been waiting when they arrived. The two griped at each other like a pre-teen brother and sister. She nearly ordered them to opposite corners of the room. She would not have been a good mother of more than one child. Something she knew all too well. She hadn't managed to be a good mother to the one she had.

When the receptionist finally said, 'You and your daughter can take him in now, Mrs Blackwell,' Frankie couldn't stifle the burble of hysterical laughter.

'Ha ha,' Hannah said.

Thankfully Dr Lanier appeared to have been briefed on the entire situation as he greeted Hannah by her first name and Frankie by hers and did not try and determine who was Mrs Blackwell or who wasn't, or even if they might both be.

Lanier's office decor matched that of the waiting room with a desk of pale wood, perhaps maple or faux maple; the floors were the same, complemented by pale gray walls.

'Mr Blackwell.' Dr Lanier stood and leaned over his pristine desk to shake Charley's hand. 'I've reviewed your tests.'

He sat once more and motioned for them to take the three guest chairs.

Again Frankie wound up in the middle.

'Are you old enough to be doing this?' Charley asked.

Lanier didn't look a day over twenty-five, though Frankie found it difficult to determine ages any more. She'd meet someone she thought was older than her only to discover they were younger. Of course, whenever she peeked in the mirror and saw her graying hair and well-lined face she experienced a tinge of surprise. She still felt twenty-five herself most days.

'Yes, sir. I have the school loans to prove it.'

'How long have you been out of school?' Hannah asked.

Dr Lanier didn't appear insulted by their questions. He probably got them all the time.

He was tall, gangly, with a prominent Adam's apple and nose. His hands were large, his knuckles too. His hair was short, brown and pin-straight. His eyes, also brown, seemed the oldest thing about him. He'd seen a lot of sad with those eyes. Unless he changed professions, he was going to see a lot more.

'I started here five years ago.'

Which put him in his mid to late thirties depending on how long he'd interned and if he'd done any fellowships.

'We had an appointment with Arnold Kettering at the Mayo Clinic,' Hannah said.

Lanier's heavy eyebrows lifted. 'You saw Arnie?'

'We did not.' Hannah's voice was clipped.

'Charley didn't want to travel,' Frankie said. 'You know Dr Kettering?'

'He was my supervisor. I interned at Mayo.'

'I heard he's the best,' Hannah said.

'He was until me.'

Silence fell over the room, unbroken until Charley laughed. 'I like a man with confidence. Especially one who's going to be messing around with my brain.'

'I'm really very good.' Lanier turned his attention to Hannah. 'You can ask Dr Kettering.'

'I will.'

'Why is she here again?' Charley asked.

'I'd be happy to have Arnie consult,' the doctor continued. 'In a case like this, I usually get his opinion anyway.'

'A case like what?' Frankie asked.

'I see you served in Vietnam, Mr Blackwell.'

'Call me Charley. I did, yes. What does that matter?'

'I wanted to point out that there's been a lot of research into cancers that are a result of Agent Orange. The most prevalent ones are multiple myeloma, leukemia, non-Hodgkin lymphoma, sarcomas, respiratory cancers.'

'You're saying Charley got this in Vietnam?' Hannah asked.

'Not necessarily. Though some studies are leaning toward including brain tumors and cancers on the list of diseases that are accelerated by exposure to Agent Orange, a definite link has not been made.'

'Yet,' Frankie said.

'Yet,' Lanier agreed. 'However, we are coming to a time where the veterans of Vietnam might be getting illnesses just because of their age rather than their service.'

'I'm not that old,' Charley muttered.

Sixty-three *wasn't* that old. Of course Charley thought he was in his thirties, regardless of the evidence to the contrary.

'Do you know if any of the men in your unit from Vietnam were diagnosed with cancer?'

Charley frowned. 'I . . . uh . . .'

'One,' Frankie said. 'He had bone cancer.'

'Multiple myeloma?' Lanier asked.

'That sounds familiar. Maybe.'

'Was he African American?'

'How'd you know?'

'Multiple myeloma is more common in that population.'

'Jim Colby?' Charley asked.

Charley had been the one to tell Frankie. She'd barely registered the news as it had come in the months after Lisa died, which explained why Charley didn't remember.

'Yes.'

'He's gone?' Charley sounded lost again.

Frankie could only nod.

'Anyone else?' Lanier asked.

Frankie glanced at Hannah, who shrugged. She didn't know anything.

'Do I have a tumor or is it cancer?' Charley asked.

'A benign brain tumor is considered non-cancerous. A malignant tumor is cancerous. Most malignant brain tumors are secondary cancers, which means they've traveled to the brain from a primary cancer, such as breast, lung, skin or blood cancer. The PET scan you had after you were admitted to the hospital revealed no primary cancer.'

'Then his tumor isn't malignant?' Frankie asked, getting pretty excited. A non-malignant tumor might have him on a plane and out of her life this week.

'I didn't say that. There are primary brain cancers. They're just rare.'

Rare in the same sentence as brain cancer could not be good. Frankie's hope withered and died.

'I have a rare, primary brain cancer?' Charley asked.

'I believe so. Yes.'

'You don't know?'

'Without a biopsy, we can't be sure.'

'Give him a biopsy,' Hannah ordered.

'You first,' Charley said.

Dr Lanier shook his head. 'No biopsy. Your tumor is in a difficult place for surgery. Removing it could cause more harm than good.'

'What kind of harm?'

'Vegetative state.'

'No, thank you,' Charley said.

'What, exactly, does he have?' Frankie asked.

'From the images we took, I recognize a tumor of the glioma group called a Glioblastoma-multiforme.' He paused, took a deep breath and wrung his large hands together. Several knuckles popped. 'It's the most lethal of the glioma tumors, I'm afraid.'

'How long does he have?' Hannah's voice was hoarse; her face now matched the gray wall behind her.

'I don't like to give life expectancies,' Lanier said. 'That can be pre-determinative.'

In other words, by saying someone had three months to live, they died in three months because they, and everyone around them, expected them to.

'We'll do more tests today,' the doctor continued. 'Then we'll get started on radiation, followed by chemotherapy.'

Hannah grabbed the arms of her chair. She appeared as if she might face-plant on to the floor. She wasn't taking this well. Not that she should, but how was she going to deal with Charley if she could barely function herself?

'Are you all—?' Lanier began.

'You're certain about this?' she interrupted.

'Even without the results of the scan, which very clearly shows the mass in the limbic system, his memory issues would make me think he had a tumor of the glioma group.'

'Hold on a sec.' Charley was rubbing his forehead again. 'What memory issues?'

Everyone went silent.

Frankie sat back and flipped her hands upward. Let the supremely confident doc handle that one.

Dr Lanier stood. 'Why don't you go into the exam room, Charley, and my nurse will get you set up for those tests?'

Charley allowed Lanier to urge him toward a door that connected the office to an exam room. That Charley went without argument was almost as disturbing as his being here in the first place. The room beyond was white and chrome – electric clean – a stark contrast to the almost homey atmosphere of the office.

Lanier handed him off to a nurse who appeared about Charley's age, but who knew?

The door closed behind him and Lanier returned to his seat. 'Did you want me to finish what I was saying or did you have specific questions?'

'Both.' Frankie waved for him to continue.

Hannah seemed dumbstruck. Had she not believed Frankie when she said Charley had a mass? Had she been expecting a specialist to say it had all been a mistake? If so, Frankie could almost feel sorry for the death of her optimism. As Frankie recalled, that really hurt.

'The limbic system processes memory,' Lanier went on. 'The hippocampus, located in the limbic system, is responsible for the transfer of memories from short to long term.'

'Could a tumor there cause someone to remember long term as short term?' Frankie asked.

'Apparently, though I've never seen it before.'

'You've never seen memory loss like Charley's?'

'No. It's intriguing. The reason I'd suspect a tumor of the glioma group, even before further testing, is that those types of tumors spread along white matter pathways, resembling multiple tumors, putting pressure in multiple places and causing myriad symptoms. For instance, the temporal lobe processes faces. I suspect a spread of Charley's tumor there, though I didn't see it on the CT scan, which is common for small tumors. If we did an MRI, it might be visible.'

'Should you do one?'

'Considering Charley's difficulty with such tests, I don't think so. Knowing that the tumor has spread isn't going to affect what we'll do for it.'

'Why do you think it's spread to the temporal lobe?' Frankie asked.

'He recognizes you, but he sees you as you were, not as you are. He sees himself the same. He doesn't recognize his wife at all. It's fascinating.'

'He's not a lab rat,' Hannah snapped.

This was the most emotion Frankie had seen from her, and it was about time. The wan, pale, scared Hannah wasn't working for her.

'Of course not,' Lanier agreed.

Hannah's hands, still clenched on the arms of her chair, tightened and the faux wood crunched. 'How long does he have?' she repeated.

The doctor opened his mouth and Hannah continued, 'I won't tell him, but I need to know.'

'Median survival rate of fifteen months.'

Hannah flinched.

'Four per cent survival at five years.'

'I'm not sure I can do this again,' she said.

'Again?' Lanier glanced at Frankie.

Frankie didn't explain about Hannah's twin. Wasn't her place.

'He's going to die.' Hannah's pupils had dilated until she looked like she was on something, and her voice seemed to have reverted two decades to the soft, shy timbre Frankie remembered.

Frankie had thought she wanted that Hannah back, but now she wasn't so sure. This Hannah – or was she *that* Hannah – seemed more like a child and Frankie had already had, and lost, the only child she ever wanted.

'I'll do everything I can to postpone that,' Dr Lanier said.

'But, eventually, he'll die.'

'Eventually, we all die. Despite every medical advance, life is still terminal.' He stood. 'I'm going to examine your . . .' he paused, glancing back and forth between the two of them, then settling on: 'Charley.'

Hannah snorted.

'He and I will come back in when we're done and discuss a timetable.'

The doctor went through the connecting door. He locked it and the click split the silence between them like a gunshot in the dead of night.

'I'm sure you can get a referral from Lanier for an equally gung-ho oncologist in DC,' Frankie said.

'You think Charley's going to get on a plane to DC any easier than he got on one to Rochester?'

Frankie had been trying *not* to think about it.

'He'll have to stay here.' Hannah's eyes seemed less drugged; her voice had reverted to its clipped, businesslike tones.

'I suppose you can work anywhere,' Frankie said.

'You suppose wrong.'

Frankie didn't like the way this conversation seemed headed.

'Private nurses are very good these days, I hear.' She'd heard nothing of the sort.

'Be that as it may,' Hannah murmured, and Frankie couldn't help it, she laughed.

Then Hannah laughed too.

They both stopped pretty fast, but for a minute there Frankie almost liked her. It didn't last.

'Charley isn't going to come with me; he doesn't know me. Despite your fairy tale to explain why I'm here, he still doesn't like me. No matter who I leave him with, he's going to keep running back to you.'

'Well, he's not staying with me.'

'Why not?'

'Because – well, no!'

'Not a reason.' Hannah's hand lay atop her phone where it rested in a pouch on the side of her purse. She hadn't taken it out yet, though she obviously wanted to.

'I don't need a reason! I am not babysitting my ex-husband.'

'He thinks he's your husband.'

'That's his problem.'

'Is it?'

'Yes! And yours.'

'I'm trying to solve it the best way I can for everyone.'

Charley living with Frankie was definitely not the best for Frankie. If she wasn't remembering the good times – a spontaneous Christmas day, their dinners at DelMonicos, the sex – she was remembering the bad – no example necessary. She'd started to wonder if the lure of the good times was somehow worse. She'd learned to steel herself against memories of Lisa and the child's loss, but she'd never had to fight her fond memories of Charley. Once he'd left, he'd been Hannah's Charley. Another man. Not *her* man. And she'd definitely not been fond of him.

Now he was behaving like the love of her life again – he thought he was. What if he convinced her to think it too?

'No,' Frankie murmured, a general negation for pretty much everything that had been happening since Charley showed up at her door.

Hannah ignored her, stroking her phone with fingernails that should have been manicured, but weren't. 'My magazine isn't doing well.'

'I heard.'

Hannah's clipped, bare, short fingernails clicked against her cell phone once. 'Where?' Then understanding filled her eyes. 'Irene Pasternak.'

Frankie shrugged. She doubted Irene was the only one who knew.

'I can't stay here.' Hannah began to pace. 'Even if I brought him back with me, I'd only be hiring people to deal with him, because I can't.'

Frankie had to shift in her chair so she could see Hannah, who continued to pace behind her – face set, eyes a bit wild. Was that sweat running down her cheek?

Hannah's twin brother had died not too long after Lisa. All that dying had been the reason Charley and Hannah had gotten so close. Or at least that's what Charley had said. Frankie thought they'd been close for a while before that. By then the reasons, the truth, hadn't mattered.

'You're picking your magazine over Charley?' Frankie asked.

'Since he doesn't know me, he isn't going to care.'

'That's cold.'

Hadn't Hannah nursed her brother through AIDS? Of course

that woman and this one were very different. For that matter so was Frankie. So was Charley.

Hannah paused and leaned against the wall. 'Says the woman who kicked him when he was down.'

'That's how you see it? I kicked him?'

'Didn't you?'

Frankie wasn't getting into a discussion of who had kicked whom. Not now. Not here. Preferably not ever and not anywhere. Definitely not with her.

'You broke his heart, Francesca.'

Frankie refused to admit that he'd broken hers first.

'Let him stay with you while he's having his treatments,' Hannah said.

'No!'

Hannah kept talking as if Frankie hadn't even spoken. 'When those are done, he'll either be better – which means you'll be back in long-term memory where you belong. Or . . .' She didn't go on.

'Or he'll be dying and he won't be able to stop anyone from doing anything that they want to.'

Hannah didn't answer, but she didn't disagree.

'Why on earth would you think I'd do anything for you?'

'It wouldn't be for me and you know it.'

'Why would I do anything for him?'

'Wouldn't you have once? Done anything?'

Frankie didn't answer. She didn't need to. They both knew she would have.

Once.

'You always wanted him back,' Hannah said.

'Not always.' It had taken a while, sure, but Frankie *had* moved on. She wasn't going back. And nothing this woman could say would make her.

Hannah's phone buzzed and she glanced at the display, frowned. 'I need to take this.'

She lifted the phone in Frankie's direction, but her gaze was already on the door leading to the hall. She slipped through it as she answered. '*What* is going on now?' She shut the door before Frankie heard any more.

Silence settled over the room, broken only by the low rumble of male voices from the exam area, an occasional sally from the nurse. She probably should have gone in with them so that . . .

'Shh,' Frankie hissed. She probably should have gone anywhere but here.

Yet here she was and here she'd stay until the appointment was finished, then she needed to . . . what?

Frankie glanced at the door through which Hannah had disappeared. For a while she'd also heard the rise and fall of Hannah's side of the phone call. Now all she heard was the occasional thump and clank of someone grabbing supplies, a nurse greeting a patient, calling for a doctor.

No Hannah.

Frankie glanced into the hall. Still no Hannah.

She hailed a passing medical assistant. 'Have you seen a woman – blond, late forties, phone stuck to her ear?'

Hands full of medical supplies and obviously frazzled, the girl nodded. 'Great outfit, killer heels?'

Frankie sighed. 'Yeah.'

'She left.'

'Left?' Frankie echoed.

The medical assistant headed past her, picking up speed. She lifted her chin to indicate the EXIT door. 'She ran out that one.'

Hannah had probably gone in search of coffee, maybe taken her call into the main halls of the hospital, or even outside. Perhaps she smoked.

Frankie wasn't going to chase after her. She'd come back.

Except she didn't.

After ten minutes, Frankie called Hannah's cell. It went straight to voicemail. She frowned at her own phone as if it were at fault, then tried the number again with the same result.

She went to the EXIT door, opened it and stared down a long, empty corridor. When she returned to Lanier's office, she ran into the receptionist.

'There you are. This was left for you.' She held out a folded piece of paper.

Frankie's chest suddenly felt both tight and cold.

She thanked the woman, took the paper, went into Lanier's office and shut the door. Then she opened the note.

I can't.

H

Frankie crumpled the paper and tossed it into the trash.

She considered fleeing. Oh, how she wanted to. But within the hour, Charley would only be knocking on her front door.

Charley walked into the office. 'Miss me?' He leaned over and kissed her on the head.

The déjà vu was killing her.

Charley

Disneyland, Anaheim, California. June, 1984

Charley needed to finish this assignment and head home. Not only because one more minute photographing Donald Duck's fiftieth birthday party might send him over the edge, but Frankie was due any day now.

When Ray had told him about this assignment, Charley had decided to try something new. Something cheery and festive and light instead of the massacre in Amritsar that his boss had originally suggested.

What the hell had he been thinking? This place depressed him more than Amritsar ever could.

And what did that say about him? Nothing good, he was certain.

He couldn't help it that tragedy made better pictures. Tragedy, presented just right, could change the world.

Charley fired off a few frames of Dick Van Dyke, who was hosting the television special of the parade, and smiling wider than any kid in the place. Charley had already taken shots of some of the other celebrities attending today.

Who wouldn't want to attend an extravaganza like this? Music, floats, dancing, laughter – the very air smelled like spun sugar.

It was all so fake, Charley's chest hurt. Did anyone realize the duck wasn't real? For some reason, Disneyland made him twitchy. Other assignments held the possibility of dying by landmine, pipe bomb, gun, knife – pick one. He wasn't going to get hurt or killed here, unless he did damage to himself just for the hell of it. Yet he'd slept horribly, dreamed constantly and woken up shouting more than once.

He'd also broken out in a cold sweat the instant he'd stepped out of his hotel and seen the crowds. There was nothing at Disneyland that resembled Saigon, except for those crowds and his reaction to them. Why could he photograph a riot and be A-OK as soon as he lifted his camera to his face, yet dancing ducks and hundreds of children made him weak at the knees?

A shrink could probably explain it, but who had the time?

Charley had managed to do the job he'd been assigned by begging a space in the cherry picker one of the camera crews had brought in to get shots of the parade from the air. He thought Ray would be thrilled with the different angle of his photographs, more so than those of any other shooter on the street. That Charley would probably have passed out if he'd had to be on the street was something he would keep to himself.

He rubbed a thumb over the side of his camera. None of the pictures in there mattered. At least to him. Maybe the duck would like them.

He'd flown to Milwaukee rarely since the visit that had followed Beirut. He wasn't proud of himself, but every time he saw Frankie she was bigger, rounder. She seemed like an alien. Probably because she was growing one.

And there was a thought he should keep to himself. He had a million of 'em.

Charley took a cab to the airport, shipped his film and got on a plane. He'd promised Frankie he would be home by June ninth, a week before her due date. He was afraid that if he broke that promise he might break their marriage irreparably. It had already cracked pretty deep.

He'd been back for Christmas. When he walked into the house, he thought he had the wrong one. In all the years they'd been married, they'd never had a Christmas tree, or any of the other decorations that had been placed all over the house. Where had they come from? Why were they here?

Frankie had come out of the kitchen. She was just starting to show.

It scared him. Which was the only reason for his answer when she'd asked him how the house looked.

'Like Santa's workshop puked all over it.'

Things had slid downhill from there.

When he'd gotten a call the day after Christmas about the USSR performing a nuclear test, he'd been on the next plane. Then there had been rioting in Tunis, an oil fire in Brazil, a miners' strike in the UK. He'd managed another quick trip home in April. By then he couldn't even hug Frankie without getting a belly bump, and while he had, the alien had moved.

He'd done his best to avoid hugging after that.

He knew he was hurting her. He wished he could stop.

He'd spent a lot of time talking to his old service buddy, Jim Colby. Jim had five kids. He lived in Austin and had his own business – a donut shop near the university.

'Why do you have five kids?' Charley asked.

'Because we don't want six.' Jim's chuckle dissolved into a cough. 'Although what happens, happens.'

Jim had never given up the cigarettes they'd smoked one after the other in Vietnam. Not only had smoking been something to do while waiting around to shoot or be shot, it had been one of the few constants in a world of very few. No matter where you were, you could have that cig in your mouth. Even if you couldn't light it, because you were either hunting or being hunted, you could hang one off your lip and you felt . . . like you. Or maybe you felt like every other guy.

Yes, a cigarette was a security blanket, a pacifier, an oral fixation. So what? It was Vietnam.

However, once Charley had returned to the States, he'd finished the pack he had on him and that was it. Cigarettes were Vietnam and he was done.

'What's wrong? Tell Uncle Jim all about it.'

Charley had taken to calling his friend while waiting for planes. He used to call Frankie.

'Everywhere I go I see an example of why we shouldn't bring more children into this world.'

'Like what?'

'Prejudice and bigotry, religious zealots, air strikes, riots, murder, assault.'

'If you wait for all that to be done, you'll never have a baby.'

'That was the plan.'

Jim lit up, took a deep drag, let the smoke trail out. For a minute Charley could have sworn he smelled spent tobacco hovering over that eternal scent of vegetative rot that had characterized the jungle.

'You mad at Frankie because she ain't followin' your plan?'

Was he mad at Frankie? A little.

'You're scared.'

'Hell, yes, I'm scared. What if. . . .?' He couldn't put into words what he held deep inside.

'It ain't 1866. It's 1984 – the year the future begins. Women don't die in childbirth these days.'

'You know that's not true.'

'And you know the chances are damn slim.'

He did, but he wasn't just worried about losing Frankie in childbirth. What if everything went fine and he lost her because he could not be a father? No matter how he tried to talk himself into it, he didn't want to be one.

'You're being selfish,' Jim said softly.

Why had he called Jim again?

They talked about the mundane after that – sports, the weather. Anything to pass the time until Charley's flight was called, which, eventually, it was.

He deplaned at Mitchell Airport at midday on June tenth. He was a day late, but he had left a message on their answering machine, unreasonably happy that he wouldn't have to tell her directly that he'd somehow confused the dates and was now arriving late due to a cartoon duck's birthday party parade.

Frankie was in the yard pulling weeds when the taxi dropped him off. She'd planted flowers seemingly everywhere that wasn't covered in grass, trees or bushes. The riot of colors was so bright and cheery that Charley's teeth ached.

She got to her feet. The dancing giraffe in the middle of her lemon-yellow maternity top seemed to be teetering on the edge of her enormous belly; her white Bermuda shorts were dirty. As he approached she stretched her back and grimaced.

'Should you be doing that?'

'No one else does.' She headed for the kitchen, where she poured two glasses of lemonade.

The temperature on this side of town, nearer the lake, was

sixty-five degrees. Low for June, but still not atypical. Her face appeared redder than it should be for the temperature.

'How long were you out there?'

'Not long enough. But I've got things to do in here too. How was your flight?'

'Not bad.'

Charley hated this surface talk, which was all they had these days.

'How are you . . . uh . . . feeling?'

'Like a beached whale.'

'You don't look like one.'

'Liar.' She smiled and for an instant everything felt almost normal.

Frankie picked up a broom and started sweeping the kitchen floor, which already appeared swept.

'Does that need to be done now?'

'Is there something else I should be doing?' She continued to sweep.

Only last year they would have spent the first several hours of his arrival home in bed. That hadn't happened since . . .

His gaze dropped to her massive middle then jerked away.

'We could get something to eat?' He wasn't hungry but it would waste some time. And since when was DelMonico's about hunger anyway? It was *their* place. Maybe if they went there, they'd actually enjoy being together the way they always did, at the same table they always shared.

'I just ate.'

The disappointment he felt over those three words was disproportionate to the actual words. He stood there, flexing his hands, trying to figure out what to say or do next.

Frankie swept back to the place she'd begun and started sweeping the kitchen all over again.

Charley gently pried the broom from her hand. 'Let me. Sit, OK?'

'If you really want to help, you can put together the crib.'

He stood there trying to figure out what, exactly, to say to that. Using a camera? He was the man. Using a screwdriver? Utterly inept.

'I'm probably not the best choice for that.'

Frankie slid away from him – something she seemed to be

doing not only physically lately – and sat on the arm of the sofa, sipping her lemonade. 'I should have put it together before I got so huge, but I kept thinking it was something that we . . .' She glanced at him and drank more lemonade.

She'd thought it was something they should do together. But he'd never come home.

'I'll check it out.' He already knew this wasn't going to end well, but he had to try.

Frankie gave him a little smile – either she was really tired, or she knew he was placating her. Probably both. She set down her glass, held out her hand. He stared at it for several seconds before he understood she needed help to stand.

'Sorry!' He leaped forward, smacking his hand into hers before he managed to grab it and pull.

When she was on her feet, she kept hold of his hand and led him to the stairs. It took her so long to climb them, even with his help, that he started to wonder – and worry – how the hell she'd been climbing them for the last month.

At the top, she turned into the room on the right. He followed, then stood gaping. The last time he'd been here the room had been painted white. The bed – a queen – had been covered with a peach pastel comforter; turquoise pillows had been placed here and there at the head. The walls had been dotted with photos she'd taken, surrounded by turquoise frames. Peach candles had graced the oak dresser and nightstands.

All of it was gone, replaced by white baby furniture – a chest of drawers, a changing table; the large parts of a crib were strewn across the floor. A rainbow had been painted on one wall; the others now shone the same shade of yellow as her shirt. The ceiling sported fluffy clouds and a ceiling fan where each blade represented a color on that rainbow.

'Tell me you didn't drag all that furniture out of the house by yourself.'

'Of course not!' She hauled two plastic tubs out of the closet. 'I dragged it into the spare room.'

'What about the painting?'

'I like to paint.'

He opened his mouth to . . . what? Scold her? He knew better. If he didn't want her to do things for herself, he should make sure he was here to help. Or send someone else to do so. Though

Frankie had told him on several occasions that money couldn't solve everything, it solved this kind of stuff really well.

She struggled to pull a third tub into the center of the room to join the other two. He shouldered her aside and did it himself, then pulled off the lids. Gazillions of tiny diapers, T-shirts and socks filled one; tiny footie pajamas, shorts, pants and shirts filled another, the third held towels, washcloths, receiving blankets.

'I've been hitting the rummage sales. You wouldn't believe the stuff! A bunch of these still had the tags on them.' She picked up a tiny – so, so tiny – blue sock. 'I shouldn't have bought anything in pink or blue, but some things I just had to. Babies don't know. I figured once he or she is here we can get more sex-appropriate clothes. And people will send stuff.'

She stared into the tubs, pulling out this, folding that. Her expression . . .

Where was his camera?

Downstairs in the bag with all the others. He'd been so discombobulated by everything he hadn't even thought to take one out. So unlike him, but she was behaving so unlike Frankie.

Frankie didn't clean unless she had to. She didn't go to rummage sales. She didn't overbuy. She also didn't get the look on her face that she'd just had for anyone but him.

'You didn't need to buy used clothes.' She also never did that.

'Most of them are hardly used. Babies grow like grass. Besides, it was fun to talk to people. Listen to their stories about their kids.' She smoothed her hand over a blanket with purple pastel kittens, then set the top back on the tub and closed it with a click. 'I wanted you to see that – except for the crib – I'm ready.'

He wasn't. Would he ever be?

'Have you thought of names?' she asked.

He shook his head. He'd tried not to think of it at all.

Sadness flitted through her eyes, but she forced a smile. 'I have a few, but we'll wait and see what he or she looks like first. Something might occur to us.'

She started to shove the plastic tubs back into the closet, but he shouldered her away again so that he could. By the time he finished, she was hauling the pieces of the crib into the center of the room.

'Fancy, come on!'

'What?' She seemed genuinely puzzled.

'You gotta quit lifting stuff.'

'Where is that written?'

'Didn't your doctor tell you to take it easy?'

Who was her doctor? How could he not know that?

'No. He said I should do what I usually do.'

'You usually carry big pieces of wood, haul heavy tubs of crap . . .' She frowned and seemed a little hurt, so he hurried on. 'Paint a bedroom? Weed the garden?'

'Yeah. Every damn day.'

He suddenly caught a clue. Her feelings weren't hurt; she was pissed.

'I'll put together the crib,' he said. 'You should lie down.'

'I don't want to lie down!' She threw up her hands. 'I want to put the crib together before the baby comes.'

'I think we've got time.' A thought occurred to him. 'Don't we? Are you feeling . . .?'

What would she feel? How would she feel?

Why hadn't he gone to the birthing classes with her? Because he wasn't here. He was never here.

Charley started grabbing random pieces of the crib and hoping they fit together. They did not.

'You never read the instructions.' Frankie waved them around.

'I hate instructions.'

'You also hate putting things together.'

'Things never go together right.'

'Because you don't read the instructions.' She opened the booklet. 'Find part A.'

He stared at the jumble of parts. 'How?'

Frankie threw the booklet at him. Since it was paper, it fell harmlessly on the pile of parts between them.

'You should probably calm down.'

The glare she gave him . . . Shit, why had he said that?

She clenched her fists, closed her eyes. Her face had turned an alarming shade of fuchsia. 'I feel like I'm going to explode.'

'Baby . . .' he began.

Her eyes opened. She glanced down. Her shorts were wet; so were her legs and the carpet too. *Had* she exploded?

'You're right,' she said. 'Baby. Now. We should probably go.' She started for the door.

'Go?' he echoed, hurrying after.

'To the hospital. It'll be hours yet, but Dr Creviet said to come in right away if my water broke.'

Her water had broken, so kind of an explosion, though it had been more of a trickle. He'd always thought when a woman's water broke it was like a tidal wave.

Frankie started down the stairs, waddling precariously.

'Whoa, hold on. I'll—' He tried to figure out how he could pick her up.

She waved him off. 'I outweigh you now. Forget it.' Then she doubled over. 'Ouch.'

Panicked, Charley dived forward to break her fall.

She didn't fall. She sat on the step, put her head between her knees and breathed. A minute later she straightened. 'I should have some time before the next one.'

Then she went down the rest of the stairs on her butt while Charley hovered helplessly at her side.

'My bag's in the front closet.'

He retrieved it, snatching his cameras along the way.

Frankie picked up her purse, tossed him the car keys. 'You drive.'

He opened the door. 'What would you have done if I wasn't here?'

'Same thing I always do, Charley.'

He opened the passenger door of the Dodge Caravan in the driveway.

'I handle it.' She plopped into the seat.

He closed the door. Since when did they have a mini-van?

The drive to St Michael Hospital on Villard Avenue was a blur, as was checking in and registration. He walked alongside Frankie's wheelchair, biting his lip every time she experienced a contraction.

The room was so white – walls, tile, sheets, pillows – he felt like they were in a Stanley Kubrick movie. The only color in the place was Frankie. The only color in any place was always Frankie.

He stood around feeling helpless while a nurse assisted his wife into a hospital gown, also white, then peeked beneath it. 'You're at four,' she announced. 'I'll be back to check on you. Use the call button if you need me sooner.'

Charley wanted to beg her to stay. He had no idea what he was doing.

'Where's the doctor?' he asked.

'On a gorgeous day like today, probably playing golf.'

'Shouldn't he be here?'

'Not when I'm at four.'

'What does that mean?'

'My cervix is dilated to four centimeters.'

'Ow.'

'Yeah. I can't wait to find out what ten feels like.'

'It's going to keep happening?'

'How do you think I get this basketball out of me without something . . .' She illustrated a widening circle with her hands.

Charley gulped at the thought of any part of him widening that much so something that big could come out. Why on earth did women give birth? And after they did it once, what nut job did it again?

Another contraction came and Frankie closed her eyes, breathing slowly until it was over.

'Does that help?'

'Nope. But it gives me something to do.'

'How long will this take?'

'Hours.'

He'd known that; he'd just hoped he was wrong.

'This is going to get worse before it gets better. Maybe you want to . . .'

'Yeah!' He jumped up, headed for the door. 'You're right. Thanks.'

He snatched his camera bag, found his favorite Nikon body and a wide-angle lens. He made sure he had color film in it – though with all this white . . . maybe he should shoot black and white. He pulled out a second camera, added a portrait lens, then loaded it with black and white film.

When he returned to the bed, Frankie stared at him oddly. 'What?' he asked.

'I thought . . .' Her eyes lowered. 'Never mind.'

He glanced at his bag, sitting right next to the exit, and knew what she'd thought. That he was going to keep going straight out that door. She had every right to and he felt like a slug.

'I promised I'd be here for this,' he said. 'I'm not leaving.'

'Because you promised.' Her disappointment was obvious.

She wanted him to say he was there because he wanted to be, because he was as excited about the baby as she was. But he couldn't lie. However, there was one truth he could give her.

'Because I love you, Fancy. I will always love you. Nothing will change that.' He kissed her. 'Nothing . . . As long as we both shall live, right?'

She peered into his face for a long time and he started to get scared. Then she smiled, though it was still sadder than he liked, and she took his hand. 'Right.'

The nurse returned and announced, 'Still at four.'

Hours passed that seemed like days.

A different nurse arrived and announced, 'Five!'

He thought Frankie might eat the woman alive.

He helped her walk.

She called him names.

They played some cards.

He wished he hadn't quit smoking.

Through it all, he took pictures. He couldn't help it. Pictures were what he did.

The third nurse peered between Frankie's legs and announced, 'Six. One more and I'll call the doctor.' Then she frowned at Charley and said, 'You need to put away the cameras. No one wants to see this.' She waved her hand in the general direction of Frankie.

'No,' Charley said, and kept shooting. He'd been told to put away his cameras by bigger, badder, crazier people than her.

He continued shooting right through the next few announcements.

'Seven.'

'Eight.'

'Nine!'

'Time to push.'

Another nurse said, 'You need to be coaching your wife, not playing with your new toy.'

He glanced at Frankie, who rolled her eyes and said, 'I can handle this. Do your thing.'

God, he loved her.

'We'll see what Dr Creviet has to say about this.' The nurse stalked off.

Dr Creviet merely gloved up and moved to the end of the delivery table. 'Just stay out of my way.'

Bleeding, sweating, cursing, straining. His wife was a goddess. Charley recorded all of it. He couldn't stop.

But when the tiny dark head emerged from between her legs, then the equally tiny body slid out too, he was stunned into inertia. All he could do was stare.

'You have a daughter.' Dr Creviet plopped the baby on to Frankie's belly.

Charley had thought he'd seen beauty before. He hadn't been impressed. Now he understood why.

He'd never seen beauty until right now.

'Lisa,' Frankie said. She was crying.

Strangely, the baby looked like a Lisa.

Frankie stared at the child as if she'd never be able to stop.

Charley's finger, poised on the trigger, twitched, fired.

He hadn't thought beauty could change anything. But in that moment, beauty changed him.

Hannah

Washington DC. Summer, 1991

'I miss being touched. I miss being kissed.' Heath's blue eyes were suspiciously shiny.

With tears, or with fever? Could be either one or both these days.

Hannah sat on the sofa at his side and took his hand. 'I touch you.' She kissed him on his dry, cracked lips. 'I kiss you.'

'I miss sex.'

She sat back. 'You're on your own there.'

He laughed and her heart jumped. It had been so long since he'd laughed.

Once he'd been diagnosed with AIDS, Heath's days of being the life of the party were over. Kent not only stopped seeing him, he'd fled DC. Heath's multitude of friends waned. He tried to make new ones; however, in 1991, if you were gay and emaciated, with a few leprosy lesions, no one wanted to talk to you let alone hang out.

He wasn't sick yet, or at least not really sick. The kind of sick that would only get sicker. The kind of sick so many gay men were all over the country, all over the world. They said things were getting better, but so far, Hannah wasn't convinced.

The doorbell rang.

Hannah's heart stuttered, then began to race.

'Charley!' Heath hurried to let him in, giving Hannah time to smooth her hair, blow into her palm and see if her breath was OK. Generally be the pathetic idiot she always was when Charley came to call.

He wasn't calling for her but for Heath. Still, he was here. Woo-hoo!

'Hey!' Charley clapped his big hands on Heath's shoulders and gave him a hug. 'A good one' as Heath called them – tight and long with a little shoulder rubbing at the end.

'Ready to go?' Charley smiled in her direction and she stood, hoping her white chinos didn't have a stain on them, not that Charley would notice.

He didn't notice things like that. In truth, he barely noticed her.

She picked up her purse and followed the two of them, already talking about some pitcher who'd had a perfect game. Charley had gotten Heath interested in baseball – Lord knew how. But it had been a good thing. There were baseball games on TV all the time. Heath could watch a game instead of going out with friends. Only Hannah knew that no one had called and asked.

Heath had a check-up today. Charley had asked to go along and take some shots. Whenever he was in town between assignments, he met up with them and recorded whatever was happening in Heath's 'Battle with AIDS'. So far it hadn't been much of one. She knew that wouldn't last.

Charley had gone into *You* with Heath, taken photos of him in the infamous bathroom, at his desk, talking with co-workers. When she'd seen the slides of that day, she'd had to go into her room afterward and fight not to cry. Was she the only one who noticed how Heath seemed to have an invisible bubble around him that no one would step past?

Same thing happened when Charley accompanied Heath to a club. The photo of her brother sitting at the bar with his drink – so thin and pale – while others danced in the background and the two seats on either side of him remained empty was excruciating to contemplate.

And it should be.

Charley wanted to record the truth. He wanted the world to see, to know, to understand and maybe to change, which wouldn't happen without pictures that made people squirm.

In the cab on the way to the physician's office, Charley asked Hannah how work was going.

'The same. Busy. Always something happening at *National Geographic*.'

His blue eyes narrowed. Sometimes she felt like she was being recorded and he hadn't even lifted his camera.

'Did you tell Charley how you plan to be editor-in-chief?' Heath gave her a soft arm-punch.

Hannah shrugged, embarrassed. Right now, that aim seemed impossibly high.

'Then you should probably transfer to another part of the magazine soon,' Charley said. 'The longer you stay in the photography department the harder it'll be to get out of the photography department.'

'I like my job.' And she certainly wasn't going to start a new one while all this was going on.

'You don't have to put your life on hold until I die.'

Hannah straightened as if she'd been poked in the butt with a stick. 'You're not going to die.'

'Of course I am.' Heath turned his head and stared out the window.

Charley took a picture.

For the first time ever, Hannah wanted to smack him.

'What the hell?' Heath murmured.

In front of the doctor's office, people marched back and forth with signs.

God Sent AIDS to Punish Gays.
Homos are Possessed by Demons!
Gay is NOT OK.
AIDS is Not a Disease; It's a Cure!

'You getting out?' the cab driver asked.

'Maybe we shouldn't,' Heath said.

Charley set his hand on Heath's shoulder. 'Up to you, pal.'

'Take us back to the apartment,' Heath said.

'No.'

Charley and Heath stared at Hannah as if a dog had sat up and spoken.

'Why should we leave? *They* should leave.'

'I don't think they're going to,' Charley said. 'And no one's going to make them. Right to assembly and all that crap.'

Heath's laugh sounded a bit cackly.

Hannah got out of the car.

Heath tried to grab her but he wasn't fast enough.

Hannah approached the demonstrators. If she thought her heart had pounded when Charley arrived, that was nothing compared to how it was thundering now. Was it because she was scared, or because she was so damn mad?

Yes.

When they saw her coming, they formed a line, men, women and – really? – a child, a young boy, perhaps ten years old. That almost made her as ill as the signs.

The man in the center, big all over – biceps, legs, gut, chin – jutted that chin out. 'Do you have AIDS?'

'Not your business.'

The woman next to him – as tiny as he was large – seemed dwarfed by her huge *HOMO Sex is a SIN* sign. 'IV drug use is a sin too,' she said.

'Good to know.' Hannah tried to walk past her.

Another woman – Olive Oyl skinny – stepped in her way. 'Sex outside of marriage is a sin too.'

Instead of backing up, Hannah got in her space. She was more mad now than scared and she liked it. 'What about a transfusion? Is that a sin?'

The woman exchanged an uneasy glance with the others.

'Because hemophiliacs – who are born that way and therefore made that way by God, right? – need transfusions to live. And almost all of them have AIDS now.'

More uneasy glances were exchanged.

'What about sex with a husband who fucked someone with HIV?'

The teeny woman gasped, dropped her sign and covered the

ears of the ten-year-old, whose eyes were so wide Hannah thought they might pop out of his head.

'Watch your language!' the protestor said.

'You first.'

Every one of the demonstrators appeared confused.

'In that scenario I just described, no one's gay. I suppose the husband might be a closet gay, *screwing*—' She winked at the woman who'd told her to watch her language; the woman pushed the boy behind her. 'The closet gay is *screwing* a man and he gets HIV, though he could just as easily have slept with a woman who'd been infected through no fault of her own either.'

'Adultery is a sin,' someone shouted.

'Gotcha. But the wife hasn't done anything wrong. Why would God punish the only one in that situation who is blameless?'

Silence met her question.

'Seriously. I really want to know.'

The big guy peered down his huge chin at her. 'It's not for us to decipher God's plan.'

'Exactly.' Hannah marched up to an elderly man who held the *AIDS is God's Punishment* sign and before he figured out what she meant to do – before *she* figured out what she meant to do – she snatched it out of his hand. 'So this one needs to go.'

Hannah ripped it in two. The shriek of the cardboard was so satisfying she nearly had a very sinful orgasm.

'And that's all we have time for today, folks.' Charley grabbed her by the elbow.

Heath grabbed her by the other and the two of them plowed straight for the door of the office building.

The loud mouth with the big chin put his hand on Charley's chest and shoved.

Charley released her. 'Go!'

Hannah would have stayed, but she didn't like the way some of the demonstrators were staring at Heath. She allowed him to think he was pulling her inside.

'You have every right to your opinion,' Charley said. 'And to protest. But you have no right to impede the path of a patient to their doctor.'

'She ripped my sign,' the elderly guy whined.

'I'm sure you have another. Excuse me.'

Hannah and Heath reached the door. Hannah opened it and urged Heath through.

Charley held his finger on the motor drive button of his camera, fanning the lens back and forth along the line of protestors, like Al Pacino in *Scarface*.

Say hello to my little friend.

'You can't just take pictures of us like that,' Big Chin said.

'Actually, I can.' Charley took advantage of their shock to walk toward the building. 'Public demonstration is fair game. Don't even need a release to use these all over the place. But you wanted publicity, right?'

Several of them nodded.

Hannah didn't think they wanted the kind of publicity she hoped they got, but at least they weren't chasing after them like a pike-carrying mob.

Charley ducked inside and Hannah let the door close.

'You get people to back off quicker with your camera than most could with a gun.' Heath pushed the *up* arrow on the elevator call buttons.

'Why mess with success?'

The elevator opened and they stepped inside.

Heath hugged her. 'You were amazing. I never . . . I can't believe . . .'

'That I had it in me?' Hannah was kind of surprised herself.

'You could have gotten hurt,' Charley said. 'What if that guy popped you in the mouth when you tore up his sign?'

'Then he popped me in the mouth. I couldn't take it any more.'

'There's going to be a lot more to take, Hannah.'

'I know.'

'Losing your temper isn't going to help. People like that won't change.'

'I know,' she repeated.

But it had felt so good not to sit there and take it for once that she couldn't be sorry. She *wasn't* sorry. She was so jazzed she was having a hard time keeping herself from bouncing up and down.

The three of them stood in the elevator and watched the floors light up on the monitor.

Two. Three. Four.

'Wasn't she the most spectacular thing you've ever seen?' Heath asked.

'Pretty close.'

In Charley's eyes she thought she saw admiration, respect, maybe even affection, though that was probably going a bit too far. What she was certain of was that today he was not only looking at her but seeing her too.

Hannah lost her bouncy feeling pretty quickly once they got into the doctor's office.

'Your white cell count is elevated, Heath.'

Heath's doctor, Thomas Beattritt, an infectious disease specialist whose father was one of their father's best clients, had agreed to take Heath on as a patient even though his practice was full.

And wasn't that just a kick in the head? The AIDS doctor's practice was full, and Beattritt's wasn't the only one.

'What does an elevated white cell count mean?' Hannah asked as Charley took pictures as unobtrusively as he could in a ten-by-twelve feet exam room the shade of jaundice.

Beattritt, an unassuming little man with an iffy toupee, paged through his notes.

'It could mean Heath's fighting off an infection.'

'That's good, isn't it? Fighting things off?'

'It would be better if he didn't have an infection to fight. Have you been taking the AZT?'

'Yes, though it gives me a headache, a backache too.'

Heath also had to take the drug every four hours – day and night – which contributed to his fatigue, another side effect of AZT.

Dr Beattritt nodded. 'It can do that. Aspirin help?'

'No.'

'I'll give you something a little stronger.'

'Got anything a little stronger for the AIDS?' Hannah asked.

'Hannah, please.' Heath sounded so tired he scared her.

'As a matter of fact,' Beattritt said, 'the FDA is considering approving DDI for use in AIDS patients.'

'I heard they hadn't done enough trials yet.'

Beattritt glanced over his shoulder at Charley as if he'd forgotten he were there. Charley took the opportunity to snap a photograph of the man's face. Beattritt had not only agreed to let Charley record the appointments, but he'd signed a release for his image to be used in any way to further a discussion on the AIDS epidemic.

'They haven't, but we're getting handed our asses with this disease. If we don't put a lid on it soon . . .'

'Epidemic isn't going to be just a word,' Charley finished.

'I was thinking apocalypse, but that works.'

'The FDA is going to let you give a drug to your patients that hasn't been tested enough?' Hannah asked.

'What difference does it make?' Heath asked. 'We're dying.'

'You need to quit saying that.'

'Not saying it won't make it less so. When can I try this stuff?'

'I'm hoping by fall. Until then keep taking your AZT. Eat well. Sleep. Try to avoid places with a lot of people and all their germs. Try to avoid germs.'

Charley laughed, then stopped when the doctor frowned. 'You were serious? How does he avoid germs?'

'Wash his hands obsessively. Try not to kiss anyone.'

Heath rolled his eyes at Hannah.

'Here's a box of surgical masks.' Beattritt plopped it down on the exam table next to Heath.

'I'm not—'

'Thank you.' Hannah plucked up the box. 'Are you giving him anything for the elevated white count?'

'So far his body is doing its job and fighting off the infection, hence the elevated count. But if he comes down with something, even a cold, call me. Barring that, I'll see you again in six weeks.'

'Is there anything you can do about the protestors?' Hannah asked.

'I think you did something about the protestors,' Heath said.

'Not enough.' If it had been enough they'd have scuttled off, never to return.

'Are they out there again?' The doctor sighed. 'We've called the police, but they're within their rights. You can leave by the doctors' entrance, which comes out to the rear of the building.'

'Thanks,' Hannah said.

The rear of the building spilled into a dank alley. Without any consultation, the three of them turned in the opposite direction from the one they'd arrived. As exhilarating as the confrontation with the protestors had been, no one wanted a repeat performance.

'We can catch a cab back to the apartment, then Charley and I will walk to the office,' Hannah said.

'Sorry, I have to head to the airport.'

Disappointment flooded her. 'Didn't you just get here?'

He flashed a quick, absentminded smile. 'I promised the kid we'd go to the zoo tomorrow. She likes to watch the big cats.' His face took on the expression it always did when he talked about his daughter. Dopey devotion combined with surprise. He couldn't believe he adored her as much as he did. 'And I like to watch her watch the big cats.'

'Don't you have to meet with Ray?' Hannah asked.

'No.'

'You came to town just for the appointment?'

'I said I would.'

Heath laid his hand on Charley's arm. 'You didn't have to do that.'

'If I hadn't I'd have missed Amazing Hannah.' He grinned at her. 'And the protestors.' His grin faded. 'Assholes they were, but the pictures are perfect.'

With Charley, it was always about the pictures.

'Do you take pictures of your daughter?'

'All the time. I've got thousands. She's a pretty good subject.' Charley's face went dopey again. 'But most kids are.'

'You have any in your wallet?'

Behind Charley, Heath spread his hands in a 'What the fuck?' gesture.

Wasn't it common to ask someone who talked about their kid like the second coming if they had a picture? She was pretty sure it was.

'I don't,' Charley said as if he'd never realized it before that moment.

Apparently no one else had ever asked to see one. Maybe she *was* being weird.

'I take a lot of slide film. The black and white shots that I like I print at eight by ten. I've got a box of them at home. She likes to page through.' He shrugged, sheepish. 'So do I. They're better than the school pics, which are creepy. Every kid appears the same. Stepford Kindergarten. You know?'

Hannah nodded, though she didn't know. She hadn't seen a children's school photograph since her own, and she hadn't thought they were creepy. Then again, her parents had never carried one in their wallets either.

Charley hailed a cab. It sped right past without slowing down.

'I never wanted kids,' he said, as if to himself. 'I'd seen so many horrible things.'

Heath mouthed *Vietnam* when Charley wasn't looking.

You think? Hannah mouthed back as Charley tried to hail another cab without any more success.

'It seemed like everything I saw was bad.' His lips tilted up just a bit. 'Until I saw her.'

Heath cast Hannah a glance. Why did he keep doing that?

'My wife said our kid might change the world. She certainly changed mine.'

A cab pulled up to the curb at last. Charley opened the door and motioned them in.

'You can take this one,' Hannah said. 'Don't you have a plane to catch?'

'I've got time and . . .' His blue eyes studied Heath's face, then flicked to Hannah's. He gave a tiny jerk of his head toward the cab.

Heath did appear exhausted.

She climbed in and Heath followed.

Charley shut the door, then waved as the cab pulled into traffic.

Hannah turned so she could see him out the back window. Another cab pulled over and he hopped in. DC traffic swallowed them up.

'Hannah, it'll never work.'

'You need to give AZT more of a chance.' She faced front. 'And this DDI sounds promising.'

'I'm not talking about my meds; I'm talking about Charley.'

'Charley?'

'Yeah, Charley.' He jabbed a thumb over his shoulder. 'The guy you're falling in love with.'

'I . . . What?' Her heart thundered again. She'd started to breathe too fast.

'I'm your twin. I know when you've got it bad.'

Her cheeks felt on fire. Her tongue felt too thick for her mouth.

'Not only is he head over heels for his kid, he's one of the few guys I've ever met who is genuinely, always and forever in love with his wife.'

'I know.' Her voice sounded as if someone had turned its speed to slow-mo.

'You gotta stop falling in love with him.'

She wasn't falling; she'd already fallen. But she kept that to herself.

'Is it that obvious?'

The only thing worse than Heath knowing would be Charley knowing.

'Not to him, honey, just to me.'

She let out her breath in a rush.

'But if you aren't careful, he'll figure it out. If he wasn't a man, he'd have figured it out already.'

'You're a man,' she muttered.

'But I'm special.' He put his arm around her and tugged her close.

She leaned her head on his shoulder. 'You are. Very.'

'What would you do without me?' he asked.

'Panic,' she whispered.

Frankie

Dr Lanier returned, his nose buried in a chart. It wasn't until he sat behind his desk and glanced up that he realized there were only three of them in the room, where before there had been four.

Charley hadn't noticed at all.

'Where's Mrs . . .?' Lanier paused. 'Uh, Hannah.'

'I don't know where she went,' Frankie said.

'Is she coming back?' Lanier asked.

'I don't think so.'

'Yahoo.' Charley gave a fist pump.

'Uh . . .' Lanier glanced at the door.

'Tried that already,' Frankie said. 'Wishing doesn't make her appear.'

And that she might ever wish for the appearance of Hannah Blackwell was so out of this world that Frankie felt . . . out of this world.

Dr Lanier emitted a soft sound of amusement, straightened and got down to business.

'We'll start daily radiation immediately. My reception desk can help you schedule that. This afternoon would be good, tomorrow at the latest.'

'I can't . . .' she began, then saw again the same two words on the note Hannah had left.

Lanier fixed her with a glare. 'Join me in the hall for a moment, Francesca.'

Charley had started examining a *Time* magazine he'd found on an end table and didn't seem to notice or care when they left.

'If he's to have any chance at all we need to jump right on this with both feet,' Lanier said.

'I understand, but I'm not his wife.'

'He thinks you are.'

'People need to stop saying that.' Frankie rubbed her forehead. 'I can't do this.'

'Can't or won't?'

She dropped her hand, curled it into a fist, let her fingernails bite into her palm and prayed for patience. 'Both.'

'Until you find his wife, a sibling, friend, relative or colleague who's willing to help him, I'm afraid you're stuck with him by reason of being stuck with him.'

'Can't he just go into the hospital and stay there?'

'For radiation? Hardly. Insurance barely pays for things that are necessary; they certainly aren't going to pay for what isn't.'

'You said he needed radiation.'

'That they'll pay for. As an outpatient. As an inpatient . . . I'm not really sure when they pay for that. But he has to start treatment now. Because of his memory issues, he's going to require someone to walk him through this. No one's here but you. Get him to radiation, then make some calls. If you can convince someone to take over, let me know. If we have to transfer his care elsewhere, though I'd rather not, I will.' He put his hand on her shoulder. 'OK?'

It wasn't, but what could she say? No?

Well, she could, but she wasn't going to.

'OK.'

He patted her shoulder – an *atta girl* without words – and walked away.

Just for the hell of it, Frankie dialed Hannah again before she retrieved Charley. This time when the voicemail answered, she left a message.

'You better have gotten hit by a bus. That's the only acceptable reason for you not to be answering your phone. Call me as soon as they scrape you off the pavement.' Frankie hit *end*.

Then she noticed several of the nurses, and the same medical assistant she'd spoken to, staring at her wide-eyed.

She waggled the phone. 'My ex-husband's wife.'

'Ah.' They all nodded sympathetically and scurried off.

Charley was able to get an appointment for radiation in two hours, so instead of driving home they had lunch at Café Hollander not too far from the hospital in Wauwatosa.

She started to make a mental list of people to call about Charley. His parents had died in 1983, within six months of each other. His dad had a stroke, his mom a heart attack. Charley had been shooting a story on 'modern' Cambodia when his dad died. By the time he'd gotten to a phone, the funeral was over. Frankie had been able to beg off going herself because she was pregnant with Lisa.

His mom had died when Lisa was a month old. At least Charley had been in the States when that call came through and managed to get back in time to join them in Illinois. Frankie had spent the entire funeral feeling guilty that Claire had never seen her granddaughter. They'd meant to visit, but they just . . . hadn't.

Even if his parents were still alive, they'd be in their eighties. What could they do?

His brothers, however . . . She'd call them first.

'How are Ben and David?' Frankie asked Charley.

'Still haven't talked to them.'

How could she have forgotten the estrangement that had followed their parents' deaths? Ben and David had asked for money to help with the farm. Charley had given it to them. Twice. When they asked a third time, Frankie had balked. Charley had agreed. His brothers had stopped speaking to them.

That was over thirty years ago. Shouldn't they have made up by now?

Charley wouldn't know. He thought the rift was a few years old.

She should ask Hannah.

Frankie checked her phone. If only Hannah would call back. After lunch, they returned to the hospital. When they called

Charley's name for radiation, she held out her hand. 'Leave your phone with me.'

He complied in a very un-Charley-like manner. He'd always wanted to know the *why* of everything. Today he was just going along.

Over half the names in his contacts were unfamiliar to her.

Annoyed, she hit Hannah's number from Charley's phone. Maybe she'd answer *his* call.

She didn't, and when Frankie thought about it she knew why. Charley had no idea who Hannah was beyond a supposed friend of Frankie's. He wouldn't call her. Therefore Frankie must be calling. And Hannah wasn't talking to Frankie right now.

She punched the *end* button. She'd figure out what to do about Hannah later.

Frankie found numbers for Ben and David. Who first?

Ben was at the top. Ben it was.

He didn't answer either, and he didn't have voicemail. Who didn't have voicemail?

She moved on to David. At least he answered.

'David, hi. This is Frankie.'

Dead silence.

'Charley's . . . uh . . .'

'Ex.'

'Yes.'

'Is he dead?'

He sounded a little too happy about that, and Frankie had a bad feeling this was going to go about as well as she'd expected.

'He's sick.'

'Why are you telling me?'

'You're his brother.' Though he certainly wasn't acting like one.

'I haven't talked to him since 1983. Maybe it was 1984.'

If that were the case, then how did he know she was the 'ex'?

'You two never talked after that stupid rift over money?' Sure Charley had told her the same, but lately, what did Charley know?

'It wasn't stupid to us. We lost the farm.'

'I'm sorry to hear it.'

'That was a long time ago.'

Yet he was still mad about it.

'What are you . . . uh . . . doing now?' Frankie asked.

'I sell farm equipment.'

'That sounds . . .' Awful. 'Good.'

'Sometimes.'

'What about Ben?'

'Ben drinks.'

'I'm sorry.'

'So am I. He never got over losing the farm, never figured out what to do with himself beyond farming. He hired out to other people who were able to keep their places going. But when you're a hired hand at thirty, forty, fifty . . .' He let out a long breath. 'What's wrong with Charley?'

'He has brain cancer.'

Silence met that statement.

'It's not a good one.'

David laughed – just one short, sharp bark. 'Is there a good brain cancer?'

Frankie's thoughts exactly. 'Charley's is worse than most. He needs immediate treatment and the prognosis is iffy.'

'Why are you calling me?'

'He needs help.'

David laughed again.

She really hated that laugh.

'I'll help him as much as he helped us.'

'He did help you.'

'I don't remember it that way.'

She was coming to understand that no one ever remembered anything the way anyone else did, even without a brain tumor.

'What happened to bouncy, blond sweet young thing?'

It was Frankie's turn to laugh. She never would have described Hannah that way, even when she'd still been young.

'How do you know about our divorce and Hannah if you never talked to Charley?'

'He wrote me a letter. After Lisa. I was sorry to hear about her. No one deserves that.'

'Deserves,' she echoed. What an odd thing to say. What had Charley's family wished on him? On them? She didn't want to know.

Quickly she told David the particulars of Charley's condition.

'If he thinks you're still married, then why would he need me?'

'We're not still married. He *is* still your brother.'

'Not in my mind.'

What was wrong with people?

She gave up. Even if she managed to convince David that it was his duty to take care of Charley, she didn't want him to. As he'd said: *No one deserves that.*

'Are there any uncles, aunts, cousins?'

'No.'

'None?'

'You could call them, but they aren't going to help. No one's seen or talked to Charley since he met you.'

'Me? What do I have to do with it?'

'Once he had you, he didn't need us. He never needed us. All he ever really needed, Frankie, was you.'

'Obviously that wasn't true.'

'If not, then why has he gone back in his mind to a time when it was?'

'He doesn't have a choice about how his mind works with a big, spreading, cancerous tumor in it.'

'No?'

'No!'

'Hmm.' David didn't sound convinced. 'Let me know when he dies.'

The line went dead.

Frankie stared at the phone for quite a while. She was almost afraid to call anyone else, but she had to.

She'd just found the phone number for the Waz when a nurse called her name. Well, she called 'Mrs Blackwell' but Frankie was getting used to it.

The woman appeared frazzled in a way that nurses rarely did.

Oh, crap, Frankie hadn't even considered that the machine for radiation might be similar to a CT scan.

'Did Charley freak out?'

'No, ma'am, just sick. Follow me.'

Frankie accompanied her to the treatment area, letting out a relieved breath when she saw that the radiation machine wasn't enclosed but rather a movable table, with a huge light source hanging from a tall, white lump of hard plastic.

Charley sat on a chair, fully clothed and very pale.

The nurse handed Frankie a prescription. 'Anti-nausea medicine. You can get that filled at our pharmacy so you've got it on hand if he has a reoccurrence.'

'I wanna go home, Fancy.'

'They always do.' The nurse clomped off in the colorful clogs they all seemed to wear these days instead of the white shoes they'd been wearing the last time she'd been in the hospital – when she'd had Lisa.

What a night that had been. She'd been terrified that the beginning of a new life would be the end of her old one. What if Charley walked out of the hospital and he never came back? But he'd surprised her.

She'd woken up in the gray light of dawn. Charley had been sitting in the armchair holding their daughter. He'd been whispering to her. Frankie swore she'd heard the word *Disneyland*. His expression . . .

He was never leaving either one of them.

She'd fallen back asleep secure in the belief that everything would be all right and that the beautiful life she wanted was right around the corner. And for a while it had been.

'Charley?' His eyes were closed. She shook his shoulder. If she couldn't wake him, she was going to have to get help.

His eyes opened – so, so blue in his too-white face. 'Hey, baby.'

Her heart went *ba-dum* the same way it always had whenever he'd called her 'baby'.

Shit. Irene would say she was being sucked in by Charley's delusion that she was his wife, by her own delusion that he was again 'Her Charley'. Maybe she was.

His smile was dopey and he hadn't had any dope.

She should ask about dope. Wasn't it good for cancer?

'Can you get up?'

'Why couldn't I?' He lurched to his feet, nearly overbalanced and fell on his face.

She snatched his elbow, hauled him back.

He threw his arm around her shoulders. 'Was I drinking?'

'Radiation.' She started inching toward the door.

'Right.' He came along and their steps soon got in sync. 'So far, not a fan.'

He squeezed her shoulder, pulling her more closely against him, then turned his head, kissed her temple.

She closed her eyes for an instant and it was twenty-four years ago. No one had died. No one had been betrayed. No one had left. Divorce was just a word that other people used.

He smelled the same; his body aligned with hers just the same.
If she kept her eyes closed would she hear Lisa shout . . .

She sucked in a breath and opened her eyes. 'My car.' She
lunged for the Volvo like a lifeline.

At the house, she had a difficult time waking him up; he leaned
on her heavily getting inside.

Mrs Stuckey next door stood watering the grass seed she'd
planted along the driveway. She ended up watering her shoes as
she gaped at Frankie hauling Charley up the sidewalk.

Frankie didn't wave. She didn't have an extra arm. She didn't
explain. She didn't have the extra time.

She dragged him into the hall and kicked the door shut. The
staircase loomed insurmountable.

'Living room it is. Come on, Charley, just a little farther.'

''K,' he slurred, and stumbled the few feet to the couch.

She straightened, her back growling at the abuse. She couldn't
lug him home every day. She was too damn old.

She was not going to be doing this every day. No. Way.

If Hannah continued to ignore her calls, maybe she'd contact
the police. There had to be some kind of law against abandoning
cancer-ridden veterans on their ex-wives' doorsteps. Didn't there?

Perhaps a lawyer would be a better option.

'You need anything?' she asked.

'Hmm?' Charley had his forearm over his eyes the same way
he always used to whenever he was trying to sleep and she was
trying to talk to him.

So she lifted it, the same way she always used to, and blew
into his face until he looked at her.

He gave her a lazy *hey, baby* smile. 'You know what I need.'

She dropped his arm as if she'd picked up a snake. 'Ginger ale?
Crackers? Water?' Her voice was too high and too bright. Pan
Am stewardess on crack.

He shook his head, gaze on her face, then moving up and
down her body.

Her cheeks heated like a fifteen-year-old's. 'Get some rest.' She
headed up the steps.

When she reached her room, she locked the door behind her,
then pulled out Charley's phone. Her hands shook. He was making
her crazy.

She tried Hannah again, with both their phones. Straight to

voicemail. If it wasn't after five, Frankie would call a lawyer right now. Instead she found the phone number for the Waz.

Their conversation went about as well as the one with David had. The Waz was dying too. Sarcoma. One of the cancers on Dr Lanier's Agent Orange Hit Parade. He wasn't surprised when she told him about Charley.

'It's a story I've heard too much already. You know there've been class action lawsuits. Government's covering some medical expenses. You should check into that.'

'I'll make a note of it.' For Hannah. 'You take care, Waz.'

Her only answer was a coughing fit, followed by a dial tone.

'Take cover!'

A crash punctuated the shout.

'Get back on the radio. Tell them we're here.'

Frankie was on the landing and she didn't remember having unlocked her bedroom door.

As she raced down the stairs, a heavy thud made the house shake. More disturbing was the scream.

'Incoming!'

Hannah

Washington DC. Late summer, 1991

A cold had followed Heath's low white counts. They'd returned to the doctor, but pneumonia happened anyway.

Heath tried to get better, but he just . . . couldn't. Not completely.

He got over the pneumonia, but he never gained back the weight he'd lost. He never got back the bounce he'd had.

Then, one day, when it was ninety in the shade and Heath was still so cold, they got the news that made Hannah colder.

'The most recent tests show Kaposi's sarcoma,' Dr Beattritt said.

Considering Heath's lesions were back, Hannah had feared the worst. This was it. Several steps above, or perhaps below, herpes simplex, Kaposi's sarcoma was the most common cancer for AIDS patients.

Heath's shocked intake of breath at the diagnosis started him coughing.

Hannah handed him a tissue. Lately when he coughed, there was blood. It frightened her.

'We'll use radiation on the lesions close to the surface, like in the mouth and throat.'

'Are lesions causing the . . .' She pointed at the Kleenex, spotted with red.

'Yes.'

Beattritt wasn't delivering this news from behind his desk but had instead taken a chair next to them. As soon as he'd done that, Hannah had known the news was grim.

'The radiation will help.'

She noticed he said *help*, not *cure*.

'Is DDI available yet?'

'No. I'm sorry.'

Hannah wrung her fingers together so she wouldn't curse. It only upset Heath to hear his previously 'never swear even when you smash a hammer to your thumb' twin cursing like a drunken sailor. But sometimes, swearing was all you had.

'We'll get started on radiation, followed by chemotherapy.'

'Will that fix him, save him, cure him?'

'Hannah.' Heath took her hand and she wanted to cry.

She didn't; she couldn't. Heath cried enough for both of them. She was the strong one. Someone had to be.

Heath squeezed her hand. 'This is the beginning of the end. You need to accept it. I have.'

'No,' she said, but her voice was pathetically weak. She cleared her throat and sat up straight. 'No.'

That was better. Perhaps too loud and confrontational, but she preferred the second *no* to the first that had sounded like she'd given up too. She hadn't. She wouldn't. She couldn't.

'Tell him it's not the end,' Hannah insisted.

'Of course not,' Beattritt agreed, though his voice was far too hearty.

She almost expected him to finish with 'Ho, ho, ho!'

'I wouldn't bother with radiation and chemo if it wasn't worth the trouble.'

Hannah wanted to ask about survival rates and percentages, but she knew from past experience that Beattritt wouldn't discuss them with Heath in the room. With Heath in the room, he was unfailingly upbeat, religiously optimistic, annoyingly chipper – what Hannah liked to call yippy-skippy. It made Heath laugh. Or at least it used to.

Now, when Heath laughed, he often coughed, so he'd stopped laughing, and Hannah had stopped trying to make him.

'I'll have my receptionist schedule an appointment for radiation. Tomorrow is good, this afternoon would be better.'

He went on detailing what they could expect both during the procedure and afterward.

'Possible nausea and fatigue. Wow, that's new,' Heath deadpanned.

Beattritt handed Hannah a prescription. 'Anti-nausea medicine. Best to fill that and have it on hand.'

Which meant there was no 'possible' about the nausea. Goody.

Hannah was still at *National Geographic*, though Ray had said she could work from home two days a week and today was one of those days. She knew Charley was behind the allowance, but when she'd tried to thank him he'd pretended he knew nothing about it.

They continued to live with Aunt Carol who refused to hear a word about them moving anywhere else. She was rarely at home. She said it was because she preferred to do Heath's job as well as her own; she wasn't hiring anyone to replace him. He would be back when he was well. She also had a new boyfriend and she stayed at his apartment nearly every night.

'She's afraid she'll catch something,' Heath had said.

'You know better than that.'

'Do I?'

Hannah didn't argue. Maybe he was right. The number of people who treated Heath like a leper, when before he'd been the star of every show, was staggering. Most of them were people who should know better. It made Hannah so damn mad.

The only person who continued to treat Heath exactly the same, and came around as often as he was able, was Charley. He was due in tonight from England where he'd been photographing Tim Berners-Lee, a computer scientist who had recently released his idea for something called the World Wide Web.

It was gibberish to Hannah, but a lot of people were excited. She was not looking forward to breaking the news of Heath's cancer to their friend. She wasn't looking forward to breaking the news to anyone, including their parents. Although, perhaps, the information might convince them to visit.

She wouldn't hold her breath.

Later that evening, Heath was ensconced on the couch, wrapped in blankets with the big bowl they'd once used for popcorn front and center on his lap. They should probably buy Aunt Carol a new big bowl. Heath had thrown up in this one so many times no one should ever eat out of it again.

Someone knocked on the door. Since they had a doorman who kept anyone not approved from doing just that, and Aunt Carol had a key, it could only be—

Hannah opened the door. 'Hey, Charley.'

He walked in bearing plates of hot dogs and apple pie. 'Why isn't the Yankees game on?'

'Because the Yankees are irritating,' Heath said.

'Not when they're getting slammed by the Red Sox. It's beautiful. Turn it on.' Charley set the food on the kitchen counter.

His gaze met Hannah's over Heath's head. He jerked his thumb toward the rear of the apartment. 'Gonna hit the head and be right back.'

Hannah waited until he noisily closed the bathroom door, though he still stood in the hall. She took one step after him.

'Tell him everything, OK?' Heath stared at the baseball game and not at her. 'Even what Beattritt told you when you called him later.'

Twin radar. She was going to miss it.

'Could you put that food in the fridge or something? The smell's making me wanna gack again.'

Hannah did as he asked, mortified when the scent made her stomach howl. She did not need hot dogs and apple pie. As Heath lost weight, she seemed to gain it, though she wasn't eating any more than she had before.

It was probably the drinking. Some nights after Heath fell asleep, she polished off a bottle of pinot by herself. That was often the only way she could rest.

She and Charley stepped into her bedroom and she quietly shut the door.

'What is it?' His blue gaze flitted over her face; the concern on his own made her heart stutter.

'Kaposi's sarcoma.' Her eyes sparked tears. She turned away, blinking like a forties starlet to make them stop.

'Prognosis?'

'Five-year survival rate for AIDS patients is less than ten per cent.'

'Fuck,' Charley muttered. 'Fuckety fuck.'

Hannah gave a short, sharp laugh, then stopped because laughter these days often led to tears and she was halfway there. If she started crying now, what would she do when things really got bad?

Now the laughter pressed on her throat so hard she started coughing.

'You OK?' Charley patted her shoulder.

She managed to stop. 'No.'

'Right.' He lowered his arm, stuck his hands behind his back. 'Stupid question. Are you taking care of yourself?'

'I'm not sick.'

'You will be if you keep going at the pace you have been. Maybe you should take your parents up on their offer to pay for some help.'

'No one's taking care of my brother but me.'

She might let her mother help – or maybe not. As she recalled, whenever one of them had sniffled, Mother had slept at her office until the nanny told her the coast was clear.

Since an offer from their mother to nurse her son wouldn't occur before the end of days, Hannah didn't have to worry about how she'd turn it down.

'Why don't you go out for something to eat? Heath and I will watch the game.'

'You brought something to eat.'

'Get out of the apartment for a while. Go to a coffee shop and read a book. Call a friend and meet for a drink.'

Getting out did sound appealing. If she stayed all she'd do was eat half an apple pie and listen to the two of them talk baseball. While she did enjoy listening to Charley talk about anything, she should probably stop.

Sadly, what she really needed to do was work, but she could do it at a coffee shop.

'OK. Thanks.'

He patted her again. Sometimes, around Charley, she felt like a poodle. If she bit him, would he finally notice her? Probably depended on where she bit him and how hard and if she kissed it better afterward.

Her face flooded with heat.

'You're flushed.' Charley put the back of his hand to her cheek.

She had to grit her teeth and hold very still lest she rub her cheek against him like a cat.

Too much animal imagery.

And now, she was having flashes of other animal imagery that only made her cheeks flush darker.

'Hot in here.' Hannah bustled around the room, collecting her files. 'I turned the air conditioning off because Heath is always freezing.'

'I thought you were going to relax.' Charley tapped her files. 'Not work.'

'I need to work.' The entire day had been sucked up with the doctor appointment and then radiation and then barfing from the radiation.

'Have you applied for a transfer from the photo department?'

Hannah shook her head.

'Why not?'

'I can't when Ray's being so great about my hours. I can apply later.'

She didn't say when later would be. They both knew.

Heath was asleep when they returned to the living room.

'I'll be back by ten,' Hannah whispered.

Charley nodded and picked up his camera. As she left, he took a few shots of Heath, his meds, the used Kleenex, the puke bowl, then he lifted the camera and fired off a shot of her.

She wore ancient jeans and an equally old T-shirt, no make-up; her hair was in a ponytail. She probably had barf on her elbow and lunch lettuce in her teeth. Whenever Charley took a photo of her she was a mess. Though, right now, she couldn't recall the last time she hadn't been.

Her aunt popped out of the elevator when it opened. 'Oh, hi, sweetie. Where you going?'

'Charley is with Heath. I thought I'd work at the coffee shop.' There was one right across from the apartment.

'I came to pick up a few things.' Carol blew a breath upward, causing the bangs on her new super short haircut to ruffle.

'There's something I should tell you.' She hadn't shared Heath's diagnosis with Carol yet. It wasn't something that should be imparted over the phone. Unless it was to their parents, as she'd done earlier.

The exchange of information took less than a minute, then Carol gathered Hannah into her arms and gave her a hug – quick and businesslike, but a hug nevertheless. 'You tell your parents?'

Hannah nodded.

'Are they coming?'

Hannah shook her head.

Carol sighed. 'They're not right, you know that.'

Hannah wasn't sure if Carol meant 'not right' in their behavior, or their belief that Heath was 'off'. Or maybe the *not right* was a statement of *them* being 'off'. Regardless, Hannah already knew. Had known even before this had happened.

'I'm going to have to hire someone for Heath's position.'

Hannah bit back an automatic *No!*

Carol couldn't keep doing Heath's job as well as her own forever. But she was surprised at how panicked the statement made her feel. As long as Heath's job was waiting for him to pick up right where he'd left off, well . . . so was his life.

A stupid belief, a foolish hope, but didn't she need belief and hope, however stupid and foolish? Heath certainly did.

'I'll work for you.'

Carol, who'd headed on down the hall toward the door, paused. 'What was that?'

'I'll take Heath's job until he's able to come back to it.'

'You know that you could get a job anywhere after working at *National Geographic*?'

'I don't want a job anywhere. I want a job at *You*.'

She didn't – shudder – but she was afraid of what would happen if Heath discovered his job no longer waited for him.

'If you leave *National Geographic* now, you'll have to start over again when you go back.'

Hannah shrugged, but only because she couldn't speak past the lump in her throat.

'If you're really serious, you'd save my ass.' Carol, who'd looked tired and frazzled when she'd gotten off the elevator, looked a little less tired and frazzled now.

She'd done so much for them; Hannah couldn't be depressed about doing something for her. She wouldn't be.

'You'll give notice?'

'Tomorrow.' Hannah's voice cracked and she cleared her throat.

Carol hugged her, no less businesslike than the last hug, but she added a cheek press too. The scent of her foundation, the faint whiff of her perfume still left from that morning's spritz, was pure Carol. 'Thank you.' Then she rushed off.

Hannah finished laying out a photo spread at the coffee shop. The place was deserted at nine p.m. on a weekday and she draped her stuff over two tables. She'd deliver the mock up to Ray in the morning along with her resignation. She thought he'd understand, maybe keep the door open, but who knew.

She returned to the apartment right before ten.

Heath was still sleeping. Or maybe sleeping again. A half-empty teacup sat on the table. The box of Saltines was out and open, though she couldn't tell if any had been eaten.

She heard the low rumble of Charley's voice from the back hall. He was on the phone.

She went to the refrigerator. Only one hot dog and a small slice of pie remained.

Charley ate like a Sumo wrestler and never seemed to gain an ounce. He said it was because when he was on an assignment he forgot to eat at all.

Hannah couldn't imagine forgetting to eat. Choosing not to was another story. She shut the refrigerator door, wished momentarily for a padlock.

'I'm leaving tomorrow, Fancy.'

Hannah tried not to listen, but the apartment wasn't that large. She could have moved out of the kitchen, back toward the front door, but she didn't.

'Sorry. I meant to tell you I was stopping in DC.' He paused, listened. 'You know I'm recording this on my own time.' He sighed. 'What does that have to do with anything?'

He sounded annoyed. She wished she could hear the other end of the conversation.

'I'll take Lisa to Door County, just her and me. You can have as long as you want to yourself.'

Charley's wife wanted time to herself when she could have time with Charley?

'OK, baby. I'll see you soon.'

Hannah scrambled to sit in a chair in the living room before Charley caught her eavesdropping.

'I didn't hear you come in.'

She glanced over her shoulder and smiled. 'Just got here. Everything OK?'

He tilted his head as if gauging how much she'd heard. 'I need to get home. I promised.'

Hannah nodded. What could she say?

Stay with me. I'm frightened. I don't want to do this alone. I can't bear to watch him die.

If she started admitting those things, even to Charley, when would the panic stop? Charley couldn't be here all the time. He was here too much already from the sound of things.

'I'll be back in a week or so. I'm taking the kid to our cabin.'

'Sounds fun.'

'I've never been alone with her for more than a few hours, maybe a day.' His expression became sheepish, as if that embarrassed him, but a lot of men would say the same. That might not be right, but it was the way it was.

'She's seven,' he continued. 'How hard can it be, right?'

He sounded like he needed convincing and Hannah, of all people, knew how that was.

'Right. Seven-year-olds practically take care of themselves.'

Later she'd wonder if what happened was partially her fault. Foolish thought. He'd barely seemed to be listening to her. His mind on the phone call, his wife, his child. Not Hannah.

Never Hannah.

When he left, he patted her shoulder same as always, then stared at a sleeping Heath with a worried expression before walking out without another word.

The next time she saw him, everything had changed.

Frankie

Charley lay flat on his back, staring at the ceiling. His face was gray; his lips were white. His eyes seemed incredibly blue.

'Which one?' she asked.

'Napalm.'

The napalm dream was one of the bad ones. From what Frankie had been able to piece together in the darkness following the times he'd had it, his company had been under attack by VC. His lieutenant had been killed, the radio operator as well. Their sergeant had called in an air strike, but he hadn't called in the coordinates quite right. As a result, the napalm had fallen far too close to the soldiers. The napalm had fallen *on to* some of the soldiers – the sergeant included.

'Where's Lisa?' Charley whispered, and her heart lurched.

'Gone.' Her voice sounded hoarse; her eyes ached.

'Camp. Right.' He rubbed his forehead. 'Forgot. Last time I had the napalm dream she woke me. She shouted "incoming", you know how she does?'

Frankie had forgotten that and it scared her. What else had she forgotten about her little girl while she was doing her best not to remember every second of every day that she was dead?

'Should have never taught her that,' Charley continued.

'She loved it.'

Lisa would run across the room, either launching herself into her father's arms when he came in the door, or on to the bed with him in the morning shouting, 'Incoming!'

'That morning, that dream, the end of it, right before the napalm hit, I shouted . . .' His voice tapered off.

'Incoming,' she finished. It was what he always shouted when he had that dream.

Which did make her wonder why he'd taught Lisa to shout it in joy. Maybe he'd thought it would help him to stop remembering it with terror. With Charley, who knew? Maybe he hadn't thought about it at all.

'Yeah.' He blinked and came back from wherever he'd been, perhaps the jungle in 1972. 'She startled me and I . . . well, I'd never forgive myself if I hurt her.'

Anger rose, flames licking at Frankie's throat, heat pushing at her forehead. She clenched her hands and fought for calm.

Charley had done a lot more than hurt Lisa, but what good would bringing that up do? He didn't remember. He wouldn't believe her.

'It's all right.' Frankie hadn't meant to say that. Why was she soothing him?

Old habits, they said, died hard. Or maybe they never died at all.

He got to his feet.

'I've been trying to get in touch with your family, your friends and colleagues.'

'What?' he asked. 'Why?'

'You're sick. Remember?'

'Of . . . course,' he said, except his brow furrowed.

Had the damn radiation caused him to lose that knowledge too? She could not bear to re-tell him every day that he might be dying.

'Mass in the brain.' Charley touched his head. 'They radiated it.'

Frankie let out a soft sigh of relief. 'That's right. Next there'll be chemo. You're going to need some help.'

'But . . .' His confusion deepened. 'I have you.'

'I'm not . . .' she began, then stopped, uncertain herself.

There were many things she was not.

A nurse. A caregiver. A lady of leisure.

His wife.

'I need you,' he said.

She walked out of the room, then out of the house. She kept walking, no idea where she was going until she reached a playground – new school, she'd never been here before, no memories of the place, thank God, she had enough of those dancing through her head – and sat on a swing.

Night was falling. The place was deserted. Could she stay here forever?

No. When morning came and the kids spilled from their buses, they'd be scared of the old lady on the swing, crying.

He'd never said he needed her.

Loved her. Adored her. Worshipped her. But need?

Never.

Because he hadn't needed her. If he had, he never would have left.

Frankie scrubbed the tears off her cheeks. This had to stop. All of it.

She pulled her cell phone from her pocket and called Hannah again. She nearly bungled the phone when Hannah answered.

'Where are you?' Frankie demanded.

'DC.'

'Are you fucking kidding me?' Her voice was too loud in the silent playground. She needed to keep it down or someone in the neighboring houses would call the cops.

'Why would I kid you?'

'Why would you leave your sick husband in one city and fly to another?'

'Didn't you get my note?' Rustles, movement and tiny thuds from Hannah's end revealed she was unpacking.

'"I can't?" What the *hell* does that mean?'

'Seems self-explanatory. I can't take care of Charley.'

'Why?'

'My brother. He . . . died.'

Frankie was well aware. The photographs Charley had taken of Heath Cartwright's battle with AIDS had won him another goddamn Pulitzer. They'd been published in several major magazines, as well as in a book that was on the *New York Times* Bestseller List for light years. Charley had donated his advance and his royalties to AIDS research. The attention his work brought to the disease had resulted in a lot of donations. Not long after, the landscape of AIDS research changed.

Because of Charley and his photographs of Heath? No. Though Charley's groundbreaking study had reached a lot of people and perhaps made them see, for the first time, the agony of not just the dying but of those watching them die.

All that attention for a man Frankie didn't know while she'd been mourning a child no one seemed to remember but her had infuriated Frankie. Stupid to be angry with Heath; he'd had a bum deal.

But so had Lisa.

'I took care of him, beginning to end,' Hannah continued. 'It was excruciating. I can't watch another man I love die, inch by inch. I just can't.'

'So I'm supposed to?' Frankie stood and the swing bopped her in the ass. She began to pace. She could not sit still.

'I didn't think you loved him any more.'

'I don't,' Frankie said, too fast.

'Then what's the problem? I seem to recall you saying you hoped he died screaming.'

Silence fell over the line. Had she said that? She'd said a lot of things back then. Who could blame her?

'You've got your revenge,' Hannah continued. 'Don't you want to watch?'

Who was this woman? When had she changed from the pudgy, adoring waif Charley had married into . . . whatever she was now? And why? Because of Heath? Or because of Charley?

'Listen,' Hannah said briskly. 'I've got problems here that I have to deal with. I'll be back. We'll see how he is then.'

'When?'

'I'll let you know.'

'I have problems of my own. Work of my own.'

'Get help.'

'I tried. His brothers still aren't talking to him. His army buddies are in worse shape than he is.'

'Colleagues?' Hannah asked.

'The ones I knew who are still working are working. The ones who aren't are old. Why don't you call the ones you know?'

'The ones I know are still working too. And they're . . . well, you know how they are. Like Charley. Always on the road to the next war zone, natural disaster or gorgeous landmark that everyone needs to see ten photographs of right now.'

'Yeah,' Frankie said. 'Hear ya.'

It felt weird to commiserate with Hannah, but it also felt good to talk to someone who understood. Someone to whom she didn't have to explain Charley Blackwell.

'I don't know why I thought any of them would nurse Charley.'

'Nurse!' Hannah blurted as if the word were new. 'I'll get you one.'

'What I need is a lawyer,' Frankie muttered.

'Go ahead. It'll take you longer than he's got to get any action that way.'

All her warm, fuzzy feelings of commiseration vanished.

'What is *wrong* with you?' Frankie demanded.

'Same thing that's wrong with you. Charley.'

Frankie sighed. Arguing was getting them nowhere.

'You said you two hadn't been getting along.'

A distinct chill came over the line. 'I did?'

'To Charley. At the hospital. Is something going on that I should know about?'

'Not really. I want him to take it easier. He's Charley. He won't.'

Silence descended. Frankie waited for Hannah to say goodbye or maybe just hang up but she didn't.

'You'll stay with him?' Hannah asked.

'I don't . . .'

'Remember those pictures of Lisa that Charley took?' Hannah blurted. 'From the instant she was born until . . .'

Frankie remembered very well, but how did Hannah?

'He burned them after she died.'

'No,' Hannah said. 'He didn't.'

Frankie's chest suddenly ached and burned. 'You're lying.'

'Why would I?'

'To get me to take care of Charley.'

'Will you?'

'You're bribing me?'

'Is it working?'

Frankie had mourned the loss of those pictures. Certainly she'd taken her own. Thousands of them. But the ones that Charley had taken of Lisa were quite simply works of art. They showed her in ways no one else, not even her mother, ever could. Ways that no one, now, ever would. In addition, Charley had taken photographs of Lisa and Frankie together. Frankie could count on two fingers the pictures she had of herself and her daughter in the same frame.

'Why did he lie about them?'

'You broke his heart, Francesca.'

Frankie still refused to point out that he'd broken hers first.

'You take care of Charley through his treatments and the pictures are yours.'

'I'm thinking that they might be mine anyway. Eventually.'

'Think again. I've seen his will. Everything, right down to his last camera, lens and camera bag, goes to me.'

Bastard. Why was Frankie surprised?

Because it was so unlike Charley to be vindictive. Frankie? Hell, yes. Charley? Never. Guess she'd been as wrong about that as she'd been about him being incapable of cheating.

'How do I know you have them?' Frankie asked.

'Which one's your favorite?'

'The first one he ever took of us together.'

'Right after she was born. She's lying on your chest. You're looking at her like there's nothing and no one else in the world *but* her.'

Frankie had often looked at Lisa like that. So had Charley. Frankie had mourned the loss of that picture more than any of the others, and she had thought for decades that it was gone.

'I'll send it to you by FedEx,' Hannah said. 'It'll be there tomorrow.'

She could say no. She'd lived without those photos for over two decades. Did she really need them back now?

Yes. And knowing that Hannah had them, had been able to see them while Frankie hadn't . . .

'Let's make a deal,' she said. 'I'll do what I can while he's in treatment. With a nurse, which you're paying for.'

'And then?'

'One of the many perks of divorce. I don't have to watch him die, and you can't make me.'

Hannah hesitated and Frankie waited for her to say: *Wanna bet?*

'All right,' Hannah said instead. 'Keep me informed of his progress. Best time for me to talk is midnight or later.'

'The last time I saw midnight or later I was wearing jeans two sizes smaller.'

Hannah laughed, then cut the sound off as if she couldn't believe it had come out of her mouth. Frankie was kind of shocked herself.

'You could email. Text. Whatever.'

'Fine.' Frankie did not plan to have any more conversations with Hannah than she had to.

For a second, she thought Hannah had hung up, then she heard her breathing.

'How is he?'

Frankie nearly said, 'I'll email you', but she was tired of being pissy. After a while, it just got old.

'He was tired from the radiation. He had a nightmare.' Frankie had no idea why she'd shared that. She hadn't meant to and then *babble-blurt*, there it was. 'Vietnam. The napalm dream.'

'I don't . . . He never . . . Not with me.'

'He never had a Vietnam flashback dream?'

'There were times he shouted out, but who doesn't? He never spoke to me about Vietnam much. I know he has PTSD. It's why he chases danger. He needs to reproduce the stress of that time to process what's going on in his head. He feels more alive when he's skating the line between life and death.'

'He told you this?'

Hannah made a soft sound of amusement that didn't sound at all amused. 'No. My brother . . . he did some research. Then I talked to some psychiatrists. Not like Charley was going to.'

'No,' Frankie agreed. 'So he wasn't just being a danger-loving asshole.'

'Oh, he was being an asshole, but I'm not sure he could help himself or that he knew why he was that way.'

'You didn't tell him?'

Hannah's breath whooshed out. 'What good would it do? He wasn't going to change, didn't want to change. Maybe he couldn't.'

The line clicked.

'Gotta take this call,' Hannah said, then she was gone without a goodbye.

Frankie stood on the playground until the stars popped out. She didn't want to go home, but standing here beneath the great big sky, she suddenly felt so small, so vulnerable, so lonely.

She couldn't call Irene. Her friend would blow a gasket, burst a blood vessel, flip her lid. Worse, she might hop the next plane, shove Charley into a straitjacket and drag him personally to Hannah's door.

Frankie wanted to avoid that.

She'd have to tell Irene something, sooner or later. Probably sooner. But not tonight.

She stayed where she was for as long as she could, but eventually she made her way back to the house, taking her time, breathing in slowly, deeply and then back out.

The door to the house was ajar.

'Charley?' she called.

No Charley in the living room, the kitchen or the downstairs bathroom. Not in the upstairs bathroom or the guest room, or the room that had been turned into a guest room. After.

She opened her bedroom door and breathed a sigh of relief at the sight of him in the bed.

She considered spending the night in the original guest room, as spending the night in Lisa's room was out of the question. She could paint the walls a hundred times, buy fifty new beds, seventy-five new bedspreads and sheets, tear the carpet out, put in hardwood, or the opposite. It wouldn't matter. That room would always be Lisa's and she rarely went into it.

But what if Charley became ill? What if he got confused? What if he wandered around searching for her, fell down the stairs and broke his neck?

Irene would say, *Problem solved.*

'Shut up, Irene.' Frankie went into the bathroom to change her clothes.

Before she lay next to him, she found a plastic tub, which she sat on the nightstand, just in case.

Her eyes opened to bright sunlight. The clock read 9:00 a.m. She hadn't slept past seven in a decade.

Disoriented, she stared at the arm over her shoulder. She wiggled her feet and brushed other feet. She shifted her hip and bumped . . . not a hip.

Charley kissed her ear. 'Morning, Fancy.'

He nuzzled her neck. His hand cupped her breast.

Why wasn't she rocketing out of bed and racing for the bathroom where she could lock the door and take a scalding hot shower?

Because it felt too good. Both familiar and decadent. She hadn't been held or touched in years.

She'd had boyfriends since the divorce – if you could call them that since they hadn't been boys any more than she'd been a girl. She'd had sex, many times. Especially right after. Sex had been the only way she'd been able to feel anything at all back then.

But no one had been Charley. No one could be Charley but Charley. And he was right here. What could one minute hurt?

She turned her head. Decades fell away at the touch of his lips and she let them. She wanted them to.

She shoved her fingers into his hair, coarser than before.

No. *Shh.* Same hair. Curly. Maybe salt and pepper instead of just pepper, but . . .

Shh.

'Should probably lock the door,' he murmured against her mouth, even as his hand crept beneath her sleep shirt.

'Why?'

He lifted his head.

She smiled and touched his face.

'I don't want Lisa seeing what she shouldn't way before she should.'

Frankie went cold. Her hand fell limply to the pillow. She got out of bed and headed for the door.

When she went right through, Charley said, 'Fancy, wait!'

Thankfully, the doorbell rang. She wished it had rung five minutes ago. Before he'd made her skin hum and her blood bubble and her lips itch. Before she'd remembered quite a bit of what she'd spent years forgetting.

She opened the door with one hand and scrubbed the other over her lips until they stopped feeling anything but raw.

'Ms Sicari?'

The woman on the stoop was in her forties, stout and blond. 'I am Ursula. From Nurses Now.'

She had a slight accent Frankie couldn't place. Russian maybe?

'Mrs Blackwell hired me.'

Last night seemed a long time away. At least several kisses ago.

'Right. Yeah.' Frankie pushed the door wider. 'Come in.'

'Hey, baby, what . . .'

Charley stopped halfway down the stairs. His hair was tousled. He wasn't wearing a shirt or shoes.

Ursula cast Frankie a glance.

'Not what it looks like,' Frankie said, but she couldn't help rubbing her lips again.

'Not my business, Ms Sicari.'

'What is your business?' Charley descended the remaining steps.

He didn't seem self-conscious to be standing half-naked in front of a stranger. But how many places had he been where shirt and shoes were optional?

'I'm a nurse, hired by your wife to help take care of you.'

'You hired a nurse?' His eyes flicked to Frankie.

'Not that—' Ursula began, and Frankie made a sharp, silencing gesture with her hand.

Could Hannah have hired the woman without informing her of Charley's unique memory issues?

'I did,' Frankie said slowly, holding Ursula's gaze.

The woman nodded.

'I don't need a nurse.'

'You have to go to radiation every day, and I have work.'

'I can get to the hospital on my own.'

'No.'

'What do you mean "no"?'

'N–O. I understand that you rarely hear the word, but I'm sure you know what it means.'

Ursula's head shifted back and forth as they spoke, like the bobble-headed dog Frankie's father had always kept in the back window of his Chevy. Frankie missed that dog. She missed her father.

He'd died of an aneurysm a year before Lisa. She'd always been glad he hadn't had to experience the loss of his only grandchild. Her mother had become fragile after the death of her husband. She forgot to eat most days. She wasted away. Losing Lisa had only accelerated the decline. She'd lasted two years before succumbing to pneumonia, but they hadn't been good years for anyone.

'I don't need a babysitter,' Charley said.

'What if I need you to have one?'

That stopped him.

'What if you drive to radiation and get sick afterward? How will you get back?'

'I'll take a cab.'

'Because cab drivers are famous for their understanding and compassion.' She didn't even bother to try and explain Uber. What would be the point?

'Huh?'

'If you're puking, no cabbie in the world is taking you anywhere. And you can't call me. I'm *working*.'

If anyone understood that rule, it was Charley Blackwell.

'What about Teddy Vexnard?' Charley asked.

He had made one friend in the few months he'd lived here and worked at the *Journal* – the sports writer, Teddy Vexnard.

Frankie lifted her hand and touched Charley's hair. 'He's dead.'

'No. I just talked to him.' Confusion flowed over his face. 'Didn't I?'

'I'll make you some coffee, yes?' Ursula clomped into the kitchen without waiting for an answer.

'What happened?' Charley asked. 'Why didn't anyone tell me?'

Teddy had died ten years after Lisa. If anyone had informed Charley, he hadn't come to the funeral.

Frankie had been there. She'd spent the entire time staring

at the door, both fearing and hoping that Charley would come through it.

'A car accident,' Frankie said. 'He fell asleep at the wheel coming back from *Monday Night Football.*'

'Hell,' Charley muttered.

'I'm sorry about Teddy. But will you give Ursula a chance? She'll be here when I'm not.'

'I'm not five,' Charley said with a pout that made him seem about five.

'Humor me.'

'Fine.'

'You wanna shower first?' she asked. There were two showers but she needed to talk to Ursula.

Charley nodded and drifted upstairs.

Frankie entered the kitchen to the blessed scent of coffee.

'Thank you.' She took out two cups, held up one with a lift of her eyebrows.

Ursula shook her head. 'I have had sufficient.'

Frankie filled her own, left the other next to the pot for Charley, then took a seat, waving Ursula into the other.

'I can't place your accent.'

'I was born in Ukraine.'

'You were a nurse there?'

'No. I am a nurse here.'

'You've dealt with patients like Charley before?'

'Like how?'

'Brain cancer. Memory issues.'

'The service would not have recommended me if I had not.'

Was that a yes? Frankie should probably call the service, though would they tell her anything if she wasn't the one paying them? She should probably talk to the one who was paying them.

'Excuse me a minute.'

Frankie's phone wasn't on the countertop, but she found it on her first glance into her purse, then stepped into the front hall where she quickly texted Hannah.

Nurse Ursula has arrived. You wanna send me her references?

Almost immediately her phone chimed.

Ursula's references, as well as several recommendations. Good ones, too.

By the time she'd given the nurse what background she had

on Charley's illness, told her the time of his radiation appointment and made sure she was familiar with Froedtert Hospital, Charley had returned, freshly showered and dressed.

'I'll just leave you two to talk while I get ready.'

The two of them eyed each other like rival street gang leaders. Frankie hoped a replay of *West Side Story* or Michael Jackson's 'Beat It' video wasn't on the agenda.

When she came downstairs, Charley was cleaning his cameras and Ursula was making scrambled eggs. They weren't talking but they weren't glaring at each other either.

'I'll be at the Greek Orthodox church,' Frankie said. 'I'll have my cell, though—'

'Don't call unless it is a bloody emergency,' Ursula quoted Frankie's earlier instructions back to her.

'I actually said an emergency with blood, but you get the drift.'

'Go.' Ursula flapped her hands. 'We will be fine. Yes, Charley?'

'Yes.' He squinted into the open back of a camera body. 'Don't worry a minute about me.'

The way he said it kind of made her worry, but after a slight hesitation – should she kiss him goodbye? Definitely not – she left.

She didn't think about Charley more than half a dozen times all day.

Frankie got some great shots of the church for her client. Then some even better ones of the local architecture, flowers growing through chain-link fences, kids riding their bikes home after school and a puppy that had chased a cat up a tree. The latter would sell like crazy on her stock site.

She hurried home, excited to show Charley.

A police cruiser was parked in front of her house.

Frankie pulled into the driveway too fast, the bottom of her Volvo scraping against the cement. She burst inside. Two police officers spoke with a visibly distraught Ursula.

'Where is he?' she demanded of the room at large.

'I only turned my back for an instant,' Ursula said. 'And he was gone.'

Charley

Fish Creek, Wisconsin. Late August, 1991

Charley drove into Fish Creek as the sun set on a Wednesday. Lisa was asleep, had been since just before they'd hit Green Bay nearly an hour ago. Up until then they'd sung grade school ditties, played the alphabet game, and the license plate game. If she hadn't fallen asleep, he might have.

He'd tried to stay another day in Milwaukee with Frankie, but she'd practically tossed him out the door.

'At this time of year you're going to be stuck in traffic for hours if you wait to leave until Thursday afternoon.'

'Don't people have jobs?'

'Not the last week of August in Door County.'

'It's going to be chaos, isn't it?'

'Which is why I wanted you to go in early June, but no. You were . . .' Her voice drifted off. 'Somewhere.'

'Everyone's somewhere.'

'But you go to more somewheres than anyone else.'

He cast her a quick glance but she was smiling. Lately, Frankie had been a little testy about his traveling. He didn't like it. He hoped it passed.

But she deserved a break and he had promised. Besides, he *wanted* to spend more time with Lisa. He wasn't just saying so. The child had charmed him from the moment she'd come out of the womb. She'd changed him.

Frankie was off to visit Irene. The last time the two of them had been together without Lisa had been before Lisa. Charley kind of felt sorry for Manhattan.

'Tell Irene hi.' He took his bag from Frankie, grabbed Lisa's hand.

His daughter smiled at him as if he were the newly risen sun. Sometimes that smile scared him. Sooner or later she was going to figure out he wasn't that great.

'Will do.' Frankie kissed him.

'Or maybe hold that hi.'

Irene already knew he wasn't that great. The last time he'd seen her, she'd told him so. Along with an admonition that if he hurt Frankie she'd do something he still thought was anatomically impossible even though Irene had insisted it was not.

Frankie took Lisa in her arms, holding on to the girl for so long and so tightly that Lisa finally squirmed and said, 'Mommy, stop.'

'Sorry.' Frankie kissed her with a big, silly smack. 'I'm just gonna miss you so much.'

'We won't be gone that long. And we'll talk to you every night.'

Charley had to smile at his daughter's parroting back to her mother exactly what her mother had said to her the night before when Lisa had been over tired and a little weepy at bedtime.

What was he going to do when she was tired and weepy? He hoped he wouldn't make things worse.

Frankie had seemed a little nervous as he and Lisa had pulled out of the drive. Her brow creased; she chewed on her lip. He nearly stopped and suggested she forget New York and come along with them. But he didn't.

Charley remembered when they'd bought the place a few years back. The three of them had walked through at least a dozen cabins on the bay. None had been right. Too big, too small, too expensive, too dumpy, too close to the water, not close enough. He thought he'd go mad. He hadn't wanted to own one house and now they were going to have two?

Then they'd found the small cottage with the brown paint, red trim, white windows.

'It looks like a gingerbread house,' Lisa had breathed, eyes wide.

The nautical themed interior had made Frankie's nose twitch. Red, white and blue in the living room – a lot of ship prints and a compass clock. The kitchen resembled a galley. The bathroom and one bedroom were covered in seashells. The master bedroom revealed a lot of fish – wallpaper, bedspread, even the sheets.

But what really sealed the deal was the mermaid room. The bedspread evoked a crystal clear ocean – turquoise with sparkles. The walls had been painted sea-foam green. Mermaids swam along the wallpaper border.

Lisa's mouth formed an 'o'. She'd turned to them and just pointed.

They had to buy the place then.

Fish Creek seemed much the same. Small enough to blink and miss it, but stuffed full of gift shops, taverns, restaurants, coffee shops and ice cream stands. What was he going to do with a seven-year-old for a week?

Being an only child, Lisa was pretty adept at amusing herself, or so Frankie had assured him. She had a bag of books, her sketchpad and box of crayons, dolls and, of course, her favorite stuffed animal, Black Kitty. There were games at the cottage, as well as VHS tapes of all her favorite movies. Frankie and Lisa spent a lot of time there every summer.

'There's mini-golf, paddle boats and bikes to rent,' Frankie had informed him. 'Also the cottage is on the bay.'

'I remember.'

'Just make sure she doesn't go swimming unless you're on the dock.'

'You bet,' he said.

As their cottage lay on the north side of Fish Creek, he left the town behind, squinting for the sign to Watchery Road. He almost missed it, the post nearly obscured by long grass and the sign hanging half off. He should probably fix that. Sure he was lame with a hammer, but how hard could it be?

'Lisa? We're here.'

She drew in a breath, tilted her head away from the window where it had been resting, and opened her eyes. For an instant he thought she might ask for her mother, but then she saw the cottage, which popped out of the trees like a magic house – not there and suddenly there. The bay spread behind it like a clear blue ocean, the sun sparkling on the water like silver sequins.

'Oh, Daddy,' she said.

His chest got tight as love for her welled up so suddenly it staggered him. How had he gone from not wanting children to adoring the one he had more than anything in his life except Frankie?

It was easy to deny what you'd never had. Impossible to remember why you had denied it once it was yours.

Within minutes they'd unloaded the car. Frankie had packed a cooler and boxes of food so they wouldn't have to hit the grocery store right away.

The rest of the day yawned in front of them. Lisa stared at

him expectantly. Charley got a little panicked. He glanced at the compass clock. Eleven thirty.

'You . . . uh . . . want lunch?'

'Yay!' She jumped into the air as if he'd asked if she wanted ice cream.

They should get ice cream!

His panic began to recede. He could do this. Piece of cake.

Maybe they should also get cake.

By evening he was exhausted. They'd eaten, twice. Rented bikes and ridden around town. Had ice cream. Swum in the bay.

Lisa was a very good swimmer. Frankie had said he could watch her from the dock, but today he had gone in too, just to be sure. He didn't like the chill. He preferred swimming in the Mediterranean, but who didn't?

Charley loaded the VHS of *Jungle Book* and soon Lisa was singing 'The Bare Necessities' to Black Kitty.

In the kitchen he poured himself a finger of Scotch – God bless his wife for packing the bottle in tight next to the orange juice – then called Hannah.

'How's he doing?'

He knew from the hitch to Hannah's sigh that the news wasn't good.

'He's not responding to the treatment as well as they'd hoped. The radiation isn't shrinking the lesions.'

'What will they try next?'

'Chemo.'

Charley frowned, took a sip of Scotch. 'Is he strong enough for that?'

'They discovered lesions in his gastrointestinal tract. If they don't shrink them he could get a blockage, which could kill him, if not outright, then with the surgery he'll need to get rid of it.'

'Sheesh.' Charley drank more Scotch.

Heath was a great guy, talented, fun and funny. Seeing him fade away was hard enough for Charley. For Hannah, it was devastating.

She tried to be strong. Not a tear where Heath could see. Charley hadn't seen one either. He'd been awed and amazed, not only by her strength but by her resilience, her energy and her patience.

She made phone calls, wrote letters and emails, read everything she could find, then trekked through all parts of DC and New York gathering anything and anyone that might help her brother.

She spoke with acupuncturists, massage therapists, herbalists, nutritionists. If Heath wasn't well enough to see them, she badgered them into coming to the apartment to see him. She brewed teas from things he could not identify, pounded ginger into a powder and sprinkled it on anything Heath might eat or drink. She created a spreadsheet so she could compare the best and the worst natural products as they pertained to chemotherapy side effects.

Charley wasn't sure how she got up every morning, but she did.

Someone had to deal with Heath's doctors, schedule his appointments, organize his meds, pay his bills, deal with their parents – idiots the both of them as far as Charley was concerned – as well as keeping her job at *National Geographic*. Which reminded him . . .

'I heard there's an opening in—'

'I quit.'

Charley sloshed Scotch on to his hand. 'Quit?'

'*National Geographic*. Ray understood.'

'I don't.'

'My aunt needs my help.'

'You're going to work at *You*?'

'You say that like I'm going to work at *Nazis R Us*.'

Charley laughed. She amused him, more than just about anyone did these days. At his age, not much was funny any more. Especially this.

'You can't leave *National Geographic*. It's your dream job.'

'I'll come back.'

He wasn't so sure.

'Things have a way of getting away from us. We think we'll do what we always meant to and then, poof, you're nearly forty and it's too late.'

'What haven't you done that you wanted to do, Charley?'

'I wasn't talking about myself.'

He'd done everything he wanted to. He'd never left a job unless the job he was leaving it for was one he wanted more. Well, except for that ill-fated time he'd spent at the *Milwaukee Journal*. He'd felt like a failure there. He *had* failed there; he'd hated it so damn much, he pretended it had never happened.

He was happy and he wanted Hannah to be happy too. He wished he could protect her from the sadness that was coming, but he couldn't.

'Just make sure you don't stay at *You* too long, OK?'

'Promise,' she said.

'I'll be in DC next week. I'll take Heath to lunch.'

'I'm sure he'd love to if he's up to it.'

A trickle of unease passed over Charley. 'That bad?'

Hannah didn't answer.

'If you need me before then, just call.'

Charley talked to Hannah every week or so, Heath about the same. He liked them. They were interesting, smart, tragic. He was captivated by their story – and it was *their* story. Heath might be dying, but Hannah was watching him do it.

Charley didn't think she knew that he photographed her nearly as much as her brother. She wouldn't like it when she saw the essay in the end. Then again, in the end, she wasn't going to like much.

However, the world needed to see not only the face of AIDS but the faces of those left behind because of it.

'I'll be fine,' Hannah said. 'See you next week.'

Charley noticed that she didn't say *we'll* be fine. Because *they* wouldn't be. While Hannah and Charley put on a hopeful face for Heath, his treatments weren't working and his options were nearly as exhausted as he was. Even the new AIDS drug they'd been promised would be available soon would be pointless for Heath. He'd needed it months ago.

For how many would any advancements arrive too late?

Charley saw an image of hundreds of pills pouring from the sky and on to a graveyard. He got a little chill. He could create that photograph, superimpose one shot over the other. Usually he disdained artsy stuff like that, but it might be the perfect way to get people first to look and then to *see*. A photograph of a beautiful, dying young man . . . not so much.

Charley finished his Scotch while he sketched the idea on a notepad. As if he'd ever forget that image, but better safe than sorry.

Suddenly his head lifted. When had Lisa stopped singing? Why was it so quiet in the other room?

He glanced at the wall clock. When had it gotten to be ten o'clock?

Had he locked the front door? Did Lisa know how to open it? Would she leave the cottage without telling him?

Charley stood up so fast his chair tilted, then landed back on four legs with a *thunk*. He barely heard it over the thunder of his heart.

The movie was done, the screen full of snow.

Lisa lay asleep on the couch, her head resting on Black Kitty.

The relief that filled Charley was staggering. He leaned against the wall and waited for his heart failure to pass. It took longer than he thought it would.

For the next several days Charley didn't let Lisa out of his line of sight, which wasn't easy. Seven-year-olds moved damn quick. They lost interest in activities even quicker. They changed directions like a goldfish – flit this way, then that. They were slippery too, like a goldfish, hard to get a grip on when in motion.

They spent a morning walking through Peninsula State Park. Lisa chattered all the way, telling him about school and friends and camp. Her take on life was enchanting, her fascination with everything equally so.

'What's this flower?' She yanked handfuls of purple, yellow and white wildflowers from the ground.

Probably not kosher, but too late now.

'I'm not sure. Let's call them Lisa's.'

She giggled and put a purple one behind each ear. Purple appeared to be her favorite color this week. She changed like the wind. That morning he'd thought they would never leave the house while she decided if she should wear her purple unicorn T-shirt with white shorts or black. Charley had nearly called Heath for his advice.

Lisa motioned for Charley to kneel and she stuck a few flowers into his curls. Her hands smelled both spicy and sweet. She had pollen on her nose.

She dropped the remainder of her stolen booty and ran to the nearest tree, setting her palm on the massive trunk. 'What kind of tree?'

'Pine?'

There were a lot of trees, one of them *had* to be a pine. Even in the summer the place smelled like Christmas – dusty Christmas, but still.

They had a picnic on a beach of white sand, then waded in the water.

'Oh!' Lisa pointed to a sky so blue Charley got a brain-pain staring into it.

'That's an eagle.' He lifted his camera and fired a few shots.

They saw that eagle, or maybe another one, several more times that day. The size of the bird, the size of some of the trees made Charley feel insignificant. Nature was like that.

He'd thought he would get some work done – he was eons behind in his expense accounts – after she fell asleep each night. But when Lisa's eyes closed, so did Charley's. A day with his daughter, joyous as it was, meant he couldn't stay awake. How did Frankie manage?

He asked her when she called on their last night.

'Because I'm marvelous.'

Frankie sounded happy, relaxed and for a second Charley was jealous that time with anyone but him could make her so. Stupid: time with him was fleeting and he had no one to blame but himself.

'I'm planning to leave here around ten tomorrow,' he said. 'We'll drive right to the airport to pick you up.'

'What if I'm delayed?'

'We'll have ice cream.'

'How many times have you had ice cream this week?'

'Once a day and twice on Sunday.'

'Funny.'

She thought he was kidding. Charley was glad he hadn't mentioned the three times they'd had ice cream on Saturday.

'She's going to be a handful when I get her back.'

'Sorry.'

'Don't be. She should have time with her father.'

Charley bristled at the old argument over broken promises. He'd made good on them this week. Hadn't he?

'See you tomorrow,' Frankie said.

However, in the morning getting his daughter into the car proved difficult.

'I don't wanna go. I wanna swim and then have ice cream. I wanna live here forever, with you.'

Charley had enjoyed himself, though he'd hit *cannot wait to get out of here* two days ago. The idea of living at this cottage forever made his head ache. Probably because he was grinding his teeth.

'We can get ice cream on the way out of town.'

Was that bribery? Oh well.

'Swimming first!'

'We have to pick up Mommy at the airport. You don't want her to be sitting there all alone, do you?'

'Don't care.'

He should count himself lucky that they hadn't had a battle of wills before now. According to Frankie, she and Lisa battled daily. Also, according to Frankie, he could not let Lisa win. Once lost, parental respect was very difficult to get back.

'Make sure everything's out of your room. Don't wanna leave anything behind. Especially Black Kitty, right?'

Confusion and a touch of fear at the thought of a lost Black Kitty flickered in eyes so like her mother's they surprised Charley every time he saw them. She scooted off to her room without another word.

Charley dusted off his hands. 'And that, my friends, is that.'

Distraction. Misdirection. Bribery. He had parenthood down.

Charley loaded what was left in the refrigerator into the cooler and fewer shopping bags than they'd used coming in.

Lisa was singing in her room, presumably to Black Kitty, so Charley dragged the bags, cooler and his suitcase to the car.

When he turned he caught sight of a barge in the bay. A dark stain spread out behind the flat boat like blood. Was it leaking oil?

He snatched his camera from the bag in the back seat, attached a 500-millimeter telephoto lens to the body and moved to the side of the house, lifting the viewfinder to his eye.

If that wasn't oil, it was something equally un-ecological.

Charley took pictures until the barge was out of sight, headed for Lake Michigan.

He had a few shots left on the roll, so he snapped the steps leading from the cabin to the dock. The ivy had grown wild and wound through several cracks in the graying wood. More of a Frankie shot; she would like it.

He scanned the area for anything else to photograph. What was that floating off the edge of the dock?

Charley zoomed in on something purple and out of place.

Why was Lisa's swimming suit in the water?

He zoomed in closer, then he dropped the camera and ran.

Frankie

'Is there anywhere you can think of that he might go?' Officer Andalaro asked.

He was the older of the two – graying as well as balding, his stomach larger than a police officer's should probably be. The second – Randolph – appeared fresh out of high school. As buff as Andalaro was not, dark hair and lots of it, dark eyes that remained intent on Frankie as if he were assessing her every word. She felt guilty and she wasn't sure why.

Unless it was because she'd left Charley behind and now he was gone.

'No,' Frankie answered. 'He . . . well . . .' She glanced at Ursula. 'Did you tell them about his condition?'

'He thinks it's the eighties.' Randolph said it as if he didn't believe it.

Frankie could relate.

'He had one close friend when he lived here,' she continued. 'That friend is dead.'

'He knows this?' Andalaro asked.

'I told him, yes.' But did he remember? 'I'll call Teddy's wife.' She hoped the number was still the same.

Three minutes later she ended the call. 'Teddy's widow still lives in the same house. No sign of Charley. If she sees him or hears from him, she'll let me know.'

'Anyone else you can think of?' Andalaro scribbled something in a notebook.

Frankie shook her head. Where would he go? Why would he go?

'What happened?' she asked Ursula.

'We went to radiation. He seemed fine. He laid on the couch.' She spread her hands. 'Then he was not on the couch.'

'His cell phone!' Frankie pulled out hers and hit Charley's number.

His phone immediately began to ring from where it had either been left or fallen under the coffee table.

'Shit!' Frankie punched the *off* button. If the phone was here, they couldn't even track the thing and find him that way.

'You did not see him at the church?' Ursula asked.

'No.' But she'd left the church, wandered the neighborhood. 'I'll go back.'

'We'll drive around,' Andalaro said. 'And put the word out to the other officers both here and near the Greek Orthodox church.'

'Thank you. What happens if we don't . . .' Frankie's throat suddenly closed, and she had to swallow, then clear her throat before she could continue. 'If we don't find him soon?'

'We'll check the hospitals and the mo—' Randolph paused when Andalaro cut him a glare.

'The morgue,' Frankie finished.

'Sorry, ma'am.'

'No. We have to make sure.'

The officers left. The house seemed so quiet once they'd gone.

'Would you like me to stay in case he returns?' Ursula held herself stiff, as if she expected a blow – or a firing.

'Please.' Frankie set her hand on the woman's arm. 'It's not your fault. He's . . .' Frankie's voice drifted off. She didn't know what Charley was, beyond gone.

As the shadows lengthened and night fell, Frankie drove to the Greek Orthodox church. The floodlights went on as she approached, reflecting in the pool of water out front, turning the bright white walls a soothing shade of peach. Frankie was anything but soothed.

The church was empty except for a custodian. He had not seen a man fitting Charley's description.

She drove around the area, observed a police car doing the same. She saw no sign of Charley. Was he lost and wandering?

After a half-hour of wandering herself, Frankie returned home and told Ursula to do the same. 'I'll let you know when I find him.' Frankie opened the door.

'And if you want me to come back.'

'Yes,' Frankie agreed, though that would be up to Hannah.

Hannah. Hell. Probably should have called her before now.

Prior to making that call, Frankie poured herself a huge glass of Cabernet.

'I thought you were going to text me,' Hannah answered in lieu of 'hello'.

'This isn't a text conversation.'

'Is he all right?'

'I don't know.'

'How can you not know?' Hannah demanded. 'Where is he?'

'Also don't know.'

'You lost him? Already?'

'Not lost.' Frankie gulped wine. 'Exactly.'

'What, exactly?'

'He ran off on the nurse.'

'When was this?'

'After his radiation. Maybe three o'clock.'

'And you're just telling me now?'

'We were busy trying to find him, and besides, what were you going to do?'

'Good point.'

Frankie blinked. Had Hannah agreed with her? There was a first.

'I'll assume, since you're not a moron, that you've contacted the police, hospitals and morgues.'

'Since I'm not a moron,' Frankie agreed dryly. 'Yes.'

'What next?'

'We keep searching. Any ideas where he might be?'

'In Milwaukee? Not.'

'Where would he go if he were in DC?' Perhaps he'd head to the same type of place here.

Silence spread over the line.

'Hannah?' Frankie said after a minute.

'Sorry, I . . . uh . . .' Silence again.

What was her problem? Besides the dying husband who'd forgotten her existence.

'Sometimes when he needs to think, he visits Heath.'

'Heath,' Frankie repeated. 'Your dead brother?'

'Who else?'

Frankie could think of a lot of people to visit who weren't dead, but she decided to zip it.

'I doubt he'd hop a plane to DC to visit the grave of someone he no longer remembers.'

Hannah drew in a sharp breath.

'What?' Frankie asked. 'You think of something?'

'No.' Hannah's voice sounded shaky, watery.

'Are you crying?'

'No.'

Except she still sounded like she was.

'What is it?' Frankie asked.

Hannah took several seconds to answer. 'It hadn't occurred to me that Charley wouldn't remember Heath. Stupid. I know.'

'You seem more upset about his not remembering your brother than you were about his not remembering you.'

'Maybe I am,' she said, as if just realizing it herself. 'Hardly anyone remembers Heath these days except Charley and me.' She sniffed. 'And now it's just me.'

'I'm sure more people remember him than you. What about your parents?'

'They've chosen to pretend he never existed. They don't speak of him. If I do, they change the subject or leave the room.'

Frankie heard echoes of herself. She did not speak of Lisa to anyone. It hurt too much.

'The only one who talked about him with me, who remembered him out loud, was Charley.'

She was speaking about Charley as if he were dead too, and perhaps to her he was.

'I'm sorry,' Frankie said. Hannah had obviously adored her brother; she mourned him still. She'd never get over his loss.

They had more in common than a husband.

'The pictures Charley took for the AIDS essay will keep your brother's memory alive forever.'

And why was she trying to make Hannah feel better? It was that essay that had brought Charley and Hannah together, bonded them over their losses, made them closer than Frankie and Charley could ever be again. Or so she had thought.

'You're right.' Hannah was all business once more. 'Thanks.'

The word was grudging, but Frankie understood. They were doing their best to get along. What choice did they have? But neither one of them had to like it.

'Speaking of pictures, did you get what I sent?' Hannah asked.

Frankie had forgotten Hannah was sending the photo of Lisa. She spied a FedEx envelope on the hall table.

'I did.' She picked it up, looked inside, placed the photo safely in a drawer to be stared at later.

'Good. You'll let me know as soon as you find him?'

'Of course.'

'Have you gone to . . . uh . . . where Lisa is?'

'Heaven?' Frankie asked sarcastically.

An exasperated huff traveled across the miles. 'Maybe Charley went to talk to her the way he talks to Heath.'

'He doesn't remember Lisa's dead.'

'Right. But maybe . . .'

'No.' Frankie's gaze went to the lilac-shaded urn on the middle shelf of her glass curio cabinet in the hall.

'OK. Just thought I'd—'

Frankie hung up.

She crossed the room, opened the cabinet, reached in and touched the smooth, cool side of the urn. 'Hi, sweetie. Seen Daddy?'

As expected, no answer was forthcoming.

Frankie's phone chimed with a text. She dived for the device, which she'd left next to the FedEx envelope. She didn't realize that she'd been hoping the text was from Charley until disappointment flooded her when she saw it was from Hannah.

His phone is here. How could he text you? Frankie thought.

Would he text her even if he had his phone? Texting was so post-1989.

Frankie opened Hannah's text.

I checked his credit card. He rented a car. I called the place and, according to them, he didn't say where he was going.

She'd also texted the license plate number, make and model of the car he'd rented.

Frankie was a little impressed with Hannah's detective skills. She informed the police of the new development.

'Excellent, ma'am.' Randolph sounded pretty excited. 'We'll be able to trace that car.'

'Really?'

Considering the thousands of cars on the road, the hundreds of directions he could have gone, she had her doubts.

'You'd be surprised what we can do. We'll let you know as soon as we have any news.'

It wasn't until she hung up that it occurred to Frankie that they should probably be informing Hannah.

She didn't sleep well, hoping for a phone call, listening for the knock on the front door that never came. Her bed smelled like Charley – basil and a bright blue sky. She took the pillow he'd slept on and threw it across the room.

Finally, in the darkest hour she slept, only to come awake with a gasp, pulling herself out of a dream that seemed very real.

Charley at the cottage in Door County, sitting on the dock, staring into the water that reflected a shimmering, silver full moon.

Frankie got out of bed, pulled back the bedroom curtains and stared at the exact same moon. Would he go to Door County? Why? Neither one of them had been there since . . .

In the divorce, she'd gotten the house; he'd gotten the cottage. She'd wanted nothing to do with the place ever again. He hadn't either but someone had to take the thing. Did he still own that cursed bit of real estate? She had no idea.

What did it matter? Charley would think that he did.

She began to pull on her clothes, pack a bag. The more she thought about it the more convinced she became that he was there. Wouldn't hurt to take a drive. It wasn't like she was going back to sleep. Frankie got in the car and headed north.

She wasn't one to believe in premonitions or prophesies. She had no use for mediums or tarot or psychics. If there were ghosts, wouldn't Lisa be one? And if she were, wouldn't she have appeared to Frankie by now? She hadn't, so it followed that there were no ghosts. First you were and then you were not. End of story.

Frankie shivered and turned on the heat.

Three hours later as the sun peeked over the horizon, Frankie rolled into Fish Creek. The place was deserted. Of course, who would be walking the streets of downtown Fish Creek at sunrise? Maybe a senior citizen. Like her.

She was close enough to Social Security to smell it. Weird how she still felt like she was thirty-ish. Or maybe not so weird. The last time she'd felt alive had been when her daughter was. When Charley had still been Her Charley and Lisa's Charley too.

She left the sleepy morning town behind, speeding down the two-lane road. Her sense of urgency she attributed to the fact that if Charley weren't here, she'd only have to turn right around and head home. But really, it was something more.

She had refused to come to Fish Creek then, refused to see the place where her baby had died. The sight of it would have ended her, and she'd been on the edge of that already. But suddenly she wanted to see; she needed to.

If she hadn't remembered that the turn lay across from a mile marker, she would have missed it. The path was overgrown, the battered sign to Watchery Road long gone.

The gravel churned up enough dust to coat the front of her car, the grinding sound loud in the pink-gray light of dawn.

Charley's rent-a-Chrysler sat in front of the house.

Frankie set her hand on her chest. She hadn't realized until just that minute how her heart had been pounding so hard it hurt.

She picked up her phone, planning to call the police, then Hannah, but she set it back down. Maybe she'd better lay eyes on him first.

She approached the house, which had once resembled a place Hansel and Gretel might bake a witch and now resembled a faded, overgrown place Hansel and Gretel might bake a witch, and tapped on the front door.

No one answered. He was probably asleep.

She put her hand on the knob, gave it a twist. The door opened, so she walked right in.

The decor hadn't changed in over twenty years. What had been cute but a bit tacky then appeared overtired now, the white walls yellowing, the blue sofa fraying, the red bordered wallpaper peeling.

Charley's camera bag sat on the kitchen table. He was definitely here, or had been, though she'd never known him to leave those cameras behind. However, when she walked through the place, he wasn't there.

Neither was Lisa's mermaid room. Someone had stripped it, changed everything to orange and white. The clash with how it had been was startling. Frankie wasn't sure if that made her sad or glad. Right now she couldn't really think past the panic of being here, of finding Charley.

Frankie's heart started to hurt again.

Slowly she walked to the patio door and stepped outside. The scent of fish and fresh water, the never-ending lap of the waves sent her back so fast she swayed.

Mommy, watch me!

Splash!

I'm a fish! I'm a dogfish! See me paddle?

'God,' Frankie muttered, an expletive and a prayer.

The sun hadn't risen past the towering pines; the bay still lay in shadow. There was just enough light for Frankie to distinguish the outline of a man sitting on the dock.

She wanted to leave; she wanted to run. Instead, she descended the rickety wooden steps to bay level, then walked across an equally rickety dock and sat at Charley's side.

'Hi.' His gaze didn't stray from the cool blue water.

'Hi.'

'Where's Lisa?' he asked.

Charley

Fish Creek, Wisconsin. Late August, 1991

Charley was still performing CPR three hours later when they found him. The paramedics had to drag him off the still, pale, cold body of his daughter.

He was hoarse from shouting, 'Help! Help us!' in between the breaths through tiny blue lips.

It was a gorgeous day in the neighborhood and all the neighbors were gone. A perfect time for tooling around town – if your daughter hadn't drowned.

Charley hadn't done CPR since Vietnam but the procedure came back to him – how many breaths, how many compressions.

CPR didn't work any better now than it had then.

'She's too cold,' he whispered.

'Sir?' asked the young police officer assigned to keep him out of everyone's way.

The paramedics had resumed CPR. All for show, he knew. His daughter hadn't breathed in hours. She wasn't going to start.

'She needs a blanket.'

Inane. She needed nothing any more. One part of him knew this. Another part was desperate that Lisa be kept warm.

As if he'd heard Charley's words, his thoughts, one of the paramedics pulled a blanket from his bag. He draped it over Lisa – head to toe.

'She can't breathe,' Charley said.

His babysitter, whose red hair glinted orange in the midday sun, patted Charley's shoulder. 'Is there someone I should call?'

Charley's lips formed the word *Fancy* but nothing came out.

'Your wife? Your family? A friend.'

'No,' Charley managed. If anyone called Fancy, it would be him.

The neighbors hung about in their backyards staring. Where had they been when he needed them?

Suddenly he couldn't stand on that dock another second. He walked over to the Lisa-shaped blanket.

The paramedics glanced up, their surprise replaced by unease. How many people lost their shit right about now?

'I'm sorry,' the female paramedic said. 'We did everything we could.'

Charley nodded, then bent and lifted Lisa into his arms.

'Sir, you can't . . .' The male paramedic tried to take her back.

Charley gave him a look that had the man retreating a step. Charley turned.

The red-headed cop stood in his way. 'Sir, you can't.'

'I shouldn't leave her alone.'

All three of them exchanged glances. He could read their minds.

Leaving her alone was where this all began.

'Let me take her.' The woman touched his arm. 'I promise I won't leave her alone.'

'I . . .' Charley began, then he lost his thought. He'd been about to do something. What was it?

In his arms, Lisa was so much heavier than he could ever remember her being. Still damp from the water, cold and—

'Floppy,' he said.

The three exchanged glances again as a phone began to ring inside the cottage.

'That keeps ringing,' the officer said. 'Someone should probably answer.'

Everyone stared at Charley. Apparently that someone was him.

The female paramedic stepped forward and took Lisa from him. He could have held on, but he didn't. The bundle in his arms didn't feel like his daughter. Maybe it wasn't.

Hope fluttered and he pulled the blanket away from the face.

From the neighborly onlookers came a gasp, a cry.

He dropped the blanket back where it had been. The face, both still and slack, had resembled Lisa enough to give him nightmares for the rest of his life.

Charley ran up the steps and into the house. Then he stood in the living room. What was he supposed to do?

The phone started ringing again.

Right. The phone.

He picked it up, put it to his ear. Listened.

'Hello? Who's there? Is someone there?'

'Fancy,' Charley said.

'Charley, thank God. Why are you still at the cottage?'

'Lisa . . .' he began, and then he couldn't go on.

'You two were supposed to pick me up at the airport. What happened?'

'She went swimming.'

Frankie went silent but not for long. 'You let me sit at the airport, terrified you'd had a car accident and died, because Lisa wanted to go swimming?' Her voice rose in both volume and pitch. 'I've told you before, you can't let her do anything she wants. You're the adult. She's the child.'

'She'll always be a child,' Charley whispered.

'What is wrong with you? Put the kid in the car and come home.'

'Fancy, please. I – I can't.'

'Why not?'

'They took her.'

'Charley,' Frankie said. 'You're scaring me.'

Charley knew he should tell her, but he didn't know how. He stood with the phone to his ear listening to his wife call his name with varying degrees of fear and anger, until the red-headed cop took it gently from his hand, pushed him into a chair and told her for him.

Charley heard Frankie's scream all the way across the room.

'Is there someone I can call for you?' the officer asked when she'd wound down. He waited a few seconds. 'Ma'am?' He pulled the phone away from his ear. 'She hung up.'

Charley nodded.

'She shouldn't be alone,' the young man said.

He was right. Why hadn't Charley thought of it?

Because he was thoughtless, clueless – and because of that, now he was childless.

Charley got to his feet. Picked up his keys, headed for the door.

The officer put his hand on Charley's chest. 'Where do you think you're going?'

'To my wife.'

'You have to make a statement. There'll be questions. A lot of them. Probably hours' worth. I'm sorry.' He took the keys out of Charley's hand.

'What about Fancy?'

For an instant the young man's face flickered confusion, then it cleared. 'Your wife's name is Fancy?'

Charley nodded, too tired to explain.

'Is there someone you can call? Someone who can go to your house and be with her until you can be?'

Frankie would want Irene, but it would take Irene longer to get there than it would take Charley. Maybe. Depending on the questions, and probably his answers.

'Does she have family?' the officer prompted.

Frankie's mother had become thin and frail since her husband had died. Her skin paper fine, her voice whisper-soft, she was no longer the woman she had been. Frankie had said often enough that she now felt more the mother than the child.

Would having her mother at her side only make things worse? Really, how could things get worse?

He should have known better than to even think such a question.

'Anyone right now is better than no one,' the officer continued. 'Trust me.'

What choice did Charley have?

He called Frankie's mother, and then he called Irene. Neither conversation was one he cared to repeat in his lifetime. But, bright side, he wouldn't have to since he was fresh out of children.

The police did have questions. He didn't have a lot of answers, or at least any worth giving.

He didn't know why she'd gone swimming without him. She knew better.

Yes, she could swim. No, she didn't have any medical conditions.

He hadn't left her alone near the water. He'd left her in the house.

How long? Hard to say. How long did it take a seven-year-old to die?

By the time the police were satisfied – or as satisfied as they'd get until the autopsy results came back – it was too late to drive home.

Charley didn't even try to sleep. He sat on the sofa, listened to the quiet. Couldn't stand it, went outside.

The lap of the water drew him down the stairs, across the dock. When the sun came up he still sat on the edge, staring at the water, trying to figure out how something so peaceful could be so deadly.

Then he got in the car and drove home. Or he must have, because several hours later he pulled into the driveway. He had no memory of what he'd done between Fish Creek and Whitefish Bay. If only he could erase the memory of yesterday just the same.

At the house, he paused with his hand on the doorknob. Would Frankie scream, rant, rave, throw things? Or had she curled up into a ball and gone silent? Which would be worse?

He didn't know.

The temptation to get into the car and drive until he was anywhere but here was strong, but in the end he opened the door.

Frankie's mother slept on the couch.

Frankie stood in the hall. She hadn't slept. Her brilliant green eyes were dull; the auburn streaks in her hair appeared as faded as her face. Her T-shirt and pajama pants were rumpled and stained. Even her bare feet were dirty. She smelled stale; everything did.

He had done that to her. He'd never forgive himself. He shouldn't. He did not deserve forgiveness, though he wanted it very badly.

'She—' he began.

'Don't.'

'Don't?' he repeated.

'She's gone. We lost her.'

I lost her.

'I can't . . . I don't . . .' She swallowed. 'I don't want to hear how, or why, or when. I just want . . . I just want . . .' Her eyes filled.

'What do you want, Fancy?'

She closed her eyes. One tear shimmered on the edge of her eyelashes, then fell, tumbling through the air like a sunbeam in slow motion until it hit the floor and disappeared.

'I just want her back,' Frankie said, then she walked past him up the stairs, went into their room and closed the door.

If he'd thought he'd been alone the night before, in that damp, dark cottage that still smelled of Lisa, or sitting on the dock, staring into the water that had taken her life, he'd been wrong. Alone was standing in your own home as the love of your life walked away, never once touching you at all.

Over the next week, the non-touching continued. Frankie made it into an art.

Handing him a plate of food, or a cup of coffee, avoiding even a brush of fingertips. Passing in the hall or on the stairs, dancing sideways to avoid even the most casual touch. Where once they'd slept in each other's arms, now the invisible divide between them was cavernous. If he attempted to cross it, he would fall and fall and fall.

He dreamed sometimes of just that – reaching for her, his arms closing on nothing, his foot slipping, his body glancing off one side of a cliff, then the other as he hurtled toward the sharp rocks that lay beneath. Most mornings he would have welcomed it.

Because in the mornings when they awoke, for just an instant, Frankie would stare at him the way she always used to. Like the world lay in his eyes, like he'd made the sun shine, the birds sing, the flowers bloom. Then she would remember and the Frankie he adored would be gone. He had no idea what to say to the stranger that peered out at him through her eyes.

If it hadn't been for Irene, who'd arrived an hour after Charley and taken over, he had no idea what they would have done. Perhaps sat in the house and not-touched each other for the rest of their lives.

Irene appeared exactly the same as she had the first day they'd met, on a visit to New York not long after Frankie's college graduation. Irene was short, maybe five-one, but straight and slim and ballsy. Whenever Charley saw her it took him several minutes to adjust to the fact that she wasn't the five-eleven he imagined her to be. She had the same haircut – short and to the point.

Irene had never married. Probably good because didn't sharks eat their mates, or maybe it was their young? And Irene was a shark – from the tips of her no-doubt hooved heels to the top of her too-black-to-be-natural head. The only softness in Irene Pasternak could be found in her brown eyes when she saw her best friend.

Irene walked in and folded Frankie into a hug that made Charley so jealous he could taste it, even stronger than the acid he'd been tasting at the back of his throat since he'd seen that purple swimming suit just floating, floating, floating . . .

There were so many things to attend to and neither Frankie nor Charley had a clue. Irene did everything. All they had to do was show up.

Unfortunately, what they had to show up to was Lisa's funeral.

'I don't want one.' Frankie sat at the kitchen table, a cup of coffee – all that seemed to pass her lips lately – between her hands.

'One what?' Irene had her head in the refrigerator, moving the casseroles already inside around so she could fit today's neighborhood offerings in too.

Frankie's mother had gone home once Irene had arrived. The silent tears that had run down her face nearly every waking hour had been too much for any of them to take. Irene had called a cousin to stay with her.

'A funeral,' Frankie continued. 'I don't think I can . . .'

Charley, also at the table, tried to take her hand.

She picked up her coffee and leaned back in her chair, out of his reach. 'I don't think I can manage a funeral.'

'You don't have to, *bubala*. That's why I'm here.'

'I mean I don't think I can manage to sit in a room with her. I can't look at . . . I can't see her like . . .'

'You want the casket closed?' Irene shut the refrigerator. 'Just let me know what you want.'

'I want her here. Breathing.'

Irene cast Charley a quick, concerned glance. Not concern for him. While Irene hadn't castrated him yet, he knew it was only a matter of time.

'Fancy,' he began, and she stood and walked out of the room.

When she wasn't not-touching him, she was not-seeing him
by leaving wherever he was. He deserved it, but that didn't make
it any easier to take.

Irene sighed. 'Do you think cremation would upset her less or
more?'

'I don't know.'

He had no idea what Frankie wanted besides the one thing
she could not have.

The autopsy results had come back. Lisa had died from water
in her lungs. No explanation as to why she had drowned in a
place she had swum without any problem three-dozen times
before. No bump on the head, no stray rope tangled around her
legs or weeds tangled around her feet. Maybe she'd had a cramp.
Probably she'd had a cramp, but they'd never know, and what did
it matter?

Shit happened, and this week it had happened to them.

'Do we have to have a funeral?' Charley asked. He didn't see
the point either.

'I don't think it would be good for Frankie not to,' Irene said.
'She's having a hard enough time accepting this as it is.'

'She shouldn't have to accept the death of her child.'

'She shouldn't,' Irene agreed. 'But she has to or else she'll never
move on. Funerals are the end of the end. Without one, I worry
she'll just keep waiting for Lisa to come back.'

'That's nuts.'

'Is it? What mother wouldn't grasp at any and all possibilities?'

'Even when the possibility that Lisa isn't dead is an impossibility?'

'Even when.' Irene crossed her arms over her chest.

'She needs to see the body,' Charley said.

Irene flinched.

'Or not.'

'No.' Irene's brow crinkled, her painted peach lips tightened.
'You might be right.'

Or he might not be. Who knew?

'I'll talk to her.' Irene left the room.

Charley listened to their voices rise and fall.

Eventually Irene came back downstairs. 'She'll go.'

Hope flickered. Would seeing Lisa allow Frankie to heal? Once
she healed, could he? Right now he felt as if he'd have a hole
in his chest that ached and bled every second for the rest of his

life. He couldn't imagine what Frankie felt like. He wished she'd talk to him like she used to, but she wasn't talking to anyone, even Irene.

'You want me to drive you?' Charley asked.

'Oh, I'm not going.'

'What? Why?'

'This is your responsibility,' Irene said, and he knew she wasn't just talking about driving Frankie to see Lisa.

Two hours later, Frankie and Charley stood in the preparation room at the funeral home.

'Whenever you're ready, Mrs Blackwell.' Josiah Duval, funeral director, laid his hand on the sheet that covered the Lisa-shaped lump on the table.

Frankie swallowed, nodded.

Duval glanced at Charley, perhaps waiting for him to put his arm around his wife, at the least take her hand, but he didn't. He'd tried so many times over the past week and been rebuffed. He'd give her the space she seemed to need. It was the least he could do.

The man frowned, waited a little longer, and when Charley didn't move, he lifted the sheet.

Frankie let out a small sound, not a cry, more of a moan.

Lisa looked better than she had the last time Charley had seen her. Her lips were no longer blue but she still appeared very dead.

Frankie touched their daughter's cheek gently, the way Charley wanted her to touch him. Then her eyes rolled back and her knees buckled.

Charley caught her before she hit the floor.

When she came around a few seconds later, she said in a completely rational voice, 'I wanna be sedated.'

'I'll make it happen,' Charley promised.

It wasn't as difficult as he thought. One call to her doctor, and the Valium was waiting an hour later.

Frankie started popping them as soon as she got them in her hand.

'Don't you think she should be present for this?' Irene asked as they stood in the receiving line a few days later.

At the front of a room stuffed with flowers sat the purple urn that held Lisa. Charley had made the executive decision on cremation almost immediately after the fainting.

'I think she should do whatever she has to do to get through this. We all should.'

Irene narrowed her eyes.

'What?'

'Nothing,' she said, but he caught her studying him at odd moments for the rest of that day.

Hundreds attended the funeral. The parents and grandparents of Lisa's classmates. The staff and administration at her school. Frankie's colleagues from the *Journal*. Their neighbors. The Waz and his wife flew in from Minnesota. So many flowers arrived that the attendants at the funeral home rotated the displays every hour.

Charley thought he might gag on the sweet scent of chrysanthemums. Ever after it would make him remember a day he immediately and always wanted to forget.

Irene had managed to scare up a pastor to perform the eulogy. The priest who'd performed Peter Sicari's funeral service had refused to come. Not only had Frankie and Charley not been married in the church, but Lisa had not been baptized Catholic. Lisa had not been baptized at all.

'Do you think she's in hell?' Frankie asked, her voice robotic.

The first-grade teacher whose hand she'd just shaken cast a wide-eyed glance at Charley and scurried on.

'There is no hell, honey.' Irene patted Frankie's arm.

'Just because the Jews don't believe in hell doesn't mean it doesn't exist.' Frankie's mom sniffed. 'I told you to raise her in the Church.'

Charley's fingers curled into his palms. But he couldn't punch a frail old woman.

'Just because the Catholics believe in hell doesn't mean it does exist,' Irene countered.

Lately, Charley liked Irene a whole lot better than he ever thought he could.

'Purgatory?' Frankie asked.

'Nope,' Irene said cheerfully.

'Then where is she?' Frankie cried out.

Everyone in the room froze, staring at her as if they were afraid she'd throw herself into the coffin with her child. Luckily there wasn't one.

Charley approved of the urn decision more and more as time went on.

The pastor came over and led Frankie off, murmuring words only Frankie could hear. Whatever they were, they seemed to work. Frankie sat in the front row and stopped asking questions.

The day was interminable. After the long, winding line of mourners came the service. Considering the pastor hadn't known Lisa, he did an admirable job eulogizing her.

'Lisa loved sunshine, peaches, purple, her mommy, her daddy and Black Kitty. Though those of us left behind mourn, she is in a better place.'

Frankie raised her hand.

Irene drew her arm back down.

The pastor continued as if he hadn't seen. Everyone pretended they hadn't either.

The luncheon at a nearby restaurant was packed. Both Charley and Irene tried to get Frankie to consume something other than coffee. She accepted the plate he brought her with a vague smile, moved her food around it, then appeared confused when he pointed out she hadn't eaten anything.

'I did. See?' She indicated the hole in the center of the plate.

Charley's eyes burned. That was Lisa's classic trick for avoiding anything she didn't want to eat – mostly green beans or rice of any type.

At last it was over and they went home. All three of them fell into bed.

Days passed, weeks, though he wasn't sure how. Time blended together. Charley was exhausted. Every time he closed his eyes he heard Lisa, saw Lisa. He would jerk awake and swear he could smell Lisa. Would that ever end? Did he want it to? When there came a day that he couldn't remember the sound of his daughter's voice, the tilt of her smile, would she be truly and forever dead?

She *was* truly and forever dead. Because of him.

Frankie breathed in and then out, slow and steady. She was asleep.

Charley slid his hand across the great divide, linking their fingers together.

She pulled them apart. Even in sleep she could not bear to touch him.

The bright light of the moon illuminated her face, the silver track of a single tear traced downward from her eye, across her cheek before disappearing into her hair.

He watched her all night; he couldn't help himself. He was afraid he might not have another chance.

She woke with the dawn, turning toward him with a smile. Then her eyes opened, the green so bright he was dazzled by it. An instant later they dulled and she sat up, reaching for the Valium on the nightstand.

'Don't,' Charley said.

'Do.' She picked up the bottle.

'Shouldn't you . . .?' he began.

'No.' She swallowed the pill dry.

'You can't take those forever, Fancy.'

'Wanna bet?'

The doctor would cut her off, eventually. Why didn't he just let the doctor do so?

Because she was his wife. He should take care of her. Or at least try.

She sat on the side of the bed, shoulders slumped, hair tangled around her face. 'I need them.'

'Why can't you need me?' He hadn't meant to say that out loud, but too late now.

'I did.'

Past tense. That hole in his heart seemed to tear deeper, wider; it bled faster. He even put his hand to his chest, half expecting his palm to come away red.

'I needed you to keep her safe, and you didn't.'

He grunted with the force of that blow.

'You never wanted her.'

He blinked. 'That's not—'

'Don't tell me it isn't true!' She lurched to her feet, took a few steps away, spun. Her eyes were both dull and wild. 'You told me to get an abortion.'

'Things changed. I changed. The minute I saw her I . . .' His voice broke. He reached out, needing her to take his hand, then take everything back.

She did not.

He was never sure how he'd ended up on that plane to DC.

All he knew was that they should be coming together. Instead, they were falling apart.

Hannah

Washington DC. September, 1991

Charley didn't show up in a week or so like he'd said he would.

Hannah didn't notice right away because she'd started work at *You*, and while she'd been working at a magazine for a while now, every magazine was different, and she had a lot to figure out.

Add to that Heath's continuing deterioration, faster than seemed possible for a week, and Hannah wasn't thinking about Charley. Probably a first since she'd met him. When she did realize he hadn't shown up, hadn't called, she called him.

Straight to voicemail.

He'd probably gotten a great assignment and left the country. No reason to be worried. He wasn't hers to worry over. No reason to be annoyed that he hadn't let her know, for exactly the same reason.

She waited a few more days, and then she got both worried and annoyed, especially when his phone continued to go straight to voicemail whenever she called and Heath's calls did the same.

'Call your old boss,' Heath ordered. 'It's making me twitchy.'

She called Ray Cantrell.

'Oh, God, Hannah, don't you know?' Ray's voice was hoarse.

Hannah's hands began to shake. Where had Charley gone this time? What violent mess had he walked straight into? Had someone finally taken offense to having a camera thrust in their face and bashed Charley's head in?

She tried to remember what part of the planet was on fire this week and could not. Her life was on fire and she didn't bother to watch the news.

'What happened to him? Is he . . .?' She couldn't choke out *dead* or *hurt*. She managed, 'OK?'

Heath, on the couch trying not to throw up after his latest chemo treatment, spread his hands and mouthed, *What the fuck?*

Hannah shook her head. He'd have to wait. She couldn't focus on anything but this.

'I don't think he'll ever be OK again.' Ray took a deep breath. It was the longest intake of air Hannah had ever heard.

'His daughter drowned.'

Hannah's lips opened but no sound came out.

'It was on his watch. He's in bad shape, Hannah. Really bad. So is Frankie. I don't know if . . . I don't know how they'll survive this.'

Hannah lifted her gaze to her brother. She could relate.

Heath was so thin now the bones of his face stood out starkly enough to make him seem skeletal in certain light. His hair was beginning to fall out. His hands had lesions. None of his classy clothes fit. He spent his days in sweatpants and shirts she'd purchased in much smaller sizes than usual, and still they hung on him.

She wasn't sure how she'd survive if he died. But to lose a child . . .

Hannah's head spun.

'The funeral?'

Heath made a small, choked sound and tears started to flow over the prominent bones of his cheeks.

She mouthed *Not Charley* and he laid his head back on the pillow and closed his eyes.

The tears ran down the side of his face, forgotten, soaking into the pillowcase. Sometimes she found him just like that, the tears dried into salty tracks on his skin, the pillow damp. She'd do and say everything she could think of to cheer him up – Mel Brooks movie marathons, Mel Brooks trivia contests, cutting photographs out of magazines and gluing Jennifer Aniston's clothes on Sharon Stone and Pamela Anderson's clothes on everyone. She was usually able to make him laugh. Eventually.

She doubted anything was going to make him laugh now; the idea of trying made her sick.

'The funeral is tomorrow,' Ray continued. 'Frankie's a mess. Charley said they had to sedate her. He's on indefinite compassionate leave.'

'Of course. If you hear from him . . .' She paused. What could she say? Absolutely nothing. 'Never mind. Thanks for telling me, Ray.'

They said quick goodbyes and hung up.

'What happened?' Heath asked.

'Charley's daughter drowned.'

'Oh, shit.' Heath didn't open his eyes. The words were not heated but despairing.

He said most everything in that tone these days and it scared her.

'He's on leave. His wife's having a difficult time.'

Heath opened his eyes. 'You think Mom will have a hard time when I die?'

'You're not—'

'I am, Hannah. Probably soon. And the only one who's going to be devastated by it is you.'

'That's not true! What about Charley?'

'Charley's got enough devastation right now. He's got enough devastation forever.'

Heath was right. Hannah wished that she could see Charley, do something, anything, to help him. Let him talk to her if he wanted to or just be silent if he'd rather. But she'd probably never see him again.

Taking photos of a dying man would be the least of Charley's concerns, and probably not the best of ideas, considering. Wouldn't more death only make things worse? When didn't it?

She bought a card. She had to do something. It took her ages to find the right one. While they did have a section devoted to *Death of a Child* – ugh! – the offerings there made her shudder. She finally selected a card with a cloud-filled sky – hokey but better than the one of the ocean – and a blank interior where she wrote: *We are so sorry. Contact us if you need ANYTHING. Love, Heath and Hannah.*

Her days returned to their pattern. Work at *You*, interspersed with doctor appointments and treatments for Heath. Movies to distract him. Cards. Games.

The nights had their pattern too. Wakefulness despite her exhaustion. Cleaning up after Heath, who only seemed to puke these days right after she'd fallen asleep. Thinking of Charley. Knowing he did not think of her.

Another week passed, then another.

Heath's morale had been down since Charley had stopped coming around. Hannah's was too, but she couldn't allow it to show. In fact, she seemed to get more and more upbeat with every day. Pretty soon she'd be talking as high and as fast as Alvin and the Chipmunks as she danced around the room.

'Your cancer could go into remission. It happened to that guy at the coffee shop.' Now that Hannah worked at *You* she frequented many of the places Heath once had.

'That would only mean waiting and wondering what the Fickle Wheel of AIDS fate has in store for me next.'

'Heath! Have some hope.'

'There is no hope, sis. Even if my cancer goes into remission, I have AIDS. That isn't ever going away.'

'Every day brings them one step closer to a cure.'

Heath rolled his eyes. She did sound like a commercial.

The second week of October Hannah stepped out of the elevator and found Charley standing in the hall.

He'd lost weight and his face appeared gaunt. His hair was overgrown, messy, and the gray that had only just begun to thread here and there seemed more pronounced. His eyes were glassy and red-rimmed, his clothes rumpled. He looked like hell.

Hannah threw her arms around his neck. 'I'm so sorry.'

He stiffened and she stepped back, mortified. They weren't hugging friends. What had she been thinking?

'Sorry,' she repeated.

He rubbed his jaw, the *scritch* of the stubble splitting the silence between them. 'I knocked but no one answered.'

Hannah frowned, pulling out her key. 'Heath's here.'

'I didn't want to wake him so I didn't knock again.'

Unease made her fingers tremble so she didn't get the key in the lock right away.

Charley's hand covered hers. 'Let me.'

His fingers didn't seem any steadier, and she wondered about that – lack of sleep, had he been drinking, perhaps a few drugs? – but he did manage to get the key in the lock.

Heath lay on the couch, eyes closed, TV babbling. He didn't look any better than Charley.

Hannah dropped her purse and her briefcase right where she stood and flew across the room. 'Heath?'

He didn't move.

She couldn't breathe, which made it damn hard to decipher if he was.

Charley's hand appeared again, his fingertips – shaking like a frightened dog – pressed to Heath's neck.

'Can't a guy get a nap?' Heath's eyes opened. They lit up at the sight of Charley. 'Hey, man. Great to see you.'

'You too.' Charley sat in the chair next to Heath's. 'Sorry I haven't been around.'

Heath's and Hannah's gazes met over Charley's head – just a quick flick then away. Charley seemed to want to pretend that nothing catastrophic had happened.

'No problem,' Heath said.

And apparently they were going to let him.

Heath smiled. His teeth appeared too big for his mouth. The smile that had charmed hundreds become both ghostly and ghastly. 'You're here now.' He picked up the TV controller. 'The playoffs are on. Braves and the Pirates.'

'Excellent.' Charley sat back.

'Let's order pizza.'

'Is this a party?' Hannah asked. 'I should have brought ice cream.'

Sadness flickered over Charley's face before he doused it with a bright smile that reminded her of the creepy clown in the mini-series *It* that Heath had insisted they watch. He loved that crap. She'd had nightmares for a month.

'Definitely a party,' Charley said. 'I missed you guys.'

Hannah was one of the guys. She knew that. She'd always known it. Better than nothing.

'How long can you stay?'

Charley's smile faltered again. 'I'm on leave. I can stay indefinitely.'

Heath and Hannah exchanged another glance. She wanted to ask about his wife – but they weren't that kind of friends either.

'I'm here to work on your essay.'

'Oh, Charley,' Hannah blurted. 'Do you think that's a good—?'

'What do you want on your pizza?' Charley asked.

Several hours later the game was over; the pizza was gone. Charley had nixed going for ice cream with more force than was necessary for the question. She hadn't asked.

Heath had fallen asleep, Hannah was about to.

Charley didn't seem in any hurry to leave.

'Where are you staying?' she asked.

'I . . . uh . . . didn't even think of it. I'll take a walk and book a room at the first place I see.'

'You'll stay here.' Charley seemed too zoned-out to be walking around DC at midnight.

'I couldn't.'

'Why not? Carol is at a conference in LA. She won't be back until next week, and even if she was in town, she hasn't slept here since summer. It's stupid for you to pay for a hotel.'

He hesitated and she stood. 'Not taking no for an answer. I'll grab some fresh sheets and towels.'

Hannah scurried from the room before he could argue. She half-expected him to have walked out by the time she returned but he sat where she'd left him, staring at Heath with an expression she recognized. He wanted to photograph him.

So why wasn't he?

His camera bag rested inside the door next to his overnight bag. But usually he had a camera if not in his hands, then hanging from his shoulder, or perched on the table at his side. Tonight, nothing.

'You OK?' She wished instantly that she'd said something, anything, else.

'Of course not.' He left the room.

Charley was still sleeping or pretending to when Hannah went to work the next morning. She hadn't slept a wink.

When she arrived home that evening, Charley was still there. He seemed to have forgotten her faux pas. He and Heath had had a great day from the sound of things.

'We lunched, then we strolled along the Mall.'

In DC 'the Mall' didn't mean the place where they kept the Nordstrom's, but the place where they kept the national monuments and memorials – Washington, Lincoln, Jefferson, Vietnam.

She couldn't remember the last time Heath had walked anywhere but into a doctor's office or a treatment center.

'I hope you didn't walk too far.'

'Hush, Mommy. I feel great.'

His cheeks *did* have a bit of color. Maybe it was a fever.

She resisted the urge to kiss his forehead. He'd only call her 'Mommy' again and that kind of creeped her out.

'Did you take any pictures?' she asked.

A photo of an obvious AIDS patient standing in front of any

of the founding fathers' monuments would be both powerful and classic.

Charley's gaze flicked to his camera bag, exactly where he'd left it the night before. It had not been opened.

Heath shook his head and frowned behind Charley's back.

Later, when Charley had gone to bed, she asked, 'What's going on?'

'From what I can tell, he doesn't want to use his cameras.'

'Charley always wants to use his cameras.'

'Since he's been here has he seemed very *Charley* to you?'

'What does that mean?'

'He's off, weird, not himself.'

'Should he be, considering?'

'I don't know.' Heath rubbed his eyes. 'I'd like to help him, but I don't know how.'

'Maybe just being here is helping. Otherwise, why did he come?'

Having Charley in the next bedroom created an intimacy Hannah hadn't realized she'd been pining for. Having him at home with Heath all day not only alleviated some of Hannah's stress but alleviated a lot of Heath's boredom.

What Charley was doing there, besides avoiding his life, neither Heath nor Hannah could figure out. He certainly wasn't working on the essay.

They stuck to the unspoken rule of not mentioning his daughter, his wife, his home, his job. That unopened camera bag.

She heard him, sometimes, talking in the dark of the night. Was he dreaming, on the phone, nattering to himself? She didn't know and she couldn't ask.

'He'll have to go home eventually,' Heath said one morning at the beginning of the second week.

Charley had yet to emerge from his room. He also slept a lot. A disturbing trait in a man who had previously rarely seemed to sleep at all.

'Will he?' Hannah asked.

Heath leaned over the breakfast table, where he was taking itty-bitty bites of toast, and lowered his voice to a stage whisper. 'Can you imagine not showing up for the holidays after your child has died?'

'The holidays are pretty far away.'

Heath pointed his finger at Hannah, made a twirl around gesture, which she did. Since starting to work at *You* Hannah had upped her fashion game. As she had no fashion game, that meant Heath dressed her every morning like a doll. Today he'd chosen pleated gray trousers and a blouse the shade of fog. Her black belt matched her flats. A black beaded bracelet finished off the ensemble.

'He seems in no hurry to go.' Heath gave her outfit a nod of approval. 'I'm not kicking him out. Are you?'

Hannah chewed her lip and peered at the closed door of Charley's room. They probably *should*, but she couldn't.

'Nothing's going to bring her back,' Hannah said. 'Not even Christmas.'

'Hannah.' Heath shook his head. 'Sometimes I don't even know you.'

'What possible good can it do for Charley and Francesca to sit alone in their house and try not to think of how it would have been if Lisa were there?'

'More good than it'll do either of them to be alone thinking the same damn thing.'

Still Hannah had no idea how to encourage Charley to go home without it seeming like they didn't want him there.

Charley stayed on.

Ray called a few times, trying to entice him back to work.

Charley could not be enticed. His camera bag never moved from its position near the front door.

He flew home once, returned the next day, slept for twenty hours straight.

Hannah heard him on the phone the following week.

'Frankie, I've gotta work. It's the only thing that . . .'

Hannah remembered how he'd always called her 'Fancy' before in a voice that had made Hannah yearn.

'Why would you quit your job?' He went silent, listening, but he let out several sharp, annoyed breaths. 'You're a photo-journalist.' Another pause. 'Anyone can take artsy pictures and sell them at the local festival. Don't you want to make a difference?'

Hannah shouldn't be listening to this, but she was frozen in the hall. Heath was asleep in his room, door closed. Charley hadn't closed his. Should she close it for him?

She crept closer to do just that and suddenly it opened wide. He appeared so angry she took a step back. 'Sorry, I . . .'

His head came up. He blinked at her as if he didn't know her. 'Hannah.' Charley shoved his hand through his still overly long hair. 'I suppose you heard.'

'I didn't mean to. I was going to close your door.'

'My fault. I can't remember the simplest things lately. Nothing's important. Everything seems so . . .'

She waited, but he seemed to have lost the thought.

'Pointless?'

'Huh?' He focused on her again.

'Everything seems pointless.'

'Yeah. Right. Exactly. Life is pointless without . . .'

She took his hand and he paused. She should have waited until he finished. Life was pointless without who? Or perhaps what?

'It seems like that now.' She squeezed his fingers. 'But things will get better.'

'Will they?' He removed his hand from hers, using it to push back his hair again. 'You know this from your vast experience, do you?'

Hannah felt like she'd been slapped, and for the first time, she got angry with Charley.

'I'm not just some Pollyanna off the street. I'll know all about losing someone who's another part of me very soon. And I have to hope that things will get better, otherwise why go on?'

'Sorry.' He shook his head, set his hand on her shoulder. 'That was insensitive.'

'It was.'

His lips curved, not a real smile, but something. That heady feeling she'd first had after he'd praised her layout of the basketball hoops essay returned, and she swayed in his direction.

'Whoa!' His hand still on her shoulder, he braced her, pushing her back a little.

Her cheeks burned. What had she been thinking?

Foolish things – which were all she ever thought about Charley Blackwell.

'I'm OK. Probably need to eat.'

Considering her ass, she didn't need to eat for a month, but what was she supposed to say?

You smell so good I'd like to lick you all over?

Her cheeks flamed now.

'We could go and get some—' he began.

The sound of retching had them running for Heath's room.

Charley stayed through Thanksgiving. He'd planned to go home, then his wife had called and said she was going to visit her friend in New York City.

'See the Macy's Parade.' He shrugged and glanced away when he told them. 'Everyone wants to.'

More than they wanted to spend a holiday with the love of their life?

Apparently.

Charley had finally gotten his hair trimmed at Heath's insistence, which only made it appear grayer, his face paler.

At the sight of his sad eyes, Hannah wanted to punch something. Or maybe someone.

Heath rallied on Thanksgiving, perhaps because Charley was there. He even ate turkey and kept it down.

Hannah felt a spark of hope.

'Maybe if you continue to improve, they'll prescribe DDI.'

The new drug had been approved in October. It was too early to tell if it was having much effect, but Hannah couldn't believe the Food and Drug Administration would have allowed DDI to become available if it hadn't been shown to work *somewhere* on *someone*.

'It's just a placebo to keep the rabble rousers quiet,' Heath said.

'When did you get so crabby-pants?'

'When I got the first leprosy lesion.'

'They seem a lot better.'

Heath peered at his hands, which looked like those of a very old man – something he would probably never, ever be. 'They're still there, and they most likely always will be.'

That tiny spark of hope went poof and died.

After Thanksgiving, Charley began to go into the *National Geographic* offices a few days a week.

'Since you left they've been short-staffed.'

'You're editing slides?' Hannah asked, half kidding.

'Someone has to.'

That someone should not be Charley Blackwell.

His cameras continued to gather dust next to the door.

The idea of his still being with them for Christmas was both exciting and terrifying. What did it mean?

She agonized over what to get him for a gift – over *if* she should get him a gift. She finally settled on a new camera strap, both practical and personal since she had it monogrammed.

She hadn't heard Charley talking to Frankie in a long, long time. That just meant she hadn't heard them. It certainly didn't mean he was in DC for her. She wasn't even sure he was in DC for Heath any more, though he was a great help.

The two of them spent a lot of time listening to jazz. The mellow sounds seemed to be one of the few things that calmed Heath enough to sleep.

Charley brought home a new album every other day. The most recent was by Yellowjackets. The two of them listened to their recording of 'Seven Stars' over and over again.

Hannah started to wonder if this was the way it would always be – the three of them together, though not really together, each of them wanting, needing, hoping for different things, except for that one thing they all wanted. A cure for AIDS.

Which was as likely to happen as any of the other dreams they dreamed.

The day before Christmas Eve, Charley came out of Carol's room with his bag. 'Thanks for letting me stay. Have a merry Christmas.' He winced after he said it.

How could any of them be merry this Christmas?

'How long will you be gone?' Hannah asked.

Heath cast her a disgusted glance. 'He lives there, not here.'

'I'll be back after the holidays.' His gaze went to his camera bag. 'We'll get some work done then. Fresh outlook. New Year. Start over. Right?'

The last word was so pathetically hopeful Hannah's eyes burned.

'Right!' Heath agreed, his voice hearty and loud.

Too loud because he started coughing, and then he couldn't seem to stop.

Hannah rushed to his side. 'Get some water.'

She heard Charley's bag hit the floor, the water running.

Her hands fluttered helplessly, patting Heath's shoulder, smoothing his hair, a stubble too short to need smoothing.

Should she smack his back? Would that help or hurt? She had no idea, so she did nothing.

A glass of water appeared at the edge of her vision. She took it without looking at anything but Heath.

He'd put both hands over his face, pressing the palms to his mouth as if he could stop the frenzied, hacking sounds.

'Try some water.' She pulled on one of his fingers.

His gaze, wide and scared, met hers. He lowered his hands.

They were covered in blood.

She dropped the glass. It hit the carpet with a thud and water soaked her toes. She picked up the blanket Heath usually wrapped around himself for warmth and offered it to him like a towel.

Blood had started to come out of his nose. At least he'd stopped coughing.

'Charley!' She turned and he took a picture.

She was so shocked, she stuttered. 'Wh–wh—?'

Had she meant to say 'what?' or 'why?' She had no idea because she couldn't finish the word.

Her hands closed into fists. The desire to punch someone returned. She'd been having that desire a lot lately.

'Put that down,' she said.

'It's OK.' Heath's voice was damp, thick, not his own. The blanket pressed to his face made it sound even more alien.

'It's not!' she snapped.

'That's why he's here, remember? Be glad he picked up a camera at last.'

True, but why did it have to be now?

'I should probably go to the hospital.'

'Hospital?' Her voice went as high as Alvin on speed, but with none of the chirpy-happy tone to keep it from being super annoying.

'It's not stopping.'

'Put your head on the pillow. Feet up. I'll get an ice pack for the back of your neck.'

'It's not going to help.'

'We can try!' she cried.

Heath started to get up. Dizzy, he fell back to the couch. 'Maybe by the time you get a cab, I'll . . .' His eyes fluttered closed.

'Heath!'

'We need an ambulance.'

Hannah spun.

Charley held the phone to his ear. He rattled off the situation and the address before hanging up. Then he lifted his camera and kept shooting.

'Why . . .?' she managed, though she wasn't sure what, exactly, she was asking.

Why was he taking pictures again?

Why was he here?

Why was Heath bleeding?

Why Heath? Why her? Why anyone?

Charley answered a different question altogether.

'A cab driver isn't going to allow anyone bleeding as badly as Heath is into his cab, even if we could get him from here to street level without making him worse.' Charley snapped a picture. 'And I don't think we can.'

Heath moved, moaned and she forgot everything but him.

'What happened?' he asked.

'You took a little nap.'

'No. I . . .' He tried to lift his head but it fell back. 'I heard you. Nine-one-one to the rescue.' He grimaced. 'Can you put a pillow or two under my head? The blood is backwashing.'

Hannah snatched every pillow in the room and began to build a pyramid beneath her brother's neck. 'Better?'

He gave a small nod, though from his expression, and the continued spread of the bloodstain on the blanket, he wasn't better by much.

The buzzer rang.

Moments later Charley opened the door for the EMTs. At least this time he didn't have to threaten them with a *Time* magazine exposé if they didn't do their job. They arrived gloved up, put on masks as soon as they saw Heath and did exactly what she'd planned to. Elevation of the head and feet, ice pack on the back of the neck.

They also packed his nose with gauze and gave him ice chips to suck. She wished she'd thought of that.

'You might have to have that cauterized,' the younger of the two women said.

The older woman gestured toward the door. 'Let's get a move on. You two can meet us there.'

Hannah glanced at Charley. 'You can probably still catch your plane.'

'Even if I could, I'm not.' He took her arm. 'Let's get a cab.'

Frankie

Frankie could not breathe, even before Charley asked, yet again, *Where's Lisa?*

The night fading, the moon falling, this place almost exactly the same. Him sitting there staring into the water precisely where Lisa had died. What did that mean?

'Lisa's . . .'

She tried to say *dead*. Couldn't.

Deceased. Nope.

Drowned. Same issue.

Perhaps she'd have more luck with a word that didn't begin with 'd'.

There. Lisa's there.

Couldn't say it. Tried to point. Except Lisa wasn't 'there' in the water. Technically, Lisa was in her purple urn back home.

'Gone,' she blurted. It appeared to be her go-to word.

'Camp. Right.' He flicked one finger toward his forehead then away in a mini-salute before he took her hand.

She was so discombobulated she let him.

He was warm where she was cold. Hard where she was soft. Rough where she was smooth. Crazy when she was not.

She tried to pull away. He was also strong where she was weak. He would not let go.

'I don't know why,' he said in a dreamy voice, 'but sitting here makes me feel . . .'

She held her breath. What would he say?

Sad. Guilty. Horrified. Sick. Stupid. Negligent.

'Close to her.'

Frankie choked.

He didn't seem to notice.

'Seems like years since I saw her. I miss her so much.'

Frankie had a problem breathing again. Might help if she actually breathed. She forced herself to let the air out, draw some back in. The pain in her chest eased, but it didn't go away. The pain in her chest never went away.

'Me too.'

Had she said that? She hadn't meant to.

Not that she didn't miss Lisa, but she certainly didn't talk about it. Ever. To anyone. That way lay a direct path back to the madness that had threatened right after.

At least Charley didn't comment. He just continued to stare into the water as the sun rose behind the cottage, framing it in tendrils of golden light, the way those old paintings used to frame Jesus, before peeking over the roof to cast yellow rays across the gently lapping gray-blue water.

Frankie should have done something, anything, but sit there and stare into that water too. Except sitting there *did* made Frankie feel closer to Lisa than she had since she'd actually been close to Lisa.

When Charley let go of her hand, then put his arm around Frankie's shoulder, drawing her against his side, memories rushed in, so strong that if she'd been standing she would have staggered. As it was, she sagged against him and he pulled her closer still.

They'd sat like this during the single trip they'd made here together after purchasing the property. Lisa asleep in the cabin, worn out from a day in the sun and water.

Mommy, I'm a fish!

She'd been such a good swimmer. How had . . .?

Charley kissed the top of Frankie's head and before she could stop herself, she rubbed her temple against his chin.

They'd sat here just like this, sipping wine they'd bought from a local winery. Then, after she'd run inside and checked to make sure the kid was still crashed out, they'd made love beneath the stars.

She hadn't thought of that night in a lifetime.

'You think any of the neighbors are here?' Charley asked.

She cast a quick glance at the seemingly abandoned houses on either side of them. 'Mid-week? Doubtful.'

Even when they'd been here, they hadn't *been here* but in town, on the bay, riding bikes, playing mini-golf. Frankie shouldn't still be angry about that. She should never have been angry about that. It wasn't their fault Lisa had died.

It was Charley's.

Although if she hadn't been so intent on having some *me time*,

Lisa would have been safe at home and none of this would ever have happened. So, in the end, wasn't it her fault?

Try to forget *that* in the middle of every long, lonely night.

Charley turned his head, captured her lips. Her hands came up to push him away, except she didn't.

He tasted exactly the same. Cinnamon sugar on toast – warm and sweet. How could that be? Over two decades had passed. Shouldn't he taste like lying, cheating, dying old man?

'I missed you,' he murmured into her mouth.

She'd missed him too. *This* him. Which was the only reason she kissed him back.

With his mouth on hers, with his scent, his taste all around, she could forget for a few minutes everything that had gone before.

The harsh words. The lonely nights. The lies. The betrayal. The divorce.

Her tongue swept into his mouth just as a fish leaped from the water, returning with a splash that brought back the one thing she could never forget.

The dead child.

She pulled away, this time so fast she managed to get away, scooting backward on the dock and out of his reach.

Frankie stood. 'We should head back. I think we can drop your rental in Sturgeon Bay. Green Bay for sure. No reason to drive two cars all the way to Milwaukee.'

'Nope.' Charley focused again on the water.

'What do you mean "nope"?'

'It's slang for *no*.'

'Ha-ha. Such a comedian.' Except he wasn't. Never had been. A prickle of unease traced the back of her neck. 'You need to start chemo.'

'Do I?'

'Yes!' She said the word so loudly she startled several birds from a nearby tree.

'What if I don't want to?'

'You'll . . .' She paused.

'Die? I get the impression I'm going to die anyway. I've seen people who've had chemo. I'll pass.'

'Who did you see who had chemo?'

Had he remembered Hannah's brother . . . Hell, what was his

name? Something with an H. Hannah had mentioned him just yesterday. Frankie couldn't remember shit any more. She and Charley were quite a pair.

And there was a sentence she'd never thought to think again.

'Guys at the VA.' He shrugged and stared at his hands, which were clasped together very tight. 'I did that story when I worked at the *Journal*.'

'You don't remember Hannah's brother?' she asked.

He lifted his eyes. 'Who's Hannah?'

She peered into the endless orbs of blue. If he was lying, he was superb at it. But then, he always had been.

Still, what would be the point of lying now? She couldn't figure that out.

'Never mind.'

'Good. What should we do today?'

'Go back to Milwaukee,' she said slowly.

'Nope.' He lay on the deck, hands behind his head and stared dreamily at the clouds floating by.

Frankie thought her brain might explode. 'Charley! Get up!'

He closed his eyes.

She fisted her hands in her hair and walked away. He'd always had the power to make her crazier than anyone in the world.

That had been another perk of divorce. Not having her temper rise until it pulsed behind her eyes when he stubbornly refused to do something, or stubbornly insisted *on* doing it. Her blood pressure had been pretty good for the past twenty-odd years. She'd bet it wasn't good now.

She should go inside and call Hannah. But that wouldn't help her blood pressure either. She called Officer Randolph first.

'I'm glad you found him. We hadn't gotten any hits on his car. Have you considered putting one of those tracker watches on him? I think they also have tracker shoes. There's a lot of new gadgets to help with Alzheimer's patients.'

'He doesn't have . . .' Frankie began, then stopped. He kind of did. 'I'll check that out. Thanks for your help.'

'I'm glad it ended well.'

Frankie nearly asked him how dying from brain cancer could possibly be counted as ending well, but such questions made everyone uncomfortable. They solved nothing. Maybe she had learned something in the years of her life.

Before calling Hannah, Frankie needed fortification. Unfortunately, the place hadn't been lived in for decades. If Charley still owned it – which she should probably find out – he must have paid a caretaker because the inside wasn't too dusty and the cottage wasn't falling apart. But there wasn't any coffee.

She'd passed at least two cafés in Fish Creek. She planned to head to the first one she saw. But could she leave Charley?

He still lay on the dock, eyes closed. She might make it to town and back before he noticed she was gone. But what if he did notice? What if he decided to get into his car and go somewhere else? She'd never find him this time. She was fresh out of ideas.

The idea of admitting to the police, and to Hannah, that she'd found Charley only to lose him again because she'd gone to a coffee shop was too mortifying.

She leaned out the screened door. 'Wanna go into town for coffee?'

He sat up, as if he'd been yanked on a string. 'Yep.'

They returned to the car. Charley pulled his seatbelt across his chest, then hesitated before buckling it. 'If you try and go right back to Milwaukee, I'll jump out.'

She hadn't even considered driving back without his permission and she should have.

'I'm no expert but I bet jumping out of a moving car would hurt.'

'What do I care?'

This daredevil attitude reminded her strongly of the man he'd been when they met. Willing to take any risk for a story. Go anywhere, do anything.

She felt the familiar whirl of her stomach at the thought of Charley being in danger, of being hurt.

According to Hannah, Charley's PTSD was to blame for his flirtation with danger. But having a psycho-babble explanation for his behavior, and all the pain it had caused, didn't make that pain any less real, didn't make the anger between them any less damaging.

Would either one of them ever get past the past and move on? She thought they had, or at least she had, but here they were right back in the same emotional shit storm they'd lived in so long ago.

When Charley continued to hold the seatbelt buckle above the latch, eyebrows lifted, she started the car with an annoyed flick of her wrist. 'I won't drive back to Milwaukee.'

At least not until she had her coffee.

The coffee shop on Main Street was nearly empty. Frankie ordered a dark roast; Charley ordered their flavored brew of the day, French vanilla.

Frankie slipped on to the front porch, where she could see Charley through the window, and placed the call.

'Find him?' Hannah asked.

'At the cottage. Does he still own it?'

From Hannah's end came the clatter of computer keys, the mumble of voices. Frankie glanced at her watch. 7:00 a.m. Which made it 8:00 a.m. in America's capital, but still pretty early for so much activity in the office.

'The cottage where—?'

'Yes.' Frankie cut her off before she could say it. Frankie had been thinking it enough already.

'He still owns it, but he hasn't been back since. I've been bugging him to sell. He ignores me.'

Frankie grunted. Been there.

'Why did he go to the cottage?' Hannah asked.

'You wanna ask him?'

'I'd prefer not to have a rerun of "Who the hell are you?"'

'Understandable.'

Charley had found a newspaper on the next table and commenced reading it. Since he didn't seem to be having a time warp moment, he either hadn't glanced at the date, or he had and his beleaguered brain had conveniently switched up the year. Frankie almost envied him the ability to see only what he wanted to.

'Did you just sympathize with me?' Hannah asked.

'Makes you feel a little squiggy, doesn't it?'

Hannah laughed and Frankie found herself smiling. Why was she loosening up with Charley's wife?

Oh, hell, why not?

'Do you like flavored coffee?' she asked.

'You planning on sending me some for my birthday?'

'I just . . .' Frankie watched Charley sip from his cup. 'Wondered.'

'I do.'

'Do you remember if Charley liked it when you met him?'

'I . . .' Hannah's voice drifted off. She cleared her throat and when she spoke again her words were softer than they'd been so far. 'I remember everything about Charley. Don't you?'

Frankie had thought she had, but maybe she was wrong.

'Flavored coffee?' she repeated. 'Charley like it or not?'

'He drank it from day one and never complained, although once he said something about the carafe smelling like . . .' She paused, then said the rest fast, as if she had to get the words out before she forgot them. 'Like eight-day-old burned sludge with none of the promised sweetness. Poetic for Charley.'

Those were nearly Frankie's exact thoughts about flavored coffee. Not that she'd ever considered herself poetic.

Bitchy, maybe.

'I took that to mean he *didn't* like flavored coffee,' Hannah continued, 'but he said that he'd developed a taste for it. That he hadn't liked it and now he did.'

'Interesting.'

'Why is it interesting?'

Frankie almost didn't tell her. Was it relevant? Who knew? But if she couldn't share the minutiae of Charley with Hannah, whom could she share it with?

Quickly she told her how Charley had ordered flavored coffee even though he hadn't liked it when he'd been Her Charley.

'Your Charley?'

Frankie's cheeks heated. Luckily no one could see her out here. 'It's how I distinguish the way he is now from—'

'The way he was when he was My Charley. Way back last week.'

'Yeah.'

'OK. That is interesting. And weird. You should tell his doctor.'

'If we ever see his doctor again.'

'What are you talking about?' Hannah demanded.

Frankie explained that Charley was refusing to leave.

'How are you going to get him back to Milwaukee?'

'Hog-tie him and throw him in the trunk?'

'You think you can?'

For an instant Frankie thought Hannah was serious and she stood blinking at the empty road in front of the coffee shop, wishing she'd brought a jacket. The temperature felt like a balmy fifty-five.

'Kidding,' Hannah said. 'Though there are times over the last few decades that I'd have helped you do it.'

'He has that effect.'

They shared a moment of commiserating silence. In the past, Frankie had complained about Charley to Irene, but that had only made Irene detest him more. Not what she'd been after, though *what* she'd been after she hadn't known until now.

Sympathy. Empathy. Someone who 'got' Charley the way that Frankie did. The only person who fit that description was Hannah.

'Any suggestions on what I should do?' Frankie continued. 'Any tricks of the Charley trade you care to share from your decades married to the man?'

'Tricks to get him to do something he doesn't want to? There aren't any.'

'Swell.' That had been too much to hope for, but nevertheless she had hoped. 'Too bad he can't get his treatment here.' Maybe then she'd even be able to convince him to *get* the treatment.

'Right. Where would he . . .?' Hannah's voice trailed off. 'Wait. How close are you to . . . to . . . something with a bay. Hold on.' Computer keys clattered more loudly than before. 'I was checking out Dr Lanier and I—'

'Checking out why?'

'To see if he's really as great as he thinks he is.'

'And?'

The keys stopped clattering for an instant. 'He is.'

The relief in her voice echoed Frankie's own.

'I called Kettering. He didn't have enough accolades for his protégé, said we were better off with Lanier than we'd be with him.' The clattering started again. 'Lanier just started a satellite cancer clinic in Sturgeon Bay.'

'No way.'

While Sturgeon Bay was the largest city in Door County, the county itself had fewer than 30,000 residents. This swelled astronomically during the summer season. However, a cancer clinic wasn't something folks on vacation often went searching for.

'According to the website, they serve the peninsula and Green Bay.'

'What else did the website say?' Frankie wasn't quite sure what a satellite cancer clinic was.

'The place provides care for cancer patients – radiation, chemo, counseling. Lanier has office hours there every other week.'

'Charley could continue his radiation, start his chemo and see the doctor when he's here.'

'You'll have to ask Lanier, but I'm thinking yes. Especially if the alternative is him being locked in the trunk.'

Frankie let out a half laugh.

'What about your job?' Hannah asked.

'My job is flexible.'

Right now her job was non-existent. She'd finished the assignment on the Basilica and the Greek Orthodox church, and she was fresh out of work. Usually she spent her downtime taking stock photos. She had none of Door County on her website; she could use some.

'You think you'll be OK there?'

Frankie hadn't melted down, shrieked, screamed, pounded her chest, run away. Any of the things she'd thought she'd do if she ever again saw the cottage, or that expanse of water at the end of the dock. Didn't mean her temporary bout of Zen would continue.

'I hope so.'

Considering Hannah's life, her own loss, it wasn't surprising that she understood what being here might do to Frankie.

'If you're not,' Hannah continued, 'if you just can't stand it, call me.'

'And you'll come to my rescue?'

Hannah let out a short, sharp breath. 'I don't know. Unless the chemo makes him remember me, wouldn't my coming only make things worse?'

Frankie had a feeling that the chemo was going to make Charley not care about much.

'Let's cross the bridges as we come to them.' Frankie paused. 'So if you weren't planning to come to my rescue, why would I call you?'

'Who else are you going to talk to about this? About him? Irene?'

The sarcasm as she said Irene's name should have annoyed Frankie, but Hannah was right. Talking to Irene about Charley was never productive. But could she talk to Hannah about him? A week ago the suggestion would have made her laugh. Today . . .

She didn't feel much like laughing.

Silence pulsed. Frankie waited for Hannah to say goodbye, or maybe just hang up.

'This is an impossible situation.'

Hannah sounded so adult. Really, she always had been despite Frankie's memory of her as a child.

'We've survived them before.'

'Have we?' Hannah asked.

'We're still breathing.' Even though Frankie remembered, very clearly, times she wished she wasn't.

'Breathing just means we're living,' Hannah said. 'Surviving is something else all together.'

'Fancy?'

Frankie spun. Charley stood right behind her.

When had she turned her back, taken her eyes off him? What if he'd decided to wander away?

'Who are you talking to? Irene? Don't tell her hi.' He winked.

'I . . . uh . . . I'll be right there.'

'Your coffee's cold. I'll have them warm it up for you, baby.' He leaned over and kissed her cheek, smiled, then set his palm against it too. 'I've never loved anyone the way I love you.'

The soft intake of breath from the other side of the line made Frankie wince. Hannah had heard everything, or at least the last part.

Charley strode off to have them 'warm it up for you, baby'.

Frankie stood there uncertain what to say. 'He . . . uh . . . thinks it's 1989.'

'That doesn't make it any less true.'

'Make what?'

'He never did love anyone the way he loved you.'

Charley

Fall of Saigon. April 30, 1975

Vietnamese poured from the stairwell as the helicopter lifted from the roof of the US Embassy. They raced across the concrete. A few tried to jump up and catch the landing skids.

Charley's finger tightened on his camera. The motor drive whirred. This was why he'd talked his way inside the embassy walls last night instead of heading to the *USS Mobile* with the rest of the journalists.

Now he was on the last flight out with the last of the Marines that had been guarding the place. The things he'd seen, the things he'd photographed . . . Despite the danger, Charley's blood seemed to course faster. The 'I'm so alive' feeling made him dizzy.

Charley leaned out the open door to take one last picture and—

Shots were fired. The helicopter dipped and swayed.

He was falling.

Charley woke himself shouting, 'No!'

Which was all he'd been able to shout before one of the Marines had snatched him back as he tipped over the edge, then thrown him into a seat.

'Jesus!' the man had snapped. 'You're so much trouble I'm about to toss you out myself.'

There, in the darkness of the night, in his house in Whitefish Bay, on his first visit back since the funeral, Charley wished the man had done it. If he had, Lisa would not be dead.

If he had, Lisa would never have existed. Would that have been better?

Sometimes, when the pain was almost too much, Charley thought so. Then he'd remember her laugh, her smile, her voice, her tiny fingers and equally tiny but no less perfect toes, her hair that was just like his and her eyes that were just like Frankie's, and he'd know that wasn't true.

He'd give anything if she would only exist again, but she wouldn't. How did he live with that? How did he get over that?

Maybe he didn't.

His heart still pounded; he'd broken out in a cold sweat. He could smell himself, that same rank scent of fear in the jungle. He could still hear the *whoop-whoop*, see the refugees streaming across the roof below them, feel the lurch as he fell.

In the past, whenever he'd woken screaming, sweating, panting in this house, Frankie had been there. She had held him, touched him, sung to him, soothed him.

Tonight, he was alone.

'Frankie?' he whispered.

The bed was empty, even though when he'd fallen asleep she'd been clinging to the edge, as far away from him as she could get and still remain on the same mattress.

This visit home had not gone well. His wife walked around like a wraith. She barely spoke, slept or ate that he could tell.

He crept through the house as if he were an intruder; he felt like one. This house had never been his, and now he didn't think it ever would be.

Wearing only his white boxers and white socks, a chill whispered over his damp skin. Probably because the place appeared haunted, the silver-gray light of the moon shining through every window, making the furniture cast shadows that seemed to dance like black flames.

Too bad he didn't have a camera, but he'd left them all in DC. Hadn't picked one up since . . .

On the landing, preparing to head downstairs, he glanced into Lisa's room. A shadow lurked near the window; this one did not move.

Was Lisa here?

Joy filled him. He didn't even care that she'd be a ghost; all he cared was that she might be . . .

'Nightmare?' Frankie asked.

Disappointment flooded him; shame followed. How could he be disappointed that the shadow belonged to his wife?

'Yeah.' He scrubbed his hand through his hair, surprised at the length. When had he last gotten it cut?

Before.

Would everything now be divided into before and after he'd let his little girl die?

He stepped tentatively into the room. He hated being tentative. It went against his nature. But lately, that's all he seemed to be.

'Are you . . .?' He stopped. She wasn't all right. Thanks to him.

'We used to watch movies every Saturday night.' Frankie sat in the window seat, her legs drawn up under her long flannel nightgown.

When had she started to wear flannel nightgowns? He had no idea. There were a lot of things he had no idea about. Like movies on a Saturday night.

'I'd make popcorn and Kool-Aid. Her favorite was grape.' Frankie laid her cheek on her knees, staring out the window into the silvery light and not at him. 'I'll never forget the taste of popcorn in my teeth and grape Kool-Aid on my tongue, but I'll forget the way she laughed. Won't I?'

Charley's throat hurt; he couldn't speak. Probably shouldn't.

'Her favorite movie is—' Frankie's breath caught, both pain and surprise, as if she'd stepped on a bumblebee, barefoot, in the middle of a patch of clover. 'Her favorite movie was *The Sound of Music*. Whenever it played on TV we had to make sure we were home and that there was lots of popcorn. She'd go to bed singing "My Favorite Things" and we'd change the words to sunshine on dandelions and cuddles with kittens, or some other silly combination. She would laugh so hard.'

Frankie lifted her head from her knees just a little. 'Hear that?'

All Charley heard was a car driving past on the street.

She laid her head back where it had been and continued. 'She hated hot dogs. She wanted a black kitty – a real one, just like her stuffed one.'

It was then that he noticed Frankie had Black Kitty tucked tightly between her breasts and her drawn-up knees; her chin just touched its head.

'Why didn't I get her one? Kittens are easy. But I didn't want to deal with it. I was selfish.'

'No, Fancy, you . . .'

She kept talking as if he weren't there.

'She hated it if I took a picture of her when she was crying. All I had to do to get her to stop was raise my camera. I always wanted to know why that was.' She breathed in, long and slow, then breathed out. 'Now I never will.'

Frankie's voice alternated between matter-of-fact and wondering, as if in talking about Lisa she was discovering things she'd never known either, though that couldn't be true. The only person who'd truly known Lisa Blackwell, the only person who now ever would, was Frankie.

'She always snatched the green game piece whenever we played Candyland. If she didn't draw Queen Frostine, she pouted. She snored a little sometimes. She smelled like . . .'

Charley breathed in, trying to remember. All he smelled was a ghost of the bay that had killed her.

'Graham crackers,' Frankie said.

Silence descended, broken only by the crackles and creaks of a house he didn't know any better than he'd known his own child.

'What else?' he asked.

He didn't think she'd answer, didn't think she even knew he was there.

'She thought she was a fish,' Frankie whispered, and the chill that had tickled over Charley before returned. 'But she wasn't.'

Hannah

Washington DC. January, 1992

Jazz played low and smooth nearly twenty-four-seven. Sometimes Hannah thought she might start screaming if she didn't hear a little disco.

Heath spent Christmas in the hospital. Kaposi's sarcoma now lived in his lungs. The doctors had switched up his chemo cocktail. It didn't seem to be helping.

Charley stayed on. Hannah was so grateful she nearly wept every time she saw him. But she managed not to cry, unless she was in the shower. She was taking very long showers these days.

She went into *You* every morning, leaving Charley and Heath together. Once he'd picked up his camera again, Charley never seemed to put it back down. The two of them spent their time talking, watching TV and recording *Heath's End of Days*.

In the afternoons, when Hannah came home, Charley would go out and do Lord knows what in and around DC. He always returned with rolls and rolls of exposed film in the pockets of his army jacket, as well as boxes and boxes of slides he'd had developed at a Mom and Pop place around the corner.

'Shouldn't you take a quick trip home?' Heath asked near the end of January.

'I'm good.' Charley had gone into *National Geographic* and brought back a portable light table, set it up in the corner of the dining room, and covered it with slides. Whenever he wasn't taking pictures – like now – he was editing them.

He remained on leave from the magazine. Hannah wondered

how long that would continue. She wondered how long a lot of stuff would continue.

'You are many things, my man, but right now "good" isn't one of them.' Heath reclined on the hospital bed they'd rented.

She and Charley had shoved the couch he'd previously used into her room. She tripped over it every time she checked on Heath in the night. They probably should have left it in the living room. Then she wouldn't have had to sleep in the chair so much.

'Hmm?' Charley peered at a slide through a loop, then tossed it into the box he used for garbage.

'You should go home, Charley.' Heath's voice was quiet.

Charley glanced in Heath's direction, frowning at Hannah as if he hadn't realized she was there. He probably hadn't. When she'd walked in, he hadn't responded to her hello; he hadn't even glanced up from the slides.

'There isn't . . . I wasn't . . . She doesn't . . .' He sighed, then hung his head. 'I can't.'

'Why?' Heath asked.

Hannah held her breath.

Charley got up, grabbed his camera bag and said, 'I'll be back,' before he ran away.

'That went well, don't you think?'

Hannah didn't answer. She crossed the room to stand in front of pile upon pile of slides.

'Hannah, what are you . . .?'

She flicked on the light table. Her breath whispered out. It was worse than she'd thought.

'Hey, I don't look that bad. Do I?' Heath's voice wavered.

He did look that bad and he knew it. If Hannah had thought he was skeletal before, she hadn't understood skeletal. The lesions shimmered like purple bruises on skin so pale it shone a little blue in certain lights. His lips were too red, chapped and cracked from the chemo, the throwing up from the chemo, the throwing up blood from the Kaposi's sarcoma.

'These aren't pictures of you.' She sat in Charley's chair and peered at slide after slide.

'What are they?'

'Marshall Heights, Washington Highlands.' She recognized them from their being in the news nearly every night because of a shooting, a stabbing, a rape, a drive-by.

'What?' Heath tried to sit up, coughed once, and lay back down. 'Why?'

She squinted at a few more slides. 'Maybe he's doing a story on all the murders.'

Washington DC in 1991 had racked up nearly five hundred violent deaths. January '92 hadn't shown much improvement.

'A story for who? He hasn't been to *National Geographic* in weeks, except to pick up that light table. Doesn't seem like something they'd publish anyway.'

'I think he's just . . . doing it.'

'Is he trying to get himself killed?' Heath asked.

'Maybe.'

'You gotta talk to him.'

'Me?' Hannah's heart began to jitter and dance. 'No. You're it. No backsies.'

Heath rolled his eyes. 'Grow up.'

Of all the things she would not have expected to hear out of her brother's mouth, 'grow up' was near the top of the list. Heath had never been a big fan of growing up. Now he never would.

Her eyes burned. 'I need a shower.'

'Suck it up and sit.'

Maybe 'suck it up' was near the top of that list too.

Heath patted the bed and she complied.

'There are a few things we need to discuss.' Heath sounded both stronger than he had in weeks and weaker than he ever had before.

'No, I . . .' Her gaze flicked to the bathroom door.

'I know you cry in the shower.'

Her gaze flicked back. 'Do not.'

'There are things you need to know. Things I need to ask. OK?'

No, she thought.

'OK,' she said.

'I've done some research on PTSD.'

There was another jumble of words she would not have expected to hear out of Heath's mouth.

'Why?'

'You haven't heard Charley shouting some nights?'

Of course she had. He never shouted much beyond, *No!* and *Incoming!* She hadn't been sure what to do, so she'd done nothing.

'How did you do research?'

Heath rarely left the apartment these days, and when he did it was for chemo or a doctor's appointment. Considering how those trips exhausted him, she was going to rap some heads if Charley had been dragging him to the library too.

'I can use the phone. I've talked to the VA, a counselor or two. And Ready Reference is damn handy.' Heath took a breath. 'The way he's behaving, the way he's always behaved – the dangerous assignments, pushing the non-dangerous ones toward dangerous by taking that extra step, going out and doing that.' He pointed at the slides. 'Some PTSD sufferers who were exposed to continued trauma, over and over for a long period of time, feel the need to recreate that adrenaline rush of danger to process their stress. Now he's had another trauma.'

Lisa.

'But he didn't take any pictures for months after she died. Didn't go anywhere dangerous.' Unless they counted that single trip home. Afterward his nightmares had gotten worse.

'Avoidance. Another symptom. Now he's got tunnel vision – focused on the essay about me to the exclusion of everything but . . .'

They both turned their gazes to the light table.

That.

'What do we do?'

'Ideally take him to a shrink, but I don't think he'll go.'

'Maybe you can get him to talk to you.'

'I'll try, Hannah, but I . . .' He took her hand.

She tried to pull away. She knew where this was going.

'I'm not going to make it.'

'Don't say that! Don't even think it!'

'Someone has to.'

'No! No one has to, especially you. Positive thinking, it releases . . .' She couldn't remember what it released right now.

'It releases my annoyance. Enough of that yippy-skippy Pollyanna bullshit. I have cancerous lesions in my lungs that are growing not shrinking. I cough blood, spit blood, yak blood.'

'Heath, please,' Hannah said, appalled at the despair in her voice. Who wasn't thinking positive now?

'Sooner or later I'm going to either die from the sarcoma, or the treatment for the sarcoma, or pneumonia that I get from all of the above. You know it. I know it. Hell, sweetie, everyone knows it.' He lifted one emaciated shoulder. 'Regrets, I've got a few. Truly just one. I wanted so badly to be part of *You* becoming the number-one fashion magazine. Stupid, I know.'

'It's *not* stupid,' Hannah said fiercely. 'Not if it's something you really want.'

'Thanks.' He took her hand, squeezed, or at least she thought he did. The movement was so weak it might only have been a twitch. 'There's one thing I want you to do for me.'

'I'll go and get Mom and Dad. I'll make them come.'

'God, no.' He laughed and this time it didn't make him cough. Maybe he was getting better.

And what had happened to no more of the Pollyanna bullshit?

'I don't even want them at the funeral. In fact, I request no funeral. There've been enough of them lately.'

'But what . . .?'

'I want to be cremated and spread on the runway at Fashion Week.'

'I don't know what that is.'

'Ask Carol. She . . .' He choked, tried to swallow. Couldn't.

His eyes widened. He tried to breathe. Couldn't.

For the first time ever, Hannah wished he'd cough. Apparently, he couldn't.

If possible, Heath became paler. The veins in his head bulged.

She picked up the phone, dialed 911.

'Heath! Stay with me!'

The operator came on the line, but by the time Hannah had finished giving the particulars, Heath was unconscious.

Charley found them at the hospital that night. He had a black eye.

She didn't even ask.

Heath was still unconscious. They were giving him morphine.

'You OK?' Charley asked.

'Nope.'

'How about him?'

'He's dying,' she said for the very first time.

Charley took the chair next to her. 'What did the doctor say?'

'A lot of big words.'

'Which add up to?'

'He's dying.'

Huh, the more she said it, the easier it did *not* get.

'Did he really say that?'

She shook her head. 'The chemo isn't working. The drugs aren't working. Everything they do only makes him weaker. We can keep trying, watch him puke blood for a few more weeks, maybe months, or we can . . .' Her voice broke.

Charley laid his hand on her arm. 'Let him go.'

She nodded.

'Did you ask Heath what he wanted?'

'He hasn't . . .' Her breath hitched. 'He hasn't woken up.'

'Have you called your parents?'

'Yes.'

'What do they say?'

'They'll be here tomorrow.'

'Isn't that what they said the last time you called?'

'Every time I called.' And, wonder of wonders, tomorrow never came.

'Your parents are almost as bad at parenting as I was.'

'Oh, Charley, you weren't—'

'Do they have the right to make his medical decisions?'

'No. Heath left that to me.' She stroked her brother's too pale, too still hand. 'Asshole.'

'What will happen if you do nothing but keep him comfortable?'

'Respiratory failure. Blue lips and skin.' She traced a vein in his blue-tinged arm. 'Rapid breathing. Racing heart.' The latter were symptoms she'd noticed in her brother on and off for the past few days.

The end had already begun and they hadn't even known it.

'He doesn't seem to be breathing too fast now and his heart . . .' Charley pointed at the monitor that emitted a steady and not too fast *beep-beep*.

'The morphine helps.' She didn't mention that the morphine would also increase the confusion and altered consciousness associated with respiratory failure.

'Hannah?'

Heath's eyes were closed, but his lips moved again, forming *Hannah* without sound.

'I'm right here.'

'I'll just . . .' Charley inched for the door.

'Stay,' Hannah and Heath said at the same time.

Charley hesitated, then remained near the door.

Heath opened his eyes, which appeared impossibly blue in his ice-pale face. He took a short, gaspy breath.

'I have a request.'

Hannah felt a shiver of déjà vu. Hadn't they been having this conversation right before he'd passed out?

'No funeral. I remember.'

'No.' He kicked his feet so hard he kicked off the sheet. The sight of his too-thin legs – the golden hair that had once covered them gone, the lesions that had made him cry stark and ugly – made her yank it back up. 'I want you to promise me . . .' He started to wheeze.

'You shouldn't talk. I've already promised.'

'No.' He fought to get air.

She considered calling for the doctor, but when she reached for the call button, he grabbed her hand. 'Promise . . .'

The last word came out on another wheeze and then . . .

Heath stopped breathing.

Frankie

'What the *hell*, Frankie?'

Why had she called Irene again? Oh, yeah, because she had no one else.

'Calm down.' Frankie glanced out the window of the cottage.

Charley stared into the water. So far, that water was the best babysitter she had.

They'd been here two days. She'd gotten Dr Lanier's OK to do radiation and chemo at the Sturgeon Bay outreach clinic and made an appointment to see him there next week. Once that was done, she'd cajoled, threatened and begged Charley into agreeing to attend the appointment and continue his treatments.

'Why are you letting him become your problem? *He* left *you*, remember? When you needed him the most, poof, he was off boinking the bimbo.'

Once it had felt good to say those things herself – which was where Irene had gotten them. Now, hearing her own words parroted back only made Frankie feel small and mean.

'He doesn't remember boinking the bimbo. He doesn't even remember the bimbo.'

'That doesn't mean it never happened. It doesn't mean she doesn't exist.'

Frankie had already participated in variations of this conversation several times. She still wasn't sure of the answers, so she asked the newest eternal question.

'Doesn't it?'

'Jesus Christ, Frankie.'

'Are you allowed to take a Lord's name in vain when you don't consider him a Lord?'

'Bite me.'

Frankie sighed. 'I promised I'd take care of him while he was in treatment.'

'He promised to love you forever and keep himself only for you.'

'He thinks he has.'

A growl of frustration traveled nearly a thousand miles in an instant. 'What on earth possessed you to promise her that?'

Frankie nearly told Irene about the pictures, but blackmail – or was it bribery? Definitely something illegal with a 'b' – would only make Irene crazier and Irene was crazy enough.

'Common decency?' Frankie asked.

'She should be the one rearranging her life.'

Irene was right. So why did agreeing with her feel so wrong?

'I don't have any assignments right now. I could use a break.'

'You could have an assignment if you wanted to.' Irene let out her breath on a huff. 'The only way any of this would make sense is if it's about revenge.'

'Revenge?' Frankie repeated.

Charley still stared into the water as if hypnotized. Pretty soon she was going to have to put a stop to it. He was freaking her out.

'He left you when you needed him the most. You're planning to do the same thing.'

'I . . . what?'

'At the end, when he's dying and he still thinks the two of

you are the loves of each other's lives, you leave. Bam. Slam-dunk. Perfect revenge. Isn't it what every left-behind woman dreams of?'

Frankie had dreamed of it once. Probably more than once.

She peered out the window again, her gaze resting on Charley's back. Right now it sounded like more of a nightmare.

'He said he's never loved anyone the way he loves me,' Frankie murmured.

Now a long, sad sigh traveled the miles. 'Oh, Frankie. That's what they all say.'

Frankie pled an appointment that was closer than it was to end the conversation. For the first time she could recall, she felt worse after talking to Irene instead of better.

She'd been happy, or at least content. Happy had disappeared with Lisa, and it wasn't coming back. But she enjoyed her work, her house, her garden. Until today, she'd enjoyed Irene. She enjoyed men and occasional sex. Nothing too serious. She didn't do serious. She liked good food, great wine. Life was, if not fabulous, livable.

But shouldn't it be more? Could it be more with Charley?

Stupid questions. Charley might be Her Charley now, but she was working on making him Hannah's Charley again. Then he would go back to his life, and her life would go back to what it had been.

Bland. Unexciting.

Lonely.

And when had she started to think that about her life?

When Charley had waltzed back into it.

Another option was that he never became Hannah's Charley again and died just the way Irene had said – needing Frankie, missing her, loving her, confused as to why she had left him.

Sounded so familiar.

There were other possibilities, of course. Charley beat the cancer but never remembered all he'd forgotten. They lived out their golden years, together, Frankie inventing new and creative lies every day about the whereabouts of Lisa.

Or, Charley didn't get better and died with Frankie holding his hand.

Now that she thought about it, pretty much every option sucked.

Charley came into the kitchen and started making scrambled eggs for lunch. He poured the beaten eggs into the heated skillet and they sizzled. Their buttery scent, that crackling sound, the sight of the lemon yellow liquid slowly solidifying into a fluffy scramble the shade of chick down – a vaguely disturbing thought – made her wonder. How many times had they made scrambled eggs together?

Not once since Lisa had died.

Making scrambled eggs had been an occupation reserved for whenever Daddy was home. Frankie would sit at the table, drinking her coffee, pretending to read the paper, but really enjoying the sight of the two people she loved most in the world having so much fun.

Daddy makes the best scrambled eggs!

The memory was so vivid Frankie had to grip the counter to keep from swaying. However, the recollection didn't cause the usual jackknife of pain to her chest that any sudden flashes of their daughter usually did. Instead she felt almost . . . happy for the visit.

Lisa lived on in their memories of her. Maybe Frankie had been wrong to tuck them away.

'So . . .' Charley scooped eggs on to two plates. 'Walk? Ride? Boat?'

'A walk,' she said. 'That would be nice.'

How often had the two of them strolled, contemplating the water, the woods, the sky?

Counting today? Just once.

The park at this time of the week was nearly deserted, the air a bit cool. The grass felt mossy beneath their feet. Overgrown, it brushed their calves. Wildflowers peppered the green.

They sat at a picnic table overlooking the water.

'We should have stopped and bought a bottle of wine.'

Charley mimed pulling a cork out of a bottle, pouring two glasses, handing her one. He was so comical, she picked up her camera and pressed the shutter. They 'clinked' the rims, had a 'sip'.

'Mmm, Russian River Valley. My favorite.' She took a large, imaginary gulp and closed her eyes on a sigh.

His camera fired off a few frames and she opened her eyes as he lowered it and smiled. 'Only the best for you.'

The breeze seemed to still. The water lapped against the rocks nearby, a lovely lulling sound.

Charley's gaze mesmerized. When he'd stared at her like that she'd believed that she was the only woman in the world for him. She'd been wrong, but while she'd believed it the world had been a bright and shining place, full of possibility. She missed that feeling almost as much as she'd once missed him.

Lured by the sound of the waves, that expression in his eyes, Frankie leaned forward and touched her lips to his.

She tasted red wine, smelled it too. Her head felt light. This day, this moment reminded her of the them they used to be, or perhaps the them they should have been, could have been.

If only . . .

She pulled back, set down her imaginary glass. She could have sworn she heard it *click*.

She was drunk on memories of something that had never happened.

He took her hand, oblivious. 'That was nice.'

She wasn't certain if he was talking about the kiss or the wine. If only the kiss had been as imaginary as the booze.

'Charley, we probably shouldn't . . .'

'I know.'

As he was still smiling at her as if he were half-drunk, she wasn't certain what he knew, and she didn't want to ask. She'd had enough crazy-making kooky talk to last a lifetime.

But what if it wasn't kooky talk?

'We need to get to the clinic,' she said.

They arrived for his chemo appointment with a few minutes to spare. The nurse, who appeared all of sixteen but just couldn't be, identified herself as Amy. She handed Frankie a thick packet of information; she handed Charley a single sheet of highlights.

'He's got enough on his plate without being overwhelmed.' She nodded at the packet Frankie clutched in her hand and her high and tight strawberry blond ponytail bobbed. Then she led them to the treatment room.

Frankie thought *she* had enough on *her* own plate without being overwhelmed, but she supposed someone had to be.

Not long after they had Charley hooked up to his IV, Frankie's phone buzzed. Figuring it was Irene, she nearly let it go to voicemail. Then she pulled it out of her bag.

Hannah.

'How's it going?' Hannah asked.

Frankie's gaze fell on the *No cell phones in the treatment area* sign. 'Hold on.'

Charley was asleep. To make sure, she set her hand on his arm and whispered, 'Charley?' into his ear.

Nothing.

Frankie hurried into the hall. 'He's asleep.'

'During chemo?'

'That's what I thought.' Quickly Frankie explained about premeds, as well as everything else she'd learned from Nurse Amy and the behemoth packet.

'Can you send me that packet?'

'I bet I can get another one sent to you.' Frankie wanted to read through hers again.

'Great. Thanks. So . . . uh . . . what you been doing?'

Frankie saw them toasting with imaginary wine and kissing with real-life lips.

'Nothing,' she said too quickly.

'It's impossible to do nothing.'

'TV, books, cards, walks.'

Wine. Kisses.

Hannah gave a loud, fake snore.

'I suppose you two do all kinds of exciting things.'

Why in *hell* had she asked that? She'd spent twenty-plus years forgetting him, learning not to care about anything he, she or they might be doing, and now she was asking for an update.

'No,' Hannah said. 'Or at least we don't any more. We did take a few trips at first . . . then, well . . .'

Frankie could imagine how that had gone. Charley had never been one to enjoy company when he was working, nor had he been the kind of man to take a trip for any other reason.

'We went golfing a few times.'

'No fucking way.'

Hannah laughed. 'Exactly. It didn't go any better than the times we tried bowling or reading the same book or listening to music.'

'What on earth did you two ever have in common?' Frankie wanted to bite her tongue the instant the question came out of her mouth. She certainly didn't want to hear how compatible the two had been in bed. Ick.

'We had tragedy in common. It brought Charley and I together.'

And tragedy had pulled Charley and Frankie apart.

'What kept you together?'

She couldn't believe she'd asked that. What was wrong with her? Then Hannah answered. What was wrong with *her*?

'Work.'

'You took away my husband so you could work together?'

'We don't work together. We enjoy our work. It's what we live for. We discuss it. We share it. And I didn't take him away. You threw him away.'

'I did no such thing.'

'Think back. Maybe hindsight will give you some twenty-twenty.'

'You're saying the divorce was my fault?'

'Does it have to be anyone's fault?'

'Yes,' Frankie muttered.

Hannah laughed. 'That's so twenty-four years ago.'

Frankie's lips twitched. That was something she might say.

'How do you see it?' she asked.

'Do you really want to do this?' Computer keys clattered; phones rang.

Did Hannah ever leave that office? Considering she lived for her work, stupid question.

'Let me have it,' Frankie said.

The computer keys stopped clattering. Hannah must have shut her office door, because the phones faded as well. 'The two of you were devastated. With good reason. You blamed him. You turned away from him. You didn't need him. I did. And right then, Charley needed to be needed.'

'You're saying you saved him?'

'No. He saved me.'

Frankie had known back then that Hannah's brother was dying of AIDS. She'd felt awful for both of them. Charley had been doing an essay. It was groundbreaking work. Something that needed, very badly, to be done.

Unfortunately, Charley had thought Hannah needed, very badly, to be done as well.

'My brother was a part of me. You've heard of twin telepathy? We had it. Not all the time, but it was there. Then it was gone. Like him. The silence was . . .' Hannah paused, breathed in and out. When she spoke again the pain, the panic that had crept into her voice had disappeared and she spoke briskly and matter-of-factly. 'When I lost Heath I lost more of myself than I could afford to.'

Frankie understood completely that feeling of loss and confusion, the hole inside you so big you couldn't figure out how you could possibly go on living with such a gaping maw at your center.

'I did things I shouldn't,' Hannah continued. 'I forgot things I couldn't afford to forget. Charley was there. He knew what it was like. He helped me to find the me I'd lost.'

'Sounds like quite a hero.'

'He was.'

And what young girl can resist a hero?

Hannah had been lost, alone, uncertain, devastated. So had Frankie. But it wasn't Hannah's fault that Charley had been there for her. He'd tried to be there for Frankie and she wouldn't let him.

These realizations caused the hard knot of anger she'd carried in her chest for far too long to loosen. It didn't disappear, maybe it never would, but it was better.

Nurse Amy waved from the treatment room. As she was smiling and no one was running in that direction, Frankie assumed Charley hadn't coded.

'I'm being summoned,' she said.

'Can you . . .?' Something tapped very fast on the other side of the country – *rat-a-tat-tat* – sounded like a pen or a pencil clicking against a desk to allay some nerves. 'Can you call me later and tell me everything?'

'What kind of everything?'

'Exactly what they're doing. How he seems. What he felt. If he's improving.'

'That seems like information better suited to an email.'

Hannah took a deep breath and the *rat-a-tat-tat* stopped. 'Please? It's hard to sleep when I have no idea what's going on.'

She sounded like a child and while that should have made Frankie frustrated, if not annoyed beyond redemption, instead she felt a flicker of compassion. What would she do if someone she loved was so far away, very sick and there was nothing she could do but beg for every crumb of information?

If she couldn't get the information, she'd go there and demand it in person.

What if her presence only made the loved one angry, scared, confused?

Worse.

It would be upsetting, frightening, insomnia-provoking. Hannah was doing the best she could. And if that best included bribery, blackmail, avoidance and payoffs, who was Frankie to judge? Who was anyone?

'I'll call,' Frankie said.

Hannah

Washington DC. January, 1992

'Heath!' Hannah shook him.

Her brother's head lolled.

She put her lips on his and began CPR. She wasn't very good at it. The last time she'd had any training had been at summer camp when they were fifteen years old. She couldn't remember how many breaths, how many compressions, but something was better than nothing, right?

Charley pressed the call button, answered the God-like voice that responded with: 'He isn't breathing.'

Almost immediately the loudspeaker called a code, footsteps pounded, a cart rattled.

Hannah placed her lips over Heath's once again. They already seemed cold.

She knew that couldn't be true. None of this could be true.

Someone yanked her away.

She fought to get back. 'He needs me to breathe for him.'

'Dude, can you grab her so we can do our thing?' An orderly in white scrubs shoved Hannah in Charley's direction.

Charley put his arm around her and drew her out of the way. 'Let them help him.'

'What were you thinking to put your mouth on his?' The orderly unwrapped a mouth guard and placed it between his lips and Heath's.

Hannah couldn't answer the question because she couldn't remember what she'd been thinking beyond breathing.

'You can't catch AIDS from a kiss,' Charley said. 'Or CPR.'

'You can catch it from an open wound.' The orderly put his mouth atop the guard, which was atop Heath's.

'Only if you have an open wound too.'

'Better safe than sorry.' The young man began chest compressions. One of Heath's ribs broke. He was so fragile.

'Stop!' A female doctor skidded in, followed by several minions. She motioned for them to hover in the background while she strode into the light. 'This patient has a DNR on file.'

The orderly immediately stopped life-saving measures.

'No!' Hannah cried, and tried to get back to the bed so she could do them herself. 'I have control over medical decisions.'

'This isn't one of them. A signed DNR trumps everything. It's what the patient wants.'

Hannah deflated so fast she nearly went to her knees – would have if Charley hadn't been there to hold her up.

'He wanted to die?' she whispered.

'No.' Charley pulled her against his side, and she leaned on him gladly. 'But he understood he probably would. He was tired, Hannah, so tired.'

She craned her neck to see Charley's face; he looked tired too. 'He told you that?'

'He did.'

'Why didn't he tell me?' Her voice was small, wispy, scared.

'You wanted him to fight, but he was all fought out. He didn't want to disappoint you.'

'He couldn't.'

'I know.'

She tried to get closer to the bed, but Charley held her back. 'I wanna hold his hand.'

Charley released her and she rushed forward, crowding others aside so she could wrap her fingers through her brother's. She didn't care for how he felt, like a jumble of sticks in a skin bag, but she didn't let go.

Charley stood next to her, hand on her shoulder. Having him there helped more than she thought it could. She was alone now, would always be alone in a way no one but Heath could understand. But Charley had loved him too, had known him – not in the way that she had – but better than anyone else had known him.

'Sir?' The doctor didn't pause as she scribbled on the chart. 'Could you take your daughter outside so we can finish?'

Hannah felt Charley jolt.

'He's not my father. He's a friend.'

The doctor lifted her gaze, then her eyebrows.

'Of Heath's!'

Charley snorted. 'You don't have to explain anything, honey.'

Honey? She liked that. Certainly he hadn't said it the way he said *Fancy*, but now that Hannah thought about it she hadn't heard him say *Fancy* in a long time.

'I can't leave him,' Hannah said.

'We'll just stand out of the way.' Charley drew her to the far wall and took her hand.

His felt wonderful – strong, firm; she couldn't feel the bones rubbing against the other side of his skin.

The doctor hesitated, as if she'd argue, then she shrugged and returned to her clipboard.

'I should probably take a picture,' Charley murmured.

'Of what?'

Charley tilted his head toward Heath. In the hand Hannah didn't hold, he cradled a camera.

Hannah's heart took a large leap, as if trying to escape from her chest. 'Now?'

'Before they take him away. Maybe after too, if they'll let me.'

The idea of Heath being photographed when he wasn't . . . *There.*

No. She didn't like that word, couldn't . . . fathom it. Heath was there. She could see him. End of story.

She should comb her brother's hair, fix his face, get him a better shirt. Except he didn't have a shirt. All he had was the horrible, stained and wrinkled hospital gown.

She lifted her hand to Charley's arm. 'He wouldn't want that.'

Charley's biceps flexed beneath her hold, as if he'd pull away, but he didn't. 'Heath wanted this essay to show everything – beginning to end. If it's going to mean anything, if it's going to *change* anything, I need this picture.'

The medical personnel continued to buzz around the body like flies. Pretty soon, they'd make Heath unrecognizable, if he wasn't already. She let go of Charley and nodded.

He stepped up to the foot of the bed and pressed the shutter.

The doctor spun, mouth open, eyes wide.

Charley pressed the shutter again.

'You cannot . . .' she began.

Charley reached into his pocket and pulled out the release Heath had signed, handing it to her without taking his eye from the viewfinder.

As she read the paper, her face smoothed out. 'You've been recording this from the beginning?'

Charley nodded, changed his angle, shot again.

'Good.' She returned the paper. 'Let me know when you exhibit the photographs. I'd like to see them.' She beckoned her staff. 'We'll be back in a few minutes.'

'What exhibit?' Hannah asked.

She'd never considered what Charley would do with the pictures. Because to consider that would mean that Heath was . . .

She swallowed.

'There should be an exhibit, don't you think?' Charley lowered the camera, cast her a glance, then lifted it again. 'Maybe you could work that out.'

'Me? I'm going to be busy.'

'Doing what?' Charley's camera whirred as he recorded every possible angle of the bed, the room with the abandoned crash cart, the TV still playing without the sound, Hannah still in the corner. 'Heath didn't want a funeral. You're going to have a lot of time on your hands.'

'*You* needs a lot of work.'

He lowered the camera. 'You're not going back to *National Geographic*?'

Hannah hadn't realized until just that second that she wasn't. Not yet.

'It was Heath's dream for *You* to become number one.'

'So?'

'Now it's mine.'

Charley frowned. 'He was hopped on drugs. You can't take a request made in the heat of the morphine seriously.'

'He didn't ask. He wouldn't.'

'Damn right, he wouldn't. And he wouldn't want you to give up your dream for his.'

'I want to.'

'Hannah, you're too good to waste—'

She held up her hand. 'Heath didn't think *You* was a waste. Neither does Carol.' She pursed her lips. 'I should call Carol.'

'Only if you're quitting,' he said.

'Not until *You* is number one. It shouldn't take that long.'

He lifted his eyebrows, but he didn't argue. 'Where should we show these photographs?'

She was so grateful he'd let the matter of *You* drop she didn't bother to tell him she knew nothing about photography exhibits. 'What's the biggest and best venue you know?'

'Society for the Visual Arts in Soho,' Charley said immediately. 'That might take you some time. I hear it's booked for the next century. But if you have a show there, anyone who's everyone sees it.'

'OK. That's where it'll be.'

'Where what will be?'

Hannah's mother stood in the doorway.

'Oh, shit,' Hannah said.

Charley choked, but covered by continuing to take pictures. Wasn't he out of film yet?

'Is that any way to greet your mother? Come and give me a kiss.' Belinda offered her perfectly powdered cheek.

Hannah did what she was told; it was easier.

Her mother appeared flawless, as usual. Platinum blond hair in a pageboy cut that framed her square-jawed face. Her eyes were as blue as Heath's had been; she also had Heath's height, or he'd had hers. She stood tall and slim in her navy blue pinstriped pantsuit – a white camisole just visible in the V at her neck, the waist nipped in tight.

'Where's Dad?'

'He had to catch a flight.'

'You said you were coming tomorrow. Both of you!'

'Well, I'm here. Your father will have to come next week when he gets back.'

'No,' Hannah said. 'He won't.'

Her mother hadn't noticed Heath's unusual lack of chatter, nor his odd stillness. Hannah should probably tell her before she air kissed a corpse.

Or not.

'Heath, darling, aren't you glad to see me?'

'He'd have been glad to see you any of the dozen times you promised to come before.'

Charley cast Hannah a quick, concerned glance.

She wasn't acting like herself. She didn't sound like herself.

Her voice was loud. Her words were harsh. Her hands were clenched.

She kind of liked this new self.

'Well, I'm here now.'

'He isn't.'

'Don't be ridiculous.' Belinda marched up to the bed. 'He's right . . .'

Her breath caught. She swayed. His name came out on an exhale sounding as lost as Hannah felt.

'When?' Belinda asked.

Hannah had no idea. It seemed like they'd both been here forever and that they'd only just arrived.

'About ten minutes ago, Mrs Cartwright,' Charley said.

From the way he held the camera, fingers tightening and releasing and tightening again, he badly wanted to take a picture of her mother with the body. But, so far, he'd refrained.

'Who the hell are you?'

The question was so rude Hannah flinched.

'Charley Blackwell. I'm doing an essay on AIDS.' He fired off a shot with her in it. 'Start to finish.'

Hannah expected her mother to grab the camera, smash it, at the least demand the film and that Charley leave. Instead she nodded slowly. 'About time someone did.'

'Who are you and what have you done with my mother?' Hannah asked.

Belinda's eyes narrowed but she didn't take the bait. 'I'd like a minute alone with my son.'

'Why?' Hannah demanded. 'You couldn't be bothered with him when he was alive. Now that he's dead he's suddenly worthy?'

'I admit, I didn't understand him. I didn't know why he had to be gay.'

'It wasn't a lifestyle choice; it's who he is. Was.'

'If you say so.'

Hannah ground her teeth.

'Then when all this started . . .' She waved her French manicure at the machines and tubes. 'We told him to snap out of it. Did he want to die?'

'Snap out of it,' Hannah repeated. Her head had started to throb.

'Now he's dead, and for what?'

'Have to agree with you there.'

'I should have been stronger. I should have been here.'

Hannah figured agreeing again would be redundant.

'Though I did send money. A lot of money.'

Hannah's gaze met Charley's. She couldn't think of anything to say.

'We'll pay for the funeral, of course.'

'No funeral.'

'No . . .' Belinda's brow would have crinkled if the plastic surgery would have let it. 'Well, I suppose that's best. So many of those people in such a small place, we don't want it to spread.'

Hannah opened her mouth, then shut it again. Why bother?

'This essay.' She waved at Charley's camera. 'Is it sold?'

'It isn't finished.'

She cast a meaningful glance at the bed. 'Isn't it?'

Hannah choked on a sob.

Charley took a step toward her, but Hannah's mother stood in the way. 'Could you get to the point, Mrs Cartwright?'

'I want to buy it.'

'No,' Hannah blurted.

She imagined her mother making a bonfire with the film, then no one would ever see her dying son, no one would ever know she'd had one; Heath would be erased as easily from the world as he'd seemed to be from their parents' lives.

'It's not for sale.'

'Everything's for sale.'

Charley just set his jaw and shook his head.

'Don't you want your work to reach the largest possible audience?'

Charley flicked a glance at Hannah.

'What are you talking about, Mother?'

'I'll publish the photographs in a book. There's nothing like it out there.'

Of course. Anything to make a hundred million bucks.

'Charley is going to exhibit the essay.'

'That's a fantastic idea.' She turned away from the bed as if what lay on it was dead to her.

Hannah fought not to laugh at her pun. If she started laughing now, she wouldn't stop.

'We'll drum up interest for the book with a showing. We'll sell the prints.' She lifted her hands, framing air. 'The people who can't afford one – and believe me, there'll be a lot of them – can buy the book. Whaddya say?'

'I don't . . .' Charley began.

Hannah held up her hand. 'The show takes place at the Society for the Visual Arts in Soho.'

'That's impossible. They're booked solid.'

Hannah shrugged. 'Oh, well.'

'Wait.' Belinda chewed on her lower lip. She wasn't going to have any lipstick left. 'I think I can call in a favor.'

She walked out, then almost immediately in again. She went directly to Heath, leaned over, kissed his brow, whispered something in his ear. Then she straightened, pulled the sheet over his face and left.

'What just happened?' Hannah asked.

'Your mother.'

'She bought us. It's what she does.'

'No, she gave us the best opportunity to display the essay of Heath in the most prominent place and with the widest medium.'

'It's a deal with the devil.'

'There's a reason the devil makes so many deals.'

'What's that?'

'She's good at it.'

Hannah released a watery, blubbery laugh that turned into a hiccup and then she was crying. She hated to cry and Heath wouldn't want her to. But how did one stop?

'Sit.' Charley urged her into the chair at the side of the bed, then pulled the sheet away from Heath's face.

He didn't look like Heath any more. Really, he hadn't looked like Heath for a while now.

'You want me to step out so you can say goodbye?'

She started to nod, then shook her head, waved at the camera. 'Finish this.'

'You don't want me to photograph your goodbye.'

'I do. Otherwise how will I remember it?'

Hannah wasn't certain she'd remember much of today. Maybe she didn't want to. But they did need to finish this the way that Heath had wanted it to be finished.

Hannah thought she'd be self-conscious, unable to say a true goodbye with a camera in the room. But the instant her hand touched Heath's – the skin bag of bones texture was fading to stiff and rubbery – her tears stopped and she just said what she needed to.

'Goodbye. I love you. Always will. You remember how I said I'd panic without you?' She leaned over and kissed his cheek one last time. 'I am.'

Charley lowered the camera. His eyes were a little damp.

'You want a minute too?' she asked.

He hesitated, then nodded and handed her his camera.

She retreated to the door, glanced back.

Charley stood at the bedside, shoulders slumped, the picture of someone who'd just lost his best friend.

Hannah lifted the lens.

'We need to take him now.'

Hannah bumbled the camera, nearly dropping it on to the tile floor.

The orderly was back.

'Where are you taking him?' Her voice sounded frightened and weak.

How would she make *You* into the magazine Heath wanted it to be if she talked to people like that? No one would ever take her seriously. They'd eat her alive.

'Morgue.' The orderly did some fancy maneuver with the bed wheels. There was a *click* and then a *clunk* and he began to take Heath away.

Hannah turned so she wouldn't have to watch him go. 'He wants to be cremated.'

'Have the funeral home contact the hospital.'

The rattle of the bed faded down the hall.

At the apartment, Hannah stood in the center of the room uncertain what to do first. Or maybe she was uncertain what to do at all. Her brain was empty.

'Hungry?' Charley asked.

Hannah made a face.

'Thirsty?'

She shook her head.

'Tired?'

She nodded.

'Off to bed then.' He herded her down the hall.

She stopped halfway to her room. 'I should call the funeral home.'

'It's ten o'clock at night.'

She glanced at her watch. 'Huh.'

'Morning's soon enough for phone calls.'

At the door to her bedroom he kissed her forehead and she clung.

He stiffened; she nearly spun and fled. Then his arms came around her and she laid her cheek on his chest and just let herself be held. It had been months since anyone had hugged her. Heath hadn't had the strength.

'What calls?' she asked.

He jerked a little as if he'd been thinking of something else.

Hannah wished she could think of anything but how warm he was, how good he smelled, what he might taste like if she—

'Funeral home. Medical equipment rental place. Your aunt. His friends. I'll make a list.'

'You seem to know a lot ab—' She bit off the word, wished she could bite off her tongue. Of course he knew a lot about what to do when someone died. 'I'm sorry.'

'At least the knowledge is good for something other than nightmares.' His arms dropped; he turned away. He'd gone into his room and shut the door before she made it into hers.

She surprised herself by falling immediately and deeply asleep. In her dream, the orderly from the hospital was in the apartment.

'Your brother ran off. We don't know where. Can you help us search for him?'

Her dream self knew exactly where Heath had gone – an underground tunnel, like the New York City subway system. A place that Heath would never, ever be caught dead.

Ha.

The dark, damp passageway was deserted as she hurried along to a destination both predetermined and mysterious.

A door loomed out of the darkness – heavy, iron – yet when she touched it the portal swung wide. Inside Heath lay on a bed in the corner and he beckoned for her to join him. He appeared as he had before this had all begun – golden and beautiful and so happy.

She lay down, her back to his front – spoons – the way her mother always said they'd slept as babies. His arms surrounded her; she laid her hands on his atop her stomach.

'I'm all right,' he whispered. 'Everything's all right here.'

The sorrow and pain ebbed out of her like the tide. Joy flowed in to take their place.

He was all right.

The sound of her own indrawn breath woke her, with tears trembling on her eyelashes and that feeling of joy just starting to fade.

Her brother had been there with her. She could still feel his arms around her. But that feeling of oneness she'd shared with him was fading along with the burst of joy.

They had always been a set, and now she was just one. Alone in a way no one else could ever understand.

Hannah sat up, swiped at her face. She wasn't going to go back to sleep anytime soon.

She opened her door, stepped into the hall, heard the low rumble of Charley's voice in his room.

'I don't know what you want from me, Francesca.'

Francesca. Not Frankie. Not Fancy.

'If I could turn back time, if I could make it un-happen, if I could die instead of her, don't you think I would?' His voice lifted with every phrase until the final question was a cry, a plea.

Hannah didn't realize she'd stepped toward his door, that her palm lay against the wood. There had been so much pain, so much loss. How did a person survive it?

Neither Frankie nor Charley seemed to be doing a very good job. Who did? Hannah certainly didn't think she was going to.

His voice lowered; she could no longer hear what he was saying. She shouldn't have been listening but it wasn't like she'd had her ear pressed to the door. Just her hand.

She curled that hand inward, wishing she could do something more for him, but knowing she could not.

Hannah hurried into the living room, then she wanted to hurry back out. Heath's hospital bed stood there, rumpled white sheets ghostly in the half-light. His pillow still bore the indentation of his head.

She definitely had to get all of that out of here ASAP.

She didn't want to turn on the television. The sole place to sit and watch would be Heath's bed, or the chair she'd sat in as she'd watched him die.

She'd get rid of that chair tomorrow as well.

The only other seat in the room was at the light table. Hannah took it, then she flicked on the bulb that lay inside. Expecting to see more shots of DC about to go up in flames, she stilled at the sight of Heath.

The majority of the photographs depicted scenes she was unfamiliar with because they'd been taken while she was at work. They'd done all sorts of things without her.

Her finger brushed a shot of Heath mugging for the camera in front of the giant panda cage at the National Zoo while Hsing-Hsing and Ling-Ling slept peacefully behind him. Sure, Heath had leprosy lesions and he wore a Red Sox cap because his hair was gone, but he looked happy.

She laughed out loud at the photo of him eating a hot dog at a street fair. He hated hot dogs. But many of the things he'd liked he could no longer stomach during chemo. Apparently things he'd previously hated he no longer did.

She spent hours staring at slides of her brother out and about in Washington DC. It was like he wasn't dead, because he was right here doing new things.

Every sad photo she removed from the light table and stacked it out of the way.

Heath reflected in the mirror as he shaved the last remaining strands of golden, god-like hair from his head.

Heath's beautiful blue eyes tear-filled as he held the puke bowl up to his chin; in the background brightly colored cartoon characters merrily capered across the television screen.

Heath at the bedside of one, two, three dying friends while he was still golden and god-like, their gazes on him dark, hopeless, knowing.

Heath holding up a hand covered in lesions toward the camera, his face turned away, the curve of his neck both achingly sweet and heartbreakingly sad.

There were also pictures of Hannah. She looked like crap in every one, which worked because in every one she remembered feeling like crap. She hadn't felt any other way since Heath had been diagnosed.

She moved every photograph of herself off the light table, as well, and concentrated on the ones that mattered. She sat there all night, grouping the happy pictures one way and then another. First chronologically – oldest to newest, then newest to oldest

– then she tossed them up and arranged them however they fell down, and after that she put all the black and white on the left side and all those in color on the right. Every edit revealed something she hadn't seen before.

By the time Charley walked in, appearing as if he hadn't slept either, she was jazzed and she hadn't even had any caffeine.

'Hi.' His stubble rasped when he ran a hand over his jaw. 'You . . .'

She leaped up and ran to him, grabbing his hands tightly in her own. 'Because of you, he's never going to die.'

He glanced at the light table. 'Hannah, you should get some sleep.'

'I'm fine. I'm good. I'm great.'

'You're not. You're overtired and a little nuts.'

She laughed, and she did sound a little nuts. 'I dreamed of Heath. He said he was all right.'

'OK.' He put his arm around her and tried to lead her back to her bedroom.

She ducked his arm and dragged him to the light table. 'See?' She pointed at all the happy slides. 'He lives right there.'

'Those are only half the story, and you know it.' He scowled. 'Where are the pictures of you?'

'I'm not the story.'

'I disagree.'

She crossed her arms over her chest. 'Heath's the story. He isn't truly dead because of you.'

'Heath did die. He *is* dead.' Charley's voice gentled. 'Everyone goes through denial. I did.'

'The dream felt so real.'

That feeling of bliss returned, fading now, fading fast, but still there. Heath was all right. She had to believe that.

'Hold on to any joy you can. I wish . . .' He ran a hand through his curls. 'I wish I could make this all better for you. Time warp you ahead a year or two when it doesn't hurt so much.'

His eyes were bleak; she captured his hand again. 'You can come too. In a few years it'll be—'

He cast her a quick glance and she knew that, for him, a few years wouldn't do it. A few decades? Maybe. She hoped she was still in his life to find out.

And that hope was so pathetic, she started to pull away, but he clung, and she let him. Or maybe she clung and he let her. What did it matter?

'Did you sleep?' she asked.

He shook his head.

She remembered what she'd heard as she passed his room, and saw his exhaustion for what it was.

Guilt.

His daughter had died while in his care. He was probably never going to get over that.

'I wish I could make this all better for you,' she whispered.

Their eyes met. In his she saw a spark of something new – interest, attraction.

She was imagining things.

'I'm so glad you're here.' Her hand tightened on his, and he stepped closer. She didn't move back. 'I don't know what I'd do without you. I'm a mess.'

'You're not.' He lifted his free hand and brushed her bird's nest hair away from her no doubt pasty face. But instead of letting his arm fall, he rested his knuckles against her cheek. 'You've been a rock. The first time I saw you cry was last night. That's incredible.'

'You're incredible.' God, she was *so* lame.

His breath puffed across her lips. She licked them.

His bright blue gaze followed the path of her tongue.

She was suddenly hot and dizzy with it. She swayed, her breasts just brushing his chest.

They froze.

How they wound up kissing, she never could figure out.

How they wound up fucking . . .

Was anyone's guess.

Charley

Washington DC. January, 1992

Charley awoke from an embarrassing dream with a hard-on that was harder than any he'd had in years.

He opened his eyes. He had no idea where he was.

Something moved next to him and he glanced down.

Hannah lay sound asleep at his side. She was naked.

Apparently his embarrassing dream was not a dream.

Holy hell.

He inched away so the world's greatest hard-on didn't bump her. Not that it hadn't bumped her last night – make that this morning – several times.

She'd been a virgin. That should have freaked him out enough to make him stop. But if he hadn't been freaked out by the kiss, the nakedness, the foreplay – there'd been a lot of foreplay – why should a little virginity get him down?

So to speak.

What had he been thinking?

That she was sad. The person she loved most in the world had died. Tragically. If anyone could understand that, it was Charley. He'd wanted to make it better.

So they'd made it.

Maybe he hadn't been thinking at all.

And that excuse would get him really far with his wife.

Wife. Shit.

That was what he'd been thinking before he'd come upon Hannah behaving so manic this morning. His wife could barely look at him, barely speak to him. She didn't want him around, and he didn't blame her.

For the first time, he'd been considering that maybe he should give her what she wanted. Maybe she'd be happier without him. Every time Frankie saw him, she saw her dead child. So maybe she shouldn't have to see him any more.

How many times had he listened to other cheaters say how their wives didn't understand them, didn't appreciate them, didn't want them, didn't love them, they'd be better off without them? He'd barely managed not to roll his eyes in disgust. You took a vow, you kept a vow, or you got out before you broke it. All that 'heat of the moment, couldn't help myself' was bullshit.

Yet here he was, hip deep in bullshit.

At least he'd used a condom. Heath had left behind a zillion. If Heath could see him now . . .

Charley groaned and Hannah stirred. He held his breath, praying she wouldn't wake up. What would he say?

See ya.

Oh, how he wished that he could.

But Hannah needed him. She was heartbroken, lost. And after meeting her mother he couldn't abandon her. Besides, he'd promised Heath.

One afternoon, after the poor kid had been doing his best to upchuck most of his vital organs, Heath had gripped Charley's shoulder and said, 'After I'm gone, will you do something for me? Please don't leave until Hannah's OK.'

And Charley had agreed, because how hard could it be?

He glanced down at the woman in the bed. He really needed to quit using the word 'hard'.

The clock read nearly noon. He was surprised someone hadn't called the apartment.

As if he'd conjured the sound, the phone began to ring.

Hannah stirred.

He leaped out of bed and found his jeans, pulled them on dry, wincing as the zipper scraped his semi-hard cock.

'Down boy,' he murmured. What was wrong with them both?

'Please don't say you regret this.'

Charley grabbed his shirt and shoved his arms into it, leaving the buttons undone. Saw his underwear beneath the dresser and wondered how he'd scoop it up and hide it somehow.

Hannah leaned against the headboard, clutching the sheet to her breasts, which only called attention to them, made Charley remember them. They were great breasts.

Hannah was short, round, pale and plain. Didn't matter. Because it wasn't the way she looked that attracted him. What attracted him was how *she* looked at *him*.

As if he had all the answers, as if he could fix anything. Everything.

Of course he didn't have any answers, could fix nothing. His talent lay in breaking things, breaking people. He should probably remind her of this. Then again, didn't she know?

Still she continued to look at him exactly the same way she always had. He didn't deserve it, but he found that he needed it.

Hannah's hair was tangled from his fingers, her chin red from his stubble, her mouth swollen from his kisses.

He was suddenly glad his shirt was long enough to cover the front of his pants. He felt like a dirty old man. He also felt like a very young one. The last time he'd gotten it up like this had been . . .

Who knew?

'You regret it.' She tugged the sheet closer. 'Of course you do.'

He did regret it. Or should he say he regretted it now. While it had been happening, he hadn't been thinking at all. He'd only been feeling. And what he'd been feeling was alive, in a way he hadn't felt since his daughter had died.

Shame flickered. He waited for it to flare, but it didn't. He'd felt so bad, for so long. Right now, he just didn't.

He'd never imagined adultery could be like this. He'd always thought that he'd be unable to stop envisioning the face of his wife, probably to the point of impotence.

Hadn't happened.

'I . . . uh . . .' He was so damn smooth.

'I won't tell Francesca.'

'Tell,' he repeated, turning the word over on his tongue. Was he going to?

'It won't happen again. We'll forget all about it.'

Charley's gaze flickered over her face, her hair, those breasts. He doubted that, but he could try. He should probably start by getting a hotel room.

He meant to. He truly did. But the apartment phone started ringing again, and then it didn't stop.

Hannah seemed so bewildered he stayed to help. He made her a list of people to call as he'd promised; he even called some of them.

Friends started arriving with food and drinks. Several remained and the apartment became a wake.

He certainly couldn't leave her alone with a dozen strangers, even though they weren't strangers to Heath. By the time midnight rolled around again, he was still there and he was too tired to go anywhere else.

He hadn't called Frankie. What was more disturbing was that she hadn't called him.

He'd told her about Heath; she'd said she was sorry, but he could tell by her voice she didn't really care. And that had pissed him off. It was the first time he'd been angry with her since Lisa, and it had felt good. It had felt normal.

Of course, after they'd hung up, the guilt had returned, intensified by his anger. He hadn't slept; he definitely hadn't been himself. As evidenced by the adultery.

Hannah was taking a shower. Code for sobbing uncontrollably. He took the opportunity to phone his wife.

'Hello?' Her voice was drowsy.

He'd forgotten it was midnight. Eleven p.m. in Milwaukee but past Frankie's bedtime. She was an early riser, always had been.

'Sorry. It's late. I'll let you get back to sleep.' He spoke too fast. Did he sound as guilty as he thought he did?

'No. That's OK.' Sheets rustled. 'How was your day?'

'Shitty.'

'Why's that?'

Was she that out of touch with his life? Or did she just care so little now that she forgot what he'd told her within twenty-four hours?

'Heath. Died.'

'Oh. Right. The essay. Sorry.'

His anger intensified. 'He was more than an essay.'

'Of course he was. Are you staying?'

He'd thought he should go – he *knew* he should go – yet he hadn't. And the pull of this place, of what was going on here, of Hannah, was stronger than the pull to go home. Because the house where Frankie slept had never been home. Home had always been Frankie and now she just . . . wasn't.

'I probably should. The kid – his sister – she's . . . well, you know.'

'I do,' she said. 'You think you can help her?'

'I . . .' His voice trailed off.

Was that what this was? Had he been helping Hannah? Or had she been helping him? Did he feel better or so much worse? Depended on when you asked him.

'The situation doesn't make things more difficult?' Frankie asked.

For an instant he wondered which 'situation' she was talking about. Thank God he didn't ask.

'No. Well, a little. But I understand how she feels.'

'Uh-huh,' Frankie said in the midst of a yawn.

'You don't need me home for anything?' he asked.

Frankie laughed, and Charley flinched like he'd been slapped.

She didn't need him. Probably never had. And he'd been OK with that, because it meant he could do his job and she didn't cling. Now he wanted her to, or maybe he needed her to, and she didn't know how.

'I'll let you sleep,' he said.

''Kay. Night.' She hung up without saying that she loved him. He tried to remember the last time she had.

'Everything OK?' Hannah stood in the door to his room, wearing a knee-length white terrycloth robe.

When she lifted her hands to towel dry her hair, the robe became thigh-length, and he wondered why he'd never noticed what fantastic legs she had. She was short, a tad overweight, but her legs were firm and round and . . .

'Charley?' She lowered her hands, face crinkling with concern. 'Is there something wrong?' She glanced around, as if she wasn't quite sure where she was or why she was here. 'Other than the two people we love so much being dead.'

'Other than that.' He crossed the distance and took the towel from her. 'Not one damn thing.'

Then he kissed her and everything that was wrong didn't seem as wrong, at least for the rest of the night.

The morning was always another story.

He opened his eyes, felt her beside him, felt himself harden. Again.

What was wrong with him? Most men would say, *Nothing, bro. Impressive hard-on for a man your age.*

I'm not that old.

Although, two days ago, he'd been feeling ancient.

Oddly, this morning, while he was still disgusted and guilty, he was markedly less so than yesterday.

Was cheating any less cheating if you only did it once?

No. But was it worse if you did it twice? Three times? More? There was the rub.

And it was too early for Shakespeare.

'You wanna go out for breakfast?' Hannah smiled sleepily and set her hand on his chest.

His impressive hard-on hardened.

'Because there isn't any food here.'

'The entire kitchen is full of— Ah. Sarcasm. Got it. We can do whatever you want.'

Her hand lowered. 'I can think of something I want more than breakfast.'

Charley couldn't remember the last time he'd been wanted more than breakfast.

An hour later, they strolled to a coffee shop. Charley needed to get out of the apartment.

He should probably *stay* out of the apartment. But he didn't.

With no funeral, the days blended together. Heath was gone, but Charley continued to glance into his room whenever he walked past. If he heard a sound in the apartment, his first thought was, *I should ask Heath . . .*

Charley hadn't had a friend like Heath since Vietnam. Maybe that was why he'd felt so close to him. They'd all been dying in Vietnam too.

But there was something to be said for closure. Charley certainly didn't look for Lisa in places she'd always been. Then again, he wasn't *in* the places she'd been.

After two weeks, that started to be obvious.

'Isn't life shifting toward normal by now?' Frankie asked.

Ever smooth, Charley said, 'I . . . uh . . .'

'Did she go back to work? Have you?'

'She did,' Charley answered, conveniently ignoring the second question, the answer to which was *no*. He was obsessed with finishing the essay on Heath, picking just the right photos for both the book and the showing. Hannah was helping him.

She'd returned to *You* in less than a week. Carol was desperate, or so Hannah had said. Charley just thought Hannah needed to complete the vow she'd made to fulfill Heath's dream. He'd tried again to get her to see that her brother wouldn't want that, but she wasn't hearing him. And who was he to say that working where Heath had, fulfilling her brother's goals, wouldn't heal her?

The evenings they spent together at the light table, peering at photographs of Heath, telling stories about him, laughing, editing; working together on something that meant so much to so many drew them closer. They both missed Heath. Into that void came each other.

They inevitably ended up sleeping together – if *inevitably* meant *always*.

'And what are you doing?' Frankie asked.

Her.

He bit his tongue. Literally. Had he said any of that out loud?

'Charley?' Frankie's voice was sharp.

'The showing. The book.'

'What showing? What book?'

'On Heath.' His voice was equally sharp. Did she remember nothing he told her any more?

Silence descended.

When Frankie broke it, her voice had cooled. 'You never told me about a showing or a book.'

'I must have.' Lately it seemed all he did was talk about it.

To Hannah.

Could he really have forgotten to tell Frankie about the contract with Balfour Publishing? The showing at the Society for Visual Arts in Soho?

Frankie sighed, an exhale heavy with disappointment, if not judgment, which he heard from her far too often lately. While he deserved it, nevertheless it grated every time.

'Tell me now.'

Charley did. He waited for Frankie to be thrilled. If she was, she did a great job hiding it.

'After the show next month, you'll . . . come here? Go where?'

'What do you want me to do, Frankie?'

'Whatever you want to. That's what you always do anyway.'

'Are you going to come to New York for the showing?'

'Do you want me to?'

On the one hand, he couldn't believe she even had to ask. Of course he wanted her to. This was a huge deal.

On the other hand, he only wanted her to come if she understood what a huge deal it was, and she didn't.

There was also the issue of his mistress.

Charley winced. He had a mistress. 'If you want to,' he said.

They sounded like teenagers. From her impatient huff, she was as tired of it as he was.

'I'll have to check my schedule and let you know. Is that OK?'

He wanted to ask, 'What schedule?' She'd left the *Journal*, against his advice.

'I can't do tragedy any more,' she'd said. 'I need to find beauty. Record it. Create it.'

He'd said a few things he shouldn't have then about artsy photographers and making a difference. He regretted them, but he wasn't sure how to take the words back. And if there were a way to take things back he wouldn't waste that magic on words.

'Check your schedule,' he said. 'Let me know.'

But she never brought it up again.

The night of the gala opening to *Aids: A Life and Death in Pictures*, Charley rented a tux at the request of his publisher.

'You should wear one of those more often,' Hannah said when he stepped out of the bedroom.

She'd bought a new dress. A long, flowing sheath of stretchy material the shade of a snowy midnight that felt like velvet. Against it her hair shone like a star; the shimmer of blue made her eyes bluer too.

'Wow.' He took her hands, held them out to the side. 'You should wear this more often.'

She laughed, and for the first time since Heath had died, she seemed to mean it.

His chest hurt a little. She was getting better. He should go soon.

Hannah twirled a cape over her dress. Charley had bought a trench coat. The night might be mild for late February, but it was still February and in Manhattan there would be snow on the ground.

They took the train into New York City, where a car waited to drive them to Soho.

'I could get used to this,' Charley said.

'You don't miss riding in an ox cart or a rickshaw or a helicopter?'

He opened his mouth to say *no* then realized he did.

'You do. I knew it.' She squeezed his hand.

He hadn't realized she held it.

'You need to get back to work.'

For the first time since he'd stood on that dock in Fish Creek, the urge to see new places, new people, new images framed by his camera arose within him. His fingers tingled.

'Yeah,' he said. 'I do.'

The gallery was lit up like the Fourth of July. Even the sienna-shaded brick sparkled. The windows gleamed. Had someone scrubbed the fire escapes? Or maybe the white paint was as fresh as it looked.

They were early, per Belinda's request.

'I hate it when I'm at a show and I have to wait around for the artist to arrive. So goddamn pretentious.'

Charley thought it was goddamn pretentious to call him an artist, but he refrained from mentioning it.

Inside, waiters loitered near the bar. One of them hurried over and took their coats.

While Charley had chosen the photographs, he'd left the framing, the sizes, the layout to Hannah and the gallery owner. He was astounded by the finished display.

Black and white photographs hung on barren white walls, color on a background of dark gray. Smaller photographs, which you had to step in close to see, contrasted with larger ones where you had to step back. He'd never considered how much size mattered.

Charley coughed to cover his snort.

Every photograph had been framed first by a thin strip of black matt, then a white matt that stretched to the edge of each black lacquer frame. The stark simplicity emphasized the complexity of the subject, while the similarity of borders and mountings drew the entire essay together.

'God, Hannah. It's stunning.'

She didn't answer and he cast her a quick glance. Her face was as bleak as the walls, her eyes shining like the glass in the windows.

'Hey . . .' he began, and she shook her head.

'I'm OK. This is your night.' Her eyes flicked to the photographs. '*His* night.'

Charley had created the image he'd imagined – pills pouring from a stormy sky on to a graveyard. Very artsy. They'd ended up using it for the invitations. While the picture didn't fit with the others, it did catch the eye, make the viewer pause, raise a little ruckus. The invitation had been used for a profile in the *New York Times*. People had been calling and begging to be invited ever since.

Maybe artsy had its uses.

Charley had had to fight to get Hannah to include the photographs he'd taken of her. Eventually she'd come to understand that she was as much a part of Heath's story as Heath was himself. Or at least she'd humored him.

The photographs of Hannah bathing Heath's sweaty face, feeding him in the darkest part of the night, watching him sleep as the sun streamed through the windows and across his hospital bed, scrubbing blood out of his T-shirts, sleeping in the chair at his side, tearing that protestor's signage into itty-bitty pieces drew a lot of attention.

People smiled at the picture of Hannah and the protestors.

Whenever Charley looked at it he smiled too. That was what a warrior goddess looked like.

The evening proceeded without a glitch. Hannah's mother and, for a change, her father arrived. Air kisses ensued.

They were both dressed in black. Gerald's tux nearly matched Charley's. So did almost every man's in the place.

Belinda's dress hugged her still-toned body, then swirled around her ankles whenever she walked. The diamonds at her ears, throat, wrist and finger had to be worth the gross national product of a small to mid-sized Caribbean nation.

'Hannah, keep your father company.' Belinda dragged Charley off to introduce him to executives from Balfour Publishing, art critics, reporters, reviewers.

Oddly, or maybe not considering Belinda, she didn't seem to see the photographs of her son as anything other than a commercial endeavor. While Heath's friends and co-workers, a few lovers, stared at them with damp eyes, some with damp cheeks, Belinda kept her back straight and her lip stiff.

Charley lost track of time, and when he searched for Hannah again, she was gone.

'Excuse me,' he said to an art critic who was expounding on an artist who painted only the dead.

The man nodded and continued to expound to the others unfortunate enough to stand in their circle without even missing a breath.

Hannah's father leaned against the bar with a glass of something the shade of caramel that smelled a lot like jet fuel.

'Where's Hannah?' Charley asked.

'She was staring at that picture over there.' Gerald pointed at the floor-to-ceiling photograph of a healthy, golden, tanned, grinning Heath that took up the entire entryway of the gallery. 'Then she ran out there.' He switched his pointer to a pair of doors in the corner of the gallery. 'I thought maybe she needed to piss.'

Hannah's father was crude for a Wall Street . . . whatever he was. Although Charley didn't know any other Wall Street whatevers but him.

Well, if Hannah had needed to piss she'd gone out the wrong door. The first one was unlocked and opened on to the alley. No sign of Hannah out there. The second read *Staff Only*. He went through it anyway.

He found her in what appeared to be the employee lunchroom. Tables, coffee maker, microwave, refrigerator. She stood in front of a spectacular window – all of the windows in the gallery were spectacular, which was probably why it was a gallery.

She looked perfect framed there – her hair so soft, her dress so dark, the window sparkling like a bright diamond, her face reflected in the large, pure sheet of glass.

Her eyes were dry but sad. As Charley came up behind her, he saw his eyes matched.

'What's wrong?' Charley set his hand on her shoulder. He couldn't help himself. He rubbed his thumb along the curve of her neck where her skin was so soft and it smelled like the color yellow. Sunshine, daybreak. Light in an eternity of dark. He inhaled, caught just a tinge and shivered.

She covered his hand with her own. Hers was cold.

He turned her to face him. 'Is it too hard for you to see Heath?'

'It's wonderful to see Heath. He'd be so thrilled. Center of attention. King of the show.'

Charley didn't think it would help to point out that Heath would have been mortified by many of the photographs that showed him in very bad shape. Heath had never looked at any of the pictures and Charley didn't blame him.

'If it's so wonderful, why are you in here?'

'I . . .' She glanced around with the lost expression that was becoming all too familiar. As if, without Heath, she was missing something she knew she'd never find, but couldn't stop searching for anyway.

Charley drew her into his arms.

She laid her head on his chest. She only came up to his sternum.

He pressed his lips to her hair and she relaxed into him. 'That helps so much. Thanks.'

A hug. A kiss. That helped? So simple, yet she was so grateful.

That gratitude made him feel . . . larger somehow. Was that a good word? Definitely the opposite of how much smaller and smaller he'd felt every day since he'd seen that purple swimming suit floating, floating, floating.

'I couldn't have managed all this without you.'

'What did I do?' Charley asked, then wished he could take it back.

They both knew what he'd done, what they'd done. What they should probably stop doing immediately.

He was such an asshole, except Hannah didn't think so. Hannah thought he was a hero.

'You were here for me,' she continued. 'You understand. I wish you didn't. I'd do anything so that you didn't have to feel what I feel. All this . . .' She took a breath and it hitched in the middle.

If she started crying now, he might join her.

'Loss,' he blurted, then cleared his throat. 'Devastating, never-get-over-it-in-a-lifetime loss.'

She leaned back in his arms, her rear end pressing against his wrists, her breath puffing against his chin. 'Yes,' she whispered.

He kissed her. She tasted like she smelled, of flaring heat and a cool golden moon. He licked her teeth; he pulled her closer.

He thought she gasped, except the body he held so near to his own did not make a gasping movement. It made no movement at all. In fact it stilled, as did he.

Charley lifted his head.

Hannah's eyes were still closed. He'd made her forget everything in the world but him and that made him feel strong, powerful, almost magic. Three things he hadn't felt in . . .

A shimmy in the window drew his gaze to the reflection of his wife, framed in the doorway for just an instant before she spun away and was gone.

Frankie

On the way home from the clinic, the sun put on a show as it set, painting the sky the colors of a Georgia O'Keefe masterpiece.

'Holy hell,' Charley said. 'Pull over.'

He pressed the shutter release on his camera several times. 'This is fantastic.'

They sat on the hood of her car hip-to-hip until the sun was gone recording, together, something they'd never shared. How sad was it that they'd never watched the sun go down together? How many couples did?

Probably quite a few.

Except they weren't a couple, no matter how much it might feel as though they were.

Several cars sped by. One honked and a kid leaned out the window. 'Go, Grampa!'

Charley made a soft sound of amusement. 'Kid needs his eyes checked. Won't be a grampa for another fifteen years. Twenty if I have my way. Do I need to have a talk with Lisa about boys yet?'

He needed to have a talk with Lisa about boys never, which was about the same time he'd be a grampa. Should she try to tell him the truth about their daughter?

'Charley . . .' she began.

He smiled at her with such joy, she couldn't do it. Would it be better to tell him when he was sad? When he was sick? She had no idea.

Frankie climbed off the car. 'We should get back.'

'Sure, baby.' Charley climbed docilely into his seat.

She could get used to his agreeing with her about everything, even if it was completely unlike him.

'Ice cream shop after dinner?' he asked when they drove past one.

How many times had she wanted ice cream over the past twenty-plus years? Imagining herself a lonely old woman at the ice cream shop had cured the craving every time.

'I don't think I need ice cream.'

'Who does? But you want some, don't you?' He winked, and before she could stop herself she laughed.

The sound was so light, so free and young, so the *her* she'd been so long ago that she barely recalled it, she immediately stopped.

'Don't.' He touched her forearm.

She jerked, causing the car to jerk too. 'Don't what?'

'Don't stop laughing. Ever.'

But she had. And until right now, she'd been afraid she didn't know how to start. It never would have occurred to her that she'd start again with Charley.

She could think of several things she'd like to start again. With him.

She had to be very careful. Charley might be the man she'd once loved, but she wasn't the woman who'd loved him.

She'd never be that woman again. She wasn't sure she wanted to be.

But as the days passed, and they shared many of the things they'd once loved, and many of the things they hadn't gotten a chance to share before their love had died, Frankie started to feel like that woman, and it scared her. Because she'd missed the person she'd been more desperately than she'd ever known.

She woke smiling. She laughed. A lot. She ate whatever she wanted. She drank whatever she wanted as well. It was a vacation in the land of chemo. Who'd have thought it would be so magnificent?

Summer kicked into high gear with the arrival of a bazillion tourists. She and Charley did their best to avoid them by driving to out-of-the-way places whenever they could and taking pictures together. Not so much because Charley's hands still shook – they did – but because they'd never realized how great it would be to experience together something that had always defined them.

Yes, they'd shared photography. But they hadn't really *shared* it. Not the way that they did now. With Frankie's hands atop and beneath Charley's. With her cheek next to his. He used her cameras. She used his. They photographed each other. They snapped selfies. They giggled and chortled. Some days you'd never know one of them was dying.

Other days . . . Charley couldn't get out of bed. Everything hurt. He was so tired he could barely open his eyes. He slurred his words because of the drugs. He couldn't keep anything down, even chicken broth or ginger ale, despite the anti-nausea meds. Many nights he didn't sleep.

Frankie should have stayed up with him, but he exhausted her. He always had.

Charley never mentioned that he spent the darkest hours alone and awake, but she surmised from his red-rimmed eyes and pale complexion when a night had been particularly bad.

He lost weight. His hair began to fall out. First his eyebrows, then most of his eyelashes, leaving him with a wide-eyed, overly plucked look.

'The hair everywhere else is going fast too,' he said. 'Legs, arms, chest.' He wiggled his eyebrows, even though he no longer had any. Instead his brow bones lifted, then lowered. 'Down under.'

Frankie got the picture. Vividly. 'Ugh! Stop talking.'

'Let's have a head-shaving party.'

'Doesn't sound like much of a party. What happens?'

'You shave my head. No one cries.'

'Woo-hoo,' Frankie muttered.

'I'd rather it was all gone at once rather than having pieces of myself falling out all over the place.' Charley handed Frankie his electric shaver.

Frankie had been finding chunks of his hair in the oddest places. Just that morning she'd yelped when she'd seen some on the kitchen floor and thought it was a mouse.

She turned on the shaver and finished eliminating what chemo had begun. Then she peered into the mirror along with him. His bald head shone whiter than the rest of him.

'You're going to need SPF-fifty on that dome.'

He appeared so upset she was afraid he might cry and spoil their weird party. And how weird would it be that he'd cry about his hair when he hadn't cried about anything else. Ever, as far as she knew.

'Or maybe a hat?' she continued. 'I've always loved a man in a fedora.' She'd been born twenty years too late for fedoras but she'd never stopped giving up hope that they'd come back.

Charley didn't answer.

Until today he'd been unfailingly cheerful, even when he was losing a lung in the toilet. Attitude was everything. She couldn't let his falter.

'Hey! Why don't I do mine? Then we'll match.' She lifted the shaver toward her own head.

'No!' He yanked it away, tossing the thing into the garbage can so hard it broke. 'Your hair is gorgeous.' He picked up a hunk and let it slip through his fingers the way he always used to.

She couldn't breathe.

'I've never seen colors like this.'

Her hair had no color, unless you counted the fifty shades of brown and gray.

Charley was due to have chemo next week, which would start the cycle all over again. A day, maybe two days of status quo. Another of bone pain from the shots he received to increase the white cells the chemo obliterated. Some nausea, which could be controlled fairly well by meds, but not completely. Some days of exhaustion from all of the above. All of that interspersed with a good day here and there, followed by several good days in a row leading up to being hit again with the Mack Truck that was chemotherapy.

'You want to go to Bay Beach?' He seemed to have forgotten his hair, or lack of it, at last.

Bay Beach was an amusement park on the other side of the bay in Green Bay. Frankie had taken Lisa there many times. Back in the eighties the tickets had been a dime each. Even though the tickets now cost a quarter and most of the rides required two tickets or more to ride, it was still the bargain of the century.

Charley had never gone there, though Lisa had constantly begged him to.

'Maybe we should wait until Lisa gets here. I did promise her I'd go with her next time.' Charley stared out the window at the dock. 'When's she coming again?'

Frankie was saved from answering by the shrill summons of her phone. As the only people who called her these days were Hannah or Irene she started searching for the device. The way Irene had been behaving lately, Frankie almost hoped it was Hannah.

It was.

Her cell was plugged into an outlet in the kitchen. She considered unplugging it and going into her room, but Charley went into his and shut the door. She hoped he didn't plan to peer at his new bald head in the mirror.

'Don't tell me you're calling to cancel again,' Frankie said.

'No, but . . .'

'No buts. You need to see him. Maybe the tumor is shrinking. Maybe he'll remember you.'

'Maybe,' Hannah agreed, but she didn't sound hopeful.

Was that why she'd cancelled her visit twice already? Because she was afraid Charley would stare at her blankly? Or worse, that he'd stare at her and call her 'nut bag' or some other nickname he'd come up with.

Hannah's excuse had been an emergency at work.

'A fashion magazine emergency?' Frankie asked.

'They do happen. Lately, every single day.'

Frankie knew that things weren't going any better at *You*, both because of what Hannah had said and because Irene had texted her about it. She'd seemed to be chortling, if one could chortle in a text.

'You'll be here Friday?'

'Saturday,' Hannah corrected.

'But that'll only give you a day before you have to go back.'

'I never thought I'd hear you complain about my short stay.'

'I'd like more than a day of freedom.'

'You can't leave!' Hannah's voice was so loud Frankie pulled the phone away from her ear.

'Calm down. I won't be going anywhere.' Far, that was.

Charley and Hannah should have some time alone. See what developed.

Another thought from outer space.

'This is a bad idea,' Hannah murmured.

'Don't you miss him?'

'Of course. The apartment is empty. Everything's empty.'

'Was he really in the apartment that much?'

'No. But there's not there and there's *not there*, you know?'

'Yeah.' The 'not there Charley' of after had been so much more *not there* than the 'not there Charley' of before.

'I don't even want to go to the restaurants we like alone. I've started going to new places because if he was never there I don't keep expecting him to be.'

'Hear ya.' Frankie hadn't gone to DelMonico's since 1991.

'But mostly I miss his voice, how he'd tell me about where he'd been, what he'd done.'

'His voice is the same.'

'It isn't. Not to me. Especially not the way he says "Hannah".'

Frankie remembered how Charley had said 'Fancy', how he was saying it again now exactly as he'd said it then.

She understood completely what Hannah was saying, feeling. She wasn't sure how to express that, or if she even should.

The silence that came over the line made Frankie think Hannah wanted to say something too, but was struggling with how. Join the club. A club of two.

'This is nice,' Hannah finally managed. 'Sharing him.'

Frankie choked. Even though she'd been thinking something very similar, hearing it out loud . . . She was even less sure of what to say than before.

'Are you nuts?' she asked. Probably not the best response.

'Yes. Aren't you?'

Frankie sighed. 'Yeah.'

She did feel nuts. Because everything in her life had become so. Her. Hannah. Charley. The situation.

Nuts.

'Talking about him with anyone . . . I've never been able to . . . because, well, no one knows him like we do. No one understands Charley Blackwell except us.'

The thought that soon no one else ever would flitted through Frankie's head. She kept it to herself. Hannah seemed freaked enough already. Her next words proved it.

'I'm afraid.'

'That he won't be better? That he'll still see you as a stranger, or worse, a crazy stalker stranger?'

'Wouldn't you be?'

'Yeah,' Frankie admitted. 'But maybe it'll be different. Maybe he'll take one glance at you and say "Hannah, baby, where you been?"'

Frankie could barely get the words out of her mouth and as soon as they were out, she had to clear her throat of the nasty aftertaste.

'He never calls me "baby".'

Thank God for small favors.

'Though sometimes he calls it out in the middle of the night.'

Frankie tensed. 'You don't have to . . .'

'It's then I know he's dreaming of you.'

Frankie took a deep breath. 'There's no reason to be jealous.'

Why was she trying to soothe Hannah? Because she didn't want her to cancel again, that's why. Had to be.

'Isn't there?'

'He left me for you. You've been married to him longer than I ever was.'

'Lucky me.'

Why did that sound sarcastic? Because it was.

'If things weren't so rosy, why didn't you leave him?'

For an instant Frankie thought Hannah had hung up and she wanted to yank out her too-blunt tongue.

'Because even though I wasn't the love of Charley's life, he was mine, and I would rather have what I had of him than not have him at all.'

Frankie had been happy to give him up if what she had of him was anything less than everything.

Well, not happy but less unhappy. As time went on she'd come to understand that not unhappy was the new happy.

'Have you had any issues with his insurance?' Hannah asked.

Well, that was an abrupt, random shift of subject, but Frankie was more than willing to accept it and leave the other subject behind.

'No,' she said slowly. 'Why?'

'You know how insurance companies are.'

'Not really.' So far she'd been lucky enough to avoid much contact with hers.

'They try and get out of paying whatever they can. Insist other agencies pay as much as they can.'

'Other agencies?' Frankie asked.

'The VA for instance.'

'Is he supposed to be going to the VA?' That had never occurred to Frankie.

'He doesn't have to. We have insurance. And a specialist like Lanier . . .' Her voice trailed off.

'He wouldn't be a VA doctor.' Sad but true. Veterans didn't get the pick of the litter like Lanier.

'No,' Hannah agreed. 'They're just being . . .'

'Assholes?'

Hannah gave one short, sharp bark of laughter. 'The insurance company is saying that his cancer was caused by Agent Orange and therefore the government should pay.'

'OK.' Dr Lanier had mentioned that, so had the Waz. She'd meant to relate her conversation with Charley's friend to Hannah and had forgotten. 'There were a few guys in Charley's unit who contracted Agent Orange cancers.'

'I know. Jim Colby's wife kept in touch. I informed the powers that be, but the government wasn't impressed. It's been over forty years and Charley might just have brain cancer, not Agent Orange brain cancer.'

'Lanier said that too.'

'I checked and there haven't been any studies that have proved Charley's disease is a result of all that crap they sprayed over Vietnam. But let me know if you have any problems.'

'Will do. Did you . . . uh . . . need me to help?'

'Thanks, but I've dealt with this kind of stuff before. My brother . . .' She paused, cleared her throat and soldiered on. 'Dying of AIDS in the nineties . . . the victim got blamed. Should have known better, should have taken precautions.'

'That's . . .' Frankie searched for a word, came up with: 'Horrible.' Which wasn't good enough but she'd never been good with words. Just pictures.

'Yep,' Hannah agreed. 'So just let me know if you have a problem and I'll deal with the insurance company and the government. I'm good at it. I've gotten to where I almost like making them eat every word they utter.'

Frankie couldn't help but be impressed with Hannah's skills. She hadn't even considered insurance, the bills, anything but Charley. She also admired Hannah's 'gonna make them pay' attitude. Hannah was a very different woman from the one Frankie had thought she was. The more Frankie knew her, the more she liked her and she wasn't sure how she felt about that. She also wasn't sure how to make it stop. It wasn't like they could be friends when all this was over.

Could they?

'You'll be here Saturday?' she asked.

Now Hannah did hang up. It was how a lot of their conversations ended. So, not friends, and she was fine with that. She had plenty of friends.

Well, she had Irene.

'Charley?' Frankie called, and got no response. 'Let's get ice cream!'

She was in the middle of searching for her purse when she realized he'd never responded.

She hurried to his door, tapped once and opened it. Her breath rushed out when she didn't find him dead on the bed, passed out on the rug, throwing up in the bathroom. But where was he?

She glanced out the side window. Car was still there. Maybe he was sitting on the dock again.

However, when she reached the sliding glass doors, she didn't see him in his usual place, but there was something floating off the edge. Something large. Something Charley shaped, wearing his shirt. Face down in the water.

Frankie didn't know she could still run until she ran down the steps and across the dock.

She didn't know she could still jump until she flew off the edge into the water.

She didn't know she could still swim until she took several strokes to reach what she could now see was definitely Charley.

She grabbed his arm and he erupted from the water like Nessie, spraying water in an arc that hit Frankie in the face.

'What the fuck, Charley?' She smacked him in the shoulder. 'I thought you were dead.'

'I . . .' His forehead creased, the lack of hair and eyebrows causing the wrinkles to appear more pronounced.

'Come on.' She pulled him toward the pier and together they clambered out, then sat in a heap of soaked clothes as they tried to get their breath. Frankie thought she might be having the heart attack she'd been expecting for years.

'I keep seeing her here.' Charley pointed to the gently lapping waves. 'Floating.' He shook his head. 'Why do I keep seeing that?'

Was the chemo actually working?

'What do you remember?'

'Remember?' he echoed.

'About Lisa.'

'She's at camp. She'll be here soon. She's five.' He rubbed his bald head like a talisman. 'Isn't she?'

Now was the time for the truth. Where should she start?

Despite the golden, heated rays of the sun, Charley was pale and clammy. The lines around his mouth reminded her of a very old man with dentures, holding his lips tightly shut so they didn't fall out. His hands shook; they appeared a little blue.

She took one. It was like ice.

'We need to get out of these wet clothes.' She tugged him toward the house.

He hung back. 'You know why I see her there, don't you?'

His eyes pleaded, but were they pleading for the truth or yet another lie?

'Charley, you see Lisa in the water because . . .'

His fingers tightened on hers so hard and fast several of her knuckles cracked.

'Because . . .' She couldn't find the words. Where *were* her words?

Drowned.

Dead.

Gone.

Forever.

She *hated* those words.

'Because why, Fancy?' Charley appeared old, sick, scared. When had that happened?

'Because you had a dream,' she blurted. 'They're more vivid with the drugs. Seems like a memory, doesn't it?'

His eyes captured hers, searched hers. 'It does.'

'All you can do is let it go.' She lifted her hand and touched his smooth cheek again. 'Just let it go, baby.'

She needed to take her own advice.

'OK,' he said, though he didn't sound convinced. 'I feel so close to her here.'

Not exactly letting it go, Charley.

'But I was never here with her except for that one time right after we bought the place. I regret that.'

Frankie couldn't speak through her own mountain of regrets. Why hadn't she told him?

'Remember how she liked strawberry jam on Saltines, peanut butter on apples, but the idea of mixing jam, bread and peanut butter grossed her out?'

'I . . .' Frankie began, but Charley kept talking, and she kept quiet, because everything he brought up was something she had forgotten.

How could she have forgotten?

'She wanted to move to Bali so she didn't have to wear shoes any more and she could meet a sacred monkey.' He laughed, though his haunted gaze kept flickering to the water. 'Does she still prefer wintergreen toothpaste to spearmint but spearmint gum to wintergreen? I can never tell the difference.'

Frankie could only shake her head. She'd forgotten that too. A minor detail, one that could easily slip away after twenty-odd years of buying only the toothpaste that she wanted. But, still, it bothered her.

How many other things had she forgotten about her daughter while she was trying to forget the pain of losing her? Would she ever have remembered any of it if not for Charley?

Doubtful, but she wouldn't have had to force herself to forget so much just to survive if not for Charley.

And that excuse was growing old. Like them.

It seemed both petty and vengeful to keep hating him, but shouldn't she?

Yes. Because if she stopped, she was terrified she might start loving him again.

Charley

Soho. Late February, 1992

'She saw,' Charley said, his voice devoid of emotion, even though he seemed to be feeling all of them – pain, fear, anger, love, hate, loss, remorse, guilt, embarrassment. Just listing them made him dizzy. Or maybe that had been Frankie's eyes.

Which had been devastated.

He hated himself, which seemed to be a constant lately. He'd been wondering if he'd ever be able to stop. Now he knew he would not.

Hannah's eyes opened. At first full of joy and pleasure, soon confusion filled them. 'Saw? Who? My mother?' She shrugged. 'Don't worry about her. She'd never rock the cash boat.'

'No.' Charley started toward the door through which Frankie had disappeared, moving faster and faster the closer he got. 'My wife.'

'Wife?' Hannah's voice was so loud he winced, turned back.

'I do have one.'

'And she was here.' Hannah pointed to the ground. 'She saw.' Now she flipped her finger back and forth between them.

'I have to go.' He hurried through the still-lush crowd. It was hard to believe, but he thought there were more people there now than when he'd left.

Hannah's mother tried to flag him down, but he caught a glimpse of Frankie's coat – a long, black leather job he'd brought back from Milan . . . whenever he'd been in Milan. As far as he knew, she'd never worn it. Said it was far too nice for anywhere that she went.

Why was he focusing on irrelevant details? So he didn't have to focus on the relevant ones.

Frankie had seen him kissing Hannah.

Snow had just started to tumble down. Charley skidded through the fresh fluff on his shiny black suit shoes and nearly fell.

Frankie was only a block away, headed for the subway station. If she reached it, she'd be gone. He couldn't let that happen.

'Frankie, wait!'

She didn't slow down. She didn't glance back. She didn't give any indication that she'd heard him at all.

He sped up, gritting his teeth and refusing to slide, refusing to fall. How was she managing such speed in the heels he'd never seen her wear before either?

He caught up to her at the stairs. Didn't touch her – contrary to his recent behavior he wasn't a complete idiot – just said her name once.

She paused, sighed, turned. Tears streamed down her face.

He wanted to die.

'Who is she?'

'Hannah. You know . . . that's . . . Hannah.'

'The child, the twin, the *kid*?'

Was that how he'd described her?

People streamed past them down the stairs. The snow picked up, slinging icy pellets against their skin.

Frankie gave a little flinch every time one hit her, giving the impression that she suddenly possessed a facial tic.

'We should go inside.'

She laughed and he stared at her amazed. Who laughed with a face full of tears?

Nobody but Frankie.

'I don't think I want to walk through a crowd of people who know you're boinking a bimbo.'

How tacky and cliché his life had become. Something he'd always strived to avoid.

'They don't . . . I'm not . . . She isn't . . .'

'Just shh.' Frankie flipped her hand up like a crossing guard calling *halt*.

She was wearing the leather gloves he'd bought her too. What did that mean?

Probably that it was snowing outside. Or maybe it had been a balmy minus ten when she'd left Milwaukee.

'I know what you look like when you kiss someone and you

mean it, Charley. That was it.' She let out a huff of air. 'Is there anywhere we can go that your fan club won't see us?'

'There's . . . uh . . . an alley entrance.' He reached for her arm.

She drew back, her nose wrinkling as if she smelled something rotten.

He let his hand fall to his side and just led the way, glancing back every few seconds to make sure she didn't dart into the crowd.

At the gallery, people had returned to the appetizers and champagne. He'd been afraid they would be staring out the window, trying to see what was happening. But this was New York. No one cared.

He was also afraid the side door would now be locked and he'd have to go around to the front and beg a key, but it was as open as it had been earlier. Perhaps the waiters used it for cigarette breaks.

They reached the employee lunch room. Hannah wasn't there. Charley wasn't sure if that was good or bad.

Frankie crossed the floor to the exact place he'd found Hannah earlier, standing in front of the huge window, staring at the night. 'How long?'

'Not long.'

'How. Long.' She didn't shout; she didn't need to.

'After Heath died.'

'How many others?'

'What?' He stiffened. 'None!'

She snorted.

'I swear.'

She turned at last.

He almost wished she'd stayed facing the other way. Her expression terrified him. Bad things were coming, things as bad as any that had come before.

'Pardon me, Charley, if I don't believe your professions of chastity.'

Because he was scared, because he was guilty – so, so guilty of so many things – he let anger drive his tongue. 'You act like you caught me boffing the help.'

'Didn't I? I thought she was an editorial assistant. Couldn't you manage to fuck an editor or higher?'

'When did you get so nasty?'

'When I brought my daughter home in an urn. I've been waiting for it to fade, but I don't think it's going to.'

The anger drained out of him so fast he got a head rush. 'I'm sorry. Hannah lost her brother. We shared some things.'

'More than *some* from the looks of it.'

'Would you let me finish?' He couldn't get his thoughts together when she kept sniping at him like that.

'By all means. I can't wait.'

'She needed me, Frankie. You never have.'

She appeared stunned. 'You never wanted me to.'

'I know.'

'I needed you for the past six months and you weren't there. You were here. With her.'

The two of them faced each other, close, but so far apart and suddenly Charley realized that they'd always be this far apart. She wasn't ever going to get over the loss of Lisa. She shouldn't have to.

She also shouldn't have to stay married to the man who'd been too busy with his camera to watch his daughter. Every time Frankie saw him, she'd see Lisa. Probably in a casket. Or the urn.

But, maybe, if she didn't have to see him, talk to him, live with him, pretend to love him, she could move on.

He still loved her, would always love her, and because of that he would give her this.

'I love Hannah,' he said.

And in saying it he realized he did love Hannah. He didn't want to lose her, leave her. He wasn't sure when that had happened.

Maybe the day she'd confronted the AIDS protestors. God, she'd been amazing. Her face full of fury when she'd spun on him with her fists raised, ready to battle any way she could for Heath. Or perhaps it had been when she'd slept night after night at her brother's side as he died inch by agonizing inch. Or when she'd let Charley touch her even though no man had ever touched her before.

Most likely it had been when she continued to look at him with the same adoration she always had even after he'd killed his own child.

Frankie drew in a sharp, tiny breath, as if she'd been stuck with a pin somewhere vital. 'You always called them kids.'

'They weren't. She isn't.'

'Well, not a kid, as in pedophile range, but . . .' She spread her hands.

Her gloves lay on a nearby table. When had she taken them off? She should tuck them in her pockets so she didn't leave them behind.

Silly, pointless thoughts. What was wrong with him?

Everything.

'Would it have been better if she was my age?' Charley asked.

Frankie approached slowly. He had no idea what she meant to do until her fist shot out.

His lip split against his teeth. Her knuckles did too.

'Ouch.' She shook her hand and blood spattered on to the floor.

He touched his front teeth. They felt jagged and wobbly. 'Jesus, Frankie.

'It's a good look for you. I like it.'

'Charley!' Hannah flew into the room and began to fuss. 'You need a cold towel. An oral surgeon.'

Frankie took a long step over the blood and headed for the door.

'Frankie,' he called, though it came out, 'Fwankie.'

She waved goodbye with her still-bleeding middle finger and disappeared.

'What happened?' Hannah rushed to the sink, ran water on some paper towels and rushed back.

'I told her.'

Hannah handed him several towels to hold to his lip, keeping a few to wipe the blood off his chin. 'Your shirt is toast.'

His marriage was toast, but so was his life.

'What did you tell her?'

'Everything.' His voice came out muffled, but he was learning to enunciate with a fat lip.

'What, exactly, is everything?'

'About you, me, us.' That came out 'uth' but Hannah got the drift.

Her eyes widened; her cheeks pinkened. 'There's an us?'

She really was very sweet, and she adored him. He knew he was pathetic for needing adoration, but a man could only take so much disdain. Even if he deserved it.

'Isn't there?' he asked.

She dropped the paper towels, which fell to the floor with a soft *shoosh* very similar to the falling snow. 'Yes. Of course. Whatever you want.'

Charley peered out the window. The snow had stopped as suddenly as it had started. Where did he go from here? His life had flown so far off course in so many ways.

'Did you want to go to the hospital?'

Charley shook his head. He'd had enough fat lips to know that this one wasn't serious. The bleeding had stopped; he didn't need stitches. But he was probably going to need some capped teeth.

'Let's just go.'

'I should tell my mother—'

'No.' The thought of talking to her mother, or anyone out there, was too much. Even if Hannah just said goodbye, there would be questions. And Hannah had never been very good at lies.

Unlike him.

'We're both headed out the back door. I'll disappear like the mysterious artiste that I am.'

Hannah seemed uncertain, but she went along with him. She always did.

On the train to DC, after a few questions about the show, which he answered with monosyllables, Hannah remained blessedly silent. He tried to think what he should do next.

File for divorce? He couldn't. The end had to come from Frankie, otherwise how would she ever move on?

But what if she didn't? What if she forgave him? What if . . .?

He touched his tongue to his jagged front teeth. That wasn't going to happen.

At the apartment, Hannah gazed at him with so much love, so much hope, he panicked. He'd never be the man she thought he was. Just ask Frankie.

'I have to make a call.' He kissed her forehead and urged her out of the room.

The way she glanced back, she thought he was calling his wife. This tightrope dance was exhausting already.

He called Ray Cantrell and begged for the longest, most distant assignment the man had.

'How about Zonguldak?'

'You made that up.'

'Turkey. Mine explosion. Over two hundred dead. Interested?'

He was. Very. And what did that say about him?

'I'm on the next flight.'

Hannah seemed OK with it, though as he said goodbye the next morning Charley noticed dark circles under her eyes. Had they been there before? Maybe it was the light. As far as he knew she'd slept just fine, right next to him all night.

'When will you be back?'

'I'll call you.'

He didn't. Zonguldak was a mess. He was there for over a week.

Right when he was about to leave, an earthquake hit Erzincan – eastern Turkey – and killed five hundred. Since he was already there . . .

To be honest, he was inappropriately thrilled with all the disasters. They kept him from thoughts he didn't want to have.

Two weeks after he'd left DC, his phone rang. Not Frankie. Not Hannah.

Carol.

'I'm worried about Hannah.'

Unease trickled across his skin. 'What's wrong?'

'You didn't notice how much weight she's lost?'

'I . . . uh . . .' He didn't want to admit he hadn't talked to her for two weeks, let alone seen her. 'She keeps saying she needs to drop ten pounds.'

'Not in a week.'

Was that even possible?

'She's also missed several meetings. Forgotten a deadline. Shown up for work late nearly every morning. She hasn't slept. She's a mess.'

After Lisa, Charley hadn't worked for months because he'd have been as worthless as Hannah was right now. 'I'll talk to her.'

'You think I haven't tried? She keeps insisting she's fine. But she isn't, Charley. Not even close.'

'I'll be back tomorrow.'

He hadn't planned to be. He'd planned to fly straight to Buenos Aires, where a truck bomb had killed twenty-eight at the Israeli embassy. But apparently his need to be needed overrode the new favorite in terrorist tactics, an embassy truck bombing.

'Good. Thanks.' She sounded so relieved, Charley almost believed he might be able to do something to help.

A day later he let himself into the apartment. It looked almost as bad as Erzincan.

The mail had been tossed on the hall table unopened, so much of it that a good portion had cascaded on to the floor.

The garbage can was overflowing on to the floor as well – mostly used tissues; definitely no food or it would have smelled like Erzincan too.

'Hannah?'

No response. It was after 8:00 p.m. Where could she be?

He moved through the apartment, growing increasingly concerned at the state of the place. The mess was so unlike her.

He set his bag in her room, frowning at the pile of clothes on the dresser, the chair, the floor, even the bed. They'd been tossed around as if she took out one thing, then another, unable to choose what to wear. Heath had often helped her decide. Was she now unable to do so on her own?

He checked the bathroom. Unoccupied. But all of Heath's toiletries were strewn across the countertop. Half of them were open and all of them appeared recently used, even his razor.

He headed to the bedroom to dig his phone from his bag and a soft sigh drifted from Heath's room. The hair on his arms lifted, and he flicked on the hall light. A Hannah-shaped lump became visible on the bed.

She was asleep, and from the waxy shade of her face and the eggplant smudges beneath her eyes, this was the first time in a while.

He reached to turn out the hall light and she murmured, 'Charley?'

'I didn't mean to wake you.'

'That's . . .' A huge yawn made her jaw crackle loud enough for him to hear across the space between them. 'Fine. You back already?'

'I'm sorry I didn't call.'

'You didn't? Oh, right.'

Was she that sleep deprived? Or maybe she didn't care as much as he thought she did. She was, after all, a sweet, young, talented woman. What did she need with broken old him?

She sat up. 'It's been, what, a few days?'

'Hannah.' He joined her on the bed. 'I've been gone two weeks.'
She blinked, yawned again. 'Huh.'

She didn't seem concerned about that either.

Charley knew from experience that not sleeping could cause all sorts of havoc in your brain. He hoped that's all this was.

'Go to sleep.' He tried to urge her on to the pillow.

She refused to go. 'I only slept here because my bed seems so empty.' She paused. 'The whole apartment seems empty.'

Charley remembered how empty the house in Whitefish Bay had been . . . after. One of the reasons he'd fled. It had never occurred to him how empty the place would feel to Frankie. No wonder she hated him.

Hannah took his hand, drew him up and out of Heath's room, down the hall and into her bedroom. He still didn't think of it as theirs. Maybe they should get their own place.

The thought made him uneasy and he shoved it away. He had plenty of other things on his mind.

A month later they were still there. He was still there. Charley had been too concerned about Hannah to leave.

Frankie's words – *I needed you for the past six months and you weren't there* – haunted him. He couldn't repeat his mistake. He had enough guilt already.

Hannah slept well at his side. Her dark circles were gone in a week. She put on a little weight. Some color returned to her cheeks. Carol said she was doing better at work; at least she was showing up.

There were some issues with Heath's hospital bills and insurance. While other parts of her life seemed too big for her to deal with, Hannah dealt with that like a lion protecting her cub.

'My brother isn't to blame for his condition. You wanna cause trouble. I'll show you trouble. The name of your insurance company will be splashed across every major newspaper, accompanied by photographs of a dying man and the grief you caused both him and his family. It will not be pretty. I goddamn guarantee it.'

The insurance company didn't cause any more trouble.

'Remind me not to get on your bad side,' Charley said. Sometimes she amazed him.

'That'll never happen,' she returned, but her smile was vague.

Other times she scared him to death. What would he do if something happened to her too?

Charley took a few short assignments in the country – never gone more than a day or two. He hated every one. Who cared if Ross Perot ran for President? He wasn't going to win. What difference did it make if Tiger Woods was the youngest PGA golfer in thirty-five years? The true issue, in Charley's opinion, was that he was photographing golf. Paint dried with greater zest and probably made better pictures doing it, too.

When Ray called with the news that sixty thousand gallons of crude oil had just spilled into the ocean in Mozambique, Charley nearly did an inappropriate little dance.

'I'm on it,' he said.

'You sure?'

'Yes.'

He packed his bag, went to the phone in the kitchen, planning to call Hannah and tell her he was going, then he saw there was a message on the answering machine. He pressed the *play* button. Disappointment flooded him when the message wasn't from Frankie.

He was such a fool. Frankie wouldn't be calling him. He didn't deserve for her to call him.

'Hannah, this is Joseph. You never came in so we could file your tax returns. I hope you did them on your own.'

Charley hadn't seen Hannah filling out any forms, but that didn't mean she hadn't. Still . . .

He'd been going to call her anyway; he'd just lead with the tax return question.

'I don't have to file until April fifteenth,' Hannah said.

'It's April sixteenth.'

'What?' Papers rustled, no doubt her desk calendar, which she used to update religiously according to Carol, but now did not. 'It can't be.'

'I assure you it is.'

'Shit.'

'Mmm.'

'I can file an extension.'

'Wouldn't you have had to do that before the fifteenth?'

'I don't know.'

She sounded so despairing that a tinge of concern overrode his excitement about Mozambique.

'By the time you get home, I'll figure it out.'

'Would you? Thank you! I'm buried here.'

Charley thought the problem was that Heath was buried. Well, not literally. Literally he was in the box in the cupboard while they tried to get permission to toss him around at Fashion Week. Charley didn't think it was going to happen.

He made some calls. His first was to a psychiatrist he'd done a story on while at *Time* magazine. The man specialized in grief. Considering his profession, Dr Mark Maloney was quite a cheery fellow.

'Charley! It's been ages. How are you?'

Charley probably should have called the guy after Lisa. Hadn't even entered his head.

What should he say in answer to the doc's question? Surviving? Managing? Sinking like a stone? As this call wasn't about him, he said none of them.

'I have a friend whose brother just died of AIDS.'

Mark immediately sobered. 'I'm sorry to hear it. Sorry every time I hear it, in fact, and I hear it a lot.'

The epidemic was still rampant. If Charley hadn't felt so lost, he might be even more pissed off.

'What's the problem?' Mark asked.

Charley quickly described Hannah's behavior.

'Were they twins?'

For an instant, shock rendered Charley speechless. 'How'd you know?'

'I've treated a few twin survivors. This is common. Losing a twin is losing a part of yourself. You're no longer whole but half.'

'What can I do to help her?'

'You could bring her to see me, but since I'm in LA, I'll suggest a few doctors in your area.'

'Thanks. Anything I can do myself?'

'Do whatever you can to make her feel whole.'

For a minute Charley thought that Mark had heard about Hannah and him and was making an off-color joke. But Mark wasn't the off-color joke type.

'Make her feel secure, loved, wanted. Be patient and be there. Time does heal. I promise.'

Charley wondered if time would ever heal him.

He thanked Mark, said goodbye, made a few more calls.

IRS. Accountant. Hannah was screwed. The IRS didn't care

who had died. April fifteenth was April goddamn fifteenth. She'd be fined accordingly, with interest.

The psychiatrist was nicer. He got Hannah in the next day.

Ray was more pleasant than the IRS, less pleasant than the doctor.

'Are you fucking kidding me? You should be on a plane right now.'

'I need to stay a few more days. There's some personal stuff . . .'

'You used to be the least personal-stuff guy I had. You'd go anywhere, anytime, no matter what. What the hell ha—?' He broke off.

Death had happened. Too much of it.

'I'm sorry, Charley. Do whatever you have to do. I hope Frankie is better soon.'

He hung up before Charley could correct him. Though *would* he have corrected him? What could he say?

I'm a cliché. Always will be. But at least I'm owning it.

The doorbell rang and Charley found the doorman in the hall with an envelope.

'I signed for it. Looked important so I brought it up before I left for lunch.'

'Thanks, Carl.' Charley pulled a few bills out of his pocket, his gaze on the return address.

Lamphill, Lamphill and Davis, Attorneys at Law – Milwaukee.

Charley tore it open, but he didn't need to. He knew what was inside.

The document was fairly straightforward. As Wisconsin was a no-fault state, neither party needed a reason for the divorce beyond that they were done.

And they *were* done. This proved it.

Charley sat there for the rest of the day reading the legalese over and over. It was the only way he could keep himself from either calling Frankie and begging her not to go through with it, or hopping on the next plane to Milwaukee, showing up on her doorstep and begging her not to go through with it.

He couldn't, wouldn't do that. Frankie deserved a life, and the least he could do was let her have one, even though in doing so, his life felt over.

His old life *was* over; a new life with Hannah had begun. She needed him. He couldn't leave her. Not like this. He couldn't do the same thing to the woman he loved now as he'd done to the woman he would love forever.

The apartment door opened and Hannah stepped in.

Charley shoved the documents into his duffle, then kicked it behind the couch. 'You're home early.'

Her gaze was unfocused. 'Is it?'

Charley glanced at the clock. 6:00 p.m. She wasn't the only one unfocused today. He'd spent over four hours staring at papers, as if by doing so he could make the ink on them disappear.

'I made an appointment for you with someone recommended by a friend of mine.'

'Great.' She drifted into the kitchen.

She didn't ask who, what, why? His friend could be an axe murderer, who was friends only with other axe murderers.

'Dr Benvolio. He's a grief psychiatrist.'

Hannah didn't answer. Instead she stared at the last can of ginger ale. Then she opened it and drained it in several long gulps.

'Huh.' She tossed the empty can into the trash. 'Didn't help.'

'Are you nauseous?'

'Nope.' She sat on the couch.

'Then how could ginger ale help?'

'I thought maybe it would fill this . . .' She rubbed her stomach with one hand, then set her other palm against her sternum and rubbed that too.

'Hole?'

Her gaze flicked to his. 'How'd you know?'

'Losing a twin is losing part of yourself,' he repeated.

'Yes!' The adoration that had faded from her eyes recently, replaced by sorrow and bewilderment, rushed back.

Charley hadn't realized how much he'd missed it. The pain that lived in that matching hole in the center of his chest eased just a little.

'You're lost, adrift, alone,' he said. 'Half not a whole.'

He didn't mention that sometimes it felt as if that missing chunk had been yanked out by the hand of a giant, then stomped on a bit.

'I'm the eternal maiden aunt. Though now I'll never *be* an aunt. I'll never again be one of two that together are one. I don't feel him any more.' Despair flickered in her pale blue eyes. 'I always felt him inside. There, even when he wasn't. I knew things about him when we weren't together – what he was doing, feeling, sometimes what he was eating. I was born a twosome. How do I stop needing to be a twosome?'

'You don't,' he said.

'Don't what?'

Her attention was hard to keep these days. He needed to cut to the chase. Quickly before he lost that attention and his nerve.

'You can be a twosome.' He took her hands. 'With me.'

She still looked confused.

Charley went down on one knee. It wasn't easy. His knees were not what they used to be. 'Marry me, Hannah.'

Though it was probably too soon for both of them to make such a decision, it was the perfect solution. Hannah needed to be part of a whole. Charley needed to anchor himself to this new life. Otherwise he'd keep drifting toward the old one.

Anticipation lit her eyes. She seemed almost like the Hannah she'd been before Heath died. Could he become, again, the man he'd been before Lisa had?

Doubtful. But he could try.

'Is this what you want, Charley?'

He wanted so many things, the foremost of which was a time machine. But as that wasn't going to happen, he'd have to settle for moving on.

With her.

Hannah

London. July 26, 1994

Hannah awoke, groggy. Had the earth moved?

Outside her hotel, sirens wailed, but that was nothing new in London. They had seemed to be wailing since they'd arrived yesterday.

Hannah glanced at the clock. 12:12. Was that a.m. or p.m.?

Since it was light outside, she voted for p.m. How could she still be asleep?

Then she did the math. She could still be asleep because it was six a.m. in DC. Maybe it was seven a.m. She wasn't good at math.

'Charley?'

He didn't answer. His side of the bed was cold; his camera bag was gone. That math she could do. Charley wasn't here.

He was a lot more used to jet lag than she was. He adjusted to time differences without any real adjustment at all. At least it didn't seem to bother him that she took a lot longer to get her shit together than he did.

He probably liked it. That meant that he could go out and do whatever while she slept their first day away. Hannah did her best, always, to make sure that Charley liked everything about their life together. Yet she still worried every day that he might go back to Frankie.

She told no one of this fear. Not her father – as if. Not her mother – dear God. She might have told Heath, if Heath had still been here to tell. She definitely hadn't told Charley.

The only thing worse than fearing Charley might leave her for his first wife, was him knowing that she feared he might leave her for his first wife.

Whenever Charley invited her to travel with him, she jumped at the chance. Sure, he only did so a few times a year – and that was OK because she had *You* to deal with.

She wasn't sure why Charley asked her to go along. Maybe he thought she was lonely in the too-large apartment that they'd moved into last year. But really, she spent so much time with people at work, and she worked a lot, that when she came home, she was happy for the silence.

Frankie had never traveled with Charley. Hannah didn't know if his inviting her was good or bad. Mostly she didn't ask questions like that because she didn't want to hear an answer she didn't want to hear. Probably not a healthy habit to have but it worked for them.

Hannah slid out of bed and searched for a coffee pot. None to be had. Neither was a note from her husband.

After the first time he'd left town and not told her that he had and she'd flipped out calling everyone he knew – almost – he'd never done it again. She'd felt like an idiot when it turned out he'd been in Barcelona for the Olympics. She probably should have known that, but shouldn't he also – probably – have mentioned it?

His voice when he'd called her after Ray called him – after Hannah had called Ray, crying . . .

Hannah wrapped her arms around herself. She never wanted to hear that chill, slightly annoyed tone again. So far, she hadn't.

They'd worked it out. He no longer flew off without telling her; she no longer flipped out if she woke and he wasn't right there.

She wasn't going to flip out now. This was London. It had stood through world wars and Roman invasions. The English were famous for their stoicism and fortitude. She admired that. She kind of thought Charley would admire it too. He loved it when people 'dealt with their shit' quietly, coolly, firmly without whining about any of it. The less he heard about trouble, the better Charley liked it.

Well, she wouldn't trouble him with her need for coffee and a donut. She'd just handle that herself. If she was going to be stoic, coffee was a necessity.

They were here so Charley could get a photo of Tony Blair, the newly elected Labour Party leader, but he had also been asked to get a shot of the Israeli embassy, perhaps to accompany a story on the peace talks between Jordan and Israel going on right now back in DC. For some reason, Ray wanted photos of Israeli embassies around the world. She found it ironic that the big story was taking place a few blocks from their new apartment, yet here they were across the ocean.

The sirens continued to wail outside. They seemed to be wailing a lot longer and louder than usual. Had something happened?

Then she remembered the weird shimmy that had woken her. She'd thought it was just jet lag, but maybe not.

Hannah flicked on the television.

'A car bomb has exploded in front of the Israeli embassy.' The on-air reporter appeared harried and a little scared. The glass windows in the shops just visible to his left lay all over the pavement. 'The blast has been heard up to a mile away. So far we have no report on the number of injuries or deaths.'

He touched his ear, tilted his head. Behind him, people trailed out of the embassy, dazed and confused.

'I'm hearing now that the injured are being taken to Charing Cross Hospital. More on that as I have it.'

Hannah reached for the phone. Her hand was shaking. She just knew Charley had been at that bombing, if not before it happened then immediately after.

'Right place, right time Charley,' she muttered. 'Goddamn it.'

She dialed his mobile phone. It went directly to voicemail, something it did so often she wondered why he even had the thing.

'Charley,' she said after the tone, proud of how calm her voice sounded. Had she even put a British twist on his name? Her back was straight, her upper lip very stiff. 'Please call me when you get this.'

Hannah waited as long as she could manage for a call back before she got dressed, wrote a note, then went in search of coffee near the Israeli embassy.

She smelled spent ordinance long before she reached the police line. She tried to talk her way closer. The bobbies didn't even blink in response; they certainly didn't bother to answer her request even with a *no*.

She caught a cab to Charing Cross Hospital. The place was busier than the blast sight. The number of press was atrocious. She spoke to a few of them. None had seen Charley. In direct opposition to any press she might have spoken to in the US, none of them had even heard of Charley Blackwell.

She bought a scone. Charley had said scones in the UK were much better than in the US. They still couldn't beat a donut.

Hannah returned to the hotel. What was she going to do now? Was it too soon to visit the US embassy? Probably. She still had to fight not to hail another cab and do just that.

She unlocked her door and went inside. It took her thirty seconds to realize the shower was on. Charley's camera bag was on the bed. His clothes were strewn everywhere.

She picked up his shirt. There were tiny brown pinpricks all over it.

The garment floated to the floor and whispered across her feet. She sat abruptly on the bed. He'd been so close to the blast that residue had burned his shirt.

Hannah put her head between her legs and tried to breathe. The shower went off.

Her head went up. She didn't pass out, so she stood, retrieved his shirt and trousers then tossed them into the trash.

By the time Charley walked out of the bathroom with a towel around his waist, using another to scrub at his hair, her hands had stopped shaking.

'Hey!' He gave her a kiss. Apparently *he* hadn't been worried at finding *her* gone. 'Did you have fun?'

'Fun,' she repeated stupidly.

'The concierge said you'd gone in search of coffee.' He winked. 'And a donut. How'd that go for you?'

She'd told the concierge that? She didn't remember even meeting the man. Explained why Charley wasn't worried. Although had he ever been worried about her? Would he ever be?

Another set of questions she was not going to ask.

'Found the coffee.' *Didn't find you.*

'Well, that's the important thing, right?' He tossed the towel over a chair and rooted through his suitcase for new clothes.

So that's the way they were playing it. Pretending nothing had happened.

No, thank you.

'How was the embassy bombing?' Hannah's voice was very QE2. She was so damn proud.

Charley froze with his hand on a fresh, unburned shirt. 'I . . . uh . . .'

'Yes?' Hannah prompted. That time she thought she sounded like Margaret Thatcher, unless she sounded like Julia Child.

Hannah cleared her throat.

Charley turned and she lifted one eyebrow. She'd been practising that since Heath had died and she'd finally perfected it. She understood why he'd liked the expression so much. It got results.

Charley shrugged into his shirt. 'As embassy bombings go, not the worst. Then again, what bombing could be anything but bad?'

'You have a point.'

Next question. What was the right one? Definitely not: *How close were you?* She knew that answer. *Close enough.*

How about: *Did anyone die?*

She wasn't certain she could get those words out without choking, maybe crying. She didn't cry in front of Charley. She cried in the shower. That was the way they both liked it. Besides, she could find out how many had died on the evening news for the next several days to several weeks – over and over and over again.

When they'd first married, he would come home and he would never say a word about where he'd been. She'd ask, he'd say a little, then next time a little more. The stories he'd shared had been whitewashed – that had been easy enough to see just by watching the news. But as time passed and she hadn't fainted like a seventeenth-century maiden, the accounts had become more in depth, more honest, more real. She'd had her panic attacks later, alone, and eventually she hadn't had them at all.

Charley finished dressing, cleared his throat, flicked her a sidelong glance. 'Something else you need to ask?'

The way he held himself so tense revealed he expected her to lose it. She was not going to be that woman; she would never be that wife. She would be the type of cool, collected female he admired, no matter that sometimes, inside, she was anything but. If she wanted to keep Charley, she would have to become That Hannah, both inside and out.

'You wanna help me find a donut?' she asked.

His smile was worth every agony; his kiss pure bliss, but it always was. Hannah would do anything for that kiss. She already had.

'Not yet,' he said, and pulled her on to the bed.

Later, much later, when the room had gone hazy with twilight and donuts were nothing but a memory, he told her about that morning while he played with the strands of her hair that splayed across his chest.

'A woman drove up in a gray Audi. Middle-aged. Middle Eastern. A security guard and a police officer approached her and then . . .' He used both hands to indicate *boom*.

How close were you? was again on the tip of Hannah's tongue. She bit her tongue and snuggled closer to his side.

He rewarded her by kissing her head and hugging her even tighter. 'I wound up on my ass. By the time I got to them, there were half a dozen others there already. I don't think they're dead. At least they weren't then.'

'I'm sure we can find out if you want . . .' She indicated the TV.

'No.' He kissed her head again. 'Right now I just want you.'

Her chest hurt. She loved him so much. 'Did you get the picture you went there for?'

'Yeah. Probably the last photograph of the embassy in one piece.'

Typical. Charley always got the last picture, if he wasn't getting the first picture.

'You need to get that film to Ray?'

'Already did. No reason to leave bed again today.'

They didn't.

The next morning when she woke, he handed her coffee.

'How long have you been up?'

Charley shrugged. 'A while. I walked over by the embassy. It's a mess.'

She sipped her coffee, said nothing. She hated it that he could leave the room and come back and she'd never even known it. She slept like the dead when she slept with Charley. What would she do when they had kids?

Would they have kids? That was a question she'd intended to ask, and she'd intended to ask it on this trip. But how?

'London's going to be shut down,' he began.

'They do not shut London down.'

'Right. But the places we planned to see are going to be tough. Kensington Palace had some damage. All the big tourist sites have doubled their security.'

'Good.' Hannah took another sip of coffee. 'I don't mind lines.'

Charley grimaced. Charley didn't do lines.

'We should probably . . .'

She waited for him to say 'go home', or at least say she should.

'Go to Paris.'

'Really?' She loved Paris, never thought she'd get there with him since Paris wasn't exactly a rip-roaring photojournalist's dream.

'I want to see it the way you do. You can show me around.'

'Really?'

He laughed and sat on the bed, touched her face, rubbed his thumb along her cheekbone the way he always did, the way that she loved. 'You gotta stop saying "really".'

'Really?' she whispered.

He didn't answer, just stared into her eyes for so long she started to wonder what, or maybe who, he was seeing. Would she ever stop wondering that?

'It means a lot to me that I can tell you everything.'

'Why couldn't you tell me everything?'

'I don't want to upset you, but you're stronger than that. You're not . . .'

He broke off, stood. She knew he was thinking of Frankie. What had Frankie done when he'd come home with burned shirts? Stories of bombs and bodies? More questions she would never ask.

They went to Paris and it was glorious. She showed him everything she loved. The café with the best coffee. The bakeries with the beignets and the croissants. Oh, my God, the croissants. She never even thought about donuts.

They were shameless tourists – the Arc de Triomphe, the Louvre, Notre Dame and the Eiffel Tower, the catacombs, the Seine. Charley didn't bother with his camera and he didn't seem to miss it.

'You sure?' she asked when he left it behind in the hotel yet again.

'No one in the world needs another picture of the Eiffel Tower.'

She wasn't sure the world didn't need a picture of the Eiffel Tower taken by Charley Blackwell, but she let it go. Hannah let a lot of things go.

But there was one thing she couldn't, one thing she wouldn't. On their last night in Paris, she brought it up during their dinner at the Four Seasons Hotel George V, her father's favorite restaurant. If there was one thing her father knew besides investments, it was dinner in Paris.

She waited until dessert – cheese and fruit, which Charley didn't think was dessert but after the multiple courses they'd just had was all either one of them could manage. The café au lait more than made up for any lack.

'I probably gained five pounds here.' Hannah pushed away what was left of the platter and sat back.

'Best way to gain them.' Charley finished his coffee.

'I can think of a better way.'

His brow creased. 'A better way to gain weight than Paris? You lost me.'

She hoped she didn't. 'I want to go off the pill.'

Charley had been taking a sip of water. He sprayed it all over the table. The Parisian couple next to them *tsked*.

'Did the doctor say you should?'

'Yes.'

'I'm sure we can find something else to use.'

'Not if we try to get pregnant.'

This time Charley choked without the benefit of water.

By the time he was done, the Parisian couple had left. They were virtually alone in the restaurant, except for their waiter who took one glance at Hannah's face and fled back to the kitchen.

'Hannah, I . . .' His voice trailed off, as did his gaze.

'Just one,' she said quickly. 'Maybe two.'

He winced and she hurried on. 'Twins run in families. We might get two for the price of one.'

She waited for him to tell her no. Then it would be no. Charley was all she cared about. Certainly she wanted a child. She wanted more than one, but she'd settle for whatever he could give her.

He sat there thinking for a very long time. Then he sipped some water, swallowed without choking, closed his eyes.

And then he nodded.

Charley

Washington DC. New Year's Eve, 1999

The beat of Prince's '1999' seemed to be the only song anyone was playing today. Charley had heard it in the airport, in the cab and, when he opened the door to their apartment . . . there it was again.

He crossed to the sound system and switched it off.

Hannah immediately popped out of the bedroom, head tilted as she fastened a sparkly, dangly earring into her ear. She was already dressed for the New Year's Eve party at *You* in a knee-length ice-blue dress that seemed to be made of sequins.

'You're here,' she said the same way she always did – as if his arrival were the best surprise in a lifetime of them.

He had to admit that their life so far had been a surprise. He was happy, or at least as happy as he'd ever be, and it was because of Hannah.

To Hannah he was everything. The only time he was able to stop hating himself for even an instant was when he saw his reflection in her eyes. She looked at him like he was precious, because to her he was.

He'd never killed her child. And he never would.

She finished with her earring and crossed the room to welcome him home with a kiss, a hug and then the snuggle against his chest that still made him feel cherished.

'How was Panama?'

'Hot.' He hadn't realized how hot until he'd gotten off the plane here and been cold for the first time in a week. The chill on his skin had been bliss.

'Everything go OK?'

He shrugged, nodded. 'We can talk about it later.'

The returning of the Panama Canal to Panama had officially taken place at noon that day. There had been pomp and ceremony for a week but mostly it had been a big show.

A big, boring show if you were a photographer. He couldn't wait for some small corner of the world to erupt.

But tonight was Hannah's. He'd promised to go to her Millennium Party. He was certain that something would go boom by tomorrow. It always did. And considering a portion of the world thought tonight was the *end* of the world . . . he'd place a bet on the certainty of disruption.

Charley headed for the bedroom, where Hannah had laid out his tux and a tie that matched her dress. 'You got all your computers ready for tomorrow?'

It amazed him that the biggest concern was Y2K, what everyone was calling the computer bug that might send the world back to the Stone Age. How could someone smart enough to invent computers and their programs not be smart enough to make a provision for the year 2000? Supposedly they'd caught the problem in time, but there were still people who'd spent the last several months provisioning a bunker for the Apocalypse.

Morons. When the Apocalypse came, a bunker with bottled water and canned goods wasn't going to help. He'd learned years ago that when an apocalypse happened, nothing in the world could help.

'Everything's set.' Hannah leaned close to the mirror and applied lipstick.

For a minute Charley saw the girl she'd been, the one that

hadn't known how to apply make-up, do her hair, or choose her clothes without help from Heath. Now the sophisticated outer trappings of the woman she'd become reflected the inner changes. She'd gone from being shy and timid to this take-charge, outgoing leader. Hannah did not quit. Ever. He admired her more now than he had then. He admired her more every day.

'Or at least that's what the computer techs tell me. If the clock strikes midnight and everything shuts down, then I'll know they lied. And someone's in for the ass-chewing of all time.'

She laughed a little and he marveled again at her attitude. He doubted Y2K would amount to anything, but if it did . . . Hannah would handle it. Handling it was what Hannah did best.

He'd seen some indication of who she might become when Heath was dying. The way she'd dealt with the doctors and the insurance companies and anyone who looked at Heath crosswise had been a marvel. When she'd fallen apart after her brother's death, Charley hadn't been sure she would ever recover that new and amazing part of herself. But she had. Again, she had not quit.

He still tried to get her to leave *You* every now and again, but she stubbornly refused to do so until the magazine was number one. He was starting to think that would never happen. There were too many similar magazines that had been around for a lot longer and had more recognizable names. *Glamour, Cosmo, Vogue.*

People were sheep. They did what they'd always done or what the guy or gal next to them had done. *You* suffered for it. Hannah suffered for it, though she would never say so. She'd made a vow; she'd keep that vow, no matter how long it took.

Another reason to admire her.

'You know where my black dress shoes are?' Charley stared into their closet, where there were a helluva lot of shoes, but none of them seemed to be his.

'Sorry, I put yours in the spare room.' She appeared sheepish. 'Mine are a little out of hand.'

He never would have imagined Hannah would become a woman with too many shoes. But there were a lot of things about his wife that he never would have imagined. If Heath could see her now he'd be as proud of her as Charley.

Charley missed Heath. Charley missed a lot of people.

'You OK?' Hannah's expression was concerned. 'You keep sighing.'

He did? Sometimes, lately, he didn't remember doing or saying things that people remarked on later. He hadn't let it worry him; he was always in a rush, always late for something because he wasn't finished doing something else. That kind of life made a man ditzy.

'Just tired. I'll be fine.'

'We don't have to . . .' she began.

He stood. 'You do. It's your party.'

'You don't. It's OK.'

'It isn't. I promised and I've been dreaming of dancing with you at midnight.'

Her eyes lit up and he resolved to make tonight wonderful for her. He would keep this promise; there were so many others that he'd broken.

'If I'm going to dance, I'll need those shoes.' Charley headed down the hall toward the spare room that no one ever used. They probably should have gotten a one-bedroom apartment.

He almost walked past the bed without glancing at it, intent on the closet. Then he stopped so fast his knees protested. He'd been sitting in a plane too damn long.

Several photographs of Lisa lay on the bed – Lisa on Frankie's stomach at birth; Lisa with her face pressed to the glass at the zoo, the nose of a male lion pressed to the other side; Lisa, asleep with Black Kitty.

Suddenly he was having trouble breathing.

'You find those shoes, Ch—' Hannah froze just inside the door. 'Shit.'

'Why?' was all Charley could manage.

'I . . .' Hannah quickly gathered the photographs and put them back in the box sitting on the end table. 'I'm sorry. I just . . .'

Charley hadn't looked at those photos since he'd put his daughter in that urn. He didn't deserve to. He probably should have given them to Frankie when she'd asked. Instead he'd told her he'd burned them. The idea of Frankie spending hours, days, weeks staring at the photographs of her dead daughter had made him so crazy he nearly *had* burned them. Instead he'd hidden them, though apparently not well enough.

How did one hide anything in an apartment anyway?

'I'm not pregnant.' Hannah sat heavily on the bed.

Charley swallowed.

'Again. I . . .' Her voice broke.

'I'm sorry,' he managed, his gaze flicking to that damn box of pictures again.

'I don't know why I wanted to see Lisa. Probably to poke at the pain, like your tongue on the sore tooth, you know?'

He knew.

'It has to be me that's the problem. You have a daughter.' She waved her hand at the box.

'Had.'

She hung her head. 'I made an appointment to get tested. Then we'll find out what to do next.'

'Next,' he repeated.

'IVF. Adoption. We'll talk. But not tonight. Tonight we party.'

Hell. They *should* probably talk tonight, before this really got out of control. Not that it already wasn't.

He should have told her long ago. But if he lived his life on *should haves*, he'd start with 'should have watched Lisa better' and that's where all this had started.

'You don't need to get tested.'

'Of course I do. Don't worry about it. The testing isn't dangerous or anything.'

He sat on the bed at her side, took her hand. 'Hannah.'

Her gaze was so open, honest, curious and trusting. God, he was such an ass.

'I had a vasectomy.'

'You . . . what?'

'It isn't you that's the problem, it's me.' Always me.

'You can't have. You had . . .' She looked at the box of photos again.

'I had the vasectomy after.'

Slowly she turned her head. 'After Lisa?'

He could say yes. He should say yes. It was true. Obviously.

'You told me in Paris that you wanted children,' she said.

He hadn't; he'd just let her believe that he had. In Paris, he'd made a decision. One he did not regret. His only regret was that he'd shared everything with her but this.

'I had the vasectomy after Paris.'

She blinked. 'You . . .' Her voice stopped. Her lips moved but no sound came out.

'I'm sorry. I couldn't . . . I can't . . .'

He couldn't bear it. Not again.

Silence descended. He continued to hold her hand, knowing that soon she would withdraw it from his, then she would leave. He would lose her. Which was why he hadn't told her. He'd lost enough.

He was selfish; he knew it. Cowardly. He admitted it. He couldn't change it.

'OK,' she said. 'I understand, but . . .' She bit her lip. 'You could have told me.'

'Could I?' He tightened his fingers around hers. 'Wouldn't you have left me?'

She didn't answer, seemed to be thinking.

'You'll leave me now.'

It wasn't a question because he knew the answer. He began to withdraw his hand from hers.

'No.' She snatched it back, tightened her fingers around his, harder and harder until he met her gaze.

Everything seemed to narrow to this room, this moment, this woman.

'There is nothing you can do that would ever make me leave you, Charley. Nothing.'

He doubted that was true. There was always something. He'd learned that the hard way.

'I'm sorry,' he said.

'I know.'

They sat there for a long time, just holding hands. She'd come through again. Hannah didn't quit – not her job, not her life, not their marriage.

Charley could depend on Hannah.

Hannah

Fish Creek. Late summer, 2016

It took Hannah a good portion of Saturday to get from Washington DC to the cabin on the bay. The only direct flight to Wisconsin was to Milwaukee, of course, where she'd had the choice of taking a puddle jumper to Green Bay, then renting a car and driving another hour north, or renting the car in Milwaukee and driving three hours north. As she rarely drove any more, she'd settled on the former.

Luckily, once she was out of Green Bay, the freeway was clear sailing. She suspected the previous evening would have been another story. It was peak tourist season in Door County, and if she hadn't been staying at the cabin, she wouldn't have been able to find a room to rent anywhere within a hundred miles.

Though she was anxious about seeing Charley, worried about what he'd say, do, feel, think, she was also intrigued by all she'd heard of the Wisconsin vacation Mecca. According to several websites she'd surfed, Door County was the Berkshires of the Midwest.

Hannah loved the Berkshires. She and Charley had gone there on their honeymoon. It had been blissful. She'd felt like he loved her.

Then.

When had she started to suspect that though he did love her, he wasn't *in* love with her and he never would be? He couldn't be. The only woman he could ever be *in love with* was Frankie.

She'd never said anything, was afraid to rock the boat. But as time went on, she'd changed. Become less sweet and agreeable, more disappointed with her life and cranky about it. She had to admit that her new self did a better job at *You*, though she hadn't been able to save the magazine in twenty-four years of trying. She was still trying, but soon she was going to have to admit defeat.

She'd become bitter over that, as well as the realization that her long-ago dreams would never be realized. It wasn't a good look for her.

As Hannah drove slowly through first Egg Harbor and then Fish Creek – slowly not only because the sidewalks were so packed with people they often spilled into the street, but because the number of cars on the narrow roads winding through the quaint little towns made all progress snail-like – Hannah picked out areas that would make good locations for a fashion photo shoot by force of habit.

Beach. Lighthouse. Lodge. Sailboats. Barns with quilts painted on the sides. Antique stores with their wares spilling on to the lawn. Cherry trees. Apple trees. Pine trees.

When had she realized that she was never going to return to *National Geographic*, that she would always be at *You*?

Maybe after Carol died.

It had been ten years since her aunt had keeled over with a fatal heart attack in the office. Carol had been alone, slaving into the night as she always had over her baby. Hannah had found her the next morning when she arrived bright and early to begin her daylight slaving away over a baby that could never be hers.

No baby would ever be hers.

Spilled milk. Troubled water under their marital bridge.

They hadn't even fought about the secret vasectomy. She'd been hurt, yes, but she'd understood why having another child would be unbearable to him. Right now, she wished she'd shouted and thrown a few things. In retrospect, there had been several times in her life with Charley where she wished she'd thrown a few things.

As Hannah drove along the two-lane highway, she caught glimpses of dark blue water between the evergreen trees. The colors were exquisite. Even the sky seemed bluer here. Ridiculous, but her eyes kept insisting that it was.

'Turn left,' her GPS said in an annoyingly calm, modulated voice.

Hannah caught a flash of a sign tangled in the weeds.

'Make a legal U-turn.'

'Go fuck yourself,' Hannah said in that same calm, modulated voice. She even sounded a little robotic.

Something Charley had accused her of the last time he'd been in DC. Make that the last time he'd been in DC when he remembered who she was.

They'd had a big fight. She wanted him to slow down. He was sixty-three for Christ's sake. Did he want to have a stroke in a country with shitty healthcare?

It was an old argument. One they'd been having for a few years, but this time Charley had told her to stay out of his business. She'd wondered if pretty soon she wouldn't be his wife any more, and . . .

'Voila, I'm not.' Hannah made the legal U-turn, although she wasn't sure it was actually legal on a remote two-lane road.

She braked the car enough so that she could actually *turn right* when the robot said *turn right*, then bounced over the dirt path of a driveway until she reached the cabin.

She was still Charley's wife, no matter what he thought, no matter that it felt like she wasn't every time he murmured *Fancy*.

Hannah stalked across the dry, yellowed grass to the door, her ivory slingbacks kicking up enough dust to coat the cuffs of her ivory trousers. She'd be shaking it out of her clothes for a week. She should have changed into jeans but she'd gone directly to the airport after stopping at the office one last time.

The door opened as she lifted her hand to knock, revealing Frankie on the other side of the screen. Her long, graying hair was as much of a shock now as it had been before. Would Hannah ever stop thinking of her as a flower-child beauty with hair every shade of brown and red? Why bother when Charley still saw her that way?

'You made it.' Frankie pushed open the screen door and inched back so Hannah could slip in. 'I was thinking you'd hopped a plane to Zanzibar.'

Frankie did wear jeans – a little tight in the hips, but flared at the calves and worn powder blue by repeated washing and wearing. Vintage, or pretend vintage. Her blouse recalled 1968 as well – white, loose and flowing. Her feet were bare.

Hannah felt starched up and stupid. As a result, her answer came out sounding very stick-in-the-mud. 'I don't make a habit of that.'

'I'm sure Charley made it a habit enough for both of you,' Frankie said.

Hannah didn't bother to answer; they both knew it was true. Though Charley had tried his best to let her know where he was going – or at least that he'd left – after the first time she'd lost it when he'd disappeared, believing he was dead on the street, or perhaps in someone else's bed.

Being the other woman made you sensitive to the fact that there could be another 'other woman' along soon. As far as she knew, there never had been. Until now.

Could Frankie be the other woman when she was the original woman? The only woman?

Charley sat in the kitchen, a laptop computer open in front of him. His back was to them; ear buds trailed out of his ears and connected to the computer. All his hair was gone. The back of his bare neck seemed so alien, so vulnerable, so not Charley.

'Checking email?' Hannah's voice was so full of hope she

embarrassed herself, but if he remembered email then maybe he'd remember her.

Frankie shook her head. 'He thinks I've got a prototype computer and camera. He's fascinated with digital photography.'

'He owns the most recent digital camera there is.'

'Yeah, try explaining that to him. You're welcome to my migraine.'

'How does *he* explain the digital cameras in his camera bag?'

'By insisting they aren't his and neither is the bag. Someone switched it when he was on the plane.'

'He's never let his camera bag out of his sight as long as I've known him,' Hannah said. 'How could someone have switched them?'

'I never said his explanations made sense.' Frankie tapped her forehead. 'Brain tumor.'

'It's not getting smaller?'

'He had another CT scan.'

Hannah frowned. 'How'd that go for him?'

'They sedated him this time, so not a problem. We'll get the results at his appointment with Dr Lanier on Monday. I was hoping maybe you'd stay for that.'

'You were hoping maybe I'd stay?' Hannah repeated. 'Wow, alternate universe.'

Frankie's lips twitched. 'Welcome to my nightmare.'

Charley chose that moment to turn as he removed his ear buds. 'Fancy, did you see . . .?' His eyes first widened, then narrowed on Hannah. 'What in holy hell is she doing here?'

'Shit,' Frankie muttered.

Hannah said nothing. Either the tumor hadn't shrunk, or it hadn't shrunk enough, or shrinking it wasn't going to do any good.

Besides, the sight of Charley rendered her speechless. Not only was he scowling at her with real dislike, but he looked even worse from the front – exhausted, pale, his shoulders stooped like an old man's.

'Charley, remember that I told you a friend was coming to stay with us?'

Confusion filtered over his face, and Hannah had to fight not to cry again. Charley was never confused. He was the most certain person she'd ever known. Even in the aftermath of Lisa's death, then Heath's, then his divorce, he'd always moved forward with the air of a man who knew his path and would blaze it regardless of any setbacks.

Because of him, she liked to think she'd become that kind of woman too.

'She's your friend?'

'Yes. You don't . . . uh . . . recognize her at all?'

Charley peered at Hannah, then he reached for his glasses and peered at her some more.

She stared back, searching for a flicker of recognition.

'Now that you mention it . . .'

Hannah's breath caught. Hope flared, bright and hot in her chest. She set her hand there, trying to keep it safe.

Charley took off his glasses. 'She's the one I thought was nuts. Kept saying I was her husband, but then you told me that was a ruse so she could be there with us. We don't need anyone *but* us, Fancy.' His eyes narrowed on Hannah. 'You can go.'

Hannah's hand fell back to her side as hope died.

'All righty then.' Frankie's voice was overly cheerful, just as Hannah's had been. 'I asked Hannah to come. She's isn't going anywhere.'

Charley shrugged.

He was awfully agreeable. It made Hannah twitchy.

'I'm going to go out for a bit and my friend's going to stay here with you.'

Hannah thought if Frankie called her a friend one more time she might lose it.

'Whoa.' Hannah put her hand up like a traffic cop. 'You nuts?'

'Not me.' Frankie snatched her purse and headed for the door.

'Wait! What should I . . .?' She glanced over her shoulder.

Charley had returned his attention to the computer and the ear buds to his ears.

'What should I do with him?'

'You never had a problem doing anything with him before. What's the big deal now?'

'He isn't who he was before.'

'Maybe all he needs is a little time with you to find his way back.'

'You know that's not true.'

'I don't know that at all and neither do you. Can't hurt to try.' Frankie set her hand on Hannah's arm, then frowned at it as if she were as startled by the gesture as Hannah was and pulled back. 'I'm going to the grocery store, maybe the bookstore. I'll be back in a few hours. If you need me, all you have to do is call. Around here, nothing is far enough away to prevent me from getting back toot-sweet. OK?'

If she said *no* would Frankie stay? Could she be that weak?

Hannah straightened her spine. She'd learned not to be.

'OK.'

Frankie practically ran out the door.

Hannah set down her Fendi carry-on and strolled around the cabin. Her heels clicked so loudly on the hardwood floors she kicked them off. She shrugged out of her jacket, which had been comfortable in the air-conditioned car but was no longer in a cabin that appeared to have been built in the age of no air conditioning and was proud of it.

Two of the bedrooms seemed to be in use and Hannah exhaled. Did she think they were sleeping together? What if they were? Charley thought they were married.

Frankie knew better.

Of course, Hannah had known better too, back when she'd started sleeping with Charley, but she hadn't been able to help herself. What if Frankie couldn't help herself? Who was Hannah to throw stones?

Except she'd like to. She still loved him. She would always love him.

Their life together had not been what she'd hoped. There had always been the shadow of Frankie, of Lisa, of Heath. There had been his career; there had been hers. There had been guilt, sadness and recriminations. But there had also been moments of happiness if not joy, shared goals, success, a family – of two, yes, but still a family. They'd managed; they'd made it. Or she'd thought they had.

Now this. It wasn't fair.

Hannah made a soft sound of amusement. What was? Very little in her experience.

'Are you going to stare at my back all day?' Charley asked as he removed one ear bud.

'How did you . . .?'

'Reflection in the screen.' He pointed to the computer. 'Come on over and take a look at these if you want.'

She had to admit she was curious to see if his photographs reflected the changes in him. Certainly he'd always been crazy-talented but his talent had evolved and she believed she could tell the difference between a shot he'd taken twenty years ago and one he'd taken last week.

Hannah had become a very good photo editor – of fashion, true, the thought could still make her cringe – but she had an eye, a knack, the touch. Not a good enough touch to make *You* what Heath had dreamed of, but she'd kept it going this long, and she knew without doubt or conceit that she'd done so with her vision – that indefinable knack.

Hannah sat in the kitchen chair to his right, and Charley spun the computer so she could see what he'd pulled up on the screen.

Dozens of shots of a sunset. Very unlike him. Certainly Charley had photographed sunsets but they usually backlit a bombed-out crater or the carcass of a poached rhino.

She nearly asked if they were Frankie's, but there was something about the angle that reminded her of twenty-years-ago Charley.

And then again it didn't.

'Do you like them?'

'I . . . do. Got any more?'

He hit a key on the keyboard and the screen filled with images of water – blue, green, white and black.

Huh. She pulled the computer closer. They were all the same body of water. She lifted her gaze. The one out there, visible from this window. But at different times of the day and the night. Also, more a photograph Frankie might take, and yet it wasn't.

'These all yours?' she asked.

'Yes.' His shoulders shifted. 'No. Well, sometimes Frankie has to help me steady my hands.' He lifted them and they shook.

'Oh,' Hannah whispered.

'Taking these pictures together has been interesting. I never thought I'd be able to share the act of photography with anyone, even Frankie. But she's so gifted.'

Jealousy flared. Hannah could edit pictures but she'd never been able to produce any that didn't resemble the snapshots they were.

'If you can't keep the camera steady then how . . .?'

'Either she holds my hands and we take the picture together, or I tell her what I see, then she frames it and pushes the shutter.'

The jealousy flared even hotter. Charley would never have asked Hannah to do that for him, even if he'd remembered who the hell she was. His vision was *his* vision. Never anyone else's.

'Frankie's been a rock. I love her so much.'

No crying. No crying. No.

'And Lisa. I can't wait until she gets here. You'll like her.'

'Charley, Lisa is . . .'

Charley tilted his head, waiting.

Hannah cleared her throat of the truth. She couldn't tell him. Had Frankie even tried?

'Lisa's wonderful, I'm sure.'

How did Frankie stand it? Every word had to be a dagger.

'Check out these.' Charley clicked a key again.

Picture after picture of him, of Frankie, of him and Frankie now filled the screen. Smiling, laughing. Their faces when they looked at each other . . . Talk about a dagger.

Did Frankie know that she'd fallen in love with him again? Or maybe she still loved him, had always loved him. Just as he had always loved her. All it had taken was brain cancer to get them back together.

Hannah stood so fast her chair teetered, and she had to set her hand on the back of it to make it stop.

Perhaps Frankie did know, or at least suspect. Maybe that's what her hustle-hurry to get out of here had been about.

'Lunch,' she said. 'You want some?'

Charley's blue-blue eyes contemplated her, and for an instant she thought he saw more than she wanted him to before those eyes flicked back to the screen. 'I could eat.'

Considering how thin he was, she decided she'd better get as much food into him as she could while she could.

She started opening cupboards, peered into the refrigerator. There wasn't much there. At least Frankie hadn't been lying about the grocery store.

'Mac and cheese?' she asked.

'Sure.'

Charley's gaze was once again riveted to the computer, on the photographs of him and Frankie together. He reached out a hand that trembled badly and ran a finger over Frankie's face.

Hannah busied herself heating the water. Then watched until the water boiled. Just like the adage, because she was watching the water took forever to heat.

There was something about those pictures that reminded her of the ones Charley had taken of Heath. Which made no sense because they weren't similar at all, except for the ones of Charley getting thinner, paler, weaker.

Charley didn't know it, maybe Frankie didn't either, but they'd been recording his illness, maybe his death, as well, and that gave Hannah an idea.

They ate together, the silence between them louder because there had rarely been silence between them. The time they'd spent together had been full of words – descriptions of where he'd been, what he'd done, stories of *You* and the people there. One thing they'd never lacked was conversation. Now Hannah couldn't think of a single thing to say.

Charley only ate half the bowl and when she urged him to eat it all, he got up and went outside. Concerned, she followed. What if he walked into the trees and he didn't come back? What if he went into the water and . . .

Charley cast her a narrow-eyed glare. 'I don't need a sitter.'

'I just thought I'd . . . uh . . . where are you going?'

'To the dock. You'll be able to see me from the window. Don't worry.'

She spent the next two hours watching Charley watch the water. The Charley she knew had been in constant motion. He never sat still that long. He never stared at anything for more than a few seconds before he snatched a camera and recorded it forever.

She wished she had a friend to call, but she didn't. Or at least not a friend with whom she could share this. She'd had two best friends in her life – Heath and Charley. And they were both gone.

The door opened. Paper bags rustled.

'Everything OK?' Frankie asked.

'Peachy.'

The bags clunked on to the counter. Frankie joined her at the window.

'He does this a lot?' Hannah asked.

'Is several hours a day and sometimes in the middle of the night a lot?' Frankie sighed. 'Yeah, a lot.'

'Middle of the night?'

Frankie shrugged. 'Sometimes I wake up and he's not in his bed. I find him on the dock in the dark. It always freaks me out.'

'Why does he go there?'

Frankie's gaze didn't waver from Charley. 'You know why.'

The silence that settled between them stretched out for so long, Hannah wanted to end it, but she didn't know how.

'Wine?' Frankie headed for the bags on the counter.

Hannah was liking Frankie more and more. They might have been friends if not for . . . well, everything.

She glanced at the nautical clock, which read 3:00 p.m. 'Isn't it early?'

Frankie removed a bottle of white sangria from a bag. 'In Door County on the weekends, early is before noon and sometimes not even then.'

'In that case, I'd love some.' Hannah moved into the kitchen and started unpacking the bags before she remembered that she didn't know where anything went, except for the milk, eggs, cheese and the like. She started putting them away.

Frankie pulled out a cutting board and sliced peaches and plums, tossing a few into wine glasses that resembled small bowls before pouring sangria to the rim.

'You're my kind of woman,' Hannah said.

'Understandable since we married the same man.' Frankie handed Hannah a glass.

'Wouldn't that make us opposites?'

Frankie took a big slug of wine. 'I have no idea.'

Hannah sipped hers. 'Me neither.'

They took the bottle on to the deck, where they could watch Charley watch the water.

'If he doesn't remember Lisa's gone, then why is he staring at the place where she went?' Hannah asked halfway through her second serving. She'd never have brought up Lisa otherwise.

'It's a mystery.' Frankie topped off their glasses.

'You're awfully calm about all of this.'

'I learned not to get worked up over stuff oh . . . about twenty-four years ago.'

'That was when I *started* getting worked up about stuff.' Though she'd made sure no one but herself ever knew about it.

'Understandable.' Frankie sipped her drink. 'Charley can make anyone crazy.'

'Sometimes you sound like you hate him.'

'I do.' Frankie frowned. 'Did.'

Hannah opened her mouth to say she'd seen the pictures of them together and did Frankie know she actually loved him again, then snapped her lips shut. She hadn't had enough sangria for that conversation. She wasn't certain there *was* enough sangria for that conversation.

'We need to make a plan.' Frankie picked up the bottle, let out a forlorn sigh when she saw it was empty.

'For?' Hannah's breathing became shallow as she waited for Frankie to bring up plans for Charley's exchange of custody, which would only happen when he was so close to death he couldn't run away from the woman he'd lived with for over two decades, whom he didn't even know.

'Dinner.' Frankie set down the empty bottle with a *thunk*. 'I vote we order Wild Tomato Pizza. Best in the world. Wood grilled. The vegetarian is so amazing you won't even miss the meat.'

'Have you had New York pizza?'

'Doesn't compare.'

Hannah finished off her sangria. 'Then I got to get me some of that.'

Charley drove since Hannah and Frankie were a little sloshed.

'Is he OK to drive?' Hannah whispered as they headed for the car.

'He remembers driving. He just doesn't remember you.'

'There's a lot more than me he doesn't remember.'

'*Touché.*' Frankie gave a little salute.

Hannah was nervous on the way to the restaurant, but Charley did remember driving, and he'd always been good at parking in tight spaces, which turned out to be necessary as everyone in the county seemed to be at Wild Tomato on a Saturday night.

By the time they went to bed at the unreasonable hour of 9:00 p.m., Hannah deemed the day a success. Charley hadn't called her crazy. She and Frankie hadn't argued. No one had punched anyone in the mouth. But the night was young.

A muffled shout woke her. Hannah stared at the ceiling trying to remember whose ceiling it was.

'The South Tower's falling,' Charley called.

She was up and across the hall as he started shouting. 'Go, go! We gotta get out of here before this one falls too.'

What followed was coughing, choking, wheezing. He must be reliving the dust storm that had washed over him and several of the firefighters he'd followed into the North Tower. They'd tried to get him to go back out, but when he'd refused they'd given up. They had more important things to do. Unfortunately they'd never gotten to do them. They'd made it into the area between the two towers as the debris rained down.

'Charley?' Hannah sat on the edge of the bed. 'Hey, come on. Wake up.'

Charley's eyes snapped open; they darted this way and that. He started thrashing. One of his knuckles caught Hannah in the mouth.

She tasted blood. That was going to leave a mark.

'Can't breathe.' He started gasping, then he started digging.

According to the authorities, Charley and several firefighters had dug their way out of the area between the two towers in an impressively short amount of time, considering. About twenty minutes.

Nine minutes before the North Tower fell too.

Charley had always said it felt like twenty hours. He was still pissed off that he'd lost his camera in the rubble. It had never been found, along with over eleven hundred people and, oddly, most of the furniture in the place. The largest piece of any office found was a portion of telephone keypad.

Everything was vaporized, pulverized or both, Charley's camera included. Whenever Hannah thought of how close Charley had come to being dust, she started wheezing herself.

'Charley!' She caught his wrists. She'd become adept at it. 'Wake up, sweetheart. Come on.'

His eyes, still open – that always gave her the wiggies – blinked and he was *there* again. She was so glad to see him she leaned over and kissed him on the mouth. He tasted like Her Charley – spicy cinnamon from the Dentyne gum he carried everywhere – and before she knew it she'd wrapped her arms around his neck.

'What the fuck?' Charley shoved her off the bed.

Hannah landed on the floor hard enough to leave another mark. Fat lip, bruised ass. Batting a thousand here.

'What's wrong?' Frankie stood in the doorway.

Hannah's face heated. How long had Frankie been there?

Charley cowered against the wall, shaking. 'There were firemen. Smoke. Ashes. People screaming. And then something monstrous fell and fell and fell. On me.'

Frankie stepped into the room just enough so that the moon through the window illuminated her face. She glanced at Hannah with eyebrows raised. 'World Trade Center?'

'Yes,' Charley agreed, then scowled at Hannah as if it were all her fault. 'The towers fell. Both of them.' He rubbed his forehead. 'But that didn't happen.' He dropped his hand, grabbed Frankie's, pulled her on to the bed next to him. 'Why does it seem like it happened?'

Frankie hesitated and Hannah murmured, 'No.'

Why tell him? He wouldn't believe them. She'd like to forget that day and the several that had followed when she hadn't known if Charley were dead or alive. She'd also like to forget that he hadn't been worried at all about her in DC. Of course, why would she have been at the Pentagon, but still. Charley wasn't supposed to be at the damn World Trade Center either, but he was.

'You had a dream,' Frankie said.

'I had a dream,' he repeated. 'And you didn't come. She did. She kissed me.' He rubbed the back of his hand over his mouth.

Hannah felt like a slut. She should probably get off the floor. That wasn't helping.

'I'll just . . .' She motioned toward the door and Frankie nodded absently.

Hannah stepped into the hall, but she didn't leave. She couldn't.

'You want to talk about it?' Frankie asked.

Hannah inched closer, careful to stay out of sight.

'It felt like the truth,' he said. 'Like Vietnam.'

'A flashback not a nightmare.'

'Yes.'

The covers rustled. The bed creaked.

Hannah drew quickly back. What were they doing?

Frankie started to hum.

Hannah didn't recognize the tune until Frankie began to sing 'Blowin' in the Wind.'

A war song. Maybe more of an anti-war song, which could explain why it might have helped calm Charley down from his war flashbacks. But would it work now?

She waited until Frankie began to hum again and then peeked in.

Charley rested in Frankie's arms, his back to her chest, his head on her shoulder. Her lips pressed to his temple, even as she continued to hum. The moon painted the room, the bed, them in silver, white and blue light. Every other color seemed leached away, leaving behind a stark depiction of a love so great it had never truly died.

I gotta get out of this place.

Hadn't that been one of those sixties songs too?

Hannah fled. Sat on her bed, then a chair, then the bed again. She tried to work, tried to read. Gave it up and just stared at the door until Frankie came through.

She shut it then leaned against it. 'You kissed him?'

'Seemed like a good idea at the time.'

And it had been. Right up until he'd shoved her on to the floor.

'He was himself again, or I thought he was, but . . .' Hannah spread her hands.

'He wasn't. He isn't.'

'No.'

'Did he have a lot of flashbacks?' Frankie asked.

'Only one that reoccurred. Mostly he had dreams, nightmares.'

'What's the difference?'

'According to my psychiatrist, a flashback is a reliving of an actual event – sometimes you're awake and sometimes you're asleep. A dream, a nightmare is a lot of jibber-jabber.'

'Is that a medical term?'

Hannah ignored her. 'Most of the time dreams make no sense; there might be things that actually happened, mixed with things you feared would happen or hoped would. But a flashback is a memory of what happened.'

'Charley has World Trade Center flashbacks?'

'No,' Hannah said. 'That's not his recurring memory. This is the first time he's woken up screaming about the towers falling. At least when he was with me.'

She had no idea what he did when he wasn't with her. She'd learned to live with that, even forget about it most of the time.

'But . . .' Frankie began.

'Lisa,' Hannah blurted, and Frankie emitted a startled gasp. 'His flashback was Lisa's death.'

Frankie slid along the door until she sat on the floor as if her legs had suddenly become too weak to hold her up. 'Did you help him?'

'Help?' Hannah repeated.

'I used to sing to help him forget.'

'He didn't want to forget. Even though he woke up sobbing and gasping, his chest aching, soaked with sweat, he didn't want any comfort. He didn't think he deserved it.'

Frankie flinched.

'And he wanted . . .' For a minute Hannah couldn't finish what she knew she needed to say.

'What did he want?' Frankie whispered.

'To keep having that flashback. Because if he didn't he might forget someday what she looked like.'

Frankie let out a soft sob, then slapped one palm over her mouth.

'Is that true?' Hannah asked. 'Would he have forgotten?'

Frankie's eyes were wide above her hand. She nodded but she didn't speak.

'I told him he should look at the photographs, but he wouldn't. He put them in a box and he hid them away. More punishment, I suppose.'

Slowly Frankie's hand fell away from her face until it rested limply on the floor.

'I didn't mean to kiss him,' Hannah said. 'He seemed like My Charley and I miss him.'

Why she was explaining to Frankie, she had no idea. Charley *was* still Hannah's husband, no matter what he believed, and she had every right to kiss him.

He also had every right to shove her on her ass.

'What I can't figure out . . .' Frankie said, either not hearing or not caring about Hannah's explanation. 'Does his having a *Your Charley* nightmare . . . flashback . . . whatever mean his

subconscious is remembering things, maybe the tumor is . . .?'
Frankie made a shrinking motion with both hands.

'Yes!' Hannah's voice was too loud, too perky. 'It must,' she
continued in a more sedate fashion, though she was still excited
bordering on manic. She was never going to sleep tonight. 'It
has to.'

'A tumor doesn't have to do anything.'

'But if he's worse, wouldn't he forget more instead of remember
more?'

'You'd think.'

'I guess we'll find out Monday,' Hannah said.

'You're staying?'

Hannah sighed. 'I'm staying.'

What else could she do? She'd been at Heath's side through
everything. Shouldn't she be at Charley's, even if he didn't want
her there?

She no longer knew what was right or wrong, what she should
or shouldn't do, but she did know the least she could do was
join Frankie and Charley in Dr Lanier's office on Monday.

'I'm sorry to say the chemo isn't working,' Dr Lanier informed
them as if he were a waiter imparting the sad but inevitable
information that the restaurant had run short of the house
special.

'But that can't be,' Hannah said faintly.

Charley cast her a withering glance. 'Why is she here again?'

Frankie shushed him and he actually shushed. He was so agreeable to everything Frankie said that Hannah was both disturbed
– definitely *not* Charley – and encouraged. Maybe he'd listen to
Frankie when she told him to do whatever it was that needed
to be done to save his life.

'I assure you it is,' Lanier continued, face and voice still carefully neutral.

Was that to keep people from losing their shit? Hannah
wondered how that worked for him.

'Not only is the tumor growing instead of shrinking, but it's
spreading. Have you noticed any new memory issues?'

'I didn't notice the old memory issues,' Charley muttered.

At least he still had a sense of humor.

'He had a flashback,' Frankie said.

'It was a dream,' Charley snapped. 'Not a memory. The World Trade Center never fell down in a cloud of ashes and smoke.'

Lanier's eyebrows lifted. 'I see.' His fingers tap-tapped on his laptop. 'Anything else?'

'Not yet,' Frankie said. 'What do we do now?'

'I'd like to try an experimental treatment that's had some success in this area.'

'What area?' Hannah asked. 'Failure?'

'The brain,' Lanier said dryly.

Frankie patted Hannah's hand. She felt like a chastised child.

'It's a new chemo cocktail used specifically on tumors that seem to feed on the old ones.'

'They feed?' Hannah felt a little nauseous at the image. 'On chemo?'

'It's as good a word as any for what's going on in Charley's head. It's almost like the tumor is drinking the chemo, smacking its lips and begging for more.'

Now Hannah felt a lot nauseous.

'The only problem is this cocktail makes patients a lot sicker, the sickness lasts longer and that makes them weaker.'

Wasn't that three problems?

'Oh, goody,' Charley said.

'Does it work?' Frankie asked.

'We're not sure.'

'How can you not be sure?' Hannah demanded.

Frankie patted her again. She *had* said that kind of loud.

'It's experimental. We don't have enough results to be sure.'

'You want me to be your guinea pig?' Charley asked.

'Only if you want to be.'

'I don't think I do.'

'Charley, you have to . . .' Hannah began, but he silenced her with a glare.

In his mind she shouldn't even be here; she definitely shouldn't be telling him what he had to do. Even if he had known who she was, Charley wouldn't thank her for telling him what to do. That had never bothered her, because he didn't tell her what to do either. Unless she asked.

And she had asked, in the beginning, because he'd not only been her husband but her mentor. She'd admired him, looked up to him, in addition to loving him. Her life with Charley had been an education in every way a young woman might want it to be.

She'd soaked up his advice, his knowledge, his attention, and he'd seemed to enjoy imparting it. He'd almost seemed to need to. In that first year, one of the few times she'd seen him smile was when she asked him a question that would take hours to answer. Something they could analyze and discuss, practice, improve.

How many times had they fallen asleep at the light table, the kitchen table? Some of her best memories were of her waking him or him waking her and together, hand in hand, walking to the bedroom still talking about whatever it was they'd been talking about when they'd nodded off.

Later, when she'd taken his advice, learned, grown, become her own woman and she'd stopped asking, had that bothered him? She didn't think so. He'd always said he was proud of the woman she'd become. He'd believed her capable of handling everything, so she'd done so. Even though he looked at her now as if she were dry, week-old gum on the bottom of his shoe, that didn't make her dry, week-old gum. Did it?

'I'm not going to spend the time I have left sicker than I've been already.' Charley's mouth tightened. He was so thin, the expression made him resemble a mulish old man. 'I'm just not.'

'Frankie?' Hannah's voice quivered.

Charley listened to Frankie. He did what she said in a very un-Charley-like way. If Frankie told Charley to take the chemo, would he listen?

Frankie's own lips set in a tight, pale line. Suddenly she looked older too.

Hannah took Frankie's hand, squeezed her fingers. 'Tell him.'

Frankie glanced at her once, then nodded. 'Whatever you want, Charley.'

Hannah snatched her hand back. 'That's not what I meant!'

Dr Lanier's gaze flicked between the two of them. He stood. 'Maybe we should step into the exam room.'

Hannah wasn't certain which 'we' he referred to, but she followed when he opened the door and went through. She nearly shut the door on Frankie. Guess she was coming too.

Charley had picked up a magazine and was paging through it, muttering to himself. He seemed far too nonchalant to have just signed his own death warrant.

The last time Hannah had felt this helpless, Heath had been dying. Then she'd been scared; now she was both scared and mad. 'Don't I have any rights in this?'

'You don't,' Lanier said. 'I'm sorry.'

'But—'

'He's in his right mind.'

'He has brain cancer!' Hannah sounded hysterical and she knew it.

'Yes, but he knows that. He's well aware of his condition and has every right to make his own choices regarding treatment or non-treatment.'

'He thinks it's 1989.'

Lanier shrugged. 'If he thought it was 1889, that might be different.'

Hannah made a soft cry of frustration. 'You're just going to let him die?'

'He was always going to die, Hannah.' Frankie's voice was just above a whisper. 'All he gets to choose is how.'

'This is what you wanted all along, isn't it?' She should stop talking, but it was as if a person she didn't know had taken over her mouth. 'You've been wanting him to die in agony ever since . . .'

'Don't say it.' Frankie lifted one finger and pointed it in Hannah's direction.

'It's true.'

'Just because it might have been true once, doesn't make it true any more.'

'Aha!'

Frankie rolled her eyes. 'I know you're upset. We're all upset.'

Except Frankie didn't look upset. She looked calm, cool and in control, even more so because Hannah was just the opposite. When had they switched roles? Hannah wasn't sure, but she wanted to switch back.

'Maybe I should tell you what's going to happen from now on.' The doctor spoke quickly, as if he couldn't wait to impart the information and get out of Dodge. 'He shouldn't be in pain. If he is, he can have morphine.'

Heath had had morphine. It had taken away the pain and given him hallucinations. Considering what Charley already saw without morphine, Hannah wasn't sure she wanted to be around for what his busy brain conjured up with it.

'He'll get increasingly sleepy, less coordinated, weaker, there might be headaches and seizures, mood swings. Since his tumor is affecting his memories, he might lose some of the ones he has, have trouble forming new ones, or mix up different memories altogether.'

'Might that be why he had a flashback of the fall of the World Trade Center when he doesn't remember it's gone?' Frankie asked.

'Probably,' Lanier agreed, then moved on as if it didn't really matter, and at this point did it? 'There's a local medical supply place where you can get a hospital bed.'

Hannah had a sudden flashback of Heath lying in one of those beds. She didn't think she could watch another man she loved die.

Lanier pulled a card from his pocket. 'Call the visiting nurse. Get things set up for when he needs meds.'

'How long?' Hannah managed, a cold sweat beading her forehead as her stomach did a frightening pitch and roll.

Lanier stared first at his shoes, then into her eyes. 'Not long.'

Hannah barely reached the wastebasket before she threw up.

Frankie

'I used to throw up whenever Charley was in life-threatening danger.' Frankie set her hand atop the roof of Hannah's rental car and leaned down so she could see in the open driver's side window.

Why was she telling Hannah that? Had she ever told anyone but Charley? There were a lot of things she was sharing with Hannah that she'd never shared with anyone but Charley, including Charley. And, really, who would understand any of these things *but* Hannah? There was a camaraderie here that Frankie had never felt with anyone before, with good reason. She wasn't sure she liked it, but she didn't *not* like it either.

Hannah's fingers curled around the steering wheel like claws. She still seemed overly pale, even for her.

'Are you sure you're OK to drive?'

'I'm fine.'

She wasn't. None of them were. Charley was the least fine of them all.

He'd fallen asleep on the way home from the clinic. Walked into the cottage and gone straight to bed.

When Lanier had said 'not long' he couldn't have meant tomorrow. Could he?

'I'll be back by the end of the week,' Hannah said. 'There are some things I gotta do in DC before I . . .'

She looked so forlorn, Frankie wanted to pat her again, but she should probably stop. Patting not only made Frankie feel like a blue-haired old lady, but every once in a while Hannah glanced at her when she did it as if she might want to curl up in Frankie's lap and never leave.

Frankie wasn't sure how she felt about that.

'Are you going to be able to do this?' Frankie asked.

'I'll have to.' Hannah started the car. 'I'll bring the photographs along with me.'

Frankie almost asked, 'What photographs?' How could she have forgotten the reason she was here?

Except it wasn't really the reason any more.

Frankie backed away without another word, just lifted her hand in goodbye, which Hannah ignored.

'Text me when you reach the airport,' she called.

'I've already got a mother,' Hannah muttered.

'I heard that.'

'You were supposed to.'

Frankie gave her the finger.

Hannah actually laughed, which made Frankie feel a little better about her driving all the way to Green Bay after she'd lost her breakfast – or what appeared to be several weeks' worth of breakfasts – into the garbage can at the clinic.

Frankie's cell started to vibrate in her pocket and she went on to the deck to answer it. She didn't want to wake Charley.

'Is he out of your house and your life yet?' Irene asked.

It had been a while since she'd talked to Irene. Had to say she hadn't missed it.

'No.'

'When will he be?'

'Not long,' Frankie said, then had to fight a hysterical giggle at her echoing of Dr Lanier's timeline. Why was that funny?

Why was anything funny any more? *Was* anything funny any more?

'I thought the bimbo was taking over at the end.'

'Don't call her that.'

'*You* called her that.'

'I know. I shouldn't have.'

Hannah wasn't a bimbo, had never been a bimbo. Hannah had been through a lot; she'd come out on the other side not only whole but stronger. Frankie wished she could say the same about herself.

'Maybe not,' Irene allowed. 'It *was* all Charley's fault.'

'No,' Frankie said. 'It wasn't.'

'Well, it wasn't *your* fault.'

'More of it was than I realized.' Or wanted to admit.

'He left you, Frankie, when you needed him the most.'

Irene really needed to find a new tune.

'I wasn't there for him either.'

'He killed your child.'

'He did not!' Frankie snapped.

'What, exactly, *did* he do?'

'He made a mistake.' Several of them.

'You're going to forgive him?'

'It's about time, don't you think?'

'You know what I think? You need to boot him out of your life before you fall in love with him again and get your heart broken worse than before.'

'That's not possible,' Frankie said.

She didn't think she was capable of loving anyone again the way she'd loved Charley.

'I worry about you.'

'I know. It's the only reason I put up with you.'

'You want me to come out there?'

'No. Thanks. It won't be long now.'

'It won't be long until she takes over or it won't be long until he dies?'

'Yes,' Frankie said, and left it at that.

While she had the phone in her hand, Frankie called both the visiting nurse and the medical supply place and made the arrangements she needed to. When she returned to the house, Charley sat on the couch, his camera in his hands.

'You OK?'

'Nope. Dying.'

'Charley, you could try . . .'

'No.' He lifted his gaze and she found herself as captured by it today as she had been way back when.

Those eyes. They saw everything, even things you never wanted them to see.

'I love you,' he said. 'I want to spend the time I have left with you, doing what we both love.' Charley lifted the camera. 'If you'll help me.'

'Of course.'

He looked away again. 'The only way I can handle this, Fancy, is to handle it with you.'

Frankie swallowed. What was he going to think when she left him with Hannah?

Who was she kidding? She wasn't going to leave him with Hannah.

'I'm just going to ask one thing,' he said.

One thing? What could it be?

'Can you bring Lisa here so I can see her before things get too bad?'

'I . . . uh . . . don't think so.'

'Maybe we can go to her.'

'Um . . .'

Why couldn't she get the words out? How hard could it be?

Lisa's dead. Has been for almost twenty-five years. You weren't paying attention and she drowned.

What possible purpose could telling him have now?

'Please?' Charley begged. 'I know she'll probably be scared, especially when she sees me like this.' He waved at his too-skinny body. 'Maybe I should just talk to her on the phone?' His face crumpled. 'But I want to hold her one last time. What do you think?'

How many times had Frankie thought that same thing? If she could only hold Lisa one last time.

'I'll see what I can do,' Frankie said, then blinked. She hadn't wanted to tell him the truth, but she hadn't meant to lie either. What was *wrong* with her?

Charley grinned. 'Thank you.'

'It isn't going to be easy.' Understatement of a lifetime. 'She's . . . um . . . pretty far away.'

Charley seemed to have forgotten his request already. He started fiddling with the camera. 'I'd like to take some shots on Washington Island.'

Washington Island was located off the tip of the Door County peninsula where Green Bay and Lake Michigan met at a place referred to as 'Death's Door'.

Life was quite the comedian sometimes, wasn't it?

Frankie had only been to Washington Island once when the three of them had gone to Door County. They'd been so happy, so clueless as to what life had in store for them. Frankie had never gone back because she didn't want to spoil the memories of that day with anything less than happy.

Going there with Dying Charley might do that.

'We can't today. They're delivering your hospital bed.'

They were. Whew! She didn't even have to lie again.

The next day it poured. The day after that Charley woke up with a nasty headache; his right hand twitched of its own accord.

Frankie panicked and called Dr Lanier.

'That's common, though he does seem to be deteriorating fast.'

'What should I do?'

'Make him comfortable. I'll call an order for morphine to the visiting nurse.'

Frankie felt terrible about not taking him to Washington Island when he'd been well enough to go because she was afraid. This wasn't about her. Never had been.

She sat on the side of his bed and stroked his head. His hair was starting to grow back. Would he be around long enough to see if it came back as curly as it had been before it had left?

'You want an aspirin?' she asked.

'No.' He kept his eyes closed. 'Pain's fading. Can you keep doing that? It helps.'

Frankie wasn't sure how stroking his face and head could help, but she continued anyway.

'The only thing that makes me feel better is you,' he whispered.

'You haven't tried morphine yet.'

He opened his eyes, took her hand, held it to his cheek. 'Don't make fun.'

'Sorry.'

'It really does help to feel your touch, hear your voice.' He pressed his mouth to her palm, and she shivered. 'Remember how Lisa believed that you could kiss it and make it all better?'

Frankie nodded. She couldn't take her gaze from his face, or pull her fingers from his grasp.

'I think I believe it too,' he whispered, drawing her closer and closer.

Their lips met. Her gasp was audible. Frankie felt that kiss everywhere.

'Hush.' He tangled his fingers in her hair.

She hushed. She couldn't do anything else with his tongue in her mouth. Or maybe her tongue was in his mouth. It was hard to tell.

'I'm afraid,' he murmured against her neck.

'Oh, Charley,' was all she could manage.

She had no idea what to say to soothe a frightened, dying man.

It'll be all right?

It wouldn't.

You're going to a better place?

Trite. Predictable. Might even be a lie.

Don't be afraid.

Who was she to give him orders? He could be, do, say, have anything he wanted.

'I'm afraid I'll die before I make love to you one last time.'

Frankie stilled in his arms, the last place she'd been where she felt alive. She felt alive now in a way she hadn't been in so very long.

Should she? Could she?

Could he?

Charley shifted closer. Apparently, he could.

'Just once,' he said. 'It's probably all I can manage.'

Hadn't she been thinking that a frightened, dying man could be, do, say, have anything he wanted?

Since what he wanted was her . . .

She gave it to him.

Just once.

Charley

Charley woke with his arms full of Frankie. He knew it even before he opened his eyes.

That faint scent of lemon. The honeyed texture of her skin. The drift of her hair across his chest.

Why did it feel as though he hadn't held her in far too long? Because it always felt like that. Every time they'd been apart and come back together, he found it hard to let her go.

How long had it been this time? Before Africa for sure. Weeks? Maybe a month. Why couldn't he remember?

Even if it had been a month or more, he'd been gone that long before and not felt so desperate to lose himself in his wife. Not that he'd ever been happy about the separations.

Not sad either, because he loved his job. But he was always, always thrilled to get back to his wife and his little girl.

Why did it seem like he hadn't seen Lisa in even longer?

Too many thoughts. They were starting to confuse him, bring back the headache that Frankie's touch, Frankie's kiss had banished.

He opened his eyes, just as Frankie did too. He'd always loved when that happened. How long had it been since they'd managed to wake at the same, exact moment?

'Decades,' he said.

Frankie frowned as if she knew what he'd been thinking. But if she had, the word *decades* would have made as little sense to her as it did to him. And she didn't look confused at all, just . . . concerned. Maybe wary. Why?

'Morning,' he said.

'Yeah.' She sat up, pulling the sheet to her neck.

He considered convincing her to let him take a stab at round two, but the way she was fondling that sheet, it wasn't going to happen.

'Washington Island today?' he asked.

Relief flowed over her face. 'Great.'

She scampered out of the room, taking the sheet with her. What did she have to be relieved about? Had she been that excited to visit Washington Island? He felt bad that he'd been too weak to go. He wasn't sure he felt strong enough today, but since Frankie was so thrilled he would not disappoint her. He'd already disappointed her enough.

Where had that thought come from? He couldn't remember Frankie ever saying she was disappointed in him. To the contrary, she constantly told him how proud she was. He was embarrassed to admit that he soaked up every word of praise both from her and the critics, his bosses and his colleagues. He had a compulsion to be the best, to prove himself to anyone and everyone, which would not be satisfied no matter how long he was in the job, no matter how many awards he won or how much money he made.

Daddy issues, no doubt. Nothing he'd ever done had been right enough for Daddy. Honestly, the sins of the fathers. He hoped that he hadn't fucked up Lisa as badly as his dad had fucked him up.

Pain whispered behind his right eye. There was something about Lisa . . .

In the distance a phone rang and Frankie answered. Her voice raised, then raised again, then quickly lowered. A few minutes later she returned wearing a robe.

Charley really missed that sheet.

'Hannah can't come back for another week.'

'Your friend Hannah?'

Frankie nodded.

'Who cares?' He couldn't figure out why the woman kept hanging around. 'What's up with you and her? The only friend you've ever had is Irene.'

'I have friends other than Irene.'

'Who?'

'Han-nah,' she said, making the two syllables pronounced enough to reveal annoyance even if he hadn't been able to read her face better than anyone's on earth.

'I don't like her,' Charley said.

Frankie burst out laughing.

'Why is that funny?'

She stopped laughing and that concerned, wary expression returned. 'Why is anything funny any more?' Frankie asked, and left.

The shower turned on and Charley lay back to wait his turn, though maybe he should . . . No. He didn't think Frankie would welcome his company in there today as she had so many times in the past.

Instead, he contemplated the ceiling. There was something weird about Hannah. The way he caught her staring at him as if she knew him, as if she liked him – a lot. Had she hit on him at some point?

Charley rubbed his eye. Wouldn't he remember that? Except he didn't even remember her. Should he ask Frankie?

Best to let it go. While Hannah got on his nerves, Frankie seemed to like her. She treated Hannah like a child, or maybe a younger sister. They were obviously close and Frankie would need friends when he was gone.

Charley got out of bed, then sat on the side until the vertigo passed. He'd had head rushes before, usually from dehydration, but this was different and worse. He sucked down the remains of the bottle of water that sat on the white painted wood nightstand. After a few minutes he did feel better.

They set off for Washington Island after they ate some toast and Frankie drank some coffee. Charley stuck with water. Coffee no longer agreed with him.

He'd thought he would be upset about that. Coffee was his second favorite reason to get up each morning after Frankie's smile, but when it bubbled in your stomach like microwaved acid, you got over wanting it pretty fast.

Despite the summer warmth, Charley wore a sweatshirt and jeans. After losing those last five pounds, he couldn't ever seem to get warm any more. Except last night, in bed with Frankie. He'd been warm enough then.

He rubbed his hand over his stubbly head. Frankie had insisted he bring the fedora she'd bought him in Sister Bay.

'Wear that or I'm gonna put SPF eight thousand on the top of your head.'

Since he hated the way sunscreen felt in his hair, or lack of it, he took the hat.

Frankie wore jeans that ended just below her knees. His mom had called them pedal pushers. They called them something else now, but he couldn't remember what and didn't feel like exerting any of his remaining brain cells figuring it out. Her red espadrilles matched her T-shirt. *She* hadn't brought a hat. But then she had her gorgeous hair to cover her head, neck, shoulders. He loved that hair.

The roads were clear, the huge crowds that mucked them up absent during the week. The ferry wasn't busy either.

Charley meant to use his camera all the way across – pictures of Northpoint Pier, where they'd caught the ferry, pictures of the town of Ellison Bay as they pulled away, pictures of the water, fish, wildlife, then of the approach to Washington Island. Instead, he found himself waking up as they docked.

Frankie lowered her camera. He thought she'd had it pointed at him.

'What happened?' He wiped a bit of drool from his chin. He'd been out cold.

'You needed the sleep,' Frankie said briskly, though the line between her eyebrows that became more pronounced when she worried appeared deeper than usual.

'I wanted to photograph . . .' He waved his hand at everything he'd missed.

'Isn't it the same in reverse?' Frankie moved toward the stairs that would take them to their Volvo, which had also made the trip to Washington Island.

Charley glanced back at the peninsula about five miles away. 'You might have a point.'

He followed her, reaching the lower level as she strode toward the car, boxed in by several others. They'd have to wait for all the vehicles in front of them to drive on to the island before they could.

The array of cars intrigued him. Charley lifted his camera, surprised when his hands shook. He should be used to it by now, but every time he expected that shake to be gone. He rested the lens on the dashboard, peered through the viewfinder.

'What do you see?' Frankie asked.

He'd never been able to explain how he saw things, how the slight variation in angle or focus could say something completely different about the subject framed by his lens.

'Take a look.'

Frankie lifted her camera – he gritted his teeth against the jealousy that her hands were as steady as his used to be. She glanced through the lens, lowered it, shrugged. 'Meh.'

Charley liked how the cars lined up in front of the ferry exit – the door of the boat opening, a slice of sky widening. He didn't notice Frankie was photographing him until she stopped. 'What are you doing?'

'You were so involved. It was beautiful.'

Charley hadn't ever been beautiful. Now he wasn't ever going to be.

They spent part of the day at Schoolhouse Beach Park, which was one of only five smooth limestone beaches in the country.

'This is wild.' Charley snapped shot after shot of the sandless beach, using Frankie's shoulder as a prop. Her hair flying in front of the lens only made the photograph seem aged. The strands against the bright blue sky resembled cracks in a photographic plate.

'You know, there's a hefty fee if you get caught stealing one of those rocks.'

'They're rocks.' Charley set his camera on top of them, then lay down and started shooting again.

'They're glacier polished rocks, which are thousands of years old, most holding fossils.'

'Like this one.' Charley zoomed in on a stone with some kind of insect etched into the surface. 'What are those?' He indicated the cairns that dotted the area.

'When on a sand beach, sand castles must be built. When on a rock beach, you get that.'

Charley got to his feet – it wasn't as easy as it used to be but he ignored Frankie's outstretched hand – then crossed the uneven ground, stumbling several times.

Frankie caught up and took his arm. 'You dizzy?'

'No.' He wasn't right now, but his balance had gone south. He blamed the smooth stone beach.

'We should bring Lisa here.'

Charley was so fascinated by the cairns – some were very elaborate – he didn't notice that Frankie wasn't talking. When he lowered the camera, her face was so set and pale he lifted it again and took the picture.

She cast him a disgusted glance. 'Really?'

'You reminded me of the death mask of Mary, Queen of Scots.'

He'd seen a copy once in Falkland Palace in Scotland. Creepy stuff. Why would anyone make a mask of a dead person? But he'd discovered there were a lot of them floating around in museums everywhere – Ben Franklin, John Dillinger, Abraham Lincoln. He'd meant to visit more of them. And how creepy did that make him?

'Thanks,' Frankie said.

She still looked a lot like Mary.

'What's wrong, Fancy?'

She stared at the water and not at him. 'You don't remember bringing Lisa here?'

'Here?' He could swear he'd never been here before. 'When?'

'Before she . . .' She stopped, pursing her lips as if she'd sucked on the lemons she still smelled so much like. 'When we came to pick out the cottage.'

The situation she described sounded familiar. If anyone had asked him if he'd come to Door County and chosen their cottage, he'd have said yes. If they asked him when and how and what else they'd done . . .

'I got nothin',' he admitted.

She took the camera from his hands. Until she did so, he hadn't realized how heavy it was. His arms were shaking.

'You don't remember Lisa going into the water?'

There was something about Lisa going into the water, but when he thought about it he couldn't breathe. His chest hurt. His legs gave out and he collapsed on the rocks in a heap.

'Charley!' Frankie fell to her knees at his side.

The breeze off the water caused the sudden sweat that had broken out all over him to cool and he shivered. 'I don't remember her here.'

'She ran into the waves, then right back out because the stones hurt her feet. You let her wear her sneakers.'

In his mind, something about him and Lisa and water hovered just out of reach. He tried to grab it, but it only danced even farther away.

Charley shook his head.

'That's OK.' Frankie kissed his cheek.

From her face, it wasn't OK. He knew he was forgetting things, but he'd yet to hear from anyone just what it was he'd forgotten.

Something caught his eye on the water. He tried to pick up his camera from where Frankie had placed it on the stones, and he couldn't. That scared him. He didn't feel weak. He felt like he could lift that thing and then . . . it just didn't happen.

'Can you . . .' he began. 'Could you help?'

Frankie practically leaped forward and retrieved the Nikon, then handed it to him. He took it and, as he'd suspected, his arms couldn't support the weight. His hands fell back to the ground, camera on top, driving his knuckles against the stones.

'I'm sorry!' Frankie sounded so horrified, annoyance flared.

'I'll live,' he said dryly. 'Although not very long.'

'Charley, please.'

'Begging isn't going to help. I've tried.'

Had he? He thought so. He was still dying.

'Just take the camera, Fancy.'

Tentatively she lifted it.

'See out there?' He nodded at the bobbing black *something.* 'Find it. Center it.'

She did. 'It's a tire.'

'Sheesh. People are pigs.'

She began to lower the Nikon, but he used one finger to lift the lens back up. That was the most he could manage. 'Wait until a bird lands. Then *ka-ching.*'

'Money happens?' She pressed her eye to the viewfinder.

'Sometimes.'

Frankie snapped the picture and laid the camera between them.

Charley stared at the water – clear up close, then blue, green, gray all the way to the blue-gray sky.

'There are things so beautiful they make me ache,' he said.

Her glance was both surprised and guarded. 'You always said photographing beauty was a waste of time. Beauty doesn't change things.'

'I did?'

She nodded.

Charley continued to stare at the water. The ache swelled. 'I was wrong.'

'I know.'

'I suddenly want to photograph everything that makes me ache. I want to photograph all the things.'

Frankie took his hand. 'I know.'

They sat together in silence. They'd always been good at it. There were so many things they could say without ever saying them.

'I love you's had gone unvoiced. 'I need you's the same. So had 'I miss you's.

'I love you; I need you; I've missed you,' he whispered.

At first he didn't think she'd heard. Then she met his eyes and in hers he saw the whole wide world. Nothing had ever been more beautiful.

'I love you; I need you; I've missed you,' she said.

He managed to lift the camera and fire off a single shot of her face.

Why had he ever wanted to look anywhere else?

Hannah

Hannah arrived at the cottage in Fish Creek nearly two weeks after she'd left it.

No car out front. Where could they be? She hoped not the hospital, though Frankie would have called.

Hannah checked her phone again. The only missed calls were from her lawyer.

She should have phoned to say she was coming, but she'd been afraid Frankie would tell her not to bother. And while she didn't want to watch another man she loved die, she thought it would be worse *not* to watch. How could she live with herself?

Charley was her husband. She loved him; he had once loved her. Did he still, somewhere in that brilliant brain? She might never know, but she would be at his side until the end. Hers would be the last face he saw on this earth. Just let Frankie try and take that from her.

Hannah had decided, in the depths of several recent sleepless nights, that she hadn't tried hard enough to make Charley remember her. She'd brought a large manila envelope stuffed with snapshots of the two of them, a visual record of their life together – their first apartment, then their second, vacations, dinners, outings.

In most of them they were laughing. Charley had often told her he'd never laughed with anyone the way he'd laughed with her. What if she could get him to laugh again? Might he remember the other times they had? Hopefully the pictures would help.

Yes, she remembered quite well what had happened when she'd shown him their wedding photograph. But he'd been upset. She'd been angry and frightened. If she spoke to him calmly, when he was rational, maybe she could reach him. At this point, what did she have to lose?

Hannah found the spare key inside the large seashell at the edge of the driveway, right where Frankie had told her it would be the last time they'd spoken on the phone – a week ago now. They hadn't gone that long without a call since this had all started.

Hannah didn't want to admit that she'd missed Frankie's voice on the other end of the line.

They weren't friends, exactly, but they were something.

Inside she hurried to the room she'd used before, dropped her bag and turned. She froze at the sight of the hospital bed across the hall. People died in those beds. That's what they were for.

She was still standing in her room, staring into his, when Charley and Frankie returned.

'Hannah?' Frankie called.

'Here,' she said, shocked at how faint her voice had become. Anyone listening would think she was the one who was dying.

But wasn't she? Bit by bit, inch by inch, as Charley faded, so did Hannah. He was everything and when he was gone she'd have nothing.

'Stop that,' she whispered an instant before Frankie came around the corner.

She paused at the sight of Hannah's face. 'You gonna pass out?'

'Not today.' She tried to smile.

The attempt must have been dismal because Frankie grabbed her hand and tugged her toward the living room. 'Let's have wine.'

Sometimes she almost loved Frankie.

Charley sat at the kitchen table, eyes glued to the laptop screen. Since his camera was plugged into the USB port, he must be downloading from one to the other.

'Hi, Charley.' Hannah's cheeks heated. She felt as awkward as she had the day she'd met him. What had happened to the confident woman she had become?

Charley grunted.

Guess he wasn't happy to see her.

He looked a lot worse than when she'd left. Thinner, paler, shakier.

Hannah cast a concerned glance at Frankie, who avoided that glance, studiously pouring the wine.

Charley was dying, faster now since he wasn't doing anything to stop it.

Hannah shouldn't be surprised. She wasn't. What surprised her was that she'd still had hope he might pull out of this. Heath had called her Pollyanna for a reason.

'Here.' A glass of red wine appeared in front of her face.

Hannah took it and gulped.

The photographs spilling on to the computer screen caught her attention. She inched closer so she could see over Charley's shoulder. He didn't seem to mind.

Rock cairns on a rock beach, bright blue skies and waves at their back.

'Is that Scotland?' Hannah had never been but she'd always thought that was what the place would look like.

'Washington Island.' Frankie stood in the kitchen, swirling her wine in the glass, not drinking it.

'Is that Scotland?' Hannah repeated.

Charley snorted but didn't answer.

Hannah felt her cheeks heat again. He'd never made her feel like an idiot before. He'd always taught her what she didn't know with patience and love. But he wasn't that man any more, and she feared he wouldn't ever be that man again. Unless she did something soon.

'Washington Island is off the tip of the peninsula by about five miles. That's where we spent the day.'

A shadow passed over Frankie's face. Something about Washington Island disturbed her.

'Everything go OK there?' Hannah waved at the photographs, which had switched to fields of lavender so vivid she could almost smell it.

'Sure,' Frankie said too quickly.

'No,' Charley muttered.

What happened? Hannah mouthed.

'Can you . . .?' Frankie beckoned toward the rear of the house with her yet untouched glass of wine and Hannah followed her in that direction.

She glanced back at Charley; his eyes followed Frankie. He didn't even seem to remember Hannah was there.

'He's getting worse fast,' Frankie said when they reached her room. 'You should probably stay.'

'No problem.' Hannah had nowhere else to go.

'Don't you need to make arrangements for work?'

'*You* is no more.' Hannah filled her lungs with air, then let the breath out slowly. Sometimes it helped. 'I filed for bankruptcy when I was in DC. That's why it took me so long.'

Well, there had been a few other issues, but *You* had been the main time suck.

'Oh, Hannah.' Frankie set her glass on the bedside table and then set both hands on Hannah's shoulders. 'I know how much the magazine meant to you.'

Hannah searched her face for sarcasm, found none. 'It was really my brother's baby.' She had to swallow before she continued, lest the tears in her throat leak out her eyes. 'And my aunt's.'

You had ended up being her baby too, though. The only one she would ever have.

Now it was gone.

While a magazine wasn't a child, she thought she felt a bit of what Frankie had all those years ago, and she was ashamed of herself. What kind of woman sleeps with the husband of another who'd just gone through what Frankie had?

Her only excuse was that she'd been foolishly, madly in love with Charley. She still was.

'What are you going to do?' Frankie stepped back, let her arms fall.

'Take care of Charley like I promised. If you want, you could leave tonight.'

'Leave?' Frankie echoed.

'Here.' Hannah handed over the carry-on suitcase that housed all of the slides, negatives and prints Charley had of Lisa. 'If I find any more, I'll send them to you.'

Frankie took the handle, but she appeared troubled.

'Is there something else I should know?' Hannah asked.

'He's not that bad yet. It's too soon for you to take over. He'll just run away like he did with Ursula.'

Hannah shrugged. 'You said he's failing fast. I doubt he's going to be able to run very far or very long.'

Frankie peered at her as if she didn't know her. Really, she didn't.

'How can you be so cold?'

Hannah's gaze was drawn toward the living room, where Charley had begun to cough. She knew that cough. He wasn't as far away from the end as Frankie believed.

'It's the only way I'm going to survive,' she said.

'I don't think I can . . .' Frankie paused, found her wine, took a large sip. 'I can't leave tonight.' She set the glass back down. 'I'll do a grocery store run. There's no milk.'

Hannah resisted the urge to roll her eyes. If she did, Frankie just might punch her.

Though Hannah had been horrified when Frankie had punched Charley the night she'd seen them kiss, Hannah could admit now, if only to herself, that she'd also secretly admired Frankie's balls. She'd wished she could find a set of her own. A few times she'd even channeled that memory of Frankie when she'd needed to dredge up some courage.

'Fine. Get milk.' Hannah wanted to talk to Charley alone, and if Frankie was going to hang around, this might be her only chance.

Frankie left the room, murmured something to Charley, who said, 'I'll go with you.'

'No. You rest.'

Charley said something too low for Hannah to hear.

'She's not that bad.'

Hannah knew the *she* Frankie was referring to was her.

As soon as the door closed and the car started, then tires rolled on the gravel driveway, Hannah picked up the manila envelope and headed for the kitchen.

Charley still sat at the computer, scowling at what he saw there.

'Problem?' Hannah asked.

He didn't look up but his scowl deepened.

She sat in the chair next to him then glanced at the computer. The entire screen was filled with waves, artsy shot, not Charley at all. He seemed to be taking an awful lot of water photographs lately; Hannah thought she knew why.

'Where's that?'

'I . . . we . . .' He let out an exasperated sigh. 'Took it on the island. There's something about it that makes me think.' He rubbed his temple. 'Remember. There's something about Lisa and water.'

Hannah flinched and for the first time that day he glanced at her. 'What do you know?'

'I know a lot of things.'

'Fancy keeps saying Lisa's away, that she'll be here soon. Is that true?'

Hannah discovered that she couldn't lie to him. She also discovered that she couldn't tell him the truth. She didn't want to. Shouldn't have to. Wasn't going to.

'Hannah?' His expression was so intense, so determined, and the way he said her name was so 'not Charley' that she panicked and dumped the photographs of the two of them all over the table.

'What the fuck?' He grabbed the nearest one.

A photo of them on a cruise to Hawaii for their tenth anniversary. She'd had to beg and threaten and cajole to get him to go. He hated cruises, hated tours. When they'd been on Kauai, he'd turned up his nose at the helicopter ride over the Waimea Canyon and instead hired one of the locals to take them down the Wailua River in his boat.

This picture was not of that trip, which had been to her an unmitigated disaster. No bathroom, no sunscreen, no clock. They'd missed the cruise ship sail time and had to hire another local to drive them at top speed to the next port. She'd been so mad.

This was a posed photo of them at dinner on their anniversary, champagne glasses raised. By then she'd forgiven him, of course. Forgiving him was what she did best. They were laughing again. Hannah had just told the story of the Wailua River to the others at their table. She'd made it funny, left out the anger. Another thing she did very well. Across the bottom of the picture, an elaborate typeface read *Happy 10th Anniversary, Hannah and Charley! And many more!*

'Where did you get this?' His gaze flickered over the others. 'Where did you get all of these?'

'Our apartment.'

His eyes narrowed, blue fire blazing between the partially closed lids. 'You're crazy.'

'I am,' she agreed. 'I'm also your wife.'

He stood up so fast his chair fell over, then he had to grab at the table's edge to keep from falling over too.

'It's not true,' he said, but his voice wasn't as certain as it had been the first time she'd told him, and that gave her hope that this might work.

She snatched up a random photograph. 'Us with the Waz. You had a job for *Time* magazine in Minneapolis and I went along. You wanted me to meet him. We stayed at his house with his second wife. Maybe his third.' She held out the photograph. 'Remember?'

He clenched his teeth so hard, they crackled. The corners of his mouth glistened.

She wanted to wipe the spittle away. Instead she picked another photograph. 'You and my brother, Heath. You did an essay on him. He was . . .' Her voice broke and she cleared it impatiently. 'He died of AIDS. You published a book. Had a show in Soho.'

'Has this happened before?' His eyes flicked from the pictures, to her, to the window and back. 'I feel like this has happened before.'

Encouraged, she found another picture. Her sitting in his lap with a big, goofy smile; he was kissing her neck. They were both so young.

'It's not 1989, Charley. You aren't married to Frankie. You haven't been for over twenty years. And Lisa . . .' She bit her lip.

'Do you see those flashing lights?'

The picture fell from her fingers and drifted gently downward. 'Charley?'

He swayed then tumbled to the floor, eyes blinking rapidly, limbs jerking in a staccato rhythm.

'Charley!'

By the time the paramedics arrived, the seizure was winding down. Charley had stopped jerking. His eyes had stopped darting here, there, everywhere. The spittle had become drool down his chin. She kept herself occupied wiping it off, in between whispering, 'I'm sorry. I'm sorry.'

She told the two young, buff men who arrived what had happened, leaving out how she'd pushed him to remember until he'd had a seizure to forget.

'He has brain cancer?' The one with slightly longer dark hair than the other and blue eyes instead of brown scribbled on a clipboard.

'Yes.'

The second took Charley's vitals. 'He seems to be coming back pretty strong.'

'We should still take him to the hospital,' Clipboard Guy said.

'No.' Charley's voice was weak, a bit slurred. 'No hop-ital.'

'Sir, it wouldn't hurt to get checked o—'

'No!'

'I guess that's a no.'

'But . . .' Hannah began.

'Patient refused transport. Nothing we can do.'

'Help to bed,' Charley said.

His stroke-like speech scared the shit out of her. If she started screaming for them to take him to the hospital, would they? They'd probably take her there instead.

'That we can do.' The young man scooped Charley into his arms as if he weighed no more than a teenager. Perhaps now he did. 'Which way?'

Hannah pointed down the hall. 'First door on the left.'

He strode off.

'You his wife?' asked the remaining paramedic.

'Yes,' she said softly.

He handed her another clipboard. 'Sign here.'

Frankie banged through the front door, her gaze flicking around the room as frantically as Charley's had. 'What happened?' she cried, but didn't wait for an answer. Instead she raced for his room.

Hannah followed, just in time to see Frankie throw herself into Charley's arms.

Huh, that was new. Or perhaps very old.

'I thought you were his wife?' Paramedic Two, who had also followed, asked.

'I am.'

'You sure?'

She cast him a sharp glance and he held up his hands. 'Sorry. Not my business. Just looked like . . .' His gaze went to Frankie, who was whispering to Charley and holding his hand. 'Never mind.'

The paramedics left.

Hannah remained in the hall. She couldn't take her eyes off them. She waited for the jealousy, the anger. Neither came.

He was no longer Her Charley. He would never be Her Charley again. She knew that now. She just had to figure out what to do about it.

Every movement Frankie made, Charley followed with his eyes. He stared at her like a devoted dog stared at its blessed master – at least until he fell asleep.

Frankie walked into the living room. 'I'm calling Dr Lanier.'

Why hadn't Hannah thought of that?

Frankie filled him in on what had happened, or what she thought had happened. A seizure for no reason at all, beyond the brain tumor.

Hannah wondered how long she could keep Frankie believing that.

'All right,' Frankie said. 'Thank you.' She disconnected. 'Lanier says as long as he's comfortable, there's nothing he can do.' Frankie wandered the room listlessly. 'I shouldn't have left.'

At the kitchen table she paused, staring at the pile of Hannah/Charley pictures. She picked one up. 'What the hell?'

Hannah stared at the floor. 'Just once I wanted him to see me and remember.'

'This is what caused his seizure, isn't it?'

Hannah didn't answer.

Frankie tore the photograph in two.

'No!' Hannah protested.

Frankie picked up another and held it ready to rip. 'Isn't it?'

Hannah nodded.

'Honestly.' Frankie tossed the picture back on the pile unharmed. 'What is wrong with you?'

'A lot,' Hannah admitted. 'I love him.'

And he was dying. What could be more wrong than that?

'How much?'

'What kind of question is that?'

'A legitimate one after this stunt.' Frankie waved at the photographs.

'I just wanted . . .'

'Exactly. *You wanted.*'

'I'm going to be here with him; you'll be gone. What's he going to think when that happens?'

'Funny, I was wondering that too.'

'I don't follow.' And it wasn't funny.

'You don't want to stay with him. Who would?'

'I love him.' Hannah swallowed as the rest of the words tried to stick in her throat. 'Of course I want to be here for him at the end.'

She did; she didn't. She wasn't sure. What she was sure of was that she'd been there for Heath; she could do no less for Charley. It was her right, but also her duty. For better or worse. She'd promised.

'But Hannah,' Frankie said softly. 'Is being with him at the end for Charley, or is it for you?'

Frankie

Frankie held her breath.

The answer to the question was obviously 'for me', but would Hannah see that? Would she insist on remaining at Charley's side until the end, upsetting him even more than he already was?

Frankie couldn't allow that, though she wasn't sure what she'd do besides shove Hannah out of the cottage and refuse to let her back in. She'd prefer not to, not only because Hannah would make a racket that would disturb the dead, or the almost dead, but she might even call the cops.

Then Frankie would be the one shoved out of the cottage. She didn't think she could stand to hear Charley calling for her, confused, frightened, sad. Not understanding why she wasn't there, why she didn't come, why she'd let a stranger hold his hand as he died.

Once she'd imagined him dying in agony, calling for her. Then she'd imagined how she would laugh and walk away. The memory made her slightly sick.

How could someone who was so brilliant, so vibrant, cease to exist? Charley was larger than life; shouldn't he be larger than death too?

'He'll be confused.' Hannah's eyes sparkled with tears. She swallowed and started to shove the photographs into the envelope. 'He won't know me; he'll only want you.'

Once Frankie had wanted Hannah to experience the pain of losing Charley to another woman. She'd figured it would happen. Once a cheater always a cheater, right? Except, it hadn't happened. Until now.

Hannah's losing Charley to Frankie should be the perfect revenge, but somehow it just wasn't. Was Hannah really losing if Charley didn't know he'd been a prize in the first place?

Was Frankie that shallow? She had been. She might still be, except she didn't feel triumphant. She felt . . .

'Sorry,' Frankie said. 'I know it's hard. But . . .'

'This is about him. You're right. I'll . . . go.' Hannah retrieved her bag and headed for the door.

Could it be this easy?

There was no way this was going to be easy.

'I can call you,' Frankie said. 'When he's close. He probably won't know who's here then. You can come and say goodbye.'

'I'll say goodbye now.' Hannah crossed the room at a fast clip for someone with such short legs.

Frankie got to the door just as Hannah leaned over and kissed Charley's lips. She caught her breath, waiting for Charley to wake and stroke out this time.

He didn't move. If she hadn't seen his chest rising and falling in a steady, encouraging rhythm Frankie might have stroked out herself. How was she going to watch him die?

'Goodbye.' Hannah gently touched his face. 'For me, it's always been you.'

Her voice was thick with tears. However, when she walked out again, Frankie didn't see a single one.

'Wait!' Frankie hurried after, catching up as Hannah retrieved her bag and the envelope. 'I *will* call you when it's time.'

'OK.' Hannah moved toward the door.

'You're doing the right thing.'

Hannah gave one short, sharp bark of laughter. 'Am I?'

'You know you are.'

She nodded, still not looking at Frankie.

Frankie wasn't sure if the nod meant she agreed that she was doing the right thing, or that she'd given up arguing about it.

Whatever worked.

'I was always jealous of you.' Hannah tucked the envelope beneath her arm and set her hand on the doorknob.

'Why? He left me for you when I needed him the most.'

'Yet you're not leaving him when he needs you the most. Why?'

'Because I know what that feels like.'

Hannah glanced at Frankie over her shoulder. For an instant she resembled the young girl Frankie had first seen in Soho. 'Were you jealous of me?'

'God, yes.'

Hannah's lips curved, but the smile was so, so sad. 'Good.'

She opened the door and left.

'I like her,' Frankie said to the empty room.

Charley

Sometimes he woke in the night and he didn't know where he was. Vietnam? Beirut? New York? DC? In the rubble of the World Trade Center, which still felt like it had happened, even though he knew it had not.

Then he'd catch the scent of lemons and it wouldn't matter where he was as long as he was with her.

Since he'd had the seizure, he hadn't been out of his room much. He couldn't remember what had happened that whole day before he'd woken in this bed. Frankie showed him the photographs of Washington Island. They didn't help. It was as if the trip had never been. He could tell that upset Frankie, so he stopped asking about it.

Frankie had dragged a mattress into his room and slept there. He'd tried to make her stop.

'You can sleep with me.' He lifted the sheet, waggled the place on his face where his eyebrows used to be.

'I'm too big to share a single with you.'

He didn't understand why she kept saying she was big, heavy, large. 'You look exactly the same size as you did when I married you.'

Her eyes got teary and she touched his face. 'Charmer.'

Days passed. Maybe weeks. He lost track. He slept a lot, even without the morphine, which he tried not to take too much because it made life foggy and he had precious little life left to live it like that. With morphine he wasn't sure where he was even in the daytime.

He wasn't in that much pain. Sometimes he had a headache. Once in a while they got bad. But mostly he just felt weak, as if he were fading bit by bit until he'd at last fade away.

'Take some pictures,' he said.

Frankie, who'd been dozing in the chair, started. 'Of what?'

'Me.'

'Why would I do that?' she asked. 'Why would you want me to?'

'I'll be gone soon.'

'No,' Frankie began.

'Baby, you know it's true.'

She pursed her lips, wrung her hands.

He hated himself for doing this to her. He should make her leave, but she wouldn't, and in reality, he couldn't make anyone do anything, not even himself these days.

'You might want a last picture of me. If you don't take it, you won't have it. Maybe Lisa will want one. Where is she again?'

He could tell from Frankie's face that he'd asked that before. He couldn't remember what she'd said.

Frankie went to the window and opened it. 'She's away.'

'At camp!'

She turned back. 'You hungry?'

He wasn't but because she appeared so hopeful he said yes.

She returned with grilled cheese and his Nikon. 'You want to take some pictures of me?'

He discovered he didn't want to take pictures of anything. All he wanted to do these days was sleep and stare at Frankie. Those were the only times he felt at peace. Otherwise his mind spun, trying to remember . . . something. But he just couldn't.

'I thought maybe . . . you missed taking photographs,' Frankie said when he didn't answer.

'Mostly I miss Lisa.'

She sighed and handed him his camera.

He tried to lift it, couldn't and set the thing aside.

Frankie bit her lip.

'Maybe later,' he said. 'Hand over that grilled cheese.'

That seemed to please her, so he tried to eat it and failed. Everything he put in his mouth these days was hard to get down, even water. The last time the visiting nurse had come she'd said she would hook up an IV soon and give him nutrients that way.

Charley hoped Lisa arrived before that happened. He'd prefer to refuse. No reason to prolong the inevitable unless he had to.

'Where is this camp?' he asked.

'Who wants ice cream?' Frankie left the room so fast she seemed to be fleeing.

Charley drifted off before she came back.

He saw Lisa. Here, at the cottage. She laughed and ran and jumped and swam; she threw herself into his arms and hugged him so hard he could have sworn she was real.

He stood on the hill and watched a big boat trail oil across the blue water. He lifted his camera; he became transfixed by what he saw through his lens. Then he saw something through that lens that changed everything.

Charley woke up shouting, 'Lisa!'

'Charley.' Frankie sat on the bed, took him by the arms. It was dark, the silver light of the moon just beginning to trail through the window and across the floor. 'It was a dream.'

He tried to crawl into her lap. He wasn't proud. 'It . . . I . . . She . . .'

Frankie got into bed with him and held him against her chest. 'Shh. I know.'

'She was floating in the water off the dock. I was taking pictures of a boat.'

Frankie stiffened for just an instant, then started to stroke his head. 'It was a dream, Charley.'

'You promise?'

She swallowed. 'Yes.'

Something about her voice made him turn so he could see her face. 'Are you crying?'

'No.'

He swiped the single tear from her cheek. The drop shimmered on the edge of his finger for an instant before falling down.

She took his hand and held it tight. 'I'm fine.'

'You aren't.'

'Shh,' she said again and pulled him closer.

He could almost forget he was dying while lying in her arms, the scent of lemons surrounding him, the night so cool and dark and still.

'I've never loved anyone the way I love you,' he said.

For a long time she didn't answer and he thought she might have fallen asleep. He started to drift too, then her words brought him back.

'I've never loved anyone *but* you.'

'And Lisa.'

She took a long, deep breath, her chest expanding at his back, lifting his body and lowering it like a gentle, rolling wave. 'And Lisa,' she agreed.

Charley floated on that wave. His eyes fluttered closed as he whispered, 'Where is she?'

Frankie

Frankie slid out of the bed.

Charley didn't stir.

She grabbed her cell phone and went into the living room. The nearly full moon spread a path of light from the hall to the sliding glass doors of the deck. She stepped through them.

The night was cool. Autumn had arrived on the peninsula. She couldn't believe she'd been here all summer. Time had flown. Too fast, considering.

Without thought for the hour, she dialed Hannah.

Hannah answered on the second ring. 'Is he . . .?'

'No.' She hadn't thought either of what Hannah might think to receive a call at this time of night. 'But soon. You should probably head back.'

'OK.'

'Like now.'

'Sure. You bet. Be right over.'

'I just meant . . .' To her horror, Frankie started to cry.

'Crap, Frankie. I'm sorry. My sarcasm button, you always push it.'

'How did you do it?'

'Do what?'

'Watch someone you love die?'

It occurred to her that she'd just told Charley's wife that she was in love with him. But she figured Hannah already knew and, really, Hannah was the only one on this earth who could understand.

How many times had she thought that sentence in the past month?

'It's . . .' Frankie struggled for a word.

'Excruciating. Horrific. Demoralizing. Exhausting.'

'Nightmarish,' Frankie said. 'Surrealistic. He keeps asking for Lisa.'

'Shit,' Hannah muttered.

'Yeah. He had a nightmare.'

'Vietnam? Beirut? Nine eleven?'

'Lisa. He never discussed exactly how she died before.'

Which was probably why he'd told her now. Much easier to share what he believed to be a dream than reality.

'Was it hard to hear?' Hannah asked.

'No.' It hadn't been pleasant, but it had also felt good to know everything at last. She'd suspected Charley had been taking pictures when their daughter died, but she'd never known. Had never wanted to know, so she hadn't asked.

'How did you do it?' she repeated.

'I just did it. There's no one way to go about something like that. I was there for Heath until he didn't need me to be any more.'

'All right,' Frankie said. 'I can do that.' She didn't really have much choice. 'You'll catch a flight tomorrow?'

'Sure,' Hannah said, and hung up.

Frankie wasn't sure how she knew Hannah was lying, but she did. She couldn't blame her for not wanting to be here. Hannah had done this once already.

Oddly, Frankie was disappointed. She could do this. She would do this. But it would have been nice to do it with Hannah. They'd forged a connection – not a friendship, not really, or maybe just not yet – but it was a connection Frankie had with no one else.

Frankie returned to Charley's room. His breathing seemed faster than usual; some nights it seemed slower. According to the visiting nurse, this was common as the end rolled near.

She pulled the chair closer to the bed so she could hold his hand, then she laid her cheek on the mattress. She was so tired, but she didn't want him to die alone. She didn't think she could stand that.

She woke with dawn just tinting the sky. The room held a soft, pink light that reminded Frankie of a painting of heaven that Charley's mom had kept above their mantel.

Charley's eyes were open. For a minute she thought he was gone.

'Charley!' She squeezed his hand, which still lay in hers.

His fingers didn't respond. They felt far too cool. But his gaze flicked to her face. A tear popped out of the corner of one eye and trickled down.

'Lisa,' he managed, his voice hoarse and a bit lispy.

Had he had a stroke?

'I should call . . .' She started to stand.

'No!' The word was perfectly clear, but his hand in hers remained limp. 'I need Lisa.'

Frankie realized she was crying too. 'I'm sorry. She's . . .' Frankie found it hard to breathe. 'Coming. She'll be here soon, Charley. Hold on, OK?'

She didn't want him to go. She knew he would, he had to, if not now, then soon. But . . .

Not now. Please, just . . .

Not. Now.

His gaze, which had been locked on hers, suddenly shifted, and he smiled his Charley-smile. 'Oh.' He drew in a deep breath. 'There she is.'

That breath left him on a sigh.

Frankie waited for him to take another.

But he didn't.

Hannah

Hannah slipped into the cottage just as the moon died. The night was so dark in that instant before the sun rose, she thought she knew what death felt like.

She shook off that morbid thought. Wasn't death called 'going into the light'? She hoped that was true.

Inside the place was quiet as a tomb.

'Sheesh.' She really needed her brain to shut up.

When she had told Frankie she would catch a plane in the morning she'd been lying, but only because she'd never left. She'd taken a room in Green Bay and waited for Frankie to call.

She had plenty to think about. For instance, what she was

going to do with the rest of her life. *You* was gone. She was too old to start over at *National Geographic*, and she discovered she didn't really want to. That had been a dream of her youth and she wasn't young any more. These days she felt pretty old.

Then her mother had called and given her even more to think about. Good old Mom.

She'd also had a lot of calls to make regarding Charley's medical bills – the Veteran's Administration, the US Army, Dr Lanier, and finally a lawyer. She was confident that everything would be taken care of. If anyone wanted to give her trouble, she had plenty of ammunition in Charley's final photographs. They said a picture was worth a thousand words and an essay depicting the famous Charley Blackwell dying from cancer, along with a story about Agent Orange and its effects, might go a long way toward resolving any future issues for others. She'd learned how to raise a ruckus from the best in that business.

Hannah hadn't planned to come back to the cottage while Charley was alive; she didn't want him to be upset, to die confused or frightened. She didn't want him to die anything but at peace, and she'd do whatever she could to make sure that happened. Even give up the final moments at his side that were rightfully hers.

So when Frankie had called and said it would be soon, she'd stared at the ceiling for hours. But eventually she had been unable to resist driving north.

She peeked into the room. Frankie sat in a chair, her head on the bed at Charley's hip, her hand wrapped around his. She was asleep.

Charley looked asleep too, so she tried to memorize his face. She knew it would fade from her mind, as her brother's had. Luckily she'd had Charley's pictures to remind her of just the way Heath had tilted his hat and winked. The world was a lesser place without Heath Cartwright, and it would be an even lesser place without Charley Blackwell.

But his pictures . . . those could keep Charley alive in everyone's mind for a long, long time. And, perhaps, they could do some good for others as well.

Charley's eyes opened and Hannah quickly stepped back. She waited for him to shout for her to get out, get lost.

She shouldn't have come.

But he remained silent and she stood just out of sight and listened to him breathe the way she used to when they were first married and she was amazed that this man loved her.

She'd been so happy then. He had been happy too. Eventually. At first he was still mourning the loss of his child and, she could admit it now, the loss of his wife. But they'd forged a path together that had been good, if not great. And if he'd murmured 'Fancy' or 'baby' sometimes in the night, well . . . now she knew why.

In truth, she'd always known why. It didn't make Hannah love *him* any less.

The sun began to come up with a strange pinkish light. She found herself fascinated by it and she watched the dust motes dance in that light, turning every shade of dawn.

'Lisa,' Charley croaked, and Frankie answered him softly.

Hannah hovered in the hall, listening to them talk. Tears streamed down her cheeks. She didn't bother to wipe them off. She wanted to go to him so badly. But she'd only make things worse.

'Oh,' Charley said. 'There she is.'

Utter silence descended. Hannah's skin prickled as her ears strained to hear one more labored breath. But the sound was gone.

Charley was gone.

Hannah stepped to the doorway. The whole room was tinged salmon and gold. She couldn't remember seeing anything quite that color before.

Frankie's face was wet with tears, same as Hannah's, but in her eyes joy warred with sorrow. 'You heard?'

Hannah nodded and crossed the room.

They hugged each other tightly; then they rocked, back and forth, and didn't let go for a long, long time.

'Do you think she was here?' Frankie asked.

Hannah remembered that dream she'd had of Heath, how real it had felt, how much it had comforted her at the time.

'I do,' she said.

'Me, too.'

Frankie

'Do you want to keep this place?' Hannah asked.

They were still at the cottage, and it had been nice. Together they'd dealt with the minutiae of Charley's death. Irene couldn't figure them out.

'You hated her for twenty years.'

'Twenty-four.'

'And now you're BFFs?'

'Jealous?'

'Yes.'

'No one can ever replace you.'

'She replaced you,' Irene said.

She hadn't. Frankie knew that now.

'Did you forgive him in the end?' Irene asked. 'Let him off the hook, make everything OK?'

'How could I forgive him for something he didn't remember?'

Irene uttered a few curses. Apparently *she* hadn't forgiven Charley. Frankie hadn't expected that she would.

'You'd be impressed with Hannah.'

'Doubtful.'

'She's handled everything like a drill sergeant. There was some issue with Charley's insurance, but there isn't any more. They actually seem a little scared of her.'

It had been fun to watch.

Hannah was not who Frankie had believed she was. She felt a little badly about *what* she'd believed. The only way to fix that was to believe something else.

'Hannah's my friend,' she said.

'Good God,' Irene muttered.

'I'll see you at the memorial?' Frankie asked.

Irene gave a long, put-upon sigh. 'Of course.'

They were having a memorial for Charley in DC. Most of his

colleagues still worked at *National Geographic* and if they didn't, they lived nearby.

Frankie hadn't bothered to call Charley's brothers. Neither had Hannah. Only people who loved Charley were allowed. There would be plenty.

'Frankie?' Hannah spread her hands. 'The cottage? You want it?'

'I seem to recall that everything, right down to his last camera, lens and camera bag, goes to you.' Frankie shut the sliding glass door and flipped the lock.

Hannah winced. 'God, I was a bitch.'

'So was I. We had our reasons. We got over it.'

'Not completely.'

'There are some instances where being a bitch is called for.'

Hannah gave her a high five.

Frankie stood in the center of the living room and turned a slow circle. The two people she loved the most in the world had died here. While some might want to hold on to that and mourn, she wasn't one of them.

'I don't want the cottage.'

'Me either. I'll put it on the market. After.'

They were flying to DC that day. The memorial was the next morning.

'You sure you don't want to stay with me?' Hannah asked.

'Thanks, but no.'

She might be friends with Hannah now; they'd been through a lot. And in loving the same man, Frankie thought they'd learned to love each other. She'd never seen it coming.

However, she did not want to spend several days in the apartment where Hannah and Charley had lived and loved and laughed what appeared to be a helluva lot from those snapshots. She did have limits.

Hannah nodded as if she understood. Frankie was certain that she did.

'My mother retired from Balfour Publishing.'

'That was random,' Frankie said.

'Not in my head.' Hannah set her bag next to Frankie's at the door. 'I've been offered her job.'

'That's great!' Frankie had been a bit worried about what Hannah would do to occupy herself now that both *You* and

Charley were gone. To be honest, Frankie was kind of concerned about what *she* was going to do now that Charley was gone.

This time they'd had together, while difficult, had also been a gift. She'd fallen in love with him again, or maybe just admitted that she loved him still. And while that should have made losing him more painful, instead, in making his final days peaceful, she'd also found peace. Not only had she been able to forgive him, she'd been able to forgive herself. She could move on now, whereas before she'd only been treading time.

'I was thinking of publishing a compendium of Charley's work.'

'OK.' She wasn't sure why Hannah was telling her. Despite their friendship, Hannah still owned everything down to the last camera bag, which included Charley's slides, minus the ones of Lisa. Frankie had yet to go through them. But she would soon.

It was time.

'I'd like it if you worked on the book with me. Nobody understands him like we do.'

Hannah had said something similar to her once before and Frankie had thought *soon no one else ever would*. But if they did the book, then wouldn't everyone?

The idea of a book with all three of their names on it was intriguing. Besides, the world should always be able to see itself the way that Charley had.

'I'd like that too.' Frankie picked up the urn that held Charley, took one step toward the door, then held it out. 'You want him?'

Hannah opened the door and picked up their bags. 'How about we take turns?'

Whatever anger or jealousy they'd once harbored for each other seemed to have melted away in their shared goal to allow Charley to die at peace. Frankie knew how hard it must have been for Hannah to leave him with her, to not stand at his side at the end, but she'd done it for Charley. Hannah understood how hard it was for Frankie to stay with him, to pretend that everything was all right when it hadn't been for years, to lie to him until his last, dying second about Lisa. But Frankie had done it for Charley.

They stepped out of the cottage and Hannah put down the bags to lock up. The wind swirled in, stirring their hair, and both of them stilled.

'You smell that?' Frankie asked.

'Graham crackers.' Hannah sniffed. 'And basil.'

Then the wind died as suddenly as it had come and all Frankie could smell were the pines.

'Goodbye,' Frankie whispered.

'Goodbye.' Hannah picked up the bags.

The sun was just peeking over the trees to the east, casting bright yellow rays across the cottage, the water and them.

'A whole new day,' Frankie said.

'It's a whole new world,' Hannah agreed.

Together, they went into the light.

Acknowledgments

This book has been a true labor of love for me, one that haunted me for years before I wrote it. I have several people to thank.

My agent, Robin Rue, who adored *Just Once* from the beginning and became an untiring advocate to see it published. Also Robin's assistant, Beth Miller, who read the manuscript on the subway and wept, proving I'd hit the mark.

The team at Severn House that has understood my vision for the book from day one and never wavered: Kate Lyall Grant, Sara Porter, Claire Ritchie and all those who have worked behind the scenes to make my dream for *Just Once* a reality.

My go-to medical gurus: Dr Joan Handeland of Prevea Health in Green Bay (also a wonderful sister in law!) and Laura Iding, Risk Management at Froedtert Hospital in Milwaukee. All mistakes are, of course, my own.

My father, Buck Miller, a photographer whose vision the world misses almost as much as I miss him.

Last but never least, my husband who never wavers in his belief that I am the most talented, beautiful, best at everything woman. He's delusional, but we'll let him keep those delusions.

And thank you, readers, for coming along with me on this new journey. May it be long and full of books!